'Erast Petrovich Fando... reactions, a probing ana... concealed weaponry . . . ... want from detective fiction: murderous dexterity acquired after long years of suffering; exotically lethal weaponry (including a Velodog – a revolver designed for cyclists to kill dogs without ever having to take their feet off the pedals); treachery in high places and detective genius, but Akunin is a fine novelist as well' *Daily Telegraph*

'This fourth book in Akunin's series of detective novels starring dashing hero Erast Fandorin will not disappoint fans of the first three, or indeed any connoisseur of detective fiction . . . a witty, rip-roaring thrill-fest' *Time Out*

'Akunin is a sensation. He has created a popular hero to equal Sherlock Holmes and James Bond . . . Akunin's finest creation and the star of his titles is Erast Fandorin – genius, gentleman, polyglot, kickboxer, and all-round inordinately lucky bloke' *The Times*

'With *The Death of Achilles*, the hilarious and dashing Erast Fandorin, Akunin's debonair Russian Sherlock Holmes, just seems to get better and better . . . I can't get enough of [Akunin] and I don't even really like thrillers or crime novels. Akunin is more like Agatha Christie meets James Bond: his plots are intricate and tantalizing, full of obscured fingerprints, poisoned darts and international agents . . . They are unputdownable and great fun . . . a stunning continuation of form from a Russian author whose thriller writing is world-class' *Sunday Express*

'A winning combination of crime fiction and adventure story as if Flashman were frisking through a tale by Dostoevsky' *Independent*

'Written with great assurance and much invention'
Scotsman

'*The Death of Achilles* may be historical pastiche but its wit and invention are a source of constant wonder . . . All in all, a delicious confection'   *Evening Standard*

Boris Akunin is the pseudonym of Grigory Chkhartishvili. He has been compared to Gogol, Tolstoy and Arthur Conan Doyle, and his Erast Fandorin books have sold over ten million copies in Russia alone. He lives in Moscow.

By Boris Akunin

The Winter Queen
Murder on the Leviathan
Turkish Gambit
The Death of Achilles

The Death of Achilles

BORIS AKUNIN

Translated by Andrew Bromfield

PHOENIX

A PHOENIX PAPERBACK

First published in Great Britain in 2005
by Weidenfeld & Nicolson
This paperback edition published in 2006
by Phoenix,
an imprint of Orion Books Ltd,
Orion House, 5 Upper St Martin's Lane,
London WC2H 9EA

First published in Russian as SMERT AKHILLESA
by Zakharov Publishers, Moscow, Russia
and Edizioni Frassinelli, Milan, Italy.
All rights reserved.

Published by arrangement with Linda Michaels Limited,
International Literary Agents.

1 3 5 7 9 10 8 6 4 2

Copyright © Boris Akunin 1998
Translation © Andrew Bromfield 2005

The Orion Publishing Group's policy is to use papers
that are natural, renewable and recyclable products and
made from wood grown in sustainable forests. The logging
and manufacturing processes are expected to conform to
the environmental regulations of the country of origin.

A CIP catalogue record for this book
is available from the British Library.

ISBN-13 978-0-7538-2046-9
ISBN-10 0-7538-2046-3

Printed and bound in Great Britain by
Clays Ltd, St Ives plc

www.orionbooks.co.uk

PART ONE
Fandorin

Chapter One

The morning train from St Petersburg, still enveloped in the
swirling smoke from its locomotive, had scarcely slowed to a
halt at the platform of Nikolaevsky Station, the conductors
unfolded the short flights of steps and raised their hands to
their peaked caps in salute, when a young man attired in quite
remarkable style leapt out of one of the first-class carriages.
He seemed to have sprung straight from some picture in a
Parisian magazine devoted to the glories of the 1882 summer-
season fashion: a light suit of sand-coloured wild silk, a wide-
brimmed hat of Italian straw, shoes with pointed toes, white
spats with silver press-studs, and in his hand an elegant silver-
topped walking cane. However, it was not so much the passenger's foppish attire that attracted attention as his overall
appearance, which was quite imposing, one might almost say
spectacular. The young man was tall, with a trim figure and
wide shoulders; he regarded the world through clear blue eyes,
and his slim moustache with curled ends sat quite extraordinarily well with his regular features, which included one
distinctive peculiarity: the neatly combed black hair shaded
intriguingly into silver-grey at the temples.

The porters made short work of unloading the young
man's luggage, which is itself worthy of special mention. In
addition to suitcases and travelling bags they carried out on
to the platform a folding tricycle, gymnastic weights and
bundles of books in various languages. Last of all there

3

emerged from the carriage a short, bandy-legged Oriental gentleman with a compact physique and an extremely solemn face with fat cheeks. He was dressed in green livery, combined discordantly with wooden sandals and a gaudy paper fan that hung around his neck on a silk string. This squat individual was clutching a quadrangular lacquered box in which there grew a tiny pine tree, looking for all the world as though it had been transported to the Moscow railway station from the kingdom of Lilliput.

Running his eye over the distinctly uninspiring structures of the railway terminus with a rather puzzling air of excitement, the young man inhaled the sooty station air and whispered: 'My God, six long years.' However, he was not permitted to indulge his reverie for long. The passengers from the St Petersburg train were already under siege by cabbies, most of whom were attached to Moscow's various hotels. Battle was joined for the handsome dark-haired gentleman – who appeared to be a most desirable client – by knights of the road from the four hotels regarded as the most chic in Russia's old capital: the Metropole, the Loskutnaya, the Dresden and the Dusseaux.

'Come and stay at the Metropole, sir!' the first cabby exclaimed. 'An absolutely modern hotel in the genuine European style! And the apartment has a special box room for your Chinee here!'

'He is not Chinese, but J-Japanese,' the young man explained, incidentally revealing that he spoke with a slight stammer. 'And I would prefer him to lodge with me.'

'Then your honour should come to us at the Loskutnaya,' said the next cabby, shouldering his competitor aside. 'If you take an apartment for five roubles or more, we drive you for free. I'll get you there quick as a flash!'

'I stayed in the Loskutnaya once,' the young man declared. 'It's a good hotel.'

'What would you want with that old ant heap, your

honour,' said a third cabby, joining the fray. 'Our Dresden's a perfect haven of peace and quiet, so elegant too – and the windows look out on Tverskaya Street, straight at His Excellency the Governor's house.'

The passenger pricked up his ears at that: 'Indeed? That is most convenient. You see, it just happens that I shall be working for His Excellency. I think perhaps—'

'Hey there, your honour!' shouted the last of the cabbies, a young dandy in a crimson waistcoat, with a parting brilliantined so painstakingly that his hair gleamed like a mirror. 'All the best writers have stayed at the Dusseaux: Dostoevsky and Count Tolstoy – even Mr Krestovsky himself.' This psychologist of the hotel trade had spotted the bundles of books and chosen his ruse well.

The handsome, dark-haired young man gasped: 'Even Count Tolstoy?'

'Why, of course: His Excellency comes straight round to us first thing, the moment he reaches Moscow.' The crimson cabby had already picked up two suitcases. He barked briskly at the Japanese: 'You carry, walky-walky follow me!'

'Well then, the Dusseaux it is,' the young man said with a shrug, little knowing that his decision would be the first link in a fateful chain of events to follow.

'Ah, Masa, how Moscow has changed,' the handsome passenger repeated again and again in Japanese, as he continually twisted round on the leather seat of the droshky. 'I can hardly recognise it. The road is completely paved with cobblestones, not like Tokyo. And how many clean people there are! Look, there's a horse-drawn tram; it follows a fixed route. Why, and there's a lady upstairs, in the Imperial! They never used to allow ladies upstairs. Out of a sense of decency.'

'Why, master?' asked Masa, whose full name was Masahiro Shibata.

'Why, naturally, so that no one on the lower level can peep while a lady is climbing the steps.'

'European foolishness and barbarism,' said the servant with a shrug. 'And I have something to say to you, master. As soon as we arrive at the inn we need to summon a courtesan for you straight away, a first-class one. Third-class will do for me. The women are good here. Tall and fat. Much better than Japanese women.'

'Will you stop your nonsense!' the young man said angrily. 'It's revolting.'

The Japanese shook his head disapprovingly. 'How long can you carry on pining for Midori-san? Sighing over a woman you will never see again is pointless.'

Nonetheless, his master did sigh again, and then yet again, after which, clearly seeking distraction from his melancholy thoughts, he turned to the cabby (they were driving past the Strastnoi Monastery at the time) and asked: 'Whose statue is that they've put up on the boulevard? Not Lord Byron, surely?'

'It's Pushkin – Alexander Sergeevich Pushkin,' the driver said reproachfully, turning round as he spoke.

The young man blushed and again began jabbering away to his slanty-eyed short-arsed companion in that funny foreign language. The only word the cabby could make out was 'Pusikin', repeated three times.

The Hotel Dusseaux was maintained after the manner of the very finest Parisian hotels – with a liveried doorman at the main entrance, a spacious vestibule with azaleas and magnolias growing in tubs and its own restaurant. The passenger from the St Petersburg train took a good six-rouble suite with windows overlooking Theatre Lane, signed the register as 'Collegiate Assessor Erast Petrovich Fandorin' and walked over inquisitively to the large blackboard on which the names of the hotel's guests were written in chalk, in the European fashion.

At the top, written in large letters complete with hooks and scrolls, was the date: *25 June, Friday – 7 juillet, vendre-*

di. A little lower, in the most prominent position, was the calligraphic inscription: *Adjutant-General and General of Infantry M.D. Sobolev – No. 47*.

'I don't believe it!' the collegiate assessor exclaimed. 'What a piece of luck!' Turning back to the reception clerk, he enquired: 'Is His Excellency in at present? He is an old accquaintance of mine!'

'Yes, he is indeed, sir,' the clerk said with a bow. 'His Excellency only arrived yesterday. With his retinue. They took an entire corner section; everything beyond that door over there is theirs. But he is still sleeping, and we have been instructed not to disturb him, sir.'

'Michel? At half past eight in the morning?' Fandorin exclaimed in amazement. 'That's not like him. But then, I suppose people change. Be so good as to inform the general that I am in apartment number twenty – he is certain to want to see me.'

The young man turned to go, but at that very moment there occurred the coincidence that was destined to become the second link in Fate's cunningly woven design. The door leading into the corridor occupied by the honoured guest suddenly opened a little and out glanced a Cossack officer with dark eyebrows, a long forelock, an aquiline nose and hollow cheeks blue with unshaven stubble.

'Hey, my man!' he bellowed, shaking a sheet of paper impatiently. 'Have this telegram sent to the telegraph office for dispatch. Look lively now!'

'Gukmasov, is that you?' said Erast Petrovich, spreading his arms wide in joyful greeting. 'After all these years! Still playing Patroclus to our Achilles? And already a captain! Congratulations!'

This effusive declaration, however, made no impression at all on the Cossack officer, or if it did, it was an unfavourable one. The captain surveyed the young dandy with a withering glance from his gypsy-black eyes and slammed the door shut

7

without saying another word. Fandorin was left frozen to the spot with his arms flung out to both sides in a ridiculous posture – as if he had been about to launch into a dance but had changed his mind.

'Yes, indeed,' he muttered in embarrassment, 'everything really has changed. Not only the city, but the people as well.'

'Will you be ordering breakfast in your suite, sir?' the reception clerk asked, pretending not to have noticed the collegiate assessor's discomfiture.

'No, I shan't,' the guest replied. 'Have them bring up a pailful of ice from the cellar instead. In fact, make it t-two pailfuls.'

Once in his spacious and luxuriously appointed apartment, Fandorin began behaving in a most unusual manner. He stripped naked, stood on his hands and pushed himself up from the floor ten times with his legs scarcely even touching the wall. The Japanese servant was not surprised in the least by his master's behaviour. Taking the two pails full of chipped ice from the floor attendant, the Oriental carefully tipped the rough grey cubes into the bath, added some cold water from the bronze tap and waited for the collegiate assessor to complete his bizarre gymnastic routine.

A few moments later Fandorin, flushed from his exertions, walked into the bathroom and resolutely immersed himself in the fearsome font of ice.

'Masa, get my dress uniform. And decorations. In the little velvet boxes. I shall go to introduce myself to the prince.' He spoke curtly, through clenched teeth. His manner of bathing evidently required a significant effort of will.

'To the Emperor's viceroy, your new master?' Masa enquired respectfully. 'Then I shall get your sword as well. You must have your sword. There was no need for you to stand on ceremony with the Russian ambassador in Tokyo. But the governor of such a big stone city is a quite different matter. Do not even try to argue.'

He disappeared and soon returned with a state functionary's ceremonial sword, carrying it reverentially in his outstretched hands.

Evidently realising that it was indeed pointless to argue, Erast Petrovich merely sighed.

'Now, how about that courtesan, master?' Masa enquired, gazing in concern at Erast Petrovich's face, which was blue from cold. 'Your health comes first.'

'Go to hell.' Fandorin stood up, with his teeth chattering. 'A t-towel and my c-clothes.'

'Come in, dear fellow, come in. We've been waiting for you. The membership of the secret sanhedrin, so to speak, is now complete, heh-heh.' These were the words with which Mother Moscow's all-powerful master, Prince Vladimir Andreevich Dolgorukoi, greeted the smartly decked-out collegiate assessor. 'Well, don't just stand there in the doorway! Come and sit down over here, in the armchair. And there was no need to get dolled up in that uniform or bring your sword. When you come to see me, you can dress simply, in a frock coat.'

During the six years that Erast Petrovich had spent on his foreign travels, the old governor-general's health had seriously declined. His chestnut curls (quite evidently of artificial origin) stubbornly refused to agree terms with a face furrowed by deep wrinkles, his drooping moustache and luxuriant sideburns were suspiciously free of grey hairs, and his excessively upright, youthful bearing prompted thoughts of a corset. The prince had governed Russia's old capital for a decade and a half – governed it with a grip that was gentle but firm.

'This is our guest from foreign parts,' said the governor, addressing the two important-looking gentlemen, a military man and a civilian, who were already seated in armchairs beside the immense desk. 'My new deputy for special assignments, Collegiate Assessor Fandorin. Appointed to me from

St Petersburg, and formerly employed in our embassy at the far end of the world, in the Japanese empire. Allow me to introduce you, my dear fellow,' said the prince, addressing Fandorin. 'Moscow's chief of police, Evgeny Osipovich Karachentsev. A bulwark of law and order.' He indicated a red-headed general of the royal retinue, whose slightly slanting brown eyes held an expression that was both calm and keen. 'And this is my Petrusha – Pyotr Parmyonovich Khurtinsky to you – a court counsellor and head of the secret section of the governor-general's chancellery. When anything happens in Moscow, Petrusha hears about it immediately and reports to me.'

A portly gentleman of about forty, his hair combed across the elongated form of his head with exquisite precision, plump jowls propped up on a starched collar and drowsy eyelids half-closed, nodded sedately.

'I specially requested you to come on Friday, my dear fellow,' the governor declared cordially. 'At eleven o'clock on Fridays it is my custom to discuss various matters of a secret and delicate nature. At this very moment we are about to touch on the delicate question of where to obtain the money to complete the murals in the cathedral. God's work, and a cross I have borne for many years.' He crossed himself piously. 'Malicious intrigue is rife among the artists, and there's no lack of pilfering either. We shall be considering how to squeeze a million roubles out of Moscow's fat moneybags for a holy cause. Well now, my secret gentlemen, there used to be two of you, and now there will be three. My blessings on this union, as they say. Mr Fandorin, you have been appointed to me especially for secret matters, have you not? Your references are quite excellent, especially considering your age. You are clearly quite a man of the world.'

He glanced searchingly into the newcomer's eyes, but Fandorin withstood his look without appearing particularly perturbed.

'I do remember you, you know,' Dolgorukoi continued, transformed once again into a benign uncle. 'Of course I do; I was at your wedding. I remember everything, yes ... You've matured, changed a great deal. Well, I'm not getting any younger either. Sit down, my dear fellow, sit down; I'm no lover of formalities ...'

As though inadvertently, he drew the newcomer's service record closer to him – he had remembered the surname but the first name and patronymic had slipped his mind, and the highly experienced Vladimir Andreevich knew that in such matters even the slightest faux pas was quite impermissible. Any man was likely to take offence if his name were remembered incorrectly, and there was absolutely no point in offending his subordinates unnecessarily.

Erast Petrovich – that was what they called this young Adonis. Glancing at his open service record, the prince frowned, because something was definitely not right. The record had a whiff of danger about it. The governor-general had already looked through his new associate's personal file several times, but things had not become any clearer as a result. Fandorin's file really did read most enigmatically. Let's see, twenty-six years of age, Orthodox Christian by confession, hereditary nobleman and native of Moscow. So far, so good. On graduating from grammar school, at his own request appointed by decree of the Moscow police to the rank of collegiate registrar and given a position as a clerk in the Criminal Investigation Department. That was clear enough too. But then followed a series of absolute marvels. What was this, for instance, only two months later? *'For outstanding devotion to duty and superlative service graciously promoted by His Majesty to the rank of titular counsellor without regard to seniority and attached to the Ministry of Foreign Affairs.'* And further on, in the 'awards' section, something even more outlandish: *'Order of St Vladimir, fourth class, for the "Azazel" case (secret archive of the Special Gendarmes Corps)'*; *'Order of St Stanislav, third class, for the "Turkish Gambit" case (secret archive of the Ministry of War)'; 'Order of St Anne for the "Diamond Chariot" case (secret archive of the Ministry of Foreign Affairs)'.* Nothing but one secret after another!

Erast Petrovich cast a tactful but acute glance at his superior and formed his first impression in a moment. On the whole it was a positive one. The prince was old, but he was not yet in his dotage and apparently quite capable of playing whatever part he might choose. Nor did the struggle that was reflected in His Excellency's face as he looked through the service record escape the collegiate assessor's attention. Fandorin sighed sympathetically, for although he had not read his own file, he could more or less imagine what might be written in it.

Erast Petrovich also took advantage of the pause in the conversation to steal a look at the two functionaries whose duty it was to know all of Moscow's secrets. Khurtinsky squinted at him cordially, smiling in an apparently friendly manner, but really only with his lips and somehow not exactly at Fandorin but at daydreams of his own. Erast Petrovich did not return the court counsellor's smile; he was only too familiar with people of this kind and disliked them intensely. However, he quite liked the look of the chief of police and smiled briefly at the general, although without the slightest hint of servility. The general nodded courteously, and yet the glance he cast at the young man seemed strangely tinged with pity. Erast Petrovich did not allow this to bother him – everything would be made clear in good time – and he turned back to the prince, who was also participating in this silent ritual of mutual inspection, conducted circumspectly within the bounds of due propriety.

One especially deep wrinkle had appeared on the prince's brow in testimony to his state of extreme preoccupation. The main thought in His Excellency's mind at that precise moment was: 'Could you possibly have been sent by the camarilla, my pretty young fellow? To undermine my position, perhaps? It looks very much like it. I have enough trouble already with Karachentsev.'

The police chief's pitying glance, however, resulted from considerations of an entirely different nature. Lying in Karachentsev's pocket was a letter from his direct superior, the director of the Department of State Police, Vyacheslav Konstantinovich Plevako. Karachentsev's old friend and mentor had written in a private capacity to tell him that Fandorin was a sound individual of proven merit who had formerly enjoyed the confidence of the deceased monarch, and in particular of the chief of gendarmes, but during his years of foreign service he had lost touch with high-level politics and had now been dispatched to Moscow because no use could be found for him in the capital. At first glance Karachentsev had rather taken a liking to the young man, with that piercing gaze and dignified bearing of his. The poor fellow was unaware that the supreme authorities had given him up for lost and he meant no more to them than an old galosh destined for the rubbish heap. Such were General Karachentsev's thoughts.

As for Pyotr Parmyonovich Khurtinsky – God only knew what he might be thinking. That enigmatic individual's thoughts followed far too devious a path.

This dumbshow was ended by the appearance of a new character, who emerged silently from the depths of the governor's inner apartments. He was a tall, emaciated old man in threadbare livery with a shiny, bald cranium and sleek, neatly combed sideburns. He carried a silver tray with several small bottles and glasses on it.

'Time to take your constipation remedy, Excellency,' the servant announced grumpily. 'You'll only be complaining afterwards that Frol didn't make you take it. Have you forgotten the terrible way you were moaning and groaning yesterday? Well then. Come on now, open wide.'

The very same kind of tyrant as my Masa, thought Fandorin, *although he could hardly look more different. What do we do to deserve such affliction?*

'Yes, yes, Frolushka,' said the prince, capitulating immediately. 'I'll take it, I'll take it. Erast Petrovich, this is my valet, Frol Grigorich Vedishchev. He has looked after me since I was a baby. Now, how about you, gentlemen? Would you care to try it? A most splendid herbal infusion. It tastes horrible, but it is supremely effective against indigestion and stimulates the functioning of the intestines quite superbly. Frol, pour them some.'

Karachentsev and Fandorin refused the herbal mixture point-blank, but Khurtinsky drank it and even declared that it tasted rather pleasant in an odd sort of way.

To follow, Frol gave the prince a decoction of sweet fruit liqueur and a slice of bread and butter (he did not offer these to Khurtinsky) and wiped His Excellency's lips with a cambric napkin.

'Well now, Erast Petrovich, what special assignments am I to occupy you with? I really can't think,' said Dolgorukoi, shrugging and raising his greasy hands. 'As you can see, I already have enough advisers on secret matters. But never mind, don't you fret. Settle in, get to know your way around …' He gestured vaguely, thinking to himself: *And meanwhile we'll see what sort of chap you are.*

At this point the antediluvian clock with the bas-relief chimed sonorously eleven times and the third and final link was added to the fatal chain of coincidences. The door that led into the reception room swung open without any knock, the contorted features of a secretary appeared abruptly in the gap and the atmosphere in the study was galvanised by the invisible but unmistakable charge of a Catastrophe.

'Disaster, Your Excellency!' the secretary declared in a trembling voice. 'General Sobolev is dead! His personal orderly Captain Gukmasov is here.'

This news affected the individuals present in different ways, each in accordance with his own temperament. The governor-general waved his hand at the grief-stricken messenger, as if to say: Away with you, I refuse to believe it – and then crossed himself with that same hand. The head of the secret department momentarily opened his eyes as wide as they would go and then rapidly lowered his eyelids again. The red-headed chief of police leapt to his feet, and the young collegiate assessor's face reflected two feelings in succession: initial extreme agitation, followed immediately by an expression of deep thought, which he retained throughout the scene that followed.

'Send in the captain, will you, Innokenty,' Dolgorukoi ordered his secretary in a low voice. 'What a terrible business!'

The same valiant officer who the day before in the hotel had declined to throw himself into Erast Petrovich's embrace entered the room with a precisely measured stride, jingling his spurs. He was clean-shaven now, and wearing his Life-Cossack dress uniform with an entire icon-screen of crosses and medals.

'Your Excellency, senior orderly to Adjutant-General Mikhal Dmitrich Sobolev, Captain Gukmasov!' the officer introduced himself. 'Woeful news ...' He controlled himself with an effort, twitched his black bandit's moustache and continued. 'The commander of the Fourth Army Corps arrived yesterday from Minsk en route to his estate in Ryazan and put up at the Hotel Dusseaux. This morning Mikhal Dmitrich was very late leaving his room. We became concerned and began knocking, but he did not answer. Then we ventured to enter, and he ...' The captain made one more titanic effort and managed after all to complete his report without allowing his voice to tremble. 'The general was sitting in an armchair. Dead ... We called a doctor. He said that there was nothing to be done. The body was already cold.'

'Ai-ai-ai,' said the governor, propping his cheek on his

palm. 'How could it happen? Mikhail Dmitrievich is so young. Not even forty yet, I suppose?'

'He was thirty-eight, not yet thirty-nine,' Gukmasov replied, his strained voice on the verge of breaking and his eyes blinking rapidly.

'But what was the cause of death?' asked Karachentsev, frowning. 'The general was not unwell, was he?'

'Not in the least. He was perfectly hale and hearty, in excellent spirits. The doctor suspects a stroke or a heart attack.'

'Very well. You may go now, go,' said the prince, dismissing the orderly. He was shaken by the news. 'I'll see to everything and inform His Majesty. Go.' But when the door closed behind the captain, he sighed mournfully. 'Ah, gentlemen, now there'll be a fine to-do. This is a serious business – a man like that, loved and admired by the whole of Russia. And not only Russia – the whole of Europe knows the White General … And I was planning to call on him today … Petrusha, you send a telegram to His Highness the Emperor; you can work out what needs to be said for yourself. No, show it to me first. And afterwards make arrangements for the period of mourning, the funeral and … well, you know all about that. And you, Evgeny Osipovich, maintain order for me. The moment the word spreads, everyone in Moscow will go rushing to the Dusseaux. So make sure that no one gets crushed while feelings are running high. I know the people of Moscow. You must maintain discipline and decorum.'

The chief of police nodded and picked up a folder from an armchair.

'Permission to leave, Your Excellency?'

'Off you go. Oho, what an uproar there'll be now, what an uproar,' said the prince, then he started, struck by a sudden thought. 'But it is likely, is it not, gentlemen, that His Majesty himself will come? He is certain to come. After all, this is not just anybody: it is the hero of Plevna and

Turkestan who has surrendered his soul to God. A knight without fear or reproach, deservingly dubbed the Russian Achilles for his valour. We must prepare the Kremlin Palace. I shall deal with that myself ...'

Khurtinsky and Karachentsev started towards the door, intent on carrying out their instructions, but the collegiate assessor remained seated in his armchair as though nothing had happened, regarding the prince with a strange air of bafflement.

'Ah, yes, Erast Petrovich, my dear fellow,' said Dolgorukoi, suddenly remembering the newcomer. 'As you can see, I have no time for you just now. You can get your bearings in the meantime. Yes, and stay close at hand. I may have instructions for you. There will be plenty of work for everyone. Oh, what a terrible calamity.'

'But Your Excellency, surely there will be an investigation?' Fandorin asked unexpectedly. 'Such an important individual. And a strange death. It ought to be looked into.'

'Come now, what investigation?' the prince replied with a frown of annoyance. 'I told you, His Majesty will be coming.'

'Nonetheless, I have grounds to suppose that foul play is involved,' the collegiate assessor declared with astounding equanimity.

His calm words produced the impression of an exploding grenade. 'What kind of absurd fantasy is this?' cried Karachentsev, instantly abandoning the slightest shred of sympathy for this young fellow.

'Grounds?' Khurtinsky snapped derisively. 'What grounds could you possibly have? How could you possibly know anything at all?'

Without even glancing at the court counsellor, Erast Petrovich continued to address the governor: 'By your leave, Your Excellency. I happen by chance to be staying at the Dusseaux. That is one. I have known Mikhail Dmitrievich for a very long time. He always rises with the dawn, and it is quite impossible to imagine that the general would remain in bed until such a late hour. His retinue would have become alarmed at six in the morning. That is two. And I saw Captain Gukmasov, whom I also know very well, at half past eight. He was unshaven. That is three.'

Here Fandorin paused significantly, as though the final point were of particular consequence.

'Unshaven? Well, what of it?' the chief of police asked, puzzled.

'The point, Your Excellency, is that never, under any circumstances whatever, could Gukmasov be unshaven at half past eight in the morning. I went through the B-Balkan campaign with that man. He is punctilious to the point of pedantry, and he never left his tent without having shaved, not even if there was no water and he had to melt snow. I suspect that Gukmasov already knew his superior was dead first thing in the morning. If he knew, then why did he keep silent for so long? That is four. This business needs to be investigated. Especially if His M-Majesty is going to be here.'

This final consideration seemed to impress the governor more powerfully than any other. 'What can I say? Erast Petrovich is right,' said the prince, rising to his feet. 'This is a matter of state importance. I hereby inaugurate a secret investigation into the circumstances of the demise of Adjutant-General Sobolev. And, clearly, there will also have to be an autopsy. But take care, Evgeny Osipovich, tread carefully; no publicity. There will be rumours enough as it is ... Petrusha, you will gather the rumours and report to me personally. The investigation will be led, naturally, by Evgeny Osipovich. Oh yes, and don't forget to give instructions to embalm the body. A lot of people will want to say goodbye to their hero, and it is a hot summer. God forbid that he should start to smell. And as for you, Erast Petrovich, since the hand of Fate has already placed you in the Dusseaux, and since you knew the deceased so well, try to get to the bottom of this business in your own way, acting in a personal capacity, so to speak. It is fortunate that you are not yet known in Moscow. You are, after all, my deputy for special assignments – and what assignment could possibly be more special than this?'

Chapter Two

Erast Petrovich's way of setting about his investigation into the death of the illustrious general and people's favourite was rather strange. Having forced his way into the hotel with considerable difficulty, since it was surrounded on all sides by a double cordon of police and grieving Muscovites (from time immemorial mournful rumours had always spread through the ancient city more rapidly than the voracious conflagrations of August), the young man, glancing neither to the right nor the left, walked up to apartment number 20 and flung his uniform cap and sword at his servant without speaking, answering all of his questions with a brief nod of the head. Well used to his ways, Masa bowed in understanding and promptly spread out a straw mat on the floor. He respectfully wrapped the short little sword in silk and placed it on the sideboard. Then, without saying a word, he went out into the corridor, stood with his back to the door and assumed the pose of the fearsome god Fudomyo, the Lord of Fire. Whenever anybody came walking along the corridor, Masa pressed his finger to his lips, clucked his tongue reproachfully and pointed either to the closed door or to the approximate position of his own navel. As a result, the rumour instantly spread through that floor of the hotel that the occupant of apartment 20 was a Chinese princess who was due to give birth, and perhaps she was even giving birth at that very moment.

Meanwhile Fandorin was sitting absolutely motionless on the mat. His knees were parted; his body was relaxed; his hands were turned with their palms upwards. The collegiate assessor's gaze was directed at his own belly or, more precisely, at the bottom button of his uniform jacket. Somewhere beneath that twin-headed gold eagle there lay the magical *tanden*, the point that is the source and centre of spiritual energy. If he could renounce all thoughts and immerse himself completely in apprehending his own self, then enlightenment would dawn in his spirit and even the most complex and puzzling of problems would appear simple, clear and soluble. Erast Petrovich strove with all his might for renunciation and enlightenment, a very difficult goal that can only be achieved following long training. His natural liveliness of thought and the restless impatience that it bred made this exercise in inward concentration particularly difficult. But, as Confucius said, the noble man does not follow the road that is easy, but the one that is hard, and therefore Fandorin obstinately continued staring at that cursed button and waiting for something to happen.

At first his thoughts absolutely refused to withdraw; on the contrary, they fluttered and thrashed about like little fish in shallow water. Then all external sounds gradually began to recede until they disappeared completely, the fish swam away to deeper waters, and his head was filled with swirling fog. Erast contemplated the crest on the circle of metal and thought of nothing. A second, a minute, or perhaps even an hour later, the eagle suddenly quite clearly nodded both its heads, the crown began sparkling brightly and Erast Fandorin roused himself. His plan of action had composed itself of its own accord.

The collegiate assessor's subsequent movements were confined to the limits of the hotel, following a route from the foyer to the doorman's lodge to the restaurant. His conversations with the hotel staff occupied rather more than a mere hour or two, and so when Erast Petrovich eventually found himself at the door leading into what was already known in the Dusseaux as 'the Sobolev section', it was almost evening; the shadows had already lengthened and the sunlight was as thick and syrupy as lime-flower honey.

Fandorin gave his name to the gendarme guarding the entrance to the corridor and was immediately admitted into a realm of sorrow, where people spoke only in whispers and walked only on tip-toe. Apartment 47, into which the valiant general had moved the previous day, consisted of a drawing room and a bedroom. In the first of these a rather large company of people had gathered: Erast Petrovich saw Karachentsev with high-ranking gendarme officers, the deceased's adjutants and orderlies, the manager of the hotel and Sobolev's valet, Lukich, a character famous throughout the whole of Russia, who was standing in the corner with his nose thrust into the door curtain and sobbing quietly. Everyone kept glancing at the closed door of the bedroom, as if they were waiting for something.

The chief of police approached Fandorin and said in a quiet, deep voice: 'Welling, the professor of forensic medicine, is performing the autopsy. Seems to be taking a very long time. I wish he'd get a move on.'

As though in response to the general's wish, the white door with carved lions' heads gave a sudden jerk and creaked open. The drawing room immediately went very quiet. A grey-haired gentleman with fat, drooping lips and a disgruntled expression appeared in the doorway, wearing a leather apron surmounted by a glittering enamel Cross of St Anne.

'Well now, Your Excellency, of course,' the fat-lipped man – evidently Professor Welling himself – declared gloomily, 'I can present my findings.'

The general looked round the room and spoke in a rather more cheerful voice: 'I shall take in Fandorin, Gukmasov and you.' He jerked his chin casually in the direction of the hotel manager. 'The rest of you please wait here.'

The first thing that Erast Petrovich saw on entering the abode of death was a mirror in a frivolous bronze frame draped with a black shawl. The body of the deceased was not lying on the bed, but on a table that had evidently been brought through from the drawing room. Fandorin glanced at the form vaguely outlined by the white sheet and crossed himself, forgetting about the investigation for a moment as he remembered the handsome, brave, strong man he had once known, who had now been transformed into an indistinct, oblong object ...

'An obvious case,' the professor began dryly. 'Nothing suspicious has been discovered. I will analyse some samples in the laboratory as well, but I am absolutely certain that vital functions ceased as a result of paralysis of the heart muscle. There is also paralysis of the right lung, but that is probably a consequence, not a cause. Death was instantaneous. Even if a doctor had been present, he would not have been able to save him.'

'But he was so young and full of life; he had been through hell and back!' Karachentsev exclaimed, approaching the table and folding back a corner of the sheet. 'How could he just up and die like that?'

Gukmasov turned away in order not to see his superior's dead face, but Erast Petrovich and the hotel manager moved closer. The face was calm and solemn. Even the famous sideburns, the subject of so much humorous banter by the liberals and scoffing by foreign caricaturists, had proved fitting in death: they framed the waxy face and lent it even greater grandeur.

'Oh, what a hero, a genuine Achilles,' the hotel manager murmured, burring the letter 'r' in the French manner.

'Time of death?' asked Karachentsev.

'Sometime during the first two hours after midnight,' Welling replied confidently. 'No earlier, and definitely no later.'

The general turned to the Cossack captain: 'Right, now that the cause of death has been established, we can deal with the details. Tell us what happened, Gukmasov, with as much detail as possible.'

The captain evidently did not know how to describe events in great detail. His account was brief, but nonetheless comprehensive.

'We arrived here from the Bryansk Station after five o'clock. Mikhal Dmitrich rested until the evening. At nine we dined in the restaurant here, then we went for a ride to look at Moscow by night. We did not stop off anywhere. Shortly after midnight Mikhal Dmitrich said that he wished to come back to the hotel. He wanted to make some notes; he was working on some new rules of engagement ...' Gukmasov cast a sidelong glance at the bureau by the window. There were sheets of paper laid out on the fold-down writing surface and a chair casually standing where it had been moved back and a little to one side.

Karachentsev walked across, picked up a sheet of paper covered in writing and nodded his head respectfully. 'I'll give instructions for it all to be gathered together and forwarded to the Emperor. Continue, Captain.'

'Mikhal Dmitrich dismissed the officers, telling them they were free to go. He said he would walk the rest of the way back; he felt like taking a stroll.'

Karachentsev pricked up his ears at that: 'And you let the general go off on his own? At night? That's rather strange!'

He glanced significantly at Fandorin, but the collegiate assessor appeared entirely uninterested in this detail – he walked over to the bureau and ran his finger over the bronze candelabrum for some reason.

'There was no arguing with him,' said Gukmasov, with a bitter laugh. 'I tried to object, but he gave me such a look, that ... After all, Your Excellency, he was used to strolling around on his own in the Turkish mountains and the Tekin steppes, never mind the streets of Moscow ...' The captain twirled one side of his long moustache gloomily. 'Mikhal Dmitrich got back to the hotel all right. He just didn't live until the morning ...'

'How did you discover the body?' asked the chief of police.

'He was sitting here,' said Gukmasov, pointing to the light armchair. 'Leaning backwards. And his pen was lying on the floor ...'

Karachentsev squatted down and touched the blotches of ink on the carpet. He sighed and said: 'Yes, indeed, the Lord moves ...'

The mournful pause that followed was unceremoniously interrupted by Fandorin. Half-turning towards the hotel manager and continuing to stroke that ill-starred candelabrum, he asked in a loud whisper: 'Why have you not installed electricity here? I was surprised about that yesterday. Such a modern hotel, and it doesn't even have gas – you light the rooms with candles.'

The Frenchman tried to explain that candles were in better taste than gas, that there was already electric lighting in the restaurant, and it would definitely appear on the other floors before autumn; but Karachentsev cut short this idle chatter that had nothing to do with the case by angrily clearing his throat.

'And how did you spend the night, Captain,' he asked, continuing with his cross-examination.

'I paid a call to an army comrade of mine, Colonel Dadashev. We sat and talked. I got back to the hotel at dawn and collapsed into bed immediately.'

'Yes-yes,' Erast Petrovich interjected, 'the night porter told me that it was already light when you got back. You also sent him to get a bottle of seltzer water.'

'That's correct. To be quite honest, I had drunk too much. My throat was parched. I always rise early, but this time, as luck would have it, I overslept. I was about to barge in with a report for the general, but Lukich told me that he had not risen yet. I thought Mikhal Dmitrich must have worked late into the night. Then, when it got to half past eight, I said, "Come on, Lukich, let's wake him or he'll be angry with us. And this isn't like him, anyway." We came in here, and he was stretched out like this' – Gukmasov flung his head back, screwed up his eyes and half-opened his mouth – 'and cold already. We called a doctor and sent a telegram to the army corps ... That was when you saw me, Erast Petrovich. I apologise for not greeting an old comrade but – you understand, I had other things to deal with.'

Rather than acknowledge the apology, which in any case was absolutely unnecessary under the circumstances, Erast Petrovich inclined his head slightly to one side, put his hands behind his back and said: 'But you know they told me in the restaurant here that yesterday a certain lady sang for His Excellency the general and apparently even sat at your table. An individual well known in Moscow, I believe? If I am not mistaken, her name is Wanda. And it appears that all of you, including the general, left with her?'

'Yes, there was a chanteuse of some sort,' the captain replied coldly. 'We gave her a lift and dropped her off somewhere. Then we carried on.'

'Where did you drop her off – at the Anglia Hotel on Stoleshnikov Lane?' the collegiate assessor asked, demonstrating how well informed he was. 'I was told that is where Miss Wanda resides?'

Gukmasov knitted his menacing brows and his voice became so dry it virtually grated: 'I don't know Moscow very well. Not far from here. It only took us five minutes to get there.'

Fandorin nodded, evidently no longer interested in the captain – he had noticed the door of a wall safe beside the bed. He walked over to it, turned the handle, and the door opened.

'What's in there – is it empty?' asked the chief of police.

26

Erast Petrovich nodded: 'Yes, indeed, Your Excellency. Here's the key sticking out of the lock.'

'Right then,' said Karachentsev, tossing his red head of hair, 'seal up any papers that we find. We'll sort out later what goes to the relatives, what goes to the ministry and what goes to His Majesty himself. Professor, you send for your assistants and get on with the embalming.'

'What, right here?' Welling asked indignantly. 'It's not like pickling cabbage, you know, General.'

'Do you want me to ferry the body all the way across the city to your academy? Look out of the window; look how tightly they're crammed together out there! I'm afraid not; do the best you can here. Thank you, Captain, you are dismissed. And you,' he said, turning to the hotel manager, 'give the professor everything he asks for.'

When Karachentsev and Fandorin were left alone, the red-headed general took the young man by the elbow, led him away from the body under the sheet and asked in a low voice, as though the corpse might overhear: 'Well, what do you make of it? As far as I can tell from the questions you ask and the way you behave, you weren't satisfied with Gukmasov's explanations. Why do you think he was not being honest with us? He explained his unshaven condition this morning quite convincingly, after all, or don't you agree? He slept late after a night of drinking – nothing unusual about that.'

'Gukmasov could not have slept late,' Fandorin said with a shrug. 'His training would never allow it. And he certainly wouldn't have gone barging in to see Sobolev, as he says he did, without tidying himself up first. The captain is lying, that much is clear. But the case, Your Excellency—'

'Call me Evgeny Osipovich,' the general interrupted, listening with rapt attention.

'The case, Evgeny Osipovich,' Fandorin continued, bowing politely, 'is even more serious than I thought. Sobolev did not die here.'

'What do you mean, not here?' gasped the chief of police. 'Where, then?'

'I don't know. But permit me to ask one question: Why did the night porter – and I have spoken with him – not see Sobolev return?'

'He could have left his post and doesn't want to admit it,' Karachentsev objected, more for the sake of argument than as a serious suggestion.

'That is not possible, and in a little while I shall explain why. But here is a mystery for you that you will definitely not be able to explain. If Sobolev had returned to his apartment during the night, then sat down at the desk and written something, he would have had to light the candles. But take a look at the candelabrum – the candles are unused!'

'So they are!' said the general, slapping his hand against a thigh tightly encased in military breeches. 'Oh, well done, Erast Petrovich. And what a fine detective I am!' He smiled disarmingly. 'I was only recently appointed to the gendarmes; before that I was in the Cavalry Guards ... So, what do you think could have happened?'

Fandorin raised and lowered his silky eyebrows, concentrating hard. 'I would not like to guess, but it is perfectly clear that after supper Mikhail Dmitrich did not return to his apartment, since it was already dark by then and, as we already know, he did not light the candles. The waiters also confirm that Sobolev and his retinue left immediately after their meal. And the night porter is a reliable individual who values his job very highly – I don't believe that he could have left his post and missed the general's return.'

'What you do or don't believe is no argument,' Evgeny Osipovich teased the collegiate assessor. 'Give me the facts.'

'By all means,' said Fandorin with a smile. 'After midnight the door of the hotel is closed on a spring latch. Anyone who wishes to leave can easily do so, but anyone who wishes to enter has to ring the bell.'

'Now that is a fact,' the general admitted. 'But please continue.'

'The only moment at which Sobolev could have returned is when our d-dashing captain sent the porter to get some seltzer water. However, as we know, that happened when it was already dawn – that is to say, no earlier than four o'clock. If we are to believe Mr Welling (and what reason have we to doubt the judgement of that venerable gentleman?), by that time Sobolev had already been dead for several hours. What, then, is the conclusion?'

Karachentsev's eyes glinted angrily. 'Well, and what is it?'

'Gukmasov sent the porter away so that he could bring in Sobolev's lifeless body without being noticed. I suspect that the other officers of the retinue were outside at the time.'

'Then the scoundrels must be thoroughly interrogated,' the police chief roared so ferociously that they heard him in the next room, where the vague drone of voices immediately ceased.

'Pointless. They have already conspired. That is why they were so late in reporting the death: they needed time to prepare.' Erast Petrovich gave the general a moment to cool down and absorb what he had said, then turned the conversation in a different direction. 'Who is this Wanda that everybody knows?'

'Well, perhaps not everybody, but in certain circles she is a well-known individual. A German woman from Riga. A singer and a beauty, not exactly a courtesan, but something of the kind. A sort of *dame aux camélias*.' Karachentsev nodded briskly. 'I see where your thoughts are leading. This Wanda will clear everything up for us. I'll give instructions for her to be brought in immediately.' The general set off resolutely towards the door.

'I wouldn't advise it,' said Fandorin, speaking to his back. 'If anything did happen, this individual will certainly not confide in the police. And she is certainly included in the officers' conspiracy. That is, naturally, if she is involved at all in what happened. Let me have a talk with her myself, Evgeny Osipovich. In my private capacity, eh? Where is the Anglia Hotel? The corner of Stoleshnikov Lane and Petrovka Street?'

'Yes, just five minutes from here.' The chief of police was regarding the young man with evident satisfaction. 'I shall be waiting for news, Erast Petrovich. God be with you.' He made the sign of the cross and the collegiate assessor left the room bearing the blessing of high authority.

Chapter Three

IN WHICH FANDORIN PLAYS HEADS OR TAILS

However, Erast Fandorin did not manage to reach the Anglia Hotel in five minutes. Waiting for him in the corridor outside the fateful apartment number 47 was a sullen-faced Gukmasov.

'Be so good as to step into my room for a couple of words,' he said to Fandorin and, taking a firm grasp of the young man's elbow, he drew him into the apartment next door to the general's.

The apartment was exactly the same as the one that Fandorin himself was occupying. There was already a large group of men in it, scattered around on the divan and the chairs. Erast Petrovich glanced round the faces and recognised the officers from the dead man's retinue whom he had seen only recently in the drawing room next door. The collegiate assessor greeted the assembled company with a slight bow, but no one made any response, and there was evident animosity in the gazes that they turned towards him. Fandorin crossed his arms on his chest and leaned back against the doorpost and the expression on his face also changed – from polite greeting to cold hostility.

'Gentlemen!' Captain Gukmasov announced in a severe, almost ceremonial voice. 'Allow me to introduce Erast Petrovich Fandorin, with whom I have had the honour of being acquainted from the time of the Turkish war. He is now working for the governor-general of Moscow.'

Again not even a single officer so much as inclined his head in greeting. Erast Petrovich refrained from repeating his own greeting to them and waited to see what would happen next.

Gukmasov turned towards him and said: 'And these, Mr Fandorin, are my colleagues: Senior Adjutant Lieutenant-Colonel Baranov, Adjutant Lieutenant Prince Erdeli, Adjutant Staff-Captain Prince Abadziev, Orderly Captain Ushakov, Orderly Cornet Baron Eichgolz, Orderly Cornet Gall, Orderly Lieutenant Markov.'

'I shan't remember them all,' responded Erast Petrovich.

'That will not be necessary,' snapped Gukmasov. 'I have introduced all these gentlemen to you because you owe us an explanation.'

'Owe you?' Fandorin echoed derisively. 'Oh, come now!'

'Yes, indeed, sir. Be so good as to explain in front of every-one here the reason for the insulting interrogation to which you subjected me in the presence of the chief of police.'

The captain's voice was menacing, but the collegiate assessor remained unperturbed and his constant slight stam-mer suddenly disappeared.

'The reason for my questions, Captain, is that the death of Mikhail Dmitrievich Sobolev is a matter of state importance; indeed it is an event of historical significance. That is one.' Fandorin smiled reproachfully. 'But you, Prokhor Akhrameevich have been trying to make fools of us, and very clumsily too. That is two. I have instructions from Prince Dolgorukoi to get to the bottom of this matter. That is three. And you may be certain that I shall get to the bottom of it, you know me. That is four. Or are you going to tell me the truth after all?'

A Caucasian prince in a white Circassian coat with silver cartridge belts – if only Fandorin could remember which of the two he was – leapt up off the divan.

'One-two-three-four! Gentlemen! This sleuth, this lousy civilian, is jeering at us! Prosha, I swear on my mother that I'll—'

'Sit down, Erdeli!' Gukmasov barked, and the Caucasian immediately did so, twitching his chin nervously.

'I certainly do know you, Erast Petrovich. I know you and I respect you.' The captain's expression was grave. 'Mikhal Dmitrich also respected you. If his memory is dear to you, do not interfere in this matter. You will only make things worse.'

Fandorin replied no less sincerely and seriously: 'If it were merely a matter of myself and my own idle curiosity, then I would certainly accede to your request; but I am sorry, in this case I cannot – it is a matter of duty.'

Gukmasov cracked the knuckles of the fingers that he had linked together behind his back and began walking round the room, jingling his spurs. He halted again in front of the collegiate assessor.

'Well now, I cannot accept that either. I cannot allow you to continue with your investigation. Let the police try – but not you, never. This is the wrong case for you to apply your talents to, Mr Fandorin. Be informed that I shall stop you by any means possible, regardless of the past.'

'Which means, for instance, Prokhor Akhrameevich?' Erast Petrovich enquired.

'I'll give you an excellent means!' Lieutenant Erdeli interjected yet again, jumping to his feet. 'You, my dear sir, have insulted the honour of the officers of the Fourth Army Corps, and I challenge you to a duel! Pistols, here, this very minute. To the death, handkerchief terms!'

'As far as I recall the rules of duelling,' Fandorin said dryly, 'the terms of combat are set by the party who is challenged. So be it, I will play this stupid game with you, but later, when I have concluded my investigation. You may send your seconds to me; I am staying in apartment number twenty. Goodbye, gentlemen.'

He was about to turn round and leave, but, with a cry of 'Then I'll make you fight!' Erdeli bounded over and attempted to slap him across the face. With amazing agility, Erast Petrovich seized the hand that had been raised to strike and squeezed the prince's wrist between his finger and thumb – apparently not very hard, but the lieutenant's face contorted at the pain.

'You scoundr-rel!' the Caucasian shrieked in a high falsetto, flinging out his left hand.

Fandorin pushed the overeager prince away and said fastidiously: 'Don't trouble yourself. We shall regard the blow as having been struck. I challenge you and I shall make you pay for the insult with your blood.'

'Ah, excellent,' said the phlegmatic staff officer whom Gukmasov had introduced as Lieutenant-Colonel Baranov. It was the first time he had opened his mouth. 'Name your terms, Erdeli.'

Rubbing his wrist, the lieutenant hissed malevolently: 'We fight now. Pistols. Handkerchief terms.'

'What does that mean – "handkerchief terms"?' Fandorin enquired curiously. 'I have heard about this custom, but I must confess that I do not know the details.'

'It's very simple,' the lieutenant-colonel told him politely. 'The opponents take hold of the opposite corners of an ordinary handkerchief with their free hands. Here, you can take mine if you like; it is clean.' Baranov took out of his pocket a large red-and-white-checked handkerchief. 'They take their weapons. Gukmasov, where are your Lepage pistols?'

The captain picked up off the table a long case that had obviously been lying there in readiness and opened the lid. The long barrels with inlaid decoration glinted in the light.

'The opponents draw lots to take a pistol,' Baranov continued, smiling peaceably. 'They take aim – although what need is there at that distance? On the command, they fire. That is really all there is to it.'

'Draw lots?' Fandorin enquired. 'You mean to say that one pistol is loaded and the other is not?'

'Naturally,' said the lieutenant-colonel with a nod. 'That is the whole point. Otherwise it would not be a duel but double suicide.'

'Well then,' said the collegiate assessor with a shrug. 'I feel genuinely sorry for the lieutenant. I have never once lost at drawing lots.'

'All things are in God's hands, and it is a bad omen to talk like that; it will bring you bad luck,' Baranov admonished him.

He seems to be the one in charge here, not Gukmasov, thought Erast Petrovich.

'You need a second,' said the morose Cossack captain. 'If you wish, as an old acquaintance, I can offer my services. And you need have no doubt that the lots will be drawn honestly.'

'Indeed I do not doubt it, Prokhor Akhrameevich. But as far as a second is concerned, you will not do. If I should be unlucky, it will appear too much like murder.'

Baranov nodded. 'He is quite right. How pleasant it is to deal with a man of intelligence. And you are also right, Prokhor: he is dangerous. What do you propose, Mr Fandorin?'

'Will a Japanese citizen suit you as my second? You see, I only arrived in Moscow today and have had no time to make any acquaintances ...' The collegiate assessor spread his arms in a gesture of apology.

'A Papuan savage will do,' exclaimed Erdeli. 'Only let's get on with it!'

'Will there be a doctor?' asked Erast Petrovich.

'A doctor will not be required,' sighed the lieutenant-colonel. 'At that distance a shot is fatal.'

'Very well. I was not actually concerned for myself, but for the prince ...'

Erdeli uttered some indignant exclamation in Georgian and withdrew into the far corner of the room.

Erast Petrovich expounded the essence of the matter in a short note written in bizarre characters running from the top to the bottom of the page and from right to left, and asked for the note to be taken to apartment number 20.

Masa was not quick to come – fifteen minutes passed before he arrived. The officers had begun to feel nervous and appeared to suspect the collegiate assessor of not playing fair.

The appearance of the offended party's second created a considerable impression. Masa was a great enthusiast of duels, and for the sake of this one he had decked himself out in his formal kimono with tall starched shoulders, put on white socks and girded himself with his finest belt, decorated with a pattern of bamboo shoots.

'What kind of macaque is this?' Erdeli asked with impolite astonishment. 'But who gives a damn anyway. Let's get down to business!'

Masa bowed ceremonially to the assembled company and held out that accursed official sword at arm's length to his master. 'Here is your sword, my lord.'

'How sick I am of you and your sword,' sighed Erast Petrovich. 'I am fighting a duel with pistols. With that gentleman there.'

'Pistols again?' Masa asked disappointedly. 'What a barbaric custom. And who are you going to kill? That hairy man? He looks just like a monkey.'

The witnesses to the duel stood along the walls and Gukmasov, having turned away and juggled with the pistols for a moment, offered the opponents a choice. Erast Petrovich waited as Erdeli crossed himself and took a pistol, then casually picked up the second pistol with his finger and thumb.

Following the captain's instructions, the duellists took hold of the corners of the handkerchief and moved as far as possible away from each other, which even with fully outstretched arms was a distance of no more than three strides. The prince raised his pistol to shoulder level and aimed directly at his opponent's forehead. Fandorin held his weapon by his hip and did not aim at all, since at that distance it was entirely unnecessary.

'One, two, three!' the captain counted quickly, and stepped back.

The hammer of the prince's pistol gave a dry click, but Fandorin's weapon belched out a vicious tongue of flame. The lieutenant fell and began rolling around on the carpet, clutching at his right hand, which had been shot through, and swearing in desperate obscenity.

When his howling had subsided to dull groans, Erast Petrovich chided him: 'You will never again be able to slap anyone's face with that hand.'

There was a clamour in the corridor, with people shouting. Gukmasov opened the door slightly and told someone that there had been an unfortunate accident – Lieutenant Erdeli had been unloading a pistol and had shot himself in the hand. The wounded man was sent to be bandaged up by Professor Welling, who fortunately had not yet left to fetch his embalming equipment, and then everyone returned to Gukmasov's suite.

'Now what?' asked Fandorin. 'Are you satisfied?'

Gukmasov shook his head: 'Now you will fight a duel with me. On the same terms.'

'And then?'

'And then – if you are lucky again – with everyone else in turn. Until you are killed. Erast Petrovich, spare me and my comrades this ordeal.' The captain looked almost imploringly into the young man's eyes. 'Give us your word of honour that you will not take part in the investigation, and we shall part friends.'

'I should count it an honour to be your friend, but what you demand is impossible,' Fandorin declared sadly.

Masa whispered in his ear: 'Master, I do not understand what this man with the red moustache is saying to you, but I sense danger. Would it not be wiser to attack first and kill all these samurai while they are still unprepared? I have your little pistol in my sleeve, and those brass knuckles that I bought for myself in Paris. I would really like to try them out.'

'Masa, forget these bandit habits of yours,' Erast Petrovich told his servant. 'I am going to fight these gentlemen honestly, one by one.'

'Oh-oh, then that will take a long time,' the Japanese said, drawing out the words emphatically. He moved away to the wall and sat down on the floor.

'Gentlemen,' said Fandorin, attempting to make the officers see reason, 'believe me, you will achieve nothing. You will simply be wasting your time ...'

'Enough speechifying,' Gukmasov interrupted him. 'Does your Japanese know how to load duelling pistols? No? Then you load them, Eichgolz.'

Once again the opponents took their pistols and stretched the handkerchief out between them. The captain was morose and determined, but if anything Fandorin seemed rather embarrassed. On the command (Baranov was counting this time), Gukmasov's pistol misfired with a dry click, but Erast Petrovich did not fire at all.

The captain, deadly pale now, hissed through his teeth: 'Shoot, Fandorin, and be damned. And you, gentlemen, decide who is next. And barricade the door so that no one can get in! Don't let him out of here alive.'

'You refuse to listen to me, and that is a mistake,' said the collegiate assessor, waving his loaded pistol in the air. 'I told you that you will achieve nothing by drawing lots. I possess a rare gift, gentlemen – I am incredibly lucky in games of chance. An inexplicable phenomenon. I resigned myself to it a long time ago. Evidently it is all due to the fact that my dear departed father was unlucky to an equally exceptional degree. I always win at every kind of game, which is why I cannot stand them.' He ran his clear-eyed glance over the officers' sullen faces. 'You don't believe me? Do you see this imperial?' Erast Petrovich took a gold coin out of his pocket and handed it to Eichgolz. 'Toss it and I will guess, heads or tails.'

After glancing round at Gukmasov and Baranov, the baron, a young officer with the first vague intimations of a moustache, shrugged and tossed the coin.

It was still spinning in the air when Fandorin said: 'I don't know … Let's say, heads.'

'Heads,' Eichgolz confirmed, and tossed it again.

'Heads again,' the collegiate assessor declared in a bored voice.

'Heads!' exclaimed the baron. 'Good Lord, gentlemen, just look at that!'

'Right Mitya, again,' Gukmasov told him.

'Tails,' said Erast Petrovich, looking away.

A deadly silence filled the room. Fandorin did not even glance at the baron's outstretched palm.

'I told you so. *Masa, ikoo. Owari da.* [Let's go, Masa. It's over.] Goodbye, gentlemen.'

The officers watched in superstitious terror as the functionary and his Japanese servant walked to the door.

As they were leaving, the pale-faced Gukmasov appealed to Erast Petrovich: 'Fandorin, promise me that you will not employ your talent as a detective to the detriment of the fatherland. The honour of Russia is hanging by a thread here.'

Erast Petrovich paused before answering. 'I promise, Gukmasov, that I will do nothing against my own honour and that, I think, is sufficient.'

The collegiate assessor walked straight out through the door, but Masa turned round in the doorway and bowed ceremonially, from the waist, to the officers before following him.

Chapter Four

IN WHICH THE USEFULNESS OF ARCHITECTURAL
EXTRAVAGANCE IS DEMONSTRATED

Whilst the apartments in the Anglia Hotel were a match for the respectable Dusseaux in the magnificence of their appointments, in terms of architectural fancy they actually surpassed it, although the presence of a somewhat dubious, or at least frivolous, quality might possibly have been detected in the sumptuous gilded ceilings and marble volutes. On the other hand, however, the entrance was radiant with bright electric light, one could ride up to the top three floors in a lift, and from time to time the foyer resounded to the shrill jangling of that fashionable marvel of technology, the telephone.

After taking a stroll round the grand foyer with its mirrors and morocco-leather divans, Erast Petrovich halted in front of the board showing the names of the guests. The people who stayed here were a more varied bunch than at the Dusseaux: foreign businessmen, stockbrokers, actors from successful theatres. However, there was no songstress named Wanda to be found on the list.

Fandorin cast a keen eye over the hotel staff darting backwards and forwards between the reception desk and the lift and selected one particularly brisk and efficient waiter with mobile features suggestive of intelligence.

'Tell me, does Miss Wanda n-no longer reside here?' the collegiate assessor asked, feigning slight embarrassment.

'Why certainly the lady does,' the fellow responded eagerly and, following the handsome gentleman's gaze, he pointed to the board. 'Right there, sir: Miss Helga Ivanovna Tolle – that's the lady in question. Uses the name Wanda for the euphonious sound of it. She lives in the annexe. You just go out through that door there, sir, into the yard; Miss Wanda has an apartment there with a separate entrance. Only the lady's not usually in at this time, sir.'

The waiter was about to slip away, but Erast Petrovich rustled a banknote in his pocket, and the good fellow suddenly froze, as if he were rooted to the ground.

'Is there some little errand you'd like done, sir?' he asked, giving the young gentleman a look of affectionate devotion.

'When does she get back?'

'It varies, sir. The lady sings at the Alpine Rose. Every day apart from Mondays. I'll tell you what, sir: you take a seat for a while in the buffet, have a drink of tea or whatever, and I'll make sure to let you know when the mamselle shows up.'

'And what is she like?' asked Erast Petrovich, twirling his fingers vaguely in the air. 'To look at? Is she really so very pretty?'

'A perfect picture, sir,' said the waiter, smacking his plump, red lips. 'Highly respected in these parts. Pays three hundred roubles a month for her apartment and very generous with tips, sir.'

At this point he paused with practised psychological precision and Fandorin slowly took out two one-rouble notes – but then thrust them into his breast pocket with a distracted air.

'Miss Wanda doesn't receive just anybody in her rooms – she's very strict about that, sir,' the waiter declared significantly, his gaze boring into the gentleman's frock coat. 'But I can announce you, seeing as I enjoy her special confidence.'

'Take that then,' said Erast Petrovich, holding out one of the notes. 'You'll g-get the other when Mademoiselle Wanda comes back. Meanwhile I'll go and read a newspaper. Where did you say your buffet was?'

On 25 June 1882 the *Moscow Provincial Gazette* wrote as follows:

A TELEGRAM FROM SINGAPORE

The renowned explorer N.N. Miklukha-Maklai intends to return to Russia on the clipper *Marksman*. Mr Miklukha-Maklai's health has been seriously undermined, he is extremely thin and suffering from constant fevers and chronic neuralgia. For the most part his state of mind is also gloomy. The traveller informed our correspondent that he is sick and tired of wandering and dreams of reaching his native shores as soon as possible.

Erast Petrovich shook his head, vividly picturing to himself the emaciated, twitching face of the martyr of ethnography. He turned over the page.

THE BLASPHEMY OF
AMERICAN ADVERTISING

An inscription in letters half the height of a man recently appeared above Broadway, the main street of New York: 'THE PRESIDENT IS CERTAIN TO DIE'. Dumbfounded passers-by halted, rooted to the spot, and only then were they able to read what was written below in smaller letters: '... in our treacherous climate, if he does not wear warm woollen underwear from Garland and Co.' A representative of the White House has taken the firm to court for exploiting the presidential title for base commercial ends.

Thank God things have not reached that state here and are never likely to, the collegiate assessor thought with some satisfaction. *After all, His Majesty the Emperor is more than some mere president.*

As a man with a certain interest in belles-lettres, he was naturally drawn to the following headline:

LITERARY TALKS

A large number of listeners were attracted to the spacious hall at the home of Princess Trubetskaya for a talk on contemporary literature given by Professor I. N. Pavlov, which was devoted to an analysis of the recent works of Ivan Turgenev. With the help of illustrative examples, Mr Pavlov demonstrated the depths to which this great talent has sunk in the pursuit of a tendentious and spurious reality. The next reading will be devoted to analysing the works of Shchedrin as the leading representative of the crudest and most fallacious form of realism.

Fandorin was dismayed to read that. Among the Russian diplomats in Japan it was considered good form to praise Turgenev and Shchedrin. How very far he had fallen behind the literary scene in Russia during his absence of almost six years! But what was new in the field of technology?

TUNNEL UNDER THE ENGLISH CHANNEL

The length of the railway tunnel under the English Channel is already approaching 1,200 metres. The engineer Brunton is excavating the galleries with a ram-drill powered by compressed air. According to the plans, the total length of the underground passage should be a little over thirty versts. The initial design envisaged that the English and French galleries would link up after five years,

but sceptics claim that the labour-intensive work of facing
the walls and laying the rails will delay the opening of the
line until at least 1890 ...

With his keen sensitivity to progress, Fandorin found the digging of the Anglo-French tunnel quite fascinating, but something prevented him from reading this interesting article to
the end. A certain gentleman in a grey two-piece suit, whom
Fandorin had only recently spotted beside the head porter in
the vestibule, had been hovering around the buffet counter
for several minutes. The isolated words that reached the collegiate assessor's ears (and his hearing was quite excellent),
seemed to Fandorin so curious that he immediately stopped
reading, although he continued to hold the news-sheet in
front of his face.

'Don't you try putting one over on me,' the grey-suited
gentleman pressed the man behind the counter. 'Were you on
duty last night or not?'

'I was asleep, yer onner,' droned the man, a fat-faced, rosy-
cheeked hulk with a greasy beard combed to both sides. 'The
only one here from the night shift is Senka.' He jerked his
beard in the direction of a boy serving cakes and tea.

The man in grey beckoned Senka to him. *A police sleuth*,
Erast Petrovich thought with unerring accuracy and without
any great surprise. So our chief of police Evgeny Osipovich
was feeling jealous and he didn't want all the laurels to go to
the governor's deputy for special assignments.

'Now tell me, Senya,' the inquisitive gentleman said
ingratiatingly, 'was there a general and some officers at
Mamselle Wanda's place last night?'

Senya twitched his nose, fluttered his white eyelashes and
asked: 'Lasnigh'? A gen'ral?'

'Yes, yes, a gen'ral,' said the sleuth, nodding.

''Ere?' asked the boy, wrinkling up his forehead.

'Yes, here, here, where else!'

'But does gen'rals drive out at nigh'?' Senka enquired suspiciously.

'And why wouldn't they?'

The boy replied with deep conviction: 'Nah, gen'rals sleeps at nigh'. 'At's what gen'rals does.'

'You just watch it, you ... little idiot!' the man in grey exclaimed furiously. 'Or I'll take you down to the station and soon have you singing a different tune.'

'I'm an orphan, mister,' Senka responded swiftly, and his foolish eyes were instantly flooded with tears. 'You can't take me down the station; it gives me the swoons.'

'Are you all in this plot together, or what?' the police agent snapped viciously and stamped out, slamming the door loudly behind him.

'A serious gent'man,' said Senka, looking at the door.

'Yesterday's were more serious,' the counter-man whispered and smacked the lad on the back of his close-cropped head. 'The sort of gentlemen who'd rip your head off without any police or such like. You take care, Senka, keep your mouth shut. Anyway, they probably slipped you something, didn't they?'

'Prof Semyonich, by Christ the Lord,' the boy jabbered, blinking rapidly. 'May I swear on a sacred holy icon! All they give me was fifteen kopecks, and I took that to the chapel and lit a candle for the peace of me mother's soul ...'

'What d'you mean, fifteen kopecks! Don't give me any of your lies. Took it to the chapel!' The man raised his hand to strike Senka, but the boy dodged away nimbly, picked up his tray and dashed off to answer a summons from a customer.

Erast Petrovich set aside his *Moscow Gazette* and went up to the counter. 'Was that man from the police?' he asked with an air of great displeasure. 'I haven't come here just to d-drink tea, my dear fellow; I am waiting for Miss Wanda. Why are the police interested in her?'

The counter-man looked him up and down and asked cautiously: 'You mean to say you've got an appointment, sir?'

'I should say I do have an appointment! Didn't I tell you I am waiting?' The young man's blue eyes expressed extreme concern. 'But I don't want anything to do with the police. Mademoiselle Wanda was recommended to me as a respectable girl, and now I find the p-police here! It's a good job I'm wearing a frock coat and not my uniform.'

'Don't you start fretting, yer onner,' the counter-man reassured the nervous customer. 'The young lady's not some kind of yellow-ticket girl; it's all top-class service with her. There's others come in their uniform and don't count it no shame.'

'In uniform?' The young man couldn't believe it. 'What, even officers?'

The counter-man and young Senka, who had reappeared, exchanged glances and laughed.

'Aim a bit higher,' the boy chortled. 'Even gen'rals comes visiting. And the manner of their visiting is a sight to see. Arrives on their own two feet, they does; then afterwards they 'as to be carried out. That's the kind of jolly mamselle she is!'

Prof Semyonich gave the joker a clout round the ear. 'Don't you go talking nonsense, Senka. I told you to keep your mouth shut.'

Erast Petrovich frowned squeamishly and went back to his table, but he did not feel like reading about the tunnel any longer. He was far too impatient to have a talk with Mademoiselle Helga Ivanovna Tolle.

The collegiate assessor's wait was mercifully brief. After about five minutes the waiter he had spoken to came darting into the buffet, bent down and whispered in his ear: 'The lady's arrived. How shall I announce you?'

Fandorin took a visiting card out of his tortoiseshell wallet and after a moment's thought wrote several words on it with a little silver pencil. 'There, g-give her that.'

The waiter carried out his commission and was back in a trice to announce: 'She asks you to come. Kindly follow me. I'll show you through.'

Outside it was already getting dark. Erast Petrovich examined the annexe in which Mademoiselle Wanda occupied the entire ground floor. It was clear enough why this lady required a separate entrance: her visitors evidently preferred things to remain confidential. Protruding above the tall ground-floor windows was a first-floor balcony, perched on the shoulders of an entire brood of caryatids. To Fandorin's eye, the amount of moulding on the façade was clearly excessive, in keeping with the bad taste of the 1860s, when all the signs indicated that this frivolous building had been erected.

The waiter rang the electric bell and, having received his rouble, withdrew with a bow, striving so diligently to display absolute tact and understanding that he actually tip-toed all the way back across the yard.

The door opened, and Fandorin saw before him a slim, frail woman with high-combed, ash-blonde hair and huge, tantalising green eyes – although at that moment he read caution rather than mockery in the gaze of their owner.

'Come in, mysterious visitor,' the woman said in a low, resonant voice for which the most fitting epithet would have to be the poetic term 'bewitching'. Despite the tenant's German name, Fandorin did not catch even the slightest trace of an accent in her speech.

The apartments occupied by Mademoiselle Wanda consisted of a hallway and a spacious drawing room, which apparently also served the function of a boudoir. It occurred to Erast Petrovich that in view of his hostess's profession this was entirely natural, and he felt embarrassed at the thought, for Mademoiselle Wanda did not resemble a woman of easy virtue. She showed her visitor through into the room, sat down in a soft Turkish armchair, crossing one leg over the other, and stared in anticipation at the young man, who had halted motionless in the doorway. The electric lighting gave Fandorin an opportunity to examine Wanda and her accommodation more closely.

She was not a classic beauty – that was the first thing that Erast Petrovich noted. A little too snub-nosed, he thought, and her mouth was a little too wide, and her cheekbones protruded more noticeably than was required by the classical canon. But none of these imperfections weakened the overall impression of quite uncommon loveliness – on the contrary, in some strange manner they actually reinforced it. He felt as if he could simply go on and on looking at this face – there was so much life and feeling in it, as well as that magical quality known as femininity, which defies description in words but is unerringly discerned by any man. Well then, if Mademoiselle Wanda was so popular in Moscow, it meant that Muscovite taste was not so very bad, reasoned Erast Petrovich, and regretfully tore himself away from the contemplation of this amazing face to look carefully round the room. An absolutely Parisian interior in the colour range of claret to mauve, with a fluffy carpet, comfortable and expensive furniture, numerous table and floor lamps with colourful shades, Chinese figurines, and on the wall – the very latest chic – Japanese prints of geishas and Kabuki theatre actors. In the far corner there was an alcove behind two columns, but a sense of delicacy obliged Fandorin to avert his gaze from that direction.

'What is "everything"?' asked his hostess, breaking a silence that had clearly lasted too long, and Erast Petrovich shivered at the almost physical sensation of that magical voice setting the secret, rarely touched strings of his heart quivering.

The collegiate assessor's face expressed polite incomprehension, and Wanda declared impatiently: 'Mr Fandorin, on your card it said "I know everything". What is "everything"? And who are you, as a matter of fact?'

'Deputy for special assignments to Governor-General Prince Dolgorukoi,' Erast Petrovich replied calmly. 'Assigned to investigate the circumstances of the demise of Adjutant-General Sobolev.'

Seeing his hostess's slim eyebrows shoot up, Fandorin remarked: 'Only do not pretend, madam, that you did not know about the general's death. As for the note on my card, that was written to deceive you. I know far from everything, but I do know the most important thing: Mikhail Dmitrievich Sobolev died in this room at about one o'clock this morning.'

Wanda shuddered and put her thin hands to her throat, as though she suddenly felt cold, but she said nothing.

Erast Petrovich nodded in satisfaction and continued: 'You have not given anyone away, mademoiselle, or broken the word that you gave. The officers themselves are to blame – they covered their own tracks far too clumsily. I shall b-be frank with you in the hope of receiving equal frankness in return. I am in possession of the following information.' He closed his eyes in order not to be distracted by the subtly nuanced pattern of white and pink tones that had appeared on the woman's agitated face. 'From the Dusseaux restaurant you came directly here with Sobolev and his retinue. It was then shortly before midnight. An hour later the general was already dead. The officers carried him out of here, pretending that he was drunk, and took him back to the hotel. If you will complete the picture of what happened, I will try to spare you interrogation at the police station. And by the way, the police have already been here – the hotel staff will probably tell you about it. So let me assure you that it would be much better to make your explanations to me.'

The collegiate assessor paused, calculating that more than enough had already been said. Wanda rose abruptly to her feet, took a Persian shawl from the back of a chair and threw it across her shoulders, although the evening was warm, even a little sultry. She walked round the room twice, glancing from time to time at the expectant functionary.

Finally she stopped, facing him. 'Well, at least you do not look like a policeman. Take a seat. This story might take some time.' She indicated a plump divan covered with embroidered cushions, but Erast Petrovich preferred to take a seat on a chair. *An intelligent woman*, he decided. *Strong. Coolheaded. She won't tell me the whole truth, but she won't lie to me either.*

'I met the great hero yesterday, in the restaurant at the Dusseaux,' Wanda said, taking a small brocade pouffe and sitting beside Fandorin – positioning herself, in fact, so close to him that she was looking up into his face from below. In this foreshortened perspective she appeared alluringly helpless, like some Oriental slave girl at the feet of a pasha.

Erast Petrovich shifted uncomfortably on his chair, but to move away would have been ridiculous.

'A handsome man. Of course, I had heard a lot about him, but I never suspected that he was so very good-looking. Especially his cornflower-blue eyes.' Wanda pensively ran one hand across her eyebrows, as if she were driving away the memory. 'I sang for him. He invited me to sit at his table. I don't know what you have been told about me, but I am certain that a lot of it is lies. I am no hypocrite; I am a free, modern woman, and I decide for myself who to love.' She glanced defiantly at Fandorin and he saw that now she was talking without pretence or affectation. 'If I take a liking to a man and decide that he must be mine, I don't drag him to the altar, the way your "respectable women" do. No, I am not "respectable" – in the sense that I do not accept your definition of respectability.'

This is no slave girl, there is no defencelessness here, Erast Petrovich thought in astonishment, looking down at those sparkling emerald-green eyes; *she is more like the Queen of the Amazons*. He could easily imagine her driving men insane with these impetuous transitions from arrogant defiance to submissiveness and back again. 'Could you please stick more c-closely to the subject,' Fandorin said dryly out loud, trying hard not to give way to inappropriate feelings.

'I could hardly be closer,' the Amazon queen teased him. 'It is not you who buy me; it is I who take you, and I make you pay me for it! How many of your "respectable" women would be only too happy to be unfaithful to their husbands with the White General in secret, skulking like thieves? But I am free and I have no need to hide. Yes, I found Sobolev attractive,' she said, suddenly changing her tone of voice again, from challenging to cunning. 'Yes, why should I pretend I was not flattered by the idea of adding such a big, bright specimen to my butterfly collection? And after that ...' Wanda twitched her shoulder. 'It was the usual thing. We came here, drank some wine. But what happened then, I don't remember very well. My head was spinning. Before I knew what was happening, we were over there, in the alcove.' She laughed hoarsely, but almost immediately her laughter broke off and the light in her eyes faded. 'After that it was horrible; I don't want to remember it. Don't make me tell you the physiological details, all right? You wouldn't wish that on anyone ... A lover in the very height of his passion suddenly stopping like that and falling on you like a dead weight ...' Wanda sobbed and angrily wiped away a tear.

Erast Petrovich followed her expression and intonation carefully. She appeared to be telling the truth. After an appropriate pause, Fandorin asked: 'Did your meeting with the general take place by chance?'

'Yes. That is, of course, not entirely. I heard that the White General was staying at the Dusseaux. I was curious to take a look at him.'

'And did Mikhail Dmitrievich drink a lot of wine here with you?'

'Not at all. Half a bottle of Château d'Yquem.'

Erast Petrovich was surprised. 'Did he bring the wine with him?'

'No, what makes you think that?'

'Well you see, mademoiselle, I knew the deceased quite well. Château d'Yquem was his favourite wine. How could you have known that?'

Wanda fluttered her slim fingers indefinitely. 'I didn't know it at all. But I am also fond of Château d'Yquem. It would seem that the general and I had many things in common. What a pity that the acquaintance proved to be so short,' she laughed bitterly and cast a seemingly casual glance at the clock on the mantelpiece.

The movement was not lost on Fandorin and he deliberately paused for a moment before continuing with the interrogation.

'Well, what happened next is clear. You were frightened. You probably screamed. The officers came running in, they t-tried to revive Sobolev. Did they call a doctor?'

'No, it was obvious that he was dead. The officers almost tore me to pieces.' She laughed again, this time in anger rather than bitterness. 'One of them was especially furious – in a Circassian coat. He kept repeating that it was a disgrace, a threat to the entire cause, shouting about death in a cheap whore's bed.' Wanda smiled disagreeably, revealing her white, perfectly even teeth. 'And there was a Cossack captain who threatened me too. First he sobbed a bit; then he said he would kill me if I said anything and offered me money. I took his money, by the way. And I took his threats seriously too. You never know, I might go down in history as some kind of new Delilah. What do you think, Monsieur Fandorin; will they write about me in the grammar-school textbooks?' And she laughed again, this time with a clear note of defiance.

'Hardly,' Erast Petrovich said pensively.

The overall picture was clear now. And so was the reason

for the obstinacy with which the officers had tried to protect their secret. A national hero could not die like that. It was so improper. Not Russian, somehow. The French would probably have forgiven their idol, but here in Russia it would be regarded as a national disgrace.

Well then, Mademoiselle Wanda had nothing to worry about. It was up to the governor, of course, to decide her fate, but Fandorin was willing to guarantee that the authorities would not harass the free-spirited songstress by opening an official investigation.

It might have seemed that the case could be regarded as closed, but Erast Petrovich was an inquisitive man and there was one small circumstance that was still nagging away at him. Wanda had already glanced stealthily at the clock several times, and the collegiate assessor thought that he could sense a mounting anxiety in those fleeting glances. Meanwhile the hand on the clock was gradually approaching the hour – in five minutes it would be exactly ten. Could Mademoiselle Wanda perhaps be expecting a visitor at ten o'clock? Could this circumstance be the reason for her being so frank and forthcoming? Fandorin hesitated. On the one hand, it would be interesting to discover who his hostess was expecting at such a late hour. On the other hand, Erast Petrovich had been taught from an early age not to foist his company on ladies. In a situation like this a cultured man said his farewells and left, especially when he had already obtained what he came for. What should he do?

His hesitation was resolved by the following common-sense consideration: if he were to linger until ten and wait for the visitor to arrive, then he would probably see him, but unfortunately in Erast Petrovich's presence no conversation would take place – and he wanted very much to hear what that conversation would be about. Therefore Erast Petrovich got to his feet, thanked his hostess for her frankness and took his leave, which was clearly a great relief to Mademoiselle

Wanda. However, once outside the door of the annexe, Fandorin did not set out across the yard. He halted, as if he were brushing a speck of dirt off his shoulder and looked round at the windows to see if Wanda was watching. She was not – which was only natural: any normal woman who has just been left by one guest and is expecting another will dash to the mirror, not the window.

Erast Petrovich also surveyed the brightly lit windows of the hotel's apartments, just to be on the safe side, then set his foot on the low, protruding border of the wall, nimbly levered himself against the slanting surface of the window sill and pulled himself up. A moment later he was above the window of Wanda's bedroom-cum-drawing room, half-lying on a horizontal projection that crowned the upper border of the window. The young man arranged himself on his side on the narrow cornice, with his foot braced against the bust of one caryatid and his hand grasping the sturdy neck of another. He squirmed to and fro for a moment and froze – that is, applying the science of the Japanese ninjas, or 'stealthy ones', he turned to stone, water, grass. Dissolved into the landscape. From a strategic point of view the position was ideal: Fandorin could not be seen from the yard – it was too dark, and the shadow of the balcony provided additional cover – and he was even less visible from the room. But he himself could see the entire yard and through the window, left open in the summer warmth, he could hear any conversation in the drawing room. Given the desire and a certain degree of double-jointed elasticity, it was even possible for him to hang down and glance in through the gap between the curtains.

There was one minus: the uncomfortable nature of the position. No normal man would have held on for long in such a contorted pose, especially on a stone support only four inches wide. But the supreme degree of mastery in the ancient art of the 'stealthy ones' does not consist in the ability to kill the enemy with bare hands or to jump down from a high fortress wall – oh no. The highest achievement for a ninja is to master the great art of immobility. Only an exceptional master can stand for six or eight hours without moving a single muscle. Erast Petrovich had not become an exceptional master, for he had been too old when he took up the study of this noble and terrible art; but in the present case he could take comfort in the fact that his fusion with the landscape was unlikely to last for long. The secret of any difficult undertaking is simple: one must regard the difficulty not as an evil, but as a blessing. After all, the noble man finds his greatest pleasure in overcoming the imperfections of his nature. That was what one should think about when the imperfections were particularly distressing – for instance, when a stone corner was jabbing fiercely into one's side.

During the second minute of this delectable pleasure, the back door of the Anglia Hotel opened and the silhouette of a man appeared – thickset, moving confidently and rapidly. Fandorin caught only a glimpse of the face, just as the man entered the rectangle of light falling from the window in front of the door. It was an ordinary face, with no distinctive features: oval, with close-set eyes, light-coloured hair, slightly protruding superciliary arches, a moustache curled in the Prussian manner, an average nose, a dimple in the square chin. The stranger entered Wanda's residence without knocking, which was interesting in itself. Erast Petrovich strained his ears to catch every sound. Voices began speaking in the room almost immediately, and it became clear that hearing alone would not be enough; he would also have to call on his knowledge of German, for the conversation was conducted in the language of Schiller and Goethe. In his time as a grammar-school boy, Fandorin had not greatly excelled in this art, and so the main focus in the overcoming of his own imperfections shifted quite naturally from the discomfort of his posture to intellectual effort. However, it's an ill wind … The sharp stone corner was miraculously forgotten.

'You serve me badly, Fräulein Tolle,' a harsh baritone declared. 'Of course, it is good that you have come to your senses and done as you were ordered. But why did you have to be so obstinate and cause me such pointless nervous aggravation? I am not a machine, after all; I am a live human being.'

'Oh, really?' Wanda's voice replied derisively.

'Really, just imagine. You carried out your assignment after all – and quite superbly. But why did I have to learn about it from a journalist I know, and not from you? Are you deliberately trying to anger me? I wouldn't advise it!' The baritone acquired a steely ring. 'Have you forgotten what I can do to you?'

Wanda's voice replied wearily: 'No, I remember, Herr Knabe, I remember.'

At this point Erast Petrovich cautiously leaned down and glanced into the room, but the mysterious Herr Knabe was standing with his back to the window. He took off his bowler hat, revealing a couple of minor details: smoothly combed hair (a third-degree blond with a slight reddish tinge, Fandorin ascertained, applying the special police terminology) and a thick red neck (which appeared to be at least size six).

'All right, all right, I forgive you. Come on, don't sulk.' The visitor patted his hostess's cheek with his short-fingered hand and kissed her below the ear. Wanda's face was in the light and Erast Petrovich saw her subtle features contort in a grimace of revulsion.

Unfortunately, he was obliged to curtail his visual observation – one moment longer, and Fandorin would have gone crashing to the ground, which under the circumstances would have been most unfortunate.

'Tell me all about it.' The man's voice had assumed an ingratiating tone. 'How did you do it? Did you use the substance that I gave you? Yes or no?'

Silence.

'Obviously not. The autopsy did not reveal any traces of poison – I know that. Who would have thought that things would go as far as an autopsy? Well then, what actually did happen? Or were we lucky and he simply died on his own? Then that was surely the hand of Providence. God protects our Germany.' The baritone quavered in agitation. 'Why do you not say anything?'

Wanda said in a low, dull voice: 'Go away. I can't see you today.'

'More woman's whimsicality. How sick I am of it! All right, all right, don't glare at me like that. A great deed has been accomplished, and that is the main thing. Well done, Fräulein Tolle, I am leaving. But tomorrow you will tell me everything. I shall need it for my report.'

There was the sound of a prolonged kiss and Erast Petrovich winced, recalling the look of revulsion on Wanda's face. The door slammed.

Herr Knabe whistled as he cut across the yard and disappeared.

Fandorin dropped to the ground without a sound and straightened up in relief, stretching his numbed limbs, before he set off in pursuit of Wanda's acquaintance. This case was acquiring an entirely new complexion.

Chapter Five

'... And my p-proposals come down to the following,' said Fandorin, summing up his report. 'Immediately place the German citizen Hans-Georg Knabe under secret observation and determine his range of contacts.'

'Evgeny Osipovich, would it not be best to arrest the blackguard?' asked the governor-general, knitting his dyed eyebrows in an angry frown.

'It is not possible to arrest him without any evidence,' the chief of police replied. 'And it's pointless: he's an old hand. I'd rather bring in this Wanda, Your Excellency, and put her under serious pressure. You never know, it might turn up a few leads.'

The fourth participant in the secret conference, Pyotr Parmyonovich Khurtinsky, remained silent.

They had been in conference for a long time already, since first thing that morning. Erast Petrovich had reported on the events of the previous evening and how he had followed the mysterious visitor, who had proved to be the German businessman Hans-Georg Knabe, the Moscow representative of the Berlin banking firm Kerbel und Schmidt, with a residence on Karetny Ryad. When the collegiate assessor related the sinister conversation between Knabe and Wanda, his report had to be interrupted temporarily, because Prince Dolgorukoi became extremely agitated and began shouting and waving his fists in the air.

'Ah, the villains, ah, the blackguards! Were they the ones who murdered the noble knight of the Russian land? What heinous treachery! An international scandal! Oh, the Germans will pay for this!'

'That will do, Your Excellency,' the head of the secret section, Khurtinsky, murmured reassuringly. 'This is too dubious a hypothesis. Poison the White General! Nonsense! I can't believe the Germans would take such a risk. They are a civilised nation, not treacherous Persian conspirators!'

'Civilised?' exclaimed General Karachentsev, baring his teeth in a snarl. 'I have here the articles from today's British and German newspapers, sent to me by the Russian Telegraph Agency. As we know, Mikhail Dmitrievich was no great lover of either of these two countries, and he made no secret of his views. But compare the tone! With your permission, Your Excellency?' The chief of police set his pince-nez on his nose and took a sheet of paper out of a file. 'The English *Standard* writes:

Sobolev's compatriots will find him hard to replace. His mere appearance on a white horse ahead of the line of battle was enough to inspire in his soldiers an enthusiasm such as even the veterans of Napoleon I hardly ever displayed. The death of such a man during the present critical period is an irreparable loss for Russia. He was an enemy of England, but in this country his exploits were followed with scarcely less interest than in his homeland.'

'Indeed, frankly and nobly put,' said the prince approvingly.

'Precisely. And now I will read you an article from Saturday's *Börsen Kurier*.' Karachentsev picked up another sheet of paper. 'Mm ... Well, this piece will do:

The Russian bear is no longer dangerous. Let the pan-Slavists weep over the grave of Sobolev. But as for us

Germans, we must honestly admit that we are glad of the death of a mettlesome enemy. We do not experience any feelings of regret. The only man in Russia who was genuinely able to act upon his word is dead …

'And so on in the same vein. How's that for civilisation, eh?'

The governor was outraged. 'Shameless impudence! Of course, the anti-German feelings of the deceased are well known. We can all remember how his speech in Paris on the Slav question caused a genuine furore and almost provoked a serious falling-out between the Emperor and the Kaiser. "The road to Constantinople lies through Berlin and Vienna!" Strongly put, with no diplomatic niceties. But to stoop to murder! Why, it's quite unheard of! I shall inform His Majesty immediately! Even without Sobolev we'll give those sausage-eaters a dose of medicine that will—'

'Your Excellency,' said Evgeny Osipovich, gently interrupting the fuming governor in full flow, 'should we not first listen to the rest of what Mr Fandorin has to say?'

After that they had heard Erast Petrovich out without interrupting, although his culminating proposal to limit themselves to placing Knabe under observation was clearly a disappointment to his listeners, as the remarks adduced above testify.

To the chief of police Fandorin said: 'To arrest Wanda would mean a scandal. By doing that we would dishonour the m-memory of the deceased and would be unlikely to achieve anything. We would only frighten Herr Knabe off. And in any case, I got the distinct impression from their conversation that Mademoiselle Wanda did not kill Sobolev. After all, Professor Welling's autopsy did not reveal any traces of poison.'

'Precisely,' Khurtinsky said emphatically, addressing himself exclusively to Prince Dolgorukoi. 'An entirely banal paralysis of the heart, Your Excellency. Most regrettable, but these things happen. Even in the very prime of life, as in the deceased's case. I wonder whether the collegiate assessor might not have misheard. Or even – who knows – fantasised a little? After all, he himself admitted that German is not exactly his forte.'

Erast Petrovich gave the speaker a particularly keen look, but said nothing in reply.

However, the red-headed gendarme jumped in. 'What do you mean, fantasised! Sobolev was in the very rudest of health! He hunted bears with a forked pole and bathed in a hole in the ice! Are you trying to say that he lived through a hail of fire at Plevna and survived the desert of Turkestan, but he couldn't survive a bit of lovemaking? Rubbish! You should stick to gathering the city's tittle-tattle, Mr Khurtinsky, and not meddle in matters of espionage.'

Fandorin was surprised at this open confrontation, but the governor was apparently well used to such scenes. He raised a conciliatory hand.

'Gentlemen, gentlemen, do not argue. My head is already spinning without that. So many things to do after this death. Telegrams, condolences, deputations; they've covered the whole of Theatre Lane with wreaths – you can't get through on foot or by carriage. There are important individuals coming to the funeral; they have to be met and accommodated. This evening the war minister and the head of the general staff will arrive. Tomorrow the Grand Duke Kirill Alexandrovich will arrive and go directly to the funeral. And today I have to call on the Duke of Lichtenberg. He and his wife happened by chance to be in Moscow. His wife, the Countess Mirabeau, is the sister of the deceased, and I must go and offer them my condolences. I have already sent ahead to warn them. You come with me, Erast Petrovich, my dear chap; you can go over everything with me once again in the carriage. We'll consider together what best to do. And you, Evgeny Osipovich, please take on the job of following both of them for the time being: this German and the girl. It would be good to intercept that little report that Knabe mentioned. I'll tell you what: let him write the report for his spymasters and then catch him red-handed with the evidence. And as soon as you have issued instructions for the surveillance, come straight back here to me, if you please. When Erast Petrovich and I get back, we'll take a final decision. We can't afford to make a mess of things. This business has the whiff of war about it.'

The general clicked his heels and went out, and Khurtinsky immediately darted across to the governor's desk. 'Urgent papers, Your Excellency,' he said, bending right down to the prince's ear.

'Are they so very urgent?' the governor growled. 'You heard me, Petrusha: I'm in a hurry, the duke's waiting.'

The court counsellor set his open hand against the decoration on his starched breast. 'They must be dealt with immediately, Vladimir Andreich; look here, this is an estimate for completing the painting of the cathedral. I suggest awarding the commission to Mr Gegechkori, a most excellent painter and a man with a very sound way of thinking. The amount he is asking is certainly not small, but then he will do the work on time – he is a man of his word. All that's required is your signature here, and you can consider the matter completed.'

Pyotr Parmyonovich deftly set a sheet of paper in front of the governor and drew a second one out of his folder. 'And this, Vladimir Andreich, is a plan for the excavation of an underground metropolitan, following the example of London. The contractor is Commercial Counsellor Zykov. A great business. I had the honour of reporting to you about it.'

'I remember,' Dolgorukoi growled. 'So now they've dreamed up some metropolitan railway or other. How much money does it require?'

'A mere pittance. Zykov is only asking half a million for

the surveying work. I've looked at the estimate and it's perfectly sound.'

'*Only*,' sighed the prince. 'When did you get so rich, Petka, that half a million became a mere pittance?' Then, noticing Fandorin's amazement at observing the governor's dealing in such a familiar fashion with the head of his secret section, he explained: 'Pyotr Parmyonovich and I talk like close relatives. But you know, he was raised in my house. My deceased cook's little son. If only Parmyon, God rest his soul, could hear how casually you dispose of millions, Petrusha!'

Khurtinsky gave Erast Petrovich an angry sideways glance, evidently displeased at this reminder of his plebeian origins. 'And this concerns the prices for gas. I've drawn up a memorandum, Vladimir Andreich. It would be good to reduce the tariff in order to make street lighting cheaper. To three roubles for a thousand cubic feet. They're taking too much as things are now.'

'All right, give me your papers, I'll read them in the carriage and sign them,' said Dolgorukoi, getting to his feet. 'It's time to be going. It's bad form to keep an important individual waiting. Let's go, Erast Petrovich, we can discuss things along the way.'

In the corridor Fandorin enquired with great politeness: 'But tell me, Your Excellency, will the Emperor himself not be coming? After all, it is Sobolev who has died, not just anybody.'

Dolgorukoi squinted at the collegiate assessor and declared with emphasis: 'He did not consider it possible. He has sent his brother, Kirill Alexandrovich. But why is not for us to know.'

Fandorin merely bowed without speaking.

They were not able to 'discuss things' along the way. When they were already seated in the carriage – the governor on soft cushions and Erast Petrovich facing him on a leather-upholstered bench – the door suddenly swung open and the prince's valet, Frol Vedishchev, clambered in, panting and gasping. He seated himself unceremoniously beside the prince and shouted to the driver: 'Off you go, Misha, off you go!'

Then, without paying the slightest attention to Erast Petrovich, he swung round to face Dolgorukoi. 'Vladimir Andreich, I'm going with you,' he declared in a tone that brooked no objections.

'Frolushka,' the prince said meekly, 'I've taken my medicine, and now please don't interfere, I have important business to talk over with Mr Fandorin.'

'Never mind, your talk can wait,' the despot declared with an angry wave of his hand. 'What were those papers that Petka slipped you?'

'Here they are, Frol,' said Vladimir Andreevich, opening his folder. 'A commission for the artist Gegechkori to complete the murals in the cathedral. The estimate has been drawn up, see? And this is a contract for the merchant Zykov. We're going to dig a railway underneath Moscow, so that people can get around more quickly. And there's this – about reducing the prices for gas.'

Vedishchev glanced at the papers and announced determinedly: 'You mustn't give the cathedral to this Gegechkori; he's a well-known swindler. Better give it to one of our own artists, from Moscow. They have to make a living too. It will be cheaper and every bit as beautiful. Where are we going to get the money from? There isn't any money. Gegechkori promised your Petka that he would decorate his dacha in Alabino, that's why Petka's taking so much trouble.'

'So you think we shouldn't give the commission to Gegechkori?' Dolgorukoi asked pensively, and put the paper to the bottom of the pile.

'It doesn't even bear thinking about,' snapped Frol. 'And this metropolitan railway is sheer stupidity. What's the point of digging a hole in the ground and sending a steam engine down it? It's just throwing the treasury's money away. What an idiotic idea!'

'Well, you're wrong about that,' the prince objected. 'The metro is a good thing. Just look what the traffic's like – we're barely crawling along.'

It was true: the gubernatorial carriage was stuck at the turn on to Neglinnaya Street and, despite making desperate efforts, the convoy of gendarmes was quite unable to clear the road which, on a Saturday, was packed solid with the carts and wagons of traders from Okhotny Ryad.

Vedishchev shook his head, as though the prince himself ought to realise that his stubbornness was wrong-headed.

'But you know the councillors in the City Duma will say old Dolgorukoi's finally lost his mind completely. And your enemies in St Petersburg won't miss their chance either. Don't sign it, Vladimir Andreich.'

The governor gave a mournful sigh and set the second paper aside. 'And what about the gas?'

Vedishchev took the memorandum, held it away from himself and began moving his lips soundlessly. 'That's all right, you can sign it. It saves the city money and it eases the burden of the people of Moscow.'

'That's what I think too,' said the prince, brightening up. He folded down the small desk with a writing set that was attached to the carriage door and affixed his sprawling signature to the document.

Erast Petrovich was astounded by this incredible scene, but he made a great effort to act as if nothing out of the ordinary were taking place, gazing out of the window with intense interest. At that very moment they arrived at the house of Princess Beloselskaya-Belozerskaya, where the Duke of Lichtenberg was staying with his wife, née Zinaida Dmitrievna Soboleva, who had been granted the title of the Countess Mirabeau in morganatic marriage.

Erast Petrovich knew that Evgeny of Lichtenberg, a major-general in the Russian Guards and commander of the Potsdam Life-Cuirassiers, was the grandson of the Emperor Nikolai Pavlovich. He had not, however, inherited the famous basilisk stare from his fearsome grandfather – His Highness's own eyes were the colour of blue Saxon porcelain and they peered out through his pince-nez with an expression of mild courtesy. The countess, on the other hand, proved to resemble her famous brother greatly. Although she might have lacked his physical stature, and her bearing was far from martial, while the oval outline of her face was delicately defined, nonetheless her blue eyes were exactly like his and she was the exact same breed, unmistakably a Sobolev.

The audience went awry from the very beginning.

'The countess and I came to Moscow on a quite diffewent matter, and then there was this tewwible calamity,' the duke began, burring his 'r's in a most engaging fashion and supporting his words by flapping motions of a hand on which the middle finger was adorned with an old sapphire.

Zinaida Dmitrievna did not allow her husband to finish: 'How, how could it have happened?' she exclaimed, and the large tears streamed down her face, which, even swollen as it was by her lamentations, remained delightful. 'Prince, Vladimir Andreevich, the grief is unbearable!'

The countess's mouth twisted and froze into the double curve of a yoke and she was unable to carry on speaking.

'Evewything is in God's hands,' the bewildered duke muttered, and glanced in panic at Dolgorukoi and Fandorin.

'Evgeny Maximilianovich, Your Highness, I assure you that the circumstances of your relative's untimely demise are being thoroughly investigated,' the governor declared in an agitated voice. 'Mr Fandorin here, my deputy for highly important assignments, is dealing with the case.'

Erast Petrovich bowed and the duke's gaze dwelt for a moment on the young functionary's face, but the countess dissolved in even more bitter tears.

'Zinaida Dmitrievna, my darling girl,' said the prince, sobbing himself now. 'Erast Petrovich was your brother's comrade in war. And as chance would have it, he put up at the same hotel, the Dusseaux. He is a very intelligent and experienced investigator; he will get to the bottom of everything and report back to me. But what's the point of crying, it won't bring him back ...'

Evgeny Maximilianovich's pince-nez glinted coldly and imperiously: 'If Mr Fandowin should discover anything important, please inform me personally about it immediately. Until Gwand Duke Kiwill Alexandwovich awwives, I wepwesent the person of His Majesty the Empewor here.'

Erast Petrovich bowed once again without speaking.

'Yes, His Majesty ...' Zinaida Dmitrievna took a crumpled telegram out of her small handbag with shaking hands. 'A telegram has arrived from His Majesty. "*Shocked and grieved by the sudden death of Adjutant-General Sobolev.*"' She sobbed and blew her nose, then continued reading. '"*This loss is a hard one for the Russian army to replace and, of course, is greatly lamented by all true soldiers. It is sad to lose such useful people who are so devoted to their work. Alexander.*"'

Fandorin raised his eyebrows slightly – the telegram had sounded rather cold to him. 'Hard to replace'? Meaning that the general could be replaced after all? 'Sad' – and nothing more?

'The lying-in-state and the funeral service are tomorrow,' said Dolgorukoi. 'Muscovites wish to pay their final tribute to their hero. Then I presume the body will be sent by train to St Petersburg? His Majesty will surely give instructions to arrange a state burial. There will be many people who wish to take their leave of Mikhail Sobolev.' The governor assumed a dignified air. 'Measures have been taken, Your Highness. The body has been embalmed, and so no problems will arise.'

The duke glanced sideways at his wife, who was wiping away her inexhaustible flow of tears, and said in a low voice, 'The thing is, Prince, the Empewor has acceded to the wishes of the family and gwanted them permission to buwy Michel *en famille* at their Wyazan estate.'

Vladimir Andreevich responded with a haste that Fandorin thought slightly excessive: 'Quite right too; things are more humane that way, without all the pomp. What a man he was, such a great heart.'

He ought not to have said that. The countess, who had begun to calm down, began sobbing even more loudly than before. The governor began blinking rapidly, took out a quite immense handkerchief and wiped Zinaida Dmitrievna's face in a fatherly manner, after which, overcome by emotion, he loudly blew his nose into it.

Evgeny Maximilianovich observed this intemperate Slavic display of emotion with a certain degree of consternation.

'How could it happen, Vladi ... Vladimir Andre ... evich?' the countess asked, falling against the prince's chest, which was squeezed up and out by his corset. 'He is only six years older than me ... Ooh-ooh-ooh,' she wailed in a quite unaristocratic, entirely demotic manner, like a peasant woman; and Dolgorukoi's composure dissolved completely.

'My dear fellow,' he said to Fandorin across the brown hair on the back of Zinaida Dmitrievna's head. 'You ... you know ... You go on. I'll stay here for a while. You go, take Frol and go. The carriage can come back for me afterwards. And you have a word there with Evgeny Osipovich. Decide things for yourselves. You can how see how things are ...'

All the way back Frol Grigorievich complained about intriguers (whom he called 'antreegars') and embezzlers of public funds.

'The things they get up to, those monsters! Every louse trying to grab a piece for himself! Say a tradesman wants to open up a shop, for instance, and sell corduroy pants. What could be simpler, you might think? Pay the fifteen roubles municipal tax and trade away. Ah, but no! Pay the local policeman, pay the exciseman, pay the sanitary inspector! And all bypassing the treasury. And the top price for the pants should be a rouble and fifty kopecks – but they go for three. This isn't Moscow – it's an absolute jungle, that's what it is.'

'What?' Fandorin hadn't understood.

'Jungle. Beast against beast. Or take vodka, for example. Oh my, sir, vodka's an entire tragedy in itself. Let me tell you ...' And there followed the dramatic history of how the merchants, in contravention of all laws human and divine, bought duty stamps from the excise officials at one kopeck a time and stuck them on bottles of home-brew in order to pass it off as state produce. Erast Petrovich had absolutely no idea what to say, but fortunately his participation in the conversation did not seem to be required.

When the carriage rumbled over the cobblestones up to the front entrance of the governor's residence, Vedishchev cut short his philippic in mid-phrase: 'You go straight up to the study. The chief of police must be tired of waiting by now. I'll get on about my business.' And with a friskiness surprising in one of such great age and with such impressive sideburns, he darted off down one of the side corridors.

The professional tête-à-tête went well. Fandorin and Karachentsev caught each other's meaning at once, which both of them found exceedingly pleasant.

The general settled himself in the armchair by the window and Erast Petrovich sat facing him on a velvet-covered chair.

'First let me tell you about Herr Knabe,' Evgeny Osipovich began, holding his folder at the ready but not glancing into it for the time being, 'an individual well known to me. I simply did not wish, in such a crowd . . .' – he made a wry face, and Fandorin realised that he was hinting at Khurtinsky. The general slapped his hand down on the folder. 'I have here a secret circular dated last year. From the department, from the Third Office which, as you know, deals with all sorts of political matters. It instructs me to keep an eye on Hans-Georg Knabe. To make sure that he doesn't overstep the mark.'

Erast Petrovich inclined his head enquiringly to one side.

'A spy,' the chief of police explained. 'According to our information, a captain of the German general staff. The head of the Kaiser's intelligence service in Moscow. Knowing that, I believed what you told us immediately and unconditionally.'

'And you haven't picked him up because a secret agent you know is better than one you don't,' the collegiate assessor stated rather than asked.

'Precisely. And there are certain rules of diplomatic propriety. If I arrest him and expel him, then what? The Germans immediately expel one of our men. What good is that to anyone? It's simply not done to touch foreign agents without specific instructions to do so. However, this particular incident goes far beyond the bounds of gentlemanly behaviour.'

Erast Petrovich could not help smiling at such an obvious understatement: 'Yes, indeed, to put it mildly.' The general smiled too.

'And so we are going to pick up Herr Knabe. The question is: where and when?'

Evgeny Osipovich's smile broadened even further. 'I think this evening, at the Alpine Rose restaurant. You see, according to information in my possession' – he slapped his hand down on the closed folder once again – 'Knabe often spends the evening there. He phoned them again today and booked a table for seven o'clock. For some reason under the name of Rosenberg, although, as you can imagine, he is very well known at the restaurant.'

'Interesting,' remarked Fandorin. 'And he really ought to be brought in.'

The general nodded. 'I have instructions from the governor-general for the arrest. I operate as a soldier: the superiors give the orders, I carry them out.'

'How do we know that Knabe t-telephoned and booked a table in a false name?' Erast Petrovich asked after a moment's thought.

'Technical progress.' The police chief's eyes glinted cunningly. 'It is possible to listen to telephone conversations from the exchange. But that is strictly between you and me. If they ever find out, I shall lose half my information. By the way, your friend Wanda will be performing at the Rose today as well. She told the porter to have a carriage at the door at six. There is an interesting evening in prospect. It would be good to pick up the pair of them together. The question is: how to proceed?'

'Resolutely, but keeping things neat and tidy.'

Karachentsev sighed. 'My dashing lads are fine when it's a matter of being resolute. But they're not so good when it comes to tidiness.'

Erast Petrovich began speaking in half-phrases. 'What if I do it? As a private individual? If anything happens – no diplomatic conflicts. Your men standing by, eh? Only, Your Excellency, no duplication, like yesterday in the Anglia.'

Well, I'll be damned if it isn't a sheer pleasure working with you, the general thought. But out loud he said: 'I apologise for yesterday. It won't happen again. But about today ... Two outside, two inside, in the hall. What do you think?'

'There should be none in the hall at all – a professional will always spot them,' the collegiate assessor declared confidently. 'But outside – one in a carriage at the front door and one at the back door. Just in case. I think that will be enough. He's an agent after all, not a terrorist.'

'How are you thinking of proceeding?'

'I honestly don't know. I'll see how it goes: take a close look, observe for a while. I don't like trying to guess ahead.'

'I understand,' said the general, nodding. 'And I have full confidence in your judgement. Do you have a weapon? Our Mr Knabe is in a desperate situation. In this case he won't get off with simple deportation, and his superiors will disown him if anything happens. He may not be a terrorist, but his nerves will probably be on edge.'

Erast Petrovich slipped his hand in under his frock coat, and a moment later there was a small, neat-looking revolver with a fluted handle worn down by frequent use lying on the palm of his hand.

'A Herstahl-Agent?' Evgeny Osipovich asked respectfully. 'An elegant little item. Do you mind if I take a look?'

The general took hold of the revolver, opened the cylinder deftly and clicked his tongue in admiration: 'No cocking notch? That's splendid! Fire off all six bullets one after another if you like. But isn't the trigger a bit too sensitive?'

'This button here is the safety catch,' said Fandorin, pointing. 'So it won't go off in your pocket. It's not all that accurate, of course, but then in our business the main thing is a rapid rate of fire. We don't need to hit a mink in the eye.'

'Perfectly true,' agreed Evgeny Osipovich, handing back the gun. 'So, will she recognise you? Wanda, I mean.'

'Please do not b-be concerned, Your Excellency. I have an entire chest full of make-up. She won't recognise me.'

Entirely satisfied, Karachentsev leaned back in his chair and, although the discussion of business had apparently been concluded, he seemed in no hurry to say goodbye. The general offered Fandorin a cigar, but the collegiate assessor took out his own, in an elegant suede case.

'Genuine Batavia, Evgeny Osipovich. Would you like to try one?'

The chief of police took a slim, chocolate-coloured wand, lit it and released a thin stream of smoke, savouring the flavour. The general very definitely liked Mr Fandorin, and that was why he took the final decision to steer the conversation in a delicate direction.

'You are new to our Moscow jungle ...' he began cautiously.

He talks about the jungle too, Erast thought in surprise, but gave no sign. He only said: 'And to the Russian jungle too.'

'Yes, indeed. While you've been on your travels things have changed a great deal ...'

Fandorin waited with an attentive smile for what would follow – all the signs suggested that the conversation in prospect would not be a trivial one.

'What do you make of our old beau?' the chief of police suddenly asked.

Erast Petrovich hesitated before replying: 'I think that His Excellency is by no means as simple as he seems.'

'Alas.' The general forcibly ejected a thick stream of smoke up into the air. 'In his time the prince was far from simple, very far indeed. It's no easy thing, maintaining a grip of iron on the old capital for sixteen years. But the old wolf's teeth have come loose. It's hardly surprising: he's over seventy now. He's grown old and lost his grip.' Evgeny Osipovich leaned forward and lowered his voice confidentially. 'He hasn't got long left. You can see for yourself, those Jacks-in-office of his, Khurtinsky and Vedishchev, can twist him round their little fingers. And that famous cathedral of his. It's sucked the city completely dry. And for what? Think of all the orphanages and hospitals you could build with money like that! No, our latter-day Cheops is determined to leave his own pyramid after him when he's gone.'

Erast Petrovich listened attentively, without opening his mouth.

'I understand that it's awkward for you to discuss this,' said Karachentsev, leaning back in his armchair again. 'But just listen to someone who is genuinely well disposed towards you. I can tell you that there is dissatisfaction with

Dolgorukoi at court. The slightest blunder from his side and it will be the end. Off into retirement, to Nice. And then, Erast Petrovich, his entire Moscow junta will fall apart. A new man will come, someone quite different. He will bring his own people. In fact, they're already here, his people. Making ready.'

'You, for instance?'

'You take my meaning at once. And that means I do not need to continue. The essence of the proposal is clear to you.'

This really is more like a jungle than the old capital city, thought Erast Petrovich, looking into the red-headed police chief's eyes, positively aglow with goodwill – to all appearances the eyes of an honest and intelligent man. The collegiate assessor smiled in a most agreeable manner and shrugged: 'I appreciate your confidence; indeed I am flattered. Perhaps Moscow would indeed be better off with a new governor. But I cannot undertake to judge, since I still understand nothing about Moscow affairs. I have, however, lived in Japan for four years, Your Excellency, and, would you believe, I have become completely Japanese – sometimes I even surprise myself. In Japan a samurai – and in their terms you and I are both samurai – must keep faith with his overlord, no matter how bad he might be. Otherwise nothing would work, the whole system would collapse. Vladimir Andreevich is not exactly my sovereign lord, and yet I cannot feel entirely free of all obligations to him. Please do not take this amiss.'

'Well, that is a shame,' sighed the general, realising that any attempt at persuasion would be futile. 'You could have had a great future. But never mind. Perhaps you still will. You can always count on my support. May I hope that this little chat will remain between the two of us?'

'You may,' the collegiate assessor replied tersely, and Karachentsev immediately believed him.

'Time to be going,' he said, getting to his feet. 'I'll issue instructions concerning the Rose and select some of my brighter deputies for you; and you, in turn ...'

They left the governor's study, discussing the final details of the forthcoming operation as they went. A second later a small door in the corner of the room opened – it led to the rest room where the old prince liked to doze after lunch. Frol Grigorievich Vedishchev emerged from behind the door, stepping silently in his thick felt slippers. His bushy grey eyebrows were knitted in a grim frown. The prince's valet walked across to the chair on which the chief of police had been sitting a minute earlier and spat savagely, depositing a brown gob of tobacco spittle on the leather seat.

Chapter Six

IN WHICH A WOMAN IN BLACK APPEARS

Back at the hotel there was a surprise in store for Erast Petrovich. As the young man approached apartment number 20, the door suddenly swung open and a buxom maid came running out towards him. Fandorin did not get a clear view of her face, since it was turned away from him, but there were certain eloquent details that did not escape the observant collegiate assessor's attention: an apron worn back to front, a lace cap that had slipped over to one side and a dress that was buttoned crookedly. Masa was standing in the doorway, looking very pleased with himself and not in the least embarrassed by his master's sudden return.

'Russian women are very good,' he declared with profound conviction. 'I suspected this before and now I know for certain.'

'For certain?' Fandorin asked curiously, surveying the glistening features of his Japanese servant.

'Yes, master. They are passionate and do not demand presents for their love. Not like the female inhabitants of the French city Paris.'

'But you don't know Russian,' said Erast Petrovich with a shake of his head. 'How did you explain yourself to her?'

'I did not know French either, but to explain oneself to a woman, words are not needed,' Masa declared with a solemn expression. 'The most important things are the breathing and the glance. If you breathe loud and fast, the woman understands that you are in love with her. And you must do this with your eyes.' He screwed up his already narrow eyes, which made them seem to sparkle in a quite astonishing fashion.

In reply Fandorin merely cleared his throat.

'After that all that is needed is to woo her a little, and a woman cannot resist any longer.'

'And how did you woo her?'

'There is a special approach for each woman, master. Thin ones like sweet things, fat ones like flowers. To the lovely woman who ran away on hearing your footsteps, I gave a sprig of magnolia, and then I gave her a neck massage.'

'Where did you get the magnolia?'

'There.' Masa pointed vaguely downwards. 'They are growing in pots.'

'And what is the point of the neck massage?'

The servant gave his master a pitying look.

'A neck massage develops into a shoulder massage, then into a back massage, then ...'

'I see,' sighed Erast Petrovich. 'You don't need to continue. Better give me that little chest with my make-up kit instead.'

Masa perked up at this. 'Are we going to have an adventure?'

'We are not; *I* am. And another thing: this morning I had no time to do any gymnastics, and I need to be in good shape today.'

The Japanese began taking off the cotton dressing gown that he usually wore when he was at home. 'Master, shall we run across the ceiling or are we going to fight again? The ceiling is best. That is a very convenient wall.'

Surveying the wallpapered wall and moulded ceiling, Fandorin felt doubtful. 'It's awfully high. At least twelve *shaku*. Never mind, let's try it.'

Masa was already standing ready in nothing but his loincloth. Round his forehead he tied a clean white rag, with the hieroglyph for 'diligence' traced out on it in red ink. After changing into a pair of close-fitting tights and rubber slippers, Erast Petrovich jumped up and down for a while, then squatted down and gave the command: 'Ichi, ni, san!'

Both of them dashed at the wall and ran up it, and when they were just short of the ceiling, pushed off from the vertical, turning a back somersault in the air and landing on their feet.

'Master, I ran higher up – as far as that rose there, but you were two roses lower,' Masa boasted, pointing at the wallpaper.

Instead of answering, Fandorin called out once again: 'Ichi, ni, san!'

The vertiginous feat was repeated, and this time the servant touched the ceiling with his foot as he tumbled head over heels.

'I reached it, and you didn't!' he declared. 'Yes, master, even though your legs are considerably longer than mine.'

'You are made of rubber,' growled Fandorin, panting slightly. 'All right, now we will fight.'

The Japanese bowed from the waist and adopted the combat position without any great enthusiasm: legs bent at the knees, feet turned out, arms relaxed.

Erast Fandorin leapt up, spun round in the air and struck his partner quite hard on the back of the head with the toe of his slipper before he had time to turn away. 'First hit!' he shouted. 'Come on!'

Masa created a distraction by tearing the white band off his forehead and tossing it to one side, and when Fandorin's gaze involuntarily followed the flying object, the servant uttered a guttural cry, launched himself across the floor like a bouncing rubber ball and tried to catch his master across the ankle with a blow from his leg. However, at the final moment Erast Petrovich leapt back, managing at the same time to strike the shorter man across the ear with the edge of his open hand. 'Second hit!'

The Japanese leapt agilely to his feet and began walking round the room with short, rapid steps, tracing out a semi-circle. Fandorin shifted his weight lightly from one foot to the other where he stood, holding his upturned palms at the level of his waist.

'Ah, yes, master, I quite forgot,' said Masa, still walking. 'It is unforgivable of me. A woman came to see you an hour ago. Dressed all in black.'

Erast Fandorin lowered his hands. 'What woman?'

He immediately received a blow from a foot to his chest. As he flew back against the wall, Masa exclaimed triumphantly: 'First hit! An old, ugly woman. Her clothes were completely black. I could not understand what she wanted and she went away.'

Fandorin stood there, rubbing his bruised chest. 'It's high time you learned some Russian. While I am out, take the dictionary that I gave you and learn eighty words.'

'Forty will be enough!' Masa exclaimed indignantly. 'You are simply taking your revenge.' And then 'I've learned two words already today: "*sweehar*", which means "dear sir" and "*chainee*" – that's Russian for "Japanese".'

'I can guess who your teacher was. Only don't ever think of calling me "sweetheart". Eighty words, I said – eighty. Then next time you'll fight fair.'

Erast Petrovich sat down in front of the mirror and started on his make-up. After considering several wigs, he selected a dark-brown one, with the hair cut to a single length and a neat centre parting. He turned down the ends of his curled black moustache and stuck a fluffy, lighter one over it, then glued on a thick, full beard cut short and square. He painted his eyebrows the appropriate colour and moved them up and down for a while, stuck out his lips, extinguished the gleam in his eyes, pinched his ruddy cheeks and sprawled back in his chair. As if at the wave of a magic wand, he was suddenly transformed into a boorish young merchant from Okhotny Ryad.

Shortly after seven in the evening a smart cab drove up to the Alpine Rose German restaurant on Sofiiskaya Street: a gleaming, lacquered droshky with steel springs, scarlet ribbons woven into the manes of the pair of blacks pulling it and the spokes of the wheels painted yellow with ochre. The dashing cabby roared out a deafening 'whoah' and cracked his whip boisterously.

'Wake up, your honour; here you are, delivered all proper and correct!'

The passenger in the back of the cab was snoring gently, sprawled out on the velvet seat – a young merchant in a long-skirted blue frock coat, crimson waistcoat and tight-fitting boots. A gleaming top hat was perched at a devil-may-care angle on the reveller's head.

The merchant opened his drowsy eyes and hiccupped: 'Delivered? Where?'

'Where you ordered, your worship. This is it, the Rose itself.'

The restaurant was famous throughout Moscow, and there was a row of cabs lined up in front of it. The coachmen watched the noisy driver of the flashy cab with annoyance – shouting and yelling and cracking his whip like that, he was likely to frighten other people's horses. One driver, a clean-shaven, highly-strung-looking lad in a shiny leather coat, walked over to the troublemaker and set about him angrily.

'What do you think you're doing, waving your whip around like that? This isn't a gypsy fair! Now you're here, stand in line like everyone else.' Then he added in a low voice. 'Off you go, Sinelnikov. You got him here, now get going; don't make yourself too obvious. I've got my carriage here. Tell Evgeny Osipovich everything's going according to plan.'

The young merchant jumped down on to the pavement, staggered and waved to the cabby: 'Off with you! I'll be spending the night here.'

The smart driver cracked his whip, whistled like a bandit and set off. The roistering trader from Okhotny Ryad took several uncertain steps and staggered.

The clean-shaven young driver was there in a flash to take him by the elbow. 'Let me help, your worship. It wouldn't do for you to go missing your step.' He took a solicitous grip on the reveller's elbow and whispered rapidly: 'Agent Klyuev, your honour. That's my carriage there, with the chestnut mare. I'll be waiting up on the coach box. Agent Neznamov is at the back entrance. Playing the part of a knife-grinder in an oilskin apron. The mark arrived just ten minutes ago. He's wearing a ginger beard. Seems very nervous altogether. He's armed too – there's a bulge under his armpit. And His Excellency told me to give you this.'

In the very doorway the 'cabby' deftly slipped a sheet of paper folded into eight into the young merchant's pocket and then doffed his cap and bowed low from the waist, but he received no tip for his pains and was left to grunt in annoyance when the door slammed in his face. To the jeers of the other drivers ('Hey, my bold lad, didn't you get your twenty kopecks, then?') he plodded back to his droshky and climbed dejectedly up on to the coach box.

The Alpine Rose restaurant was regarded on the whole as a decorous European establishment – during the daytime, that is. Moscow's Germans, both merchants and civil servants, flocked here for breakfast and lunch. They ate leg of pork with sauerkraut, drank genuine Bavarian beer and read newspapers from Berlin, Vienna and Riga. But come the evening, all the boring beer-swillers went back home to tot up the balances in their account books, have supper and get into their feather beds while it was still light, and a jollier, more open-handed public began to converge on the Rose. For the most part they were foreigners, people of easy manners who preferred to take their fun in the European style rather than the Russian. If Russians did look in, then it was more out of curiosity than anything else and also – in more recent times – to hear Mademoiselle Wanda sing.

The young merchant stopped in the white marble entrance hall, hiccupped as he surveyed the columns and the carpeted stairs, tossed his dazzling top hat to a flunky and beckoned to the maître d'hôtel.

The first thing he did was to hand him a white one-rouble note. Then, enveloping him in cognac fumes, he demanded: 'Now then, you German pepper sausage, you fix me up with a table, and not just one that happens to be standing empty, but the one I take a fancy to.'

'The place is rather crowded, sir,' the maître d'hôtel said with a shrug. He might have been German, but he spoke Russian like a true Muscovite.

'Fix me up,' the merchant said, wagging a threatening finger at him. 'Or else I'll make trouble! Oh, right, and where's your privy here?'

The maître d'hôtel beckoned a flunky across with his finger and the rowdy customer was shown with all due deference to a toilet room that was fitted out with the latest word in European technology: porcelain stools, flushing water and washstands with mirrors. But our merchant was not interested in these German novelties. Ordering the flunky to wait outside, he went in, took a folded sheet of paper out of his pocket and began reading, frowning in concentration.

It was the transcript of a telephone conversation:

17 MINUTES PAST 2 IN THE AFTERNOON.
PARTY 1 – MALE, PARTY 2 – FEMALE

P1: Young lady, give me number 762, the Anglia … This is Georg Knabe here. Could you please call Miss Wanda?

VOICE (SEX NOT DETERMINED): One moment, sir.

P2: Wanda speaking. Who is this?

P1: (Note in the margin: 'From this point on everything

is in German.') It's me. An urgent matter. Very important. Tell me one thing: did you do anything to him? You understand what I mean. Did you or didn't you? Tell me the truth, I entreat you!

P2: (Following a long pause): I did not do what you mean. Everything simply happened on its own. But what is wrong with you? Your voice sounds very strange.

P1: You really didn't do it? Oh thanks be to God! You have no idea of the position I'm in. It's like a terrible nightmare.

P2: I'm delighted to hear it. (One phrase inaudible.)

P1: Don't joke. Everyone has abandoned me! Instead of praise for showing initiative, there is only black ingratitude. And that is not the worst thing. It could turn out that a certain event of which you know will not postpone the conflict, but, on the contrary, bring it closer – that is what I have been informed. But you didn't do anything after all?

P2: I told you, no.

P1: Then where's the bottle?

P2: In my room. And it's still sealed.

P1: I must collect it from you. Today.

P2: I'm singing at the restaurant today and won't be able to get away. I've already missed two evenings as it is.

P1: I know. I'll be there. I've already booked a table. For seven o'clock. Don't be surprised – I'll be in disguise. This business has to be kept secret. Bring the bottle with you. And another thing, Fräulein Wanda. Just recently you have been tending to get above yourself. Take care, I'm not the kind of man to take liberties with.

(P2 hangs up without replying.)

Stenographed and translated from the German by Yuly Schmidt.

There was a note at the bottom in a slanting guardsman's hand: *'Make sure he doesn't get scared and do away with her! E.O.'*

The young merchant emerged from the toilet clearly refreshed. Accompanied by the maître d'hôtel, he entered the dining hall and cast a dull glance over the tables and their impossibly white tablecloths covered with gleaming silver and crystal. He spat on the brilliant parquet floor (the maître d'hôtel merely winced) and finally jabbed his finger in the direction of a table (an empty one, thank God) beside the wall. On the left of it there were two students in the company of several young milliners trilling with laughter, and on the right of it was a gentleman with a ginger beard in a check jacket, sitting there watching the stage and sipping Mosel wine.

If not for Agent Klyuev's warning, Fandorin would never have recognised Herr Knabe. Another master of disguise. But then, in view of his primary professional activity, that was hardly surprising.

Scattered but enthusiastic applause broke out in the hall. Wanda had come out on to the low stage – slim and sinuous in a dress shimmering with sequins, looking like some magical serpent.

'What a scrawny thing – not a pick on her,' a chubby milliner at the next table snorted, offended because both students were staring wide-eyed at the songstress.

Wanda swept the hall with her wide, radiant eyes and began singing quietly without any introduction in either words or music. The accompanist picked up the melody on the piano as she went along and began weaving a lacy pattern of chords around that low voice that pierced straight to the heart.

> *Beside a crossroads far way,*
> *Buried in sand a body lies.*
> *Above it blooms a dark-blue flower,*
> *The flower of the suicides.*

Chill evening wrapped the world in slumber
As at that spot I stood and sighed.
The moon shone on its gentle swaying ...
The flower of the suicides.

A strange choice for a restaurant, thought Fandorin, listening to the German words of the song. *From Heine, I think.*

The hall grew very quiet, then everyone began applauding at once, and the milliner who had recently been so jealous even shouted out 'Bravo!' Erast Petrovich realised that even he himself had perhaps slipped out of character, but nobody appeared to have noticed the inappropriately serious expression that had appeared on the young merchant's drunken features. In any case, the man with the ginger beard, sitting at the table to the right, had been looking only at the stage.

The final chords of the mournful ballad still hung in the air when Wanda began clicking her fingers to set a rapid rhythm. With a shake of his shaggy head, the pianist rushed his ending, then crashed all ten digits down on to the keys, and the audience began swaying in their chairs in time to a rollicking Parisian *chansonnette*.

Some Russian gentleman who looked like a factory owner performed a strange series of actions: he called over a flowergirl, took a bouquet of pansies out of her basket, wrapped them in a hundred-rouble note and sent them to Wanda. Without even breaking her song, she sniffed the bouquet and ordered it to be sent back, together with the hundred-rouble note. The factory owner, who so far had been acting as proud as a king, was visibly deflated and gulped down two tall wineglasses of vodka in quick succession. The people around him in the hall kept casting derisive glances in his direction.

Erast Petrovich did not forget his role again. He played the fool a little, pouring champagne into a teacup, and from there into the saucer. He puffed out his cheeks and sipped at the champagne with a loud slurping noise – but only drank a tiny amount, in order not to get tipsy. He ordered the waiter to bring some more champagne ('And not Lanvin either – the real stuff: Moët.') and roast a piglet, only it had to be still alive, and first they had to bring it and show it to him: 'I know what you Krauts are like, you'll slip me some old carcass from the ice house.' Fandorin was counting on the fact that it would take a long time to find a live piglet, and in the meantime the situation would be resolved in one way or another.

The disguised Knabe squinted across at his noisy neighbour in annoyance, but took no great interest in him. The secret agent took out his Bréguet watch four times and it was obvious that he was feeling nervous. At five minutes to eight Wanda announced that she was singing her last song before the intermission and struck up a sentimental Irish ballad about a girl called Molly, whose true love failed to return from the war. Some of the people sitting in the hall were wiping away the tears from their faces.

She'll finish the song in a moment and sit at Knabe's table, Fandorin assumed and prepared himself by lowering his forehead on to his elbow, as if he had dozed off. At the same time, he tossed back the strand of hair from over his right ear and, applying the science of concentration, shut off all his senses except for hearing. He became transformed, as it were, into his own right ear. Wanda's singing now seemed to be coming from far away, but he could hear the slightest movement made by Herr Knabe with great clarity. The German was restless: squeaking his chair, scraping his feet, then suddenly starting to drum his heels. Growing suspicious, Erast Petrovich turned his head and half-opened one eye – and was just in time to see the gentleman with the ginger beard slipping out through the side door.

The hall broke into thunderous applause. 'A goddess!' shouted a student, moved almost to tears. The milliners were clapping loudly.

Herr Knabe's stealthy withdrawal was not at all to the collegiate assessor's liking. In combination with the disguise and the false name it suggested alarming possibilities.

The young merchant rose abruptly to his feet, knocking over his chair, and declared in a confidential tone to the jolly company at the next table: 'Got the urge to relieve myself.' Swaying slightly on his feet, he headed for the side exit.

'Sir!' shouted a waiter, racing up behind him, 'the toilet room is not that way.'

'Go away,' said the barbarian, shoving the waiter aside without even turning round. 'I'll relieve myself wherever I like.'

The waiter froze on the spot in horror, and the merchant continued on his way in broad, rapid strides. Oh, this was not good. He needed to hurry. Wanda had already flitted off the side of the stage into the wings.

Just as he reached the door a new obstacle arose in the form of a desperately squealing piglet being carried towards the capricious client. 'There, just as you ordered!' said the panting chef, proudly displaying his trophy. 'Alive and kicking. Shall we roast it for you?'

Erast Petrovich looked at the piglet's terror-filled little eyes and suddenly felt sorry for the poor creature, born into the world only to end up in the belly of some glutton. The merchant growled: 'Not big enough yet; let him put on a bit of fat!'

The chef dejectedly clutched the cloven-hoofed beast to his breast as the ignorant boor stumbled against the doorpost and tumbled out into the corridor.

Right, Fandorin thought feverishly. *On the right is the entrance hall. That means the offices and Wanda's dressing room are on the left*. He set off down the corridor at a run. Round the corner he heard a scream coming from a dimly lit recess. There was some kind of commotion going on in there.

Erast Petrovich dashed towards the sound and saw the

man with the ginger beard clutching Wanda from behind, holding his hand over her mouth and bringing a narrow steel blade up towards the songstress's throat. Wanda had grabbed the broad wrist covered in reddish hair with both her hands, but the distance between the blade and her slim neck was closing rapidly.

'Stop! Police!' Fandorin cried in a voice hoarse with tension.

Displaying phenomenally rapid reactions, Herr Knabe pushed the floundering Wanda straight at Erast Petrovich who involuntarily put his arms round the singer's thin shoulders. She clung to her saviour with a grip of iron, trembling all over. In two bounds the German was past them and dashing away down the corridor, fumbling under his armpit as he ran. Fandorin saw the man's hand emerge, holding something black and heavy, and he barely had time to drag Wanda to the floor and shield her under his body. A second later and the bullet would have pierced both their bodies. For an instant the collegiate assessor was deafened by the thunderous roar that filled the narrow corridor. Wanda squealed in despair and began thrashing about underneath him.

'It is I, Fandorin!' he panted as he struggled to stand up. 'Let go of me.'

He tried to leap to his feet, but Wanda, still lying on the floor, was clutching him tightly by the ankle and sobbing hysterically: 'Why did he do that? Why? Oh, don't leave me!'

It was useless trying to pull his foot free – the songstress was clinging on tight and would not let go. Then Erast Petrovich said in an emphatically calm voice: 'You know yourself why. But God is merciful: you're safe now.'

He unclasped her fingers gently but firmly and ran off in pursuit of the secret agent. It was all right, Klyuev was at the entrance, a sound officer: he wouldn't let him go. At the very least he would delay him.

However, when Fandorin burst out of the doors of the

restaurant on to the street, he discovered that things had gone about as badly as possible. Knabe was already sitting in an 'egoist' – an English one-seater carriage – and lashing a lean, sinewy gelding with his whip. The horse flailed at the air with its front hooves and set off so sharply that the German was thrown back hard against his seat.

The sound officer Klyuev was sitting on the pavement, holding his head in his hands with blood running out between his fingers. 'Sorry, let him get away,' he groaned dully. 'I told him, "Stop," and he hit me on the forehead with the butt—'

'Get up!' Erast Petrovich tugged at the wounded man's shoulder and forced him to his feet. 'He'll get away!'

With a great effort of self-control, Klyuev smeared the dark-red sludge across his face and began hobbling sideways towards the droshky. 'I'm all right, it's just that everything's spinning,' he muttered, clambering up on to the coach box.

Fandorin leapt up beside him in a single bound, Klyuev cracked the reins, and the chestnut mare set off with its hooves clip-clopping loudly over the cobblestones, gradually picking up speed. But it was slow, too slow. The egoist already had a start of a hundred paces!

'Harder!' Erast Petrovich shouted at the listless Klyuev. 'Harder!'

At breakneck speed, with houses, shop signs and astounded pedestrians flashing past in a blur, both carriages tore along the short Sofiiskaya Street and out on to broad Lubyanka Street, where the chase began in earnest. A policeman on duty opposite Mobius's photographic studio began whistling in furious indignation and waving his fist at the lawbreakers, but that was all. *Ah, if only I had a telephone apparatus in the carriage*, Fandorin fantasised, *I could call Karachentsev and have a couple of carriages sent out from the gendarme station to cut him off*. A useless, idiotic fantasy – their only hope now was the chestnut mare, and that dear creature was giving her all, desperately flinging out her sturdy legs, shaking her mane, glancing back over her shoulder with one insanely goggling eye – as if she were asking if this was all right, or should she kick even harder. *Kick, my darling, kick*, Erast Petrovich implored her. Klyuev seemed to have recovered a little and he stood up, cracking his whip and hallooing so wildly that Mamai's entire Tartar horde seemed to be hurtling along the quiet evening street.

The distance to the egoist had been reduced a little bit. Knabe looked back in alarm once, then again, and seemed to realise that he would not get away. When there were about thirty paces remaining between them, the German agent turned round, holding out the revolver in his left hand, and fired.

Klyuev ducked. 'Damn, he's a good shot! That one whistled right past my ear! That's a Reichsrevolver he's blasting away with! Shoot, Your Excellency! Aim at the horse! We'll lose him!'

'What has the horse done wrong?' growled Fandorin, remembering the piglet. In fact, of course, the interests of the fatherland would have outweighed his compassion for the bay gelding, but the problem was that his Herstahl-Agent was not designed for accurate shooting at such a distance. God forbid, he might hit Herr Knabe instead of the horse, and the entire operation would be ruined.

At the corner of Sretensky Boulevard the German turned round once again, taking a little longer to aim before his barrel belched smoke and flame. Klyuev instantly collapsed backwards, straight on to Erast Petrovich. One eye gaped in fright into the collegiate assessor's face; the place of the other had been taken by a red hole.

'Your Excel ...' his lips began to say, but they did not finish.

The carriage swung to one side and Fandorin was obliged to shove the fallen man aside unceremoniously. He picked up the reins, and just in time, or the carriage would have been smashed to smithereens against the cast-iron railings of the boulevard. The excited chestnut mare was still trying to run on, but the left front wheel had jammed against a bollard.

Erast Petrovich leaned down over the police agent and saw that his one remaining eye was no longer frightened, but staring fixedly upwards, as though Klyuev were looking at something very interesting, far more interesting than the sky or the clouds.

Fandorin mechanically reached up to remove his hat, but he had none, for his remarkable topper had been left behind in the cloakroom at the Alpine Rose.

This was a fine result: an officer killed and Knabe allowed to escape!

But where exactly could he have escaped to? Apart from the house on Karetny Ryad, the German had nowhere else to go. He had to call in there, if only for five minutes – to pick up his emergency documents and money, and destroy any compromising materials.

There was no time to indulge in mourning. Erast Petrovich grasped the dead man under the arms and dragged him out of the droshky. He sat him with his back against the railings. 'You sit here for a while, Klyuev,' the collegiate assessor muttered and, paying no attention to the passers-by who had frozen in poses of horrified curiosity, he climbed back up on to the coach box.

The egoist was standing at the entrance of the beautiful apartment house on the third floor of which the Moscow representative of the banking firm Kerbel und Schmidt resided. The dun gelding, covered in thick lather, was nervously shifting its feet and shaking its wet head.

Fandorin dashed into the hallway.

'Stop! Where are you going?' yelled the fat-faced doorman, grabbing hold of the young man's arm, but he was immediately sent flying by a punch to the jaw, without receiving any superfluous explanations.

Upstairs a door slammed. It sounded like the third floor! Erast Petrovich bounded upwards two steps at a time, holding the Herstahl at the ready. He would have to shoot him twice, in the right arm and the left. The German had tried to slit Wanda's throat with his right hand, and he had fired with his left, which meant that he was ambidextrous.

And here was a door with a brass plaque: 'Hans-Georg Knabe'. Fandorin tugged hard on the bronze handle – it wasn't locked. After that he moved quickly, but took precautionary measures. He held the revolver out in front of him and took the safety catch off.

The long corridor was dimly lit, the only light entering from an open window at its far end. That was why Erast Petrovich, anticipating danger from ahead and from the side, but not from below, failed to notice the elongated object lying under his feet and stumbled over it, almost sprawling full length. He turned swiftly and prepared to fire, but there was no need.

Lying face down on the floor, with one hand flung out forwards, was a familiar figure in a check jacket with its back flaps parted. *Witchcraft*, was the first thought that came into Erast Petrovich's mind. He turned the man over on to his back and immediately saw the wooden handle of a butcher's knife protruding from his right side. Witchcraft apparently had nothing to do with the case. The secret agent was dead, and to judge from the blood pulsing from the wound, he had only just been killed.

Fandorin ran through all the rooms, peering intently through half-closed eyes. There was chaos everywhere, with everything turned upside down and books scattered across the floor. In the bedroom the white fluff from a slashed eiderdown was swirling in the air like snow in a blizzard. And there was not a single soul.

Erast Petrovich glanced out of the window that was intended to illuminate the corridor and saw the roof of an extension directly below him. So that was it!

Jumping down, the detective set off across the rumbling iron sheeting of the roof. The view from up there was quite marvellous: a scarlet sunset above the belfries and towers of Moscow, and a black flight of crows rippling across it. But the collegiate assessor, normally so sensitive to beauty, did not even glance at this wonderful panorama.

It was a strange business. The killer had disappeared, and yet there was absolutely nowhere he could have gone from that roof. He couldn't have simply flown away, could he?

Two hours later, the apartment on Karetny Ryad was unrecognisable. There were detective officers darting around the crowded rooms, employees of the coding section numbering and assembling in cardboard files all the papers that had been found, a gendarme photographer taking photographs of the body from various angles. The top brass – the chief of police, the head of the secret section of the governor's chancellery and the deputy for special assignments – had occupied the kitchen, where the search had already been completed.

'And what ideas do the gentlemen detectives have?' asked Khurtinsky, dispatching a pinch of tobacco into his nostril.

'The general picture is clear,' said Karachentsev with a shrug, 'a mock robbery, designed for idiots. They wrecked everything, but didn't take anything of value. And the secret hiding places haven't been touched: the weapons, the codebook, the tools – they're all still there. Evidently they were hoping we wouldn't dig too deep.'

'Atish-oo!' Court Counsellor Khurtinsky sneezed deafeningly, but no one blessed him.

The general turned away from him and continued, addressing Fandorin: 'One particularly "convincing" detail is the murder weapon. The knife was taken from over there.' He pointed to a set of hooks on which knives of various sizes were hanging. One hook was empty. 'Intended to suggest that the thief grabbed the first thing that came to hand. Typically German, rough-hewn cunning. The blow to the liver was delivered with supreme professionalism. Someone was waiting for our Herr Knabe in the dark corridor.'

'But who?' asked Pyotr Parmyonovich, carefully charging his other nostril.

The chief of police did not condescend to explain, and so Erast Petrovich had to do it: 'Probably someone from his side. There doesn't appear to be anyone else it could be.'

'The Krauts took fright; they're afraid of a diplomatic conflict,' Evgeny Osipovich said with a nod. 'The robbery is a fiction, of course. Why bother to rip open the eiderdown? No, they were just trying to muddy the waters. It's not good, *meine Herren*, not Christian, to butcher your own agent like a pig in a slaughterhouse. But I understand the reason for the panic. In this case exposure could mean more than a mere scandal – it could mean war. The general staff captain overplayed his hand a bit. Excessive zeal is a dangerous thing, and the careerist got what he deserved. In any case, gentlemen, our work is done. The events surrounding General Sobolev's death have been clarified. From here on the people at the top make the decisions. What's to be done with Wanda?'

'She has nothing to do with Sobolev's death,' said Fandorin, 'and she has been punished enough for her contacts with the German agent. She almost lost her life.'

'Leave the chanteuse alone,' Khurtynsky seconded him, 'otherwise a lot of things will surface that we'd rather didn't.'

'Well then,' the chief of police summed up, evidently considering how he would compose his report to the 'people at the top', 'in two days the investigation has reconstituted the entire chain of events. The German agent Herr Knabe, wishing to distinguish himself in the eyes of his superiors, took it into his head, at his own risk, to eliminate our finest Russian general, well known for his militant anti-Germanism, and the acknowledged leader of the Russian nationalist party. Having learned of Sobolev's forthcoming arrival in Moscow, Knabe arranged for the general to meet a *demi-mondaine*, to whom he gave a small bottle of a certain powerful poison. The female agent either chose not to use it or had no time to do so. The sealed bottle has been confiscated from her and is now in the Moscow governor's Department of the Gendarmes. The general's death was the result of natural causes; however, Knabe did not know this and hurried to report his actions to Berlin, anticipating a reward. His superiors in Berlin were horrified and, foreseeing the possible consequences of such a political murder, immediately decided to rid themselves of their overzealous agent, which they did. It is not envisaged that there will be any reason to take diplomatic action against the German government, especially since no attempt was actually made on the general's life.' Evgeny Osipovich concluded his summary in his normal, unofficial tone of voice. 'Our clever captain was destroyed by a fatal confluence of circumstances. Which was no more than the scoundrel deserved.'

Khurtinsky stood up: 'Amen to that. Now, gentlemen, you can finish up here, and with your permission I shall take my leave. His Excellency is waiting for my report.'

It was well after midnight when Erast Petrovich reached the hotel. Masa was in the corridor, standing motionless in front of the door. 'Master, she is here again,' the Japanese declared laconically.

'Who?'

'The woman in black. She came and she does not leave. I looked in the dictionary and said that I did not know when you would come back: "Master not here now. Here later." She sat down and is still sitting. She has been sitting three hours, and I have been standing here.'

With a sigh, Erast Petrovich opened the door slightly and

peered in through the gap. Sitting by the table with her hands folded on her knees was a golden-haired young woman in a mourning dress and a wide-brimmed hat with a black veil. He could see the long eyelashes lowered over her eyes, the thin, slightly aquiline nose, the delicate oval outline of her face.

Hearing the door creak, the stranger raised her eyes and Fandorin froze when he saw how beautiful they were. Instinctively recoiling from the door, the collegiate assessor hissed: 'Masa, but you said she was old. She is no more than twenty-five!'

'European women look so old,' said Masa, shaking his head. 'And anyway, master, is twenty-five years young?'

'You said she was ugly!'

'She is ugly, the poor thing. Yellow hair, a big nose and watery eyes – just like yours, master.'

'I see,' whispered Erast Petrovich, stung. 'So you're the only handsome one here, are you?' And heaving another deep sigh, but this time for a quite different reason, he entered the room.

'Mister Fandorin?' asked the young woman, rising abruptly. 'You are conducting the investigation into the circumstances of Mikhail Dmitrievich Sobolev's death, are you not? Gukmasov told me.'

Erast Petrovich bowed without speaking and gazed into the stranger's face. The combination of willpower and fragility, intelligence and femininity was one not often seen in the features of a young woman. Indeed, the lady was somehow strangely reminiscent of Wanda, except that there was not the slightest sign of cruelty or cynical mockery in the line of her mouth.

The night visitor walked up close to the young man, glanced into his eyes and in a voice trembling from either suppressed tears or fury, asked: 'Are you aware that Mikhail Dmitrievich was murdered?'

Fandorin frowned.

'Yes, yes, he was murdered.' The girl's eyes glinted feverishly. 'Because of that accursed briefcase!'

Chapter Seven

From early on Sunday morning the incessant pealing drifted across a tranquil sky, bleached almost white by brilliant sunlight. The day had apparently turned out fine, and the golden onion domes of the innumerable churches shone so brightly that it made you blink to look at them; but the heart of this city – sprawling across its low hills – was filled with a chill anguish. There was a doleful and despondent cadence to the constant droning of the far-famed bells: today the grieving people of Moscow were praying for the eternal repose of the recently departed servant of God Mikhail.

The deceased had lived for a long time in St Petersburg and only made brief, flying visits to Russia's ancient capital. Yet Moscow had loved him more intensely than cold bureaucratic Peter, loved him with a devoted, womanly love, without sparing too much thought for the true virtues of its idol – it was enough that he was dashingly handsome and famed for his victories. And above all Sobolev was beloved of Muscovites because in him they sensed a genuine Russian soul, untainted by foreign finicality and whimsy. This was the reason why lithographs of the bushy-bearded White General with his keen-edged sabre drawn hung in almost every house in Moscow, whether the inhabitants were minor functionaries, merchants or bourgeois.

Such great grief had not been manifested in the city, even in March of the previous year, when the requiem had been celebrated for the treacherously slain Emperor Alexander the Liberator, after which people had worn mourning for a whole year, without dressing up smartly, or organising any festivities, or styling their hair, or staging any comedies in the theatres.

Long before the funeral procession set out across the entire centre of the city to Krasnye Vorota, where the requiem was due to be celebrated in the Church of the Three Hierarchs, the pavements, windows, balconies and even roofs along Theatre Lane, Lubyanka Street and Myasnitskaya Street were thronged with hordes of spectators. Little boys ensconced themselves in trees, and the most audacious of them even clung to drainpipes. The forces of the city garrison and cadets from the Alexander and Junker Colleges were drawn up in ranks that lined the entire route to be travelled by the hearse. The funeral train – fifteen carriages decorated all over with flags, St George crosses and oak leaves – was already waiting at the Ryazan Station. Since St Petersburg had chosen not to bid farewell to the hero, it was Mother Russia herself who would say the final goodbye, and her heart lay midway between Moscow and Ryazan, where the White General would finally be laid to rest in the village of Spasskoe in the district of Ranenburg.

The procession extended for a good verst. There were more than twenty velvet cushions bearing the orders and decorations of the deceased, with the Star of Saint George, first class, carried by the commander of the St Petersburg military district, General of Infantry Ganetsky. And the wreaths – all those wreaths! A huge one from the traders of Okhotny Ryad, and from the English Club, and the Moscow Bourgeois Council, and the Cavaliers of St George – far too many to list them all. The hearse – a gun carriage covered with crimson velvet and surmounted by a canopy of gold – was preceded by heralds on horseback bearing inverted torches, and the masters of ceremonies, the governor-general of Moscow and war minister. The coffin was followed by a solitary rider on a black Arabian steed, the brother and personal representative of the sovereign, the Grand Duke Kirill Alexandrovich. Behind him came Sobolev's famous snow-white Akhaltekin, draped with a black blanket of mourning, with adjutants leading him by the bridle. Then came the guard of honour, marching in slow time, carrying yet more wreaths, more modest in size, and the most important guests, walking along with their heads uncovered – high officials, generals, members of the City Duma, financial magnates. It was a magnificent, quite incomparable spectacle.

Then, as though suddenly ashamed of its misplaced brightness, the June sunshine hid itself behind dark clouds and the day turned grey, and when the procession reached Krasnye Vorota, where a crowd of a hundred thousand stood sobbing and crossing itself, a fine, miserable drizzle began to fall. Nature was finally in harmony with the mood of human society.

Fandorin squeezed his way through the dense crowd, trying to find the chief of police. He had gone to the general's home on Tverskoi Boulevard shortly after seven, when it was barely light, but he had arrived too late – they had told him that His Excellency had already left for the Hotel Dusseaux. This was a serious business, a special day, and a great responsibility. And everything depending on Evgeny Osipovich.

Then there had followed a string of misfortunes. At the door of the Hotel Dusseaux a captain of gendarmes had informed Erast Petrovich that the general 'was here just this minute and went galloping off to the department'. But Karachentsev was not at the department on Malaya Nikitskaya Street either – he had dashed away to maintain order in front of the church, where there was a danger of people being crushed.

Of course, Erast Petrovich's urgent little matter of vital importance could have been decided by the governor-general. There was no need to search for him – there he was, clearly visible from all sides, at the very head of the procession, perched on his dappled-grey horse with a seat as firm as a bronze Cavalry Guard. No point in trying to get anywhere near him.

In the Church of the Three Hierarchs, which Fandorin was only able to enter thanks to the timely appearance of the prince's secretary, things were no better. By applying the science of 'the stealthy ones', Erast Petrovich was able to squeeze his way through almost to the very coffin, but there the backs closed together in a sheer, impenetrable wall. Vladimir Andreevich Dolgorukoi, with a solemn face and pomaded hair, his bulging eyes moist with old man's tears, was standing nearby with the grand duke and the Duke of Lichtenberg. It was absolutely impossible to talk with him, and even if it had been, at that moment it was unlikely that he would have appreciated the urgency of the matter.

Furious at his helplessness, Fandorin listened to the touching sermon by the Reverend Amvrosii, who was expounding the inscrutability of the ways of the Lord. A pale and agitated young cadet declaimed a long verse epitaph in a ringing voice, concluding with the words:

> And did not he our foemen proud
> Inspire with dread and trepidation?
> Though his remains lie in the ground,
> His spirit lives, our inspiration.

Not for the first time, or even the second, everybody there shed a tear, scraping their feet and reaching for their handkerchiefs. The ceremony proceeded with a lack of haste that befitted the occasion.

Meanwhile precious time was slipping away.

The previous night Fandorin had been informed of new circumstances that cast an entirely new light on the case. His night-time visitor, whom his servant, unaccustomed to the European canon of beauty, had considered old and ugly, while his romantically inclined master had thought her intriguing and quite lovely, had proved to be a teacher at the girls' grammar school in Minsk, Ekaterina Alexandrovna Golovina. Despite her frail frame and clearly agitated emotional state, Ekaterina Alexandrovna had expressed herself in a resolute and direct way most untypical of grammar-school teachers – either that was her natural manner, or grief had hardened her.

'Mr Fandorin,' she began, enunciating every syllable with deliberate clarity, 'I should explain to you immediately the nature of the relationship that bound me to the – the – deceased.' It was almost impossible for her to get the word out. A line of suffering creased her tall, clear forehead, but her voice did not tremble.

A Spartan woman, thought Erast Petrovich, *a genuine Spartan.*

'Otherwise you will not understand why I know what was not known to anyone else, not even Mikhail Dmitrievich's closest helpers. Michel and I loved each other.' Miss Golovina looked enquiringly at Fandorin and, evidently unsatisfied by the politely attentive expression on his face, felt it necessary to clarify the point. 'I was his lover.'

Ekaterina Alexandrovna pressed her clenched fists to her breast, and at that moment Fandorin thought once again that she resembled Wanda, when she was speaking about her free love – there was that same expression of defiance and readiness to be insulted. The collegiate assessor continued looking at the young lady in exactly the same way – politely and without the slightest hint of condemnation.

She sighed and explained to the dolt one more time: 'We lived as man and wife, you understand? And so he was more open with me than with others.'

'I understand that, madam; please do go on,' said Erast Petrovich, opening his mouth for the first time.

'But surely you know that Michel had a lawful wife,' said Ekaterina Alexandrovna, still feeling the need to elaborate, making it clear from her entire bearing that she wished to avoid leaving anything unsaid and was not in the least ashamed of her status.

'I know, the Princess Titova by birth. However, she and Mikhail Dmitrievich separated a long time ago and she has not even come for the funeral. Tell me about the briefcase.'

'Yes, yes,' said Golovina, suddenly confused. 'But let me start at the beginning. Because first I must explain ... A month ago Michel and I had a quarrel ...' She blushed. 'In fact, we parted and did not see each other again. He left for manoeuvres, then came back to Minsk for a day and then immediately—'

'I am aware of Mikhail Dmitrievich's movements for the last month,' Fandorin said politely but firmly, redirecting his visitor to the main theme.

She hesitated, then suddenly said very clearly: 'But are you aware, sir, that in May Michel cashed in all his shares and securities, drew all the money out of his bank accounts, mortgaged his Ryazan estate and also took a large loan from a bank?'

'What for?' asked Erast Petrovich, frowning.

Ekaterina Alexandrovna lowered her gaze. 'That I do not know. He had some secret business that was very important to him, which he did not wish to let me know about. I was angry, we quarrelled – I never shared Michel's political views: Russia for the Russians, a united Slavdom, our own non-European path and similar preposterous nonsense. Our final, conclusive quarrel was also caused in part by this. But there was something else ... I sensed that I was no longer at the centre of his life. There was something new in it, more important than me ...' She blushed. 'Or perhaps, not something, but someone … Well, that is all immaterial. The truly important thing is something else.' Golovina lowered her voice. 'All the money was in a briefcase that Michel bought in Paris during his tour in February. Brown leather, with two silver locks with little keys.'

Fandorin half-closed his eyes as he tried to remember if there had been a briefcase like that among the dead man's things during the search of apartment number 47. No, definitely not.

'He told me that he would need the money for a trip to Moscow and St Petersburg,' the teacher continued. 'The trip was due to take place at the end of June, immediately the manoeuvres were completed. You did not find the briefcase among his things, did you?'

Erast Petrovich shook his head.

'And Gukmasov says that the briefcase disappeared. Michel never let go of it, and in the hotel room he locked it in the safe – Gukmasov saw him do it. But then afterwards, after … when Prokhor Akhrameevich opened the safe, there was nothing in it except a few papers; the briefcase was not there. Gukmasov did not make anything of it, because he was in a state of shock, and anyway he had no idea what a huge sum the briefcase contained.'

'What was th-the sum?'

'To the best of my knowledge, more than a million roubles,' Ekaterina Alexandrovna said quietly.

Erast Petrovich whistled in surprise, for which he immediately apologised. This was decidedly ominous news. Secret business? What sort of secret business could an adjutant-general, general of infantry and corps commander have? And what kind of papers were they that had been lying in the safe? When Fandorin had looked into the safe in the presence of the chief of police, it had been completely empty. Why had Gukmasov taken the risk of concealing the papers from the police? This was very serious. And most importantly of all, the sum was huge, quite incredibly huge. What could Sobolev have needed it for? And the key question: where had it gone?

Peering into the collegiate assessor's preoccupied face, Ekaterina Alexandrovna began speaking quickly and passionately: 'He was murdered, I know it. Because of that accursed million roubles. And then somehow they faked a death from natural causes. Michel was strong, a genuine warrior, his heart would have withstood a hundred years of battles and turmoil, it was made for turmoil.'

'Yes,' said Erast Petrovich, with a sympathetic nod. 'That is what everybody says.'

'That is why I did not insist on marriage,' said Golovina, not listening to him. Bright pink now from the turbulence of her emotions, she continued: 'I felt that I had no right, that his mission in life was different, that he could not belong just to one woman, and I did not want his left-overs – My God, what am I saying! Forgive me ...' She put her hand over her eyes and after that spoke more slowly, with an effort. 'When the telegram from Gukmasov arrived yesterday, I dashed to the station immediately. Even then I did not believe in this "paralysis of the heart", and when I learned that the briefcase had disappeared ... He was murdered, there can be no doubt about it.' She suddenly seized hold of Fandorin's arm and he was amazed at how much strength there was in her slim fingers. 'Find the murderer! Prokhor Akhrameevich says that you are an analytical genius, that you can do anything. Do it! He could not have died of heart failure! You did not know this man as I did!'

At this point she finally began weeping bitterly, thrusting her face against the collegiate assessor's chest like a child. As he awkwardly embraced the young woman around the shoulders, Erast Petrovich remembered how only recently he had embraced Wanda, in quite different circumstances. Identically frail, defenceless shoulders, an identical scent from the hair. It seemed clear now why the general had been attracted to the songstress – she must have reminded him of his love in Minsk.

'Naturally, I did not know him as you did,' Fandorin said gently. 'But I did know Mikhail Dmitrievich well enough to doubt that his death was natural. A man of that kind does not die a natural death.'

Erast Petrovich seated the young woman, still shuddering and sobbing, in an armchair and he himself began walking around the room. Suddenly he clapped his hands loudly eight times.

Ekaterina Alexandrovna started and stared at the young man through eyes gleaming with tears.

'Pay no attention,' Fandorin hastened to reassure her. 'It is an oriental exercise to aid concentration. Very helpful in setting aside what is merely incidental and focusing on the fundamental. Let's go.' He strode resolutely out into the corridor and Golovina, dumbfounded by the suddenness of it, dashed after him.

As he went, Erast Petrovich spoke rapidly to Masa, who was waiting behind the door: 'Get the travelling bag with the tools and catch up with us.'

Thirty seconds later, as Fandorin and his companion were still descending the staircase, the Japanese was already on their heels, walking with small, quick steps and panting on the back of his master's neck. In one hand the servant was holding the travelling bag in which all the tools required for an investigation were kept – numerous items that the detective found useful and even irreplaceable.

In the vestibule Erast Petrovich called over the night porter and told him to open apartment 47.

'That's quite impossible,' the porter said with a shrug. 'The gentlemen gendarmes put up a seal and confiscated the key.' He lowered his voice: 'The dead man's in there, God rest his soul. They'll come to get him at dawn. It's the funeral in the morning.'

'A seal? Well, at least they didn't leave a guard of honour,' muttered Fandorin. 'That would have been really stupid – a guard of honour in a bedroom. All right, I'll open it myself. Follow me; you can light the candles.'

The collegiate assessor strode into the 'Sobolev' corridor and tore the wax seal from the door with an intrepid hand. He took a bundle of picklocks out of the travelling bag and a minute later he was inside the apartment.

The porter lit the candles, glancing warily out of the corner of his eye at the closed door of the bedroom and crossing himself with small, rapid movements. Ekaterina Alexandrova also looked at the white rectangle behind which the embalmed body lay. Her gaze froze, spellbound, and her lips moved soundlessly, but Fandorin had no time for the teacher and her sufferings just at the moment – he was working. He dealt with the second seal just as unceremoniously, and this time the picklock was not needed – the bedroom door was not locked.

'Well, don't just stand there!' said Erast Petrovich with an impatient glance at his servant. 'Bring the candles in.' And he stepped into the kingdom of death.

The coffin was closed, thank goodness – otherwise he would probably have had to attend to the young woman instead of getting on with the job in hand. There was an open prayer-book lying at the head of the bed, with a thick church candle guttering beside it.

'Madam,' Fandorin called, turning back towards the drawing room. 'I ask you please not to come in here. You will only be in the way.' He added in Japanese, to Masa, 'The torch, quick!'

Once equipped with the English electric torch, he moved straight to the safe. Shining the torch on the keyhole, he spoke brusquely over his shoulder: 'Magnifying glass number four.'

Well, well. They'd certainly given the door a good groping – just look at all those fingerprints! The year before last, in

Japan, with the help of a certain Professor Garding, Erast Petrovich had been successful in solving a mysterious double murder in the English settlement after taking fingerprints at the scene of the crime. The new method had created a genuine furore, but it would be years before a dactyloscopic laboratory and card index could be set up in Russia. Ah, such a pity – these were such clear prints, and right beside the keyhole. All right then, what would we find inside?

'Magnifying glass number six.'

Under strong magnification fresh scratches were clearly visible – indicating that the safe had probably been opened with a picklock instead of the key. And in addition, strangely enough, there were traces of some white substance left in the lock. Fandorin took a pinch of it with a pair of miniature forceps. On inspection, it appeared to be wax. Curious.

'Is that where he was sitting?' a thin, tense voice asked behind him.

Erast Petrovich swung round in annoyance. Ekaterina Alexandrovna was standing in the doorway, clutching her elbows in her hands as if she felt cold. The young lady was not looking at the coffin; she was even making an effort to keep her eyes turned away from it by gazing at the chair in which Sobolev had supposedly died.

There is no need for her to know where it really did happen, Fandorin thought. 'I asked you not to come in here!' he shouted sternly at the teacher, because in such a situation sternness is more effective than sympathy. Let the dead hero's lover remember why they had come here in the middle of the night – remember and take herself in hand.

Golovina turned away without speaking and walked out into the drawing room.

'Sit down!' Fandorin said loudly. 'This could take some time.'

The thorough examination of the apartment took more than two hours. The porter, who had long ago ceased being afraid of the coffin, found a comfortable perch for himself in the corner and fell into a quiet doze. Masa followed his master around like a shadow, humming a little tune and from time to time handing him the tools that he required. Ekaterina Alexandrovna did not appear in the bedroom again. Fandorin glanced out once and saw her sitting at the table, with her forehead resting on her crossed arms. As if sensing Erast Petrovich's gaze, she sat up abruptly and turned the searing glance of her immense eyes on him, but she did not ask any questions.

Not until it was already dawn, and the torch was no longer needed, did Fandorin find the clue. The faint print of the sole of a shoe could just be made out on the sill of the far-left window – a narrow print, as if it had been left by a woman, although the shoe was quite clearly a man's. Through the magnifying glass it was even possible to make out a very faint pattern of crosses and stars. Erast Petrovich raised his head. The small upper pane of the window was open. If not for the footprint, he would have thought nothing of it – the opening was far too narrow.

'Hey, my good man; come on now, wake up,' he called to the drowsy porter. 'Has the apartment been cleaned?'

'Not a bit,' the man replied, rubbing his eyes. 'How could it be? You can see for yourself, sir.' And he nodded his head at the coffin.

'And have the windows been opened?'

'I wouldn't know. But it's not very likely. They don't open the windows in dead men's rooms.'

Erast Petrovich also examined the two other windows, but failed to discover anything else worthy of note.

At half past four the search had to be called off, when the make-up artist and his assistants arrived to prepare Achilles for the final journey in his chariot.

The collegiate assessor let the porter go and said goodbye to Ekaterina Alexandrovna, still without having told her anything. She shook his hand firmly, looked enquiringly into his eyes and managed to avoid any superfluous words. He was right, she was a true Spartan.

Erast Petrovich was impatient to be left alone, in order to think over the results of the search and work out a plan of action. Despite a sleepless night, he did not feel at all drowsy, not even slightly tired. When he got back to his room, Fandorin began his analysis.

At first sight the night-time search of apartment 47 did not appear to have yielded a great deal, and yet the picture that emerged seemed clear enough.

Frankly, the claim that the people's hero had been killed for money had initially appeared improbable, or even preposterous, to Erast Petrovich. But after all, someone had climbed in through the window, opened the safe and made off with the briefcase. And it had had nothing to do with politics. The thief had not taken the papers from the safe, although these papers were so important that Gukmasov had felt it necessary to extract them before the authorities arrived. So surely the burglar had only been interested in the briefcase?

There was one thing worth noting: the thief had known that Sobolev was not in the apartment that night, and that he would not return suddenly – the safe had been opened with considerable care and no haste. But the most significant thing of all was that the safe had been not left wide open, but carefully closed again, which certainly required a great deal more time and skill than opening it. Why had the additional risk been necessary, if the loss of the briefcase would be discovered by Sobolev in any case? And why bother to climb out through the small window aperture, when the large window could have been used? Conclusions?

Fandorin stood up and started walking round the room.

The thief knew that Sobolev would not be coming back to his apartment. At least not alive. That was one.

He also knew that no one apart from the general would

miss the briefcase, since only Sobolev himself knew about the million roubles. That was two.

All of the above indicated that the criminal was quite incredibly well informed. That was three.

And also, naturally, four: the thief absolutely must be found. If only because he might be a murderer as well as a thief. A million roubles was a very serious motive.

It was all very well to say that he must be found. But how?

Erast Petrovich sat down at the table and pulled a packet of writing paper towards him.

'The brush and the inkwell?' asked Masa, dashing over to the collegiate assessor from where he had been standing motionless by the wall, even snuffling less loudly than usual in order not to prevent his master from comprehending the meaning of the Great Spiral, on to which all existent causes and consequences are threaded, from the very great to the extremely small.

Fandorin nodded, continuing his deliberations.

Time was precious. Last night someone had made himself a million roubles richer. The thief and his loot could be far away by now. But if he were clever – and everything indicated that he was a wily individual – then he would be avoiding any sudden moves and lying low.

Who would be familiar with professional safebreakers? His Excellency Evgeny Osipovich. Should Erast Petrovich pay him a visit? But then the general was sleeping, restoring his strength for the arduous day ahead. And, in addition, he presumably did not keep a card index of criminals at home. And there would be no one at the Criminal Investigation Department at such an early hour either. Should Fandorin wait until the office opened?

Oh, but did they even have a card index? Previously, when Fandorin himself used to work in the department, there had been no such subtle arrangements in place. No, there was no point in waiting until morning.

Meanwhile Masa rapidly ground up a stick of dry ink in a square lacquered bowl, added a few drops of water, dipped a brush in the ink and handed it respectfully to Fandorin, taking up a standing position behind him in order not to distract his master from his calligraphic exercise.

Erast Petrovich slowly raised the brush and paused for a second, then painstakingly traced out on the paper the hieroglyph for 'patience', trying to think of only one thing: making the form of the character ideal. The result was absolutely awful: crude lines, disharmonious elements, a blot at one side. The crumpled sheet of paper went flying to the floor. It was followed by a second, a third, a fourth. The brush moved ever faster, with ever greater assurance. The eighteenth attempt produced an absolutely irreproachable hieroglyph.

'There, keep it,' said Fandorin, handing the masterpiece to Masa.

The servant admired it, smacked his lips in approval and put it away in a special folder of rice paper.

Now Erast Petrovich knew what to do, and the simple and correct decision brought peace to his heart. Correct decisions are always simple. Has it not been said that the noble man does not embark on unfamiliar business until he has acquired wisdom from a teacher?

'Get ready, Masa,' said Fandorin. 'We are going to visit my old teacher.'

If there was anyone who might prove even more useful than a card index, it was Xavier Feofilaktovich Grushin, a former detective inspector at the Criminal Investigation Department. The youthful Erast Petrovich had begun his career as a detective under his tolerant, fatherly tutelage, and although the term of their service together had not been a long one, he had learned a great deal from it. Grushin was old now, long since retired, but he knew all there was to know about the criminal underworld of Moscow; he had studied it inside and out in his many long years of service. There had been occasions when the twenty-year-old Fandorin was walking with him through the Khitrovka slum district or, say, along Grachyovka Street, a favourite bandits' haunt, when he had been amazed to see how the grim-faced ruffians, and nightmarish ragamuffins, and pomaded fops with shifty eyes would approach the inspector, and every one of them would doff his hat, bow and greet him. Xavier Feofilaktovich would whisper for a while with one of them, give another an amiable smack on the ear and shake hands with a third. And immediately, after moving on a little, he would explain to his novice of a clerk: 'That's Tishka Siroi, a railway specialist – he works the stations, snatches suitcases out of cabs on the move. And that's Gulya, a first-class swopper.' 'A swopper?' Erast Petrovich would enquire timidly, glancing round at the respectable-looking gentleman with a bowler hat and a cane. 'Why yes, he trades in gold. He's very clever at switching a genuine ring for a fake. Shows them a gold ring and slips them a gilded copper one. A respectable trade, requires great skill.' Grushin would stop beside some 'players' – rogues who used three thimbles to empty people's pockets – then point and say: 'See that, young man, Styopka just put the little ball of bread under the left thimble? But don't you believe your eyes – the ball's glued to his fingernail, so it can never stay under the thimble.' 'Then why don't we arrest them, the swindlers!' Fandorin would exclaim passionately, but Grushin would only chuckle: 'Everyone has to live somehow, my dear fellow. The only thing I ask of them is to have a conscience and never take the last shirt off a man's back.'

The inspector was held in especially high regard among the criminals of Moscow – for his fairness, for the fact that he allowed birds of every feather to earn their living, and especially for his lack of cupidity. Unlike other police officers, Xavier Feofilaktovich did not take bribes, and therefore he had never earned enough to buy himself a stone mansion, and when he retired he had settled in a modest house with a vegetable garden in the Zamoskvorechie district. While working in the diplomatic service in distant Japan, Erast Petrovich had from time to time received news from his old boss, and when he was transferred to Moscow, he had decided that he must pay Grushin a visit just as soon as he had settled in a little. But now it seemed that he would have to pay that visit right away.

As their cab rumbled across the Moskvoretsky Bridge, bathed in the very first, uncertain rays of morning sunlight, Masa asked in concern: 'Master, is *Grushin-sensei* simply a *sensei* or an *onshi*?' And he explained his doubts, with a dis-approving shake of his head: 'For a respectful visit to a *sensei* it is still too early, and for a highly respectful visit to an *onshi* it is even more so.'

A *sensei* is simply a teacher, but an *onshi* is something immeasurably greater: a teacher to whom one feels profound and sincere gratitude.

'I would say he is an *onshi*,' said Erast Petrovich, glancing at the broad red band of dawn that extended halfway across the sky, and confessing frivolously: 'It is a little early, certainly. But then Grushin probably has insomnia anyway.'

Xavier Feofilaktovich was indeed not asleep. He was sitting at the window of the house which, although it was little, was nonetheless his own – located in the labyrinth of narrow lanes between Greater Ordynka Street and Lesser Ordynka Street – and indulging in meditations on the peculiar properties of sleep. The fact that as a man grows older he sleeps less than in his youth seemed right and proper – what was the point of wasting the time when you would catch up on your sleep for ever soon enough? But on the other hand, when you were young, you had so much more use for the time. Sometimes you would be dashing around from dawn till dusk, rushed off your feet, and if you only had just another hour or two, you could get everything done, but then you had to give away eight hours to the pillow. The feeling of regret was sometimes so keen – but what could you do about it? Nature would claim what was hers by right. And now you doze for an hour or two in the evening in the little front garden, and then you might go all night without sleeping a wink, but you have nothing to occupy your time. Times had changed; things were done differently now. The old dray horse had been retired to live out his life in a warm stall. And thanks for that, of course; it would be a sin to complain. But it was boring. His wife, may she rest easy in the ground, had passed away more than two years ago. His only daughter, Sashenka, had upped and married a loud windbag of a midshipman and taken off with her husband to the other end of the world, to the city of Vladivostok. Of course, his cook Nastasya still prepared his meals and washed his clothes, but sometimes he felt like talking too. And what could he talk about with an empty-headed woman like that? The price of kerosene and sunflower seeds?

But Grushin could still have made himself useful – oh, yes, very useful indeed. His strength was not yet completely exhausted, and his brains, thank God, hadn't begun to rust away. *You'll never hit the mark, mister chief of police. How many villains have you caught with those idiotic Bertillonages of yours? People are afraid to walk around the streets of Moscow now – the footpads will have your purse off you in an instant, and in the evenings you are as likely as not to get a cosh over the head.*

Mental wrangling with his former bosses usually left Xavier Feofilaktovich in a state of depression. The retired inspector was honest with himself: the service would get by without him somehow or other, but life without the service was unbearably tedious for him. Ah, sometimes you would go out on an investigation in the morning and everything inside you would be trembling like a spring wound up as tight as it would go. After your coffee and your first pipe your head was clear and your thoughts would lay out the entire line of action without any effort. And now he could see that that had been happiness, *that* had been living. 'Lord, you would think I'd lived long enough already and seen more than enough in my time, but if only I could live a bit longer,' sighed Grushin, glancing in disapproval at the sun peeping out from behind the roofs – the long, empty day would soon begin.

And the Lord heard him. Xavier Feofilaktovich squinted at the unpaved road with his long-sighted eyes – he thought he could see a carriage raising dust over in the direction of Pyatnitskaya Street. There were two riders: one wearing a tie, the other low and squat, wearing something green. Who could this be so early in the morning?

After the obligatory embraces, kisses and questions, to which Grushin answered at great length and Fandorin with great brevity, they got down to business. Erast Petrovich did not go into the details of the story, and in particular he did not mention Sobolev, but merely outlined the terms of the problem.

A safe had been cleaned out in a certain hotel. The signature was as follows: the lock had been picked rather sloppily – to judge from the scratches, the thief had fiddled with it for quite a while. A distinctive feature was that there were traces of wax inside the keyhole. The criminal possessed an exceptionally slender frame – he had climbed in through a small window opening, only seven inches by fourteen. He had been wearing boots or shoes with a pattern of crosses and stars on the sole, with a foot approximately nine inches long and a little less than three wide—

Before Fandorin could even finish listing the terms of the problem, Xavier Feofilaktovich suddenly interrupted the young man: 'Boots.'

The collegiate assessor cast a startled sideways glance at

Masa dozing in the corner. Had they perhaps wasted their time in coming here? Was the old *onshi* already in his dotage?'

'What?'

'Boots,' the inspector repeated. 'Not shoes. Box-calf boots, shined as bright as a mirror. He never wears anything else.'

Fandorin's heart stood still. Cautiously, as if he were afraid of alarming Grushin, he asked: 'Do you mean you know the thief?'

'I know him very well,' said Grushin, with a smile of satisfaction covering his entire soft, wrinkled face (which had far more skin than the skull required). 'It's Little Misha – can't be anyone else. Only it's strange that he fumbled with the safe for such a long time: opening a hotel safe is as simple as falling off a log for him. Misha is the only safebreaker who climbs in through the small window, and his picklocks are always lubricated with wax – his ears are very sensitive and he can't bear the sound of squeaking.'

'Little Misha? Who's th-that?'

'Everybody knows him,' said Xavier Feofilaktovich, untying his tobacco pouch and taking his time to fill his pipe. 'The king of Moscow's "businessmen". A first-rate safebreaker, and not squeamish about getting his hands bloody either. He's also a lady's man, a fence and the leader of a gang. The master of a wide range of trades, a criminal Benvenuto Cellini. Very short – only two *arshins* and two *vershoks*. Puny, but he dresses in style. Cunning, resourceful, vicious and cruel. An individual of considerable repute in Khitrovka.'

'So well known and still not doing hard labour?' Fandorin asked in surprise.

The inspector chortled and sucked on his pipe in delight – the first puff in the morning is always the sweetest. 'Just you try to put him away. I couldn't manage it, and I doubt whether the present crowd will either. The villain has his own men in the force – that's for certain. The number of times I tried to nail him. I never even got close!' Grushin waved his hand dismissively. 'He escapes from every raid. They tip him off, those well-wishers of his. And people are afraid of Misha. Oh, they're really afraid! His gang are all cut-throats and murderers. They have plenty of respect for me up in Khitrovka, but you couldn't rip a single word about Little Misha out of them with pliers. And they know I'm not going to try to do that – the worst I'll do is punch someone in the teeth; but afterwards Misha will pick them to pieces with red-hot pincers, never mind pliers. There was one time, four years ago, when I managed to get really close to him. I was using one of his working girls; she was a good girl really, still not completely lost yet. Then just before the job, when I was supposed to pick Misha up in their bandits' hideaway, some-one dumped a sack right in front of the department. Inside it was my informer – sawn up into joints, twelve of them … Eh, Erast Petrovich, the things I could tell you about his tricks; but if I understand aright, you don't have the time for that. Otherwise you wouldn't have come round at half past five in the morning.' And Xavier Feofilaktovich screwed up his eyes cunningly, proud of his perspicacity.

'I need Little Misha very badly,' Fandorin said with a frown. 'Although it seems improbable, he must be connect-ed in some way … However, I have no right … But I do assure you that it is a matter of state importance and also of great urgency. Why don't we go right now and pick up this Benvenuto Cellini of yours, eh?'

Grushin shrugged and spread his arms wide: 'That's a tall order. I know every nook and cranny of Khitrovka, but I've no idea where Little Misha spends the night. It would take a mass raid. And it would have to come from right at the very top, not through any inspectors or captains – they'd tip him off. Cordon off the whole of Khitrovka, and do every-thing right, without rushing it. And then, if we don't get

Misha himself, we might at least pick up someone from his gang or one of his girls. But that would require about five hundred constables, no less. And they mustn't be told what it's all about until the last minute. That's absolutely essential.'

And so since early that morning Erast Petrovich had been roaming around a city in the grip of mourning, dashing backwards and forwards between Tverskoi Boulevard and Krasnye Vorota, trying to find the topmost brass in town. The precious time was slipping away! With a fabulous haul like this one, Little Misha could already have made a dash for the jolly haunts of Odessa, or Rostov, or Warsaw. It was a big empire, with plenty of room for a high-spirited fellow to cut loose. Since the night before last, Misha had been sitting on loot the like of which he could never have imagined, even in his dreams. The logical thing for him to do would be to wait for a little while and see whether there would be an uproar or not. Misha was an old hand, so he was bound to understand all this. But with money like that his bandit's heart would be smarting. He wouldn't be able to hold out for long: he'd make a dash for it – if he hadn't slipped away already. Ah, what a nuisance this funeral was …

Once, as the Grand Duke Kirill Alexandrovich stepped towards the coffin and respectful silence filled the church, Fandorin caught the governor-general glancing at him and began nodding desperately to attract His Excellency's attention, but the prince merely replied by nodding in the same way, sighing heavily and raising his eyes mournfully to the flaming candles in the chandelier. However, the collegiate assessor's gesticulations were noticed by His Highness the Duke of Lichtenberg, who seemed rather embarrassed to find himself surrounded by all this gilded Byzantine finery, and was crossing himself the wrong way, from left to right, not like everybody else, and in general looking as though he felt very much out of place. Raising one eyebrow slightly, Evgeny Maximilianovich fixed his gaze on this functionary who was making such strange signs, and after a moment's thought he tapped Khurtinsky on the shoulder with his finger – the court counsellor's disguised bald spot was just peeping out from behind the governor's epaulette. Pyotr Parmyonovich proved quicker on the uptake than his superior: he realised in an instant that something out of the ordinary must have happened and jerked his chin in the direction of the side exit – as if to say, Go over there and we'll have a talk.

Erast Petrovich began slipping through the dense crowd once again, but in a different direction, not towards the centre now, but at a slant, so that now his progress was quicker. And all the while, as the collegiate assessor was forcing his way through the mourners, the deep, manly voice of the grand duke resounded under the vaults of the church, and everybody listened with rapt attention. It was not merely that Kirill Alexandrovich was the sovereign's own well-loved brother. Many of those present at the requiem knew perfectly well that this stately, handsome general with the slightly predatory, hawkish face did more than merely command the Guards, he could in fact be said to be the true ruler of the empire, for he was also in charge of the War Ministry and the Department of Police and, even more significantly, of the Special Gendarmes Corps. And most importantly of all, they said that the Tsar never took a single decision of even the slightest importance without first discussing it with his brother. As he worked his way towards the entrance, Erast Petrovich listened to the grand duke's speech and thought that nature had played a mean trick on Russia: if only one brother had been born two years sooner and the other two years later, the autocratic ruler of Russia would not have been the prevaricating, inert, morose Alexander, but the intelligent, far-sighted and decisive Kirill! Ah, how different drowsy Russian life would have been then! And what a glittering role the great power would have played on the international stage! But it was pointless to rage in vain at nature and, if you chose to vent your rage after all, then it should not be at Mother Nature, but at Providence, who never decided any matter without a higher reason, and if the empire was not destined to rise from its slumber at the command of a new Peter the Great, then it must be that the Lord did not wish it. He had some other, unknown fate in mind for the Third Rome. At least let it be a joyful and bright one. And with this thought Erast Petrovich crossed himself, something he did extremely rarely, but the movement failed to attract anybody's attention, for the people around him were all repeatedly making the sign of the cross themselves. Perhaps they were having similar thoughts?

Kirill's speech was splendid, filled with a noble, vital energy: '... There are many who complain that this valiant hero, the hope of the Russian land, has left us in such a sudden and – why not face the truth? – absurd fashion. The man who was dubbed Achilles for his legendary good fortune in battle, which saved him many times from imminent doom, did not fall on the battlefield; instead of a soldier's death, he died the quiet death of a civilian. But is that really so?' The voice assumed the ringing tone of antique bronze. 'Sobolev's heart burst because it had been exhausted by years of service to the fatherland, weakened by numerous wounds received in battles against our enemies. Achilles should not have been his name – oh no! Well protected by the waters of the Styx, Achilles was invulnerable to arrow and sword; until the very last day of his life he did not spill a single drop of his own blood. But Mikhail Dmitrievich bore on his body the traces of fourteen wounds, each of which invisibly advanced the hour of his death. No, Sobolev should not have been compared with the fortunate Achilles, but rather with the noble Hector – a mere mortal who risked his own life just as his soldiers did!'

Erast Petrovich did not hear the ending of this powerful and emotional speech, because just at that point he finally reached his goal – the side door, where the head of the secret section of the governor's chancellery was already waiting for him.

'Well then, what's happened?' the court counsellor asked, twitching the skin of his tall, pale forehead. He pulled Fandorin out after him into the yard, further away from prying ears.

Erast expounded the essence of the matter with his invariable mathematical clarity and brevity, concluding with the following words: 'We need to carry out a mass raid immediately – tonight at the very latest. That is six.'

Khurtinsky listened tensely, gasped twice and near the end of Fandorin's account even loosened his tight collar. 'You have killed me, Erast Petrovich, simply killed me,' he said. 'This is worse than the spy scandal. If the hero of Plevna was murdered for filthy lucre, we are disgraced before the entire world. Although a million roubles is not exactly a miserly sum ...' Pyotr Parmyonovich began cracking his knuckles, trying to think. 'Lord, what is to be done, what is to be done? ... There's no point in pestering Vladimir Andreevich – he is in no condition for this today. And Karachentsev won't be any help either – he hasn't got a single constable to spare at the moment. We can expect public unrest this evening in connection with the sad event, and so many important individuals have come – every one of them has to be guarded and protected from terrorists and bombers. No, my dear sir, nothing can be done about a raid tonight; don't even think of it.'

'Then we shall lose him,' Fandorin almost groaned. 'He will get away.'

'Most likely he already has,' Khurtinsky sighed gloomily.

'If he has, then the tracks are still fresh. We might just be able to p-pick up some little thread.'

Pyotr Parmyonovich took the collegiate assessor by the

elbow in an extremely tactful manner: 'You are quite right. It would be criminal to waste any more time. I am no novice when it comes to the secrets of Moscow. I also know Little Misha, and I have been trying to get close to him for ages; but he's crafty, the rogue. And let me tell you something, my dear Erast Petrovich …' The court counsellor's voice assumed an affectionate and confidential tone; the eyes that were always hooded opened to their full extent and proved to be intelligent and piercing. 'To be quite honest, I did not take a liking to you at first. Not at all. A windbag, I thought, an aristocratic snob. Hovering around prey won by others' sweat and blood. But Khurtinsky is always prepared to admit when he is wrong. I was mistaken about you – the events of the last two days have demonstrated that most eloquently. I see that you are a man of great intelligence and experience, and a first-rate detective.'

Fandorin bowed slightly, waiting to see what would follow.

'And so I have a little proposal for you. That is, of course, if you don't find it too frightening …' Pyotr Parmyonovich moved close and began whispering. 'To prevent this evening being entirely wasted, why don't you take a stroll round the thieves' dens of Khitrovka and do a little bit of reconnaissance? I know that you are an unsurpassed master of disguise, so to pass yourself off as one of the locals should be no problem at all to you. I am in possession of certain information, and I can let you know where you are most likely to pick up Misha's trail. And I will provide you with guides, some of my very finest agents. Well, I hope you are not too squeamish for this kind of work? Or perhaps you are afraid?'

'I am neither squeamish nor afraid,' replied Erast Petrovich, who actually thought that the court counsellor's 'little proposal' made rather good sense. Indeed, if a police operation was impossible, why not have a go himself?

'And if you should pick up a thread,' Khurtinsky continued, 'it would be possible to launch a raid at dawn. Just give me the word. I won't be able to get you five hundred constables, of course, but that many would not be needed. We must, after all, assume that by then you will have narrowed the scope of the search, must we not? Just send word to me with one of my men and I'll see to the rest myself. And we shall manage perfectly well without His Excellency Evgeny Osipovich.'

Erast Petrovich frowned, detecting in these last words an echo of the high-level intrigues of Moscow, which were best forgotten at this moment.

'Th-thank you for your offer of assistance, but your men will not be required,' he said. 'I am used to managing on my own, and I have a very able assistant.'

'That Japanese of yours?' asked Khurtinsky, surprising Fandorin with how well informed he was. But then, what was there to be surprised at – that was the man's job: to know everything about everybody.

'Yes. He will be quite sufficient help for me. There is only one other thing I need to ask from you: tell me where to look for Little Misha.'

The court counsellor crossed himself piously in response to the chiming of a bell high above them. 'There is a certain terrible place in Khitrovka. An inn by the name of "Hard Labour". During the day it is merely a revolting drinking parlour, but as night approaches the "businessmen" – that is what bandits are called in Moscow – gather there. Little Misha often drops in too. If he is not there, one of his cut-throats is certain to turn up. And also watch out for the landlord, a truly desperate rogue.' Khurtinsky shook his head disapprovingly: 'It is a mistake not to take my agents. That place is dangerous. It isn't the Mysteries of Paris, it's the Khitrovka slums. One slash of a knife and a man is never heard of again. At least let one of my men take you to the

Hard Labour and stand guard outside. Honestly, don't be stubborn.'

'Thank you kindly but I'll manage somehow myself,' Fandorin replied confidently.

Chapter Eight

IN WHICH DISASTER STRIKES

'Nastasya, will you stop squealing like a stuck pig?' Xavier Feofilaktovich said angrily, glancing out into the entrance hall, where the shouting was coming from.

His cook was an empty-headed woman with an intemperate tongue, who treated her master irreverently. Grushin only kept her on out of habit, and also because the old fool baked quite magnificent pies with rhubarb or liver. But her strident foghorn of a voice, which Natasya employed unsparingly in her constant squabbles with the neighbour Glashka, the local constable Silich and all beggars, had often distracted Xavier Feofilaktovich from his reading of the *Moscow Police Gazette* or his philosophical ruminations and even his sweet early-evening sleep.

Today once again the accursed woman had started kicking up such a racket that Grushin had been obliged to abandon his pleasant doze. It was a pity – he had been dreaming that he wasn't a retired police inspector at all, but a head of cabbage growing in a market garden. His head was sticking straight up out of the soil of the vegetable patch and there was a raven sitting beside it, pecking at his left temple, but it was not at all painful; on the contrary, it was all very pleasant and restful. He didn't need to go anywhere, he was in no hurry and he had nothing to worry about. Sheer bliss. But the raven had started getting carried away, gouging his head cruelly with a loud crunch, and then the villain had begun cawing deafeningly in his ear and Grushin had woken up with his head throbbing to the sound of Nastasya's screeching.

'I hope you gets all cramped up even worse,' the cook was howling on the other side of the wall. 'And you, you pagan brute, what are you squinting at? I'll give you such a slap with my duster across your greasy chops.'

Listening to this tirade, Xavier Feofilaktovich began wondering who it was out there that was all cramped up. And who could this pagan brute be? He got to his feet with a grunt and set out to restore order.

The meaning of Nastasya's mysterious words became clear when Grushin stuck his head out on to the porch. So that was it: more beggars – the kind that roamed the pitiful, narrow streets of Zamoskvorechie all day long from dawn till dusk. One of them was an old hunchback, bent over double and supporting himself on two short crutches. The other was a grubby Kirghiz wearing a greasy robe and tattered fur cap. Good Lord, you certainly saw all kinds in old Mother Moscow!

'That will do, Natasya; you're enough to deafen a man!' Grushin yelled at the rowdy woman. 'Give them a kopeck each and let them go on their way.'

'But they're asking for you!' said the enraged cook, swinging round to face him. 'This one 'ere' – she jabbed her finger at the hunchback – 'sez wake 'im up, like, we've got business with yer master. I'll give you "wake 'im up". Right, off I goes at the double! Robbing a man of his chance for a sleep!'

Xavier Feofilaktovich took a closer look at the wandering beggars. Wait! That Kirghiz looked familiar, didn't he? Yes, he wasn't a Kirghiz at all. The inspector clutched at his heart: 'What's happened to Erast Petrovich? Where is he?'

Ah, yes, he didn't understand Russian.

'You, old man, are you from Fandorin?' asked Grushin, leaning down towards the hunchback. 'Has anything happened?'

The invalid straightened up until he stood half a head taller than the retired detective. 'Well, Xavier Feofilaktovich, if you didn't recognise me, it means the disguise is a success,' he said in the voice of Erast Petrovich.

Grushin was absolutely delighted: 'How could anyone recognise you? Clever, very clever. If it wasn't for your servant, I would never have suspected a thing. But isn't it tiring walking around bent over like that?'

'That's all right,' said Fandorin, with a dismissive wave of his hand. 'Overcoming difficulties is one of life's great pleasures.'

'I'd be prepared to argue that point with you,' said Grushin, letting his guests through into the house. 'Not just at this moment, of course, but some time later, sitting round the samovar. But today, I gather, you are setting out on an expedition of some kind?'

'Yes, I want to pay a call to a certain inn in the Khitrovka district. With the romantic name of Hard Labour. They s-say that it's by way of being Little Misha's headquarters.'

'Who says?'

'Pyotr Parmenovich Khurtinsky, the head of the governorgeneral's chancellery.'

Xavier Feofilaktovich merely spread his arms: 'Well, that certainly means something. He has eyes and ears everywhere. So you're off to the Labour?'

'Yes. Tell me, what kind of inn is it, how do people behave there and, most important of all, how do we get there?' Fandorin asked.

'Sit down, my dear fellow. Best not in the armchair – over there on the bench; your get-up is a bit ...' Xavier Feofilaktovich also took a seat and lit up his pipe. 'From the beginning. Your first question: what kind of inn is it? My answer: it is owned by Full State Counsellor Eropkin.'

'How can that be?' asked Erast Petrovich, amazed. 'I had assumed that it was a d-den of thieves, a stinking sewer.'

'And you assumed correctly. But the building belongs to a general and it earns His Excellency a handsome income.

Eropkin himself is never there, of course; he rents the building out, and he has plenty of similar premises across Moscow. As you know yourself, money has no smell. In the upstairs rooms there are cheap girls for fifty kopecks, and in the basement there is an inn. But that's not the most valuable thing about the general's house. During the reign of Ivan the Terrible the site was occupied by an underground prison complete with a torture chamber. The prison was demolished long ago, but the underground labyrinth is still there. And during the last three hundred years they've dug plenty of new tunnels – it's a genuine maze, so it won't be easy trying to find Little Misha in that place.

'Now for your second question: how do people behave there?' Xavier Feofilaktovich smacked his lips in a cosy, reassuring manner. It was a long time since he had felt so exhilarated. And his head wasn't aching any more. 'People behave terribly. Like real bandits. The police and the law have no authority there. Only two species of human being survive in Khitrovka: those who fawn on someone strong, and those who oppress the weak. There is no middle way. And the Labour is where their high-society gathers. It's the place where the stolen goods circulate, and there's plenty of money, and all the big bandit bosses come calling. Khurtinsky's right: you can find Little Misha through the Labour. But how? – that's the question. You can't just go barging in regardless.'

'My third question was n-not about that,' Fandorin reminded him politely but firmly. 'It was about the location of the Labour.'

'Ah well, that I won't tell you,' said Xavier Feofilaktovich with a smile, leaning against the back of his armchair.

'Why not?'

'Because I'll take you there myself. And don't argue. I don't want to hear a word.' In response to Erast Petrovich's gesture of protest, the inspector pretended to stick his fingers in his ears. 'In the first place, without me you won't find it. And in the second place, when you do find it, you won't get in. And if you do get in, you won't get out alive again.'

Seeing that his arguments had produced no effect on Erast Petrovich, Grushin implored him: 'Show some mercy, my dear chap! For old times' sake, eh? Take pity on an old man who's all shrivelled up from doing nothing: humour him. We could take such a marvellous stroll together!'

'My dear Xavier Feofilaktovich,' Fandorin said patiently, as if he were addressing a small child, 'for goodness' sake, in Khitrovka every dog in the street can recognise you!'

Grushin smiled cunningly. 'That's nothing for you to fret over. Do you think you're the only one who knows how to dress himself up?'

And that was the beginning of a long, exhausting argument.

It was already dark as they approached Eropkin's house. Fandorin had never before had occasion to visit the infamous Khitrovka district after twilight had fallen. It proved to be an eerie, frightening place, like some underground kingdom inhabited not by living people, but by phantoms. On the crooked streets not a single lamp was lit; the plain little houses twisted either to the right or the left; the rubbish heaps filled the air with a fetid stench. Nobody walked here; they slithered or scuttled or hobbled along beside the wall: a grey shadow would dart out of an entryway or an invisible door, flash a quick glance this way and that, scurry across the street and melt away again into some little chink. *A land of rats*, thought Erast Petrovich, hobbling along on his little crutches. *Except that rats do not sing in voices hoarse from drink, or shout obscenities and weep at the tops of their voices, or mutter inarticulate threats to passers-by.*

'There it is – the Hard Labour,' said Grushin, crossing himself as he pointed to a dismal two-storey house with a malevolent glow in its half-blind windows. 'God grant we can do the job and get away in one piece.'

They entered as they had agreed: Xavier Feofilaktovich and Masa went in first and Fandorin followed a little later – such was the condition imposed by the collegiate assessor. 'Don't you worry that my Japanese doesn't speak Russian,' Erast Petrovich had explained. 'He has been in all sorts of predicaments and he senses danger instinctively. He used to be one of the *yakuza* – the Japanese bandits. His reactions are lightning-fast, and he is as skilful with his knife as the surgeon Pirogov is with his scalpel. When you are with Masa, you have no need to worry about your back. But if all three of us burst in together it will look suspicious – that would look like a police detail come to arrest someone.'

He had managed to convince the inspector.

It was pretty dark in the Labour; the local folk were not very fond of bright light. There was only a paraffin lamp on the bar – for counting the money – and a single thick tallow candle on each table of rough boards. As the flames flickered, they sent crooked shadows scurrying across the low-vaulted stone ceiling. But semi-darkness is no hindrance to the accustomed eye. Sit there and take your time, then take a look around, and you can see everything you need to see. Over in the corner a tight-lipped group of 'businessmen' was sitting at a richly spread table that actually had a tablecloth on it. They were drinking in moderation and eating even less, exchanging terse phrases incomprehensible to the outsider. These jaunty fellows definitely seem to be waiting for something to happen: either they were going out on a job or there was some serious discussion in the offing. The other characters there were a petty uninteresting bunch: a few girls, ragamuffins totally ruined by alcohol and, of course, the regular clients – pickpockets and thieves, who were doing what they were supposed to do: divvying up the swag – that is, sharing out the day's booty, grabbing at each others' chests and arguing in precise detail over who had nicked how much and how much everything was worth. They had already thrown one of their number under the table and were kicking him furiously. He was howling and struggling to get out, but they drove him back under, repeating over and over: 'Don't steal from your own, don't steal!'

An old hunchback came in. He stood in the doorway for a moment, rotated his hump to the left, then to the right, getting his bearings, and then hobbled across into the corner, manoeuvring skilfully on his crutches. Hanging round his neck the cripple had a heavy cross on a green-tarnished chain and some bizarre religious instruments of self-torment in the form of metal stars. The hunchback grunted as he sat down at a table. In a good spot, with the wall at his back and quiet neighbours: on the right a blind beggar with blank, staring wall-eyes, steadily chomping away at his supper; and on the left a girl sleeping the sleep of the dead with her black-haired head resting on the table and her hand clutching a large, half-empty square bottle – obviously one of the 'businessmen's' molls. Her clothes were a little cleaner than those of the other trollops and she had turquoise earrings, and – most significant of all – no one was molesting her. Which meant they weren't supposed to. Let the girl sleep, if she was tired. When she woke up, she could have another drink.

The waiter came across and asked suspiciously: 'Where would you be from, granddad? I don't reckon I've seen you in here before.'

The hunchback grinned, exposing his rotten teeth, and broke into a rapid patter: 'Where from? From hereabouts and thereabouts, uphill creeping and crawling, downhill tumbling and falling. Bring me some vodka, will you, me darling? Been out and about all day long. Fair worn meself out all hunched up like this. And don't you worry, I'm not short of money.' He jangled some copper coins. 'The orthodox folks take pity on a poor wretched cripple.' The lively old man winked, pulled a long roll of cotton padding out from behind his shoulders, straightened up and stretched. The hump had completely vanished. 'Oh, me bones are sore and aching from that sweaty money-making. What I need is a crust of white bread and a woman in the bed.'

Bending over to his left, the jester nudged the sleeping girl: 'Hey, little darling, me sweet plump starling! Whose might you be? Would you fancy pleasuring an old man?' And then he did something that made the waiter gasp: what a gay old granddad this was!

The waiter advised him: 'Don't you go pestering Fiska; she's not for the likes of you. If you want a bit of cuddling and coddling, get yourself up those stairs over there. And take fifty kopecks and half a bottle with you.'

The old man got his bottle, but he was in no hurry to go upstairs – he seemed to feel quite comfortable where he was. He knocked his glass over, then started humming a song in a thin little voice and darting glances in all directions out of those sharp eyes with that youthful gleam. In an instant he had examined everybody there, taken a good look at the 'businessmen' and turned towards the bar, where the innkeeper Abdul, a placid, powerfully built Tartar who was known and feared by the whole of Khitrovka, was chatting about something with an itinerant junk dealer in a low voice. The junk man was doing most of the talking, and the innkeeper was answering reluctantly, in monosyllables, as he slowly wiped a glass tumbler with a dirty rag. But the grey-bearded junk dealer, who was wearing a good-quality nankeen coat and galoshes over his boots, would not give up: he kept on whispering something, leaning in over the counter and every now and then prodding with this finger at the box hanging over the shoulder of his companion, a young Kirghiz who was glancing around cautiously with his sharp, narrow eyes.

So far everything was going according to plan. Erast

Petrovich knew that Grushin was playing the part of a dealer in stolen goods who had happened to buy a full set of fine housebreaking tools and was looking for a good buyer who knew the value of the goods. It was not a bad idea, but Fandorin was terribly alarmed by the keen attention that the 'businessmen' were paying to the junk merchant and his assistant. Could they really have spotted them? But how? Why? Xavier Feofilaktovich's disguise was magnificent – there was no way anyone could have recognised him.

Now he saw that Masa had also sensed the danger: he stood up, thrust his hands into his sleeves and half-closed his thick eyelids. He had a dagger in his sleeve, and his pose indicated readiness to repel a blow, from whichever side it might be struck.

'Hey, slanty-eyes!' one of the 'businessmen' shouted, 'which tribe would you be from then?'

The junk dealer swung round abruptly. 'He's a Kirghiz, my dear man,' he said politely but without a trace of timidity. 'A wretched orphan. The infidels cut his tongue out. But he suits me very well.' Xavier Feofilaktovich made some cunning sign with his fingers. 'I deal in gold and peddle dope, so I can do without over-talkative partners.'

Masa also turned his back to the counter, realising where the real danger lay. He closed his eyes almost completely, leaving just a small spark barely gleaming between his eyelids.

The 'businessmen' glanced at each other. The junk dealer's words seemed to have had a reassuring effect on them. Erast Petrovich was greatly relieved – Grushin was nobody's fool; he could look after himself. Fandorin sighed in relief and took the hand which had been about to grasp the handle of his Herstahl back out from under the table.

He ought not to have done that.

Taking advantage of the fact that both of them had turned their backs to him, the innkeeper suddenly grabbed a two-pound weight on a string off the counter and with a movement that looked easy and yet appallingly powerful, swung it against the round back of the Kirghiz's head. There was a sickening crunch and Masa slumped to the floor in a sitting position. Then the treacherous Tartar, who had clearly had plenty of practice, struck Grushin's left temple just as he began to turn round.

Absolutely astounded, Erast Petrovich threw his chair back and pulled out his revolver. 'Nobody move!' he shouted in a wild voice. 'Police!'

One of the 'businessmen' dropped his hand under the table and Fandorin immediately fired. The young man screamed, clutched at his chest with both hands, collapsed on the floor and began thrashing about in convulsions. The others froze.

'Anybody move and I'll fire!'

Erast Petrovich moved his gun about rapidly, shifting his aim from the 'businessmen' to the innkeeper as he tried feverishly to work out whether there would be enough bullets for all of them and what to do next. A doctor – they needed a doctor! Though the blows with the weight had been so shattering that a doctor was unlikely to be required … He glanced rapidly round the room. He had the wall at his back, and his flanks also appeared to be covered: the blind man was still sitting in the same place, merely turning his head this way and that and blinking his terrible white wall-eyes; the girl had been woken by the shot and she raised a pretty face made haggard by drink. She had gleaming black eyes – evidently a gypsy.

'The first bullet's for you, you bastard!' Fandorin shouted at the Tartar. 'I won't wait for your trial, I'll—'

He didn't finish what he was saying, because the gypsy girl raised herself up as stealthily as a cat and hit him over the back of the head with a bottle. Erast Petrovich never saw it coming. As far as he was concerned, everything suddenly just went black – for no reason at all.

Chapter Nine

IN WHICH FURTHER SHOCKS ARE
IN STORE FOR FANDORIN

Erast Fandorin came round gradually, his senses reviving one by one. The first to recover was his sense of smell, which caught the scent of something sour, mingled with dust and gunpowder. Then his sense of touch revived and he felt a rough wooden surface and a painful aching in his wrists. There was a salty taste in his mouth, which could only be from blood. Hearing and vision were the final senses to recover, and with their return his reason finally began to function.

Fandorin realised that he was lying face down on the floor with his hands twisted behind his back. Half-opening one eye, the collegiate assessor saw a revoltingly filthy floor, a ginger cockroach scuttling away from him and several pairs of boots. One pair was foppishly elegant, made of box-calf leather with little silver caps on their toes, and they were very small, as if they were intended for a juvenile. A little further away, beyond the boots, Erast Petrovich saw something that instantly brought back everything that had happened: the dead eye of Xavier Feofilaktovich staring straight at him. The inspector was also lying on the floor and the expression on his face was disgruntled, even angry, as if to say, Well, we made a real mess of that! Beside him Fandorin could see the black hair on the back of Masa's head, matted with blood. Erast Petrovich squeezed his eyes tight shut. He wanted to sink back into the blackness, where he would not see anything; he never wanted to see or hear anything again, but the harsh voices reverberating painfully in his brain would not allow it.

'... Well, ain't Abdul the smart one,' said an excited voice with a syphilitic nasal twang. 'The way that 'un started giving us the spiel, I reckoned he was the wrong 'un, but Abdul whacked 'im with that weight!'

A low, lazy voice swallowing the endings of its words in the Tartar fashion boomed: 'What d'you mean, the wrong 'un, yer numbskull? We was told: the one with the slanty-eyed Chinee – that's the one to get.'

'But that ain't no Chinee, he's a Kirghiz.'

'He's no more a Kirghiz than you are! How many slanty-eyes do we 'ave wandering round Khitrovka? An' if I'd gorrit wrong – it wouldn't 'ave mattered. We'd 'ave chucked 'im in the river, and there's an end o' the matter.'

'But how about Fiska, then?' put in a third voice that sounded ingratiating, but with a hysterical note. 'If it weren't for 'er, granddad 'ere would 'ave done for us all. But Misha, you said as there'd be two on 'em, an' see, Mish, there's three on 'em. An' they put an 'ole in Lomot over there. Lomot's dying, Mish. He burned right through 'is insides with that bullet.'

Catching the name 'Misha', Fandorin decided definitely not to sink back into the darkness. The back of his head was bruised and painful, but Erast Petrovich drove the pain away – drove it into the void, into the same darkness from which he himself had only recently emerged. This was no time for pain.

'I ought to lash my whip across your face for drinking,' declared a leisurely, languid falsetto. 'But seeing what happened, I forgive you. You caught the nark a handy swelp.'

Two scarlet morocco-leather boots moved closer and stood opposite the box-calf pair.

'Lash me across the face, if you like, Mishenka,' a rather

hoarse woman's voice declared sing-song fashion. 'Only don't drive me away. I haven't seen you for two whole days, my little falcon. I missed you so bad. Come round today and I'll give you a treat.'

'We can enjoy our treat later.' The dandified boots took a step towards Fandorin. 'But meanwhile we'll take a look-see what kind of slimy creature has come calling on us. Right, roll him over, Shukha. Look at the way his eye's glinting.'

They turned Erast Petrovich over on his back.

So this was Little Misha. Just a little taller than the gypsy girl's shoulder, and compared with the 'businessmen' he was an absolute midget. A thin, nervous face, with a twitch at the corner of the mouth. Repulsive eyes, as if it was a fish looking at you, not a man; but generally speaking, a handsome little fellow: hair parted precisely into two halves, curling up at the ends. One unpleasant detail: the black moustache was exactly the same as Erast Petrovich's own – even curled up in the same manner. Fandorin immediately took a solemn vow not to wax his moustache any longer, and was immediately struck by the thought that he would probably never get the chance.

In one hand the bandit king was holding the Herstahl, and in the other the stiletto that Fandorin wore above his ankle. So they had searched him.

'Well now, and who might you be?' Little Misha growled through his teeth. Seen from below, he didn't look little at all – quite the opposite: he seemed like a real Gulliver. 'Which station are you from? Myasnitskaya Street, is it? That's right, that's the one. That's where all my persecutors have gathered, the bloodsucking vampires.'

After registering surprise at the words 'persecutors' and 'vampires', Erast Petrovich made a mental note for the future that apparently they did not take bribes at the Myasnitskaya Street Station. It was useful information – if, of course, he was ever able to make use of it.

'Why did three of you come?' The meaning of Misha's question was not entirely clear. 'Or are you on your own, separate from those two?'

It was tempting to nod, but Fandorin decided that the right thing was to say nothing. To wait and see what would happen next.

What happened was unpleasant. Misha swung his foot back briefly and kicked the lying man in the crotch. Erast Petrovich spotted the swing and was able to prepare himself. He imagined that he was jumping at a run into a hole in a frozen river. The icy water scorched him so fiercely that by comparison the blow with the silver-tipped boot seemed a mere trifle. Fandorin did not even gasp.

'A real tough old nut,' said Misha, astonished. 'Seems like we'll have to take a bit of trouble over him. Never mind, though, that just makes things more interesting, and we've got plenty of time. Chuck him in the cellar for now, lads. We'll fill our bellies with God's bounty, and then we'll have some fun and games. I'll get all hot and bothered and afterwards Fiska can sluice me down.'

To the sound of squealing woman's laughter, Collegiate Assessor Fandorin was dragged by the legs across the floor and behind the counter, then along some dark corridor. The door of the cellar creaked, and the next moment Erast Petrovich went flying into pitch-blackness. He braced himself as best as he could, but he still landed hard on his side and shoulder.

'And here's your crutches, hunchback!' someone shouted with a laugh from the top of the stairs. 'Take a stroll and try a bit of begging down there!'

Fandorin's crutches fell on him one after the other. The dim square above his head disappeared with a crash, and Erast Petrovich closed his eyes, because he could not see anything anyway.

Flexing his hand, he fingered the bonds restraining his

wrists. Nothing to it: ordinary string. All he needed was a fairly hard, preferably ribbed surface and a certain amount of patience. What was that there? Ah, the staircase that he had just fallen on so hard. Fandorin turned so that his back was towards the steps and started rubbing the string against a wooden upright in a rapid rhythm. The job would probably keep him occupied for about thirty minutes. Erast Petrovich began counting to one thousand eight hundred, not in order to make the time pass more quickly, but to avoid thinking about things that were too horrible. But the counting was powerless to prevent black thoughts from piercing poor Fandorin's heart like needles: *What have you done now, Mr Fandorin! You can never be forgiven for this, never.*

How could he have dragged his old teacher into this animal pit! Dear old Xavier Feofilaktovich had trusted his young friend, and been delighted that he could still serve the good of the fatherland; and now look how things had turned out! It was not destiny that was to blame, or some malicious fate, but the indiscretion and incompetence of a person whom the inspector had trusted no less than he trusted himself. The jackals of Khitrovka had been waiting for Fandorin – waiting for him. Or, rather, for the man who would come with a 'Chinee'. The bungling detective Fandorin had led his close friends to certain execution. But had Grushin not warned him that the entire police force was in Little Misha's pay? The disagreeable Khurtinsky had let it slip to one of his men and he had sent word to Khitrovka. It was all very simple. Afterwards, of course, it would become clear just who the Judas in the secret section was, but that would not bring back Masa and Grushin. It was an unforgivable blunder! No, not a blunder, a crime!

Groaning in unbearable mental anguish, Erast Petrovich began moving his hands even faster, and suddenly the string parted and went slack sooner than he had expected. But the collegiate assessor was not gladdened by his success; he simply sank his face into his freed hands and burst into tears. Ah, Masa, Masa …

Four years earlier, in Yokahama, Fandorin, the second secretary at the Russian embassy, had saved the life of a *yakuza* boy. From that moment on Masahiro had been his faithful – indeed, his only – friend, and he had several times saved the life of the diplomat with a weakness for adventures; and yet he continued as before to believe himself irredeemably in his debt. *For what end, Mr Fandorin, did you drag a good man of Japan all the way to the other side of the world, to this alien place? So that he could die a futile death at the hands of a vile murderer, and all because of you?* Erast Petrovich's regret was bitter, inexpressibly bitter, and it was only the anticipation of vengeance that prevented him from beating his brains out against the slimy wall of the cellar. Oh, his vengeance on these murderers would be merciless! As a Christian, Xavier Feofilaktovich might not really care for revenge, but Masa's Japanese soul would certainly rejoice in anticipation of its next birth.

Fandorin was no longer concerned for his own life. Little Misha had had a good chance to finish him off – upstairs, when he was lying stunned on the floor, bound and disarmed. But things were different now, Your Bandit Majesty. As gamblers might say: You're holding the wrong suit.

The copper cross on a chain and the bizarre star-shaped instruments of self-torment were still hanging round the former hunchback's neck. And the numbskulls had made him a present by throwing the short crutches into the cellar. Which meant that Erast Petrovich was in possession of an entire Japanese arsenal.

He took the strange stars off his neck and separated them out. He felt the edges: they were honed as sharp as a razor. These stars were called *sharinken*, and the ability to throw them with deadly accuracy was learned during the very first stage of a ninja's training. For serious business the tips were also smeared with poison, but Fandorin had decided that he could get by without that. Now all that was left was to assemble the *nunchaka* – a weapon more terrible than any sword.

Erast Petrovich took the cross off the chain. He set the cross to one side, then opened the chain and attached his little crutches to it at both ends. The pieces of wood had special hooks on them for this very purpose. Without rising from the ground, the young man whirled the *nunchaka* through a lightning-fast figure of eight above his head and seemed entirely satisfied. The feast was ready and waiting; only the guests were missing.

He climbed up the stairs, feeling out the cross-pieces in the darkness. His head came up against a trapdoor, locked from the outside. *All right then, we'll wait. Mohammed will come to the mountain soon enough.*

He jumped back down, dropped on to all fours and began groping around on the floor with his hands. After a moment he came across some kind of rancid bundle of sackcloth with an overpowering smell of mould. Never mind; this was no time to be feeling oversensitive.

Erast Petrovich settled back with his head on the improvised pillow. It was very quiet: the only sound was of agile little animals scurrying about in the darkness – mice, no doubt, or perhaps rats. *I hope they come soon*, thought Fandorin and then, before he knew it, he plummeted abruptly into sleep – he had not had any rest the night before.

He was woken by the creak of the trapdoor being opened and immediately remembered where he was and why. The only thing that was unclear was how much time had passed.

A man in a long-waisted coat and Russian leather boots walked down the steps, swaying as he went. He was holding a candle in his hand. Erast Petrovich recognised him as one of Misha's 'businessmen'. Behind him Misha's box-calf boots with the silver toes appeared through the trapdoor.

There were five visitors in all: Little Misha and the four others that Erast Petrovich had seen recently. The only person missing to complete the pleasure was Abdul, which upset Fandorin so much that he actually sighed.

'That's right, my little police spy, have a nice little sigh,' said Misha, baring his brilliant teeth in a scowl. 'I'll soon have you yelling so loud the rats will go dashing for their holes. Cosying up to the carrion, are you? Well, that's right, you'll be the same yourself soon enough.'

Fandorin looked at the bundle that was serving him as a pillow and jerked upright in horror. Glaring up at him from the floor with its vacant eye-sockets was an ancient, decayed corpse. The 'businessmen' burst into raucous laughter. Apart from Misha, each of them was holding a candle in his hand, and one was also carrying some kind of tongs or pincers.

'You don't like the look of him, then?' the midget enquired mockingly. 'Last autumn-time we caught ourselves a spy; he was from Myasnitskaya Street too. Don't you recognise him?' More laughter, and Misha's voice turned sweet and syrupy. 'He suffered that long, the poor fellow. When we started pulling the guts out of his belly, he called out for his mummy and his daddy.'

Erast Petrovich could have killed him that very second – each of the hands he was holding behind his back was clutching a *sharinken*. But it is unworthy of the noble man to give way to irrational emotions. He needed to have a little talk with Misha. As Alexander Ivanovich Pelikan, the consul in Yokahama, used to say, he 'had a few little questions' for him. Of course, he could immobilise the retinue of His Highness of Khitrovka first. The way they were standing was most convenient: two on the right, two on the left. He couldn't see anyone with a firearm, except for Misha, who kept toying with the handy little Herstahl. But that was nothing to worry about. He did not know about the little button, and the revolver would not fire if the safety catch was not taken off.

It seemed that the best thing to do was try to find out something while Little Misha felt that he was in control. There was no way of telling if he would feel like talking afterwards. Everything about him suggested that he was the obstinate type. What if he simply wouldn't talk?

'I'm looking for a little briefcase, Mishutka lad. With huge great money in it – thousands upon thousands,' Fandorin intoned in the voice of the luckless hunchbacked swindler. 'Where'd you put it, eh?'

Misha's expression changed, and one of his lieutenants asked with a nasal twang: 'What's he gabbling on about, Mish? What thousands upon thousands?'

'He's a-lying, the bastard nark!' barked the king. 'Trying to set us agin each other. I'll have you coughing blood for that, you lousy rozzer.'

Misha pulled a long, narrow knife out of his boot and took a step forward. Erast Petrovich drew his own conclusions. Misha had taken the briefcase. That was one. No one else in the gang knew about it, so he was obviously not intending to share the loot. That was two. He was frightened by the prospect of exposure and now he was going to shut his prisoner's mouth. For ever. That was three. Fandorin had to change his tactics.

'What's the rush to make me suffer? This granddad's not a total duffer,' Fandorin rattled off. 'Slash and stab and I can't blab. Treat me nice and gentle, do, and I'll give you a little clue.'

'Don't finish him off him just yet, Mish,' said the nasal-voiced one, grabbing his leader by the sleeve. 'Let him sing a bit first.'

'Humble greetings from Mr Pyotr Parmyonovich Khurtinsky,' said Erast Petrovich, winking at Malenky and gazing into his face to see if his hypothesis were correct. But this time Misha did not even blink.

'The old man's pretending he's not right in the head.

Raving about some Parmyonich or other. Never mind, we'll soon set his brains to rights. Kur, you sit on his legs. And you, Pronya, hand me the pincers. I'll soon have this lousy crow singing like a rooster.'

Erast Petrovich realised that the monarch of Khitrovka was not going to tell him anything interesting – he was far too wary of his own men.

Fandorin gave a deep sigh and closed his eyes for an instant. Over-hasty rejoicing is the most dangerous of feelings. It causes many important undertakings to miscarry. Erast Petrovich opened his eyes, smiled at Misha and suddenly pulled first his right hand and then his left from behind his back. Whoo-oosh, whoo-oosh – the two little spinning shadows went whistling through the air. The first bit into Kur's throat, the second into Pronya's. They were both still wheezing, gushing blood and swaying on their feet – they had still not fully realised that they were dying – when the collegiate assessor snatched up his *nunchaka* and leapt to his feet. Misha had no time even to raise his hand, let alone press the safety catch before the stick of wood struck him on the top of his head – not too hard: just enough to stun him. But the burly young lout whom he had called Shukha had barely even opened his mouth when he received a powerful blow to the head that felled him like a log, and he did not move again. The last of the 'businessmen', whose name Fandorin had still not discovered, proved more adroit than his comrades. He dodged away from the *nunchaka*, pulled a Finnish knife out of the top of his boot and then swayed out of reach of a second blow as well. But the relentless figure of eight broke the arm that was holding the knife, and then smashed the agile bandit's skull. Erast Fandorin froze, carefully controlling his breathing. Two of the bandits were writhing on the ground, jerking their legs about and vainly trying to squeeze shut the gaping tears in their throats. Two were lying motionless. Little Misha was sitting on the ground, shaking his head stupidly. The burnished steel of the Herstahl glinted off to one side.

I have just killed four men and I feel no regret at all, the collegiate assessor thought to himself. His heart had been hardened by that terrible night.

To begin with Erast Petrovich took the stunned man by the collar, gave him a good shaking and slapped him hard across both cheeks – not in vengeance, but to bring him to his senses faster. However, the slaps produced a quite magical effect. Little Misha pulled his head down into his shoulders and began whining: 'Don't hit me, granddad! I'll tell you everything! Don't kill me! Spare my young life!'

Fandorin looked at the tearful, contorted, cute little face in wonder and amazement. The unpredictability of human nature never ceased to astonish him. Who would have thought that the bandit autocrat, the bane of the Moscow constabulary, would fall apart like that after just a couple of slaps on the cheeks? Fandorin experimented by gently swinging the *nunchaka*, and Misha immediately stopped his whinging, gazed spellbound at the regular swaying of the bloodied stick of wood, pulled his head back down into his shoulders and started to shudder. Well, well, it worked. Extreme cruelty was the obverse side of cowardice, Erast Petrovich thought philosophically. But that was not really surprising, for these were the very worst pair of qualities that the sons of humanity possessed.

'If you want me to hand you over to the police and not kill you right here, answer my questions,' the collegiate assessor said in his normal voice, dropping the beggar's whine.

'And if I answer, you won't kill me?' Misha asked in a pathetic whimper.

Fandorin frowned. Something was definitely not right here. A sniveller like this could not possibly have terrorised the entire criminal underworld of a big city. That required a will of iron and exceptional strength of character. Or at least something that could effectively take the place of those qualities. But what?

'Where are the million roubles?' Erast Petrovich asked darkly.

'In the same place they always were,' Little Misha replied quickly.

The *nunchaka* swayed menacingly again. 'Goodbye then, Misha. I warned you. I like it better this way, I can pay you back for my friends.'

'I swear, honest to God!' The puny, terrified little man put his hands over his head, and Fandorin suddenly found the whole situation unbearably nauseating.

'It's the honest truth, granddad; I swear by Christ Almighty. The loot is still where it was, in the briefcase.'

'And where's the briefcase?'

Misha swallowed and twitched his lips. His reply was barely audible. 'Here, in a secret room.'

Erast Petrovich threw his *nunchaka* aside – he wouldn't need it any more. He picked the Herstahl up off the floor and set Misha on his feet. 'Come on then, you show me.'

While Misha was climbing the steps, Fandorin prodded him in the backside from below with the gun-barrel and carried on asking questions. 'Who told you about the "Chinee"?'

'It was Khurtinsky.' Misha turned round and raised his little hands. 'We do what he tells us to do. He's our benefactor and protector. But he's very strict, and he takes nigh on half.'

That's wonderful, thought Erast Petrovich, gritting his teeth. *As wonderful as it possibly could be.* The head of the secret section, the governor-general's own right hand, was a major criminal boss and patron of the Moscow underworld. Now he could see why they hadn't been able to catch Misha no matter how hard they tried, and how he had become so powerful in Khitrovka. Fine work, Court Counsellor Khurtinsky!

They clambered out into the dark corridor and set off through a labyrinth of narrow, musty passages. Twice they turned to the left, and once to the right. Misha stopped in front of a low, inconspicuous door and tapped out a complicated special knock. The girl Fiska opened up in nothing but her nightshirt, with her hair hanging loose and a sleepy, drunk expression on her face. She did not seem at all surprised to see her visitors and never even glanced at Fandorin. She shuffled back across the earth floor to the bed, flopped down on to it and immediately started snoring lightly. In one corner there was a stylish dressing table with a mirror, obviously taken from some lady's boudoir, with a smoking oil lamp standing on it.

'I hide stuff with her,' said Misha. 'She's a fool, but she won't give me away.'

Erast Petrovich took a firm grip on the little runt's skinny neck, pulled him closer, stared straight into his round, fishy eyes and asked, carefully emphasising each word: 'What did you do to General Sobolev?'

'Nothing.' Misha crossed himself rapidly three times. 'May I croak on the gallows. I don't know a thing about the general. Khurtinsky said as I was to take the briefcase from the safe and make a neat job of it. He said there'd be no one there and no one would miss it. So I took it. Simple – a pushover. And he told me when things quietened down we'd split the money two ways and he'd send me out of Moscow with clean papers. But if I tried anything, he'd find me no matter where I went. And he would too; that's what he's like.'

Misha took a rug with a picture of Stenka Razin and his princess down off the wall, opened a little door behind it and began feeling about with his hand. Fandorin broke out in a cold sweat as he stood there, trying to grasp the full hideous meaning of what he had just heard.

There'd be no one there and no one would miss it.

Khurtinsky had said that to his accomplice? That meant that the court counsellor knew Sobolev would not be coming back to the Dusseaux alive!

But Erast Petrovich had underestimated the lord and master of Khitrovka. Misha was far from stupid and by no means the pitiful sniveller he had pretended to be. Glancing back over his shoulder, he could see that the detective had been shaken by his announcement and had even lowered the hand that was holding the revolver. The agile little man spun round sharply. Erast Petrovich glimpsed the barrel of a sawn-off shotgun pointing straight at him and only just managed to strike it from below in time. The barrel belched thunder and flame, a hot wind scorched his face and debris rained down from the ceiling. The collegiate assessor's finger spontaneously tightened on the trigger of his revolver and the Herstahl, its safety catch off, obediently fired. Little Misha grabbed at his stomach and sat down on the floor with a high-pitched grunt. Remembering the bottle, Erast Petrovich glanced round at Fiska, but she did not even raise her head at the thunderous roar – merely covered her ear with the pillow.

So now Misha's surprising compliance was explained. He had played his part cleverly, getting Erast Petrovich to lower his guard and leading the detective to just where he wanted him. How could he possibly have known that the speed of Erast Fandorin's reactions was famous even among the 'stealthy ones'?

The important question now was whether the briefcase was there. Erast Petrovich pushed the twitching body aside with his foot and thrust his hand into the niche. His fingers encountered a dimpled leather surface. It was!

Fandorin leaned down over Misha, who was blinking rapidly and licking fitfully at his white lips. Beads of sweat were breaking out on his forehead. 'A doctor!' groaned the wounded man. 'I'll tell you everything, I won't keep anything back!'

Erast Petrovich checked and saw that the wound was serious, but the Herstahl was only a small-calibre weapon and if Misha were taken to a hospital quickly, he might live. And an important witness such as this one had to live.

'Sit still, don't move a muscle,' Fandorin said aloud. 'I'll send for a cab. But if you try to crawl away, the life will just drain out of you.'

The inn was empty. The dim light of early morning was filtering in through the murky half-windows. A man and a woman were lying in each other's arms right in the middle of the filthy floor. The hem of the woman's skirt was pulled up – Erast Petrovich turned his eyes away. There did not seem to be anybody else. But no, there was yesterday's blind man sleeping on a bench with his knapsack under his head and his staff on the ground. There was no sign of the landlord Abdul – the one person that Fandorin badly wanted to see. But what was that? He thought he could hear someone snoring in the storeroom.

Erast Petrovich cautiously pulled aside the chintz curtain and breathed an inward sigh of relief: there he was, the scum – stretched out on a large chest, his beard jutting up in the air, his thick-lipped mouth half-open.

The collegiate assessor thrust the barrel of the revolver in his teeth and said in a low, gentle voice: 'Time to get up, Abdul. It's a bright new morning.'

The Tartar opened his eyes. They were matt-black, devoid of even the slightest expression.

'You just try to make a run for it,' Fandorin invited him, 'and I'll shoot you like a dog.'

'No point in running,' the killer replied coolly, with a wide yawn. 'I'm not the lad for running.'

'You'll go to the gallows,' said Erast Petrovich, staring with hatred into those expressionless little eyes.

'If that's what's set down for me,' the landlord agreed. 'All things are ruled by the will of Allah.'

It took all of the collegiate assessor's strength to resist the compulsive itch in his index finger. 'You dare to mention Allah, you miserable low scum! Where are the men you killed?'

'I put them away in the closet for now,' the monster replied readily. 'Reckoned I'd throw them in the river later. That's the closet there.' He pointed to a rough wooden door.

The door was bolted shut. Erast Petrovich tied Abdul's hands with his own leather belt and drew the bolt back with a wearily aching heart. It was dark inside.

After hesitating for a moment the collegiate assessor took one step, then another and received a powerful blow from the side of someone's hand to the back of his neck. Taken totally by surprise, half-stunned, he collapsed face-forwards on to the floor. Someone jumped on top of him and breathed hotly into his ear: 'Where massa? Marder dog!'

Hesitantly, with a great effort – the blow had been a heavy one, and it had landed on the bump from the day before – Fandorin stammered in Japanese: 'So you have b-been learning words, after all, you idle loafer?' And he burst into sobs, unable to restrain himself.

But that was not the last shock in store for him. When Fandorin had bandaged up Masa's broken head and found a cab, he went back to Fiska's underground chamber for Little Misha; but the gypsy girl was not there and Misha himself was no longer sitting slumped against the wall, but lying on the floor. He was dead, but he had not died from the wound in his stomach – someone had very precisely slit the bandit king's throat.

Holding his revolver at the ready, Erast Petrovich dashed off along the dark corridor, but it branched into several paths that led away into the damp darkness, where he would be more likely to get lost himself than to find anybody else.

Outside the door of the Hard Labour, Fandorin screwed up his eyes against the sun as it peeped over the rooftops. Masa was sitting in the cab, clutching the briefcase that had been entrusted to him against his chest with one hand and maintaining a firm hold on the collar of the bound Abdul with the other. Jutting up beside him was a formless bundle – the body of Xavier Feofilaktovich wrapped in a blanket.

'Off you go!' shouted Erast Petrovich, leaping up on to the coach box beside the cabby. He wanted to get out of this accursed place as soon as possible. 'Drive hard to Malaya Nikitskaya Street, to the Department of Gendarmes!'

Chapter Ten

IN WHICH THE GOVERNOR-GENERAL
TAKES COFFEE WITH A ROLL

The sergeant-major on duty at the door of the Moscow Province Gendarmes Department (20, Malaya Nikitskaya Street) cast a glance of curiosity, without any particular surprise, at the strange threesome clambering out of the cab – doing duty at a post such as that one you saw all sorts of things. The first to climb down, stumbling on the footboard, was a black-bearded Tartar with his hands tied behind his back. Behind him, pushing the prisoner in the back, came some slanty-eyed devil in a tattered *beshmet* and a white turban, holding a very expensive-looking leather briefcase. And finally a ragged old man leapt down from the coach box far too easily for his age. On taking a closer look, the sergeant-major saw that the old man had a revolver in his hand, and it wasn't a turban on the slanty-eyed devil's head after all, but a towel that was stained in places with blood. That was clear enough, then: they were secret agents back from an operation.

'Is Evgeny Osipovich in?' the old man asked in a young gentleman's voice, and the gendarme, a seasoned campaigner, asked no questions but simply saluted.

'Yes, sir, he arrived half an hour ago.'

'C-Call the duty officer, will you, b-brother,' said the man in disguise, stammering slightly. 'Let him register our prisoner. And over there,' he said gloomily, pointing to the carriage, in which they had left some very large bundle, '... over there

153

we have a dead man. They can take him to the ice room for the time being. It is Grushin, the retired detective inspector.'

'Why, your honour, we remember Xavier Feofilaktovich very well; we even served together for a few years.' The sergeant-major removed his cap and crossed himself.

Erast Petrovich walked quickly through the wide vestibule. Masa, clutching the bulging briefcase with its leather belly packed so tightly with banknotes that it was almost bursting open, could hardly keep up with him. At such an early hour the department was rather empty – it was not, in any case, the kind of place that was ever crowded with visitors. From the far end of the corridor, where the plaque on the door read 'Officers' Gymnastics Hall', came the sound of shouting and the clash of metal on metal. Fandorin shook his head sceptically: of course, knowing how to fence was obviously essential for an officer of the gendarmes. With whom? he wondered. With the bomb-throwers? It was an outmoded skill. They would do better to study jujitsu or even, at a pinch, English boxing.

Outside the entrance to the reception room of the chief of police he said to Masa: 'Sit here until you are called. Guard the briefcase. Does your head hurt?'

'I have a strong head,' the Japanese replied proudly.

'And thank God for that. Remember now: don't move from this spot.'

Masa puffed out his cheeks in offence, evidently regarding this last instruction as superfluous. Behind the tall double door Fandorin found a reception room, from where, according to the plaques, one could go either straight on, into the office of the chief of police, or to the right, into the secret section. In fact, Evgeny Osipovich Karachentsev had his own chancellery – on Tverskoi Boulevard – but His Excellency preferred the office on Malaya Nikitskaya Street: it was closer to the secret springs of the machinery of state.

'Where are you going?' asked the duty adjutant, rising to meet the ragged tramp.

'Collegiate Assessor Fandorin, deputy for special assignments to the governor-general. On urgent business.'

The adjutant nodded and dashed off to announce him. Thirty seconds later Karachentsev himself came out into the reception room. At the sight of the poor tramp he froze on the spot.

'Erast Petrovich, is that you? What an incredible transformation! What has happened?'

'A great deal.'

Fandorin went into the office and closed the door behind him.

The adjutant followed the unusual visitor in with a curious glance. He stood up and looked out into the corridor. There was nobody there, except for some Kirghiz sitting opposite the door. Then the officer tip-toed up to his superior's door and put his ear against it. He could hear the even intonation of the collegiate assessor's voice, interrupted every now and then by the general's deep-voiced exclamations. Unfortunately, those were the only words that he was able to make out. The exchange sounded like this:

'What briefcase?'

'...'

'But how could you do that!'

'...'

'And what did he say?'

'...'

'To the Khitrovka?'

At this point the door from the corridor opened and the adjutant barely had time to recoil, pretending that he had just been about to knock at the general's door, and turn back in annoyance at the intrusion. An unfamiliar officer with a briefcase under his arm threw up his open hand reassuringly and pointed to the side door, which led into the secret sec-

155

tion, as much as to say, Don't trouble yourself; I'm going that way. He strode quickly across the spacious room and disappeared. The adjutant placed his ear back against the door.

'Appalling!' Karachentsev exclaimed excitedly. Then a moment later he gasped: 'Khurtinsky! That's incredible!'

The adjutant flattened himself out across the door, hoping to make out at least something in the collegiate assessor's story; but then, as ill luck would have it, a courier came in with an urgent letter that he had to accept and sign for.

Two minutes later the general emerged from his office, flushed and excited. However, to judge from the gleam in his eyes, the news appeared not to be all bad. Karachentsev was followed out by the mysterious functionary.

'First we need to deal with the briefcase, and then we can deal with the treacherous court counsellor,' said the chief of police, rubbing his hands together. 'Where is this Japanese of yours?'

'Waiting in the corridor.'

The adjutant glanced out from behind the door and saw the general and the functionary stop in front of the tattered Kirghiz, who stood up and bowed ceremonially, with his arms at his sides.

The collegiate assessor asked him anxiously about something in an incomprehensible dialect.

The oriental bowed again and gave a reassuring answer.

The functionary raised his voice, clearly indignant about something.

The narrow-eyed face expressed confusion. Its owner seemed to be trying to justify his actions.

The general turned his head from one of them to the other. He puckered his ginger eyebrows in concern.

Clasping his hands to his forehead, the collegiate assessor turned towards the adjutant: 'Did an officer with a briefcase enter the reception?'

'Yes, sir. He went through into the secret section.'

Acting with extreme rudeness, the functionary pushed aside first the chief of police and then the adjutant, and dashed out of the side door of the reception room. The others followed him. Behind the door with the plaque there was a narrow corridor with windows looking out on to the yard. One of the windows was slightly open. The collegiate assessor leaned out over the window sill.

'Boot prints in the ground! He jumped down!' the emotional functionary groaned and smashed his fist against the frame in rage. The blow was so strong that all the glass showered out into the yard with a mournful jangle.

'Erast Petrovich, what has happened?' the general asked in alarm.

'I don't understand this at all,' said Fandorin, raising his arms in a shrug. 'Masa says that an officer came up to him in the corridor, gave him my name, handed him an envelope with a seal, took the briefcase and supposedly brought it to me. And there really was an officer, only he jumped out of this very window with the suitcase. It's like some incredible nightmare!'

'The envelope, where's the envelope?' asked Karachentsev.

The functionary roused himself and started jabbering away in some oriental tongue again. The negligent oriental, showing signs of exceptional concern, took an official envelope out of his *beshmet* and handed it to the general.

Karachentsev glanced at the seal and the address. 'Hmm. "To the Moscow Province Department of Gendarmes. From the Department for the Maintenance of Order and Public Security of the Office of the Governor-General of St Petersburg."' He opened the envelope and began reading: '"Secret. To the chief of police of Moscow. On the basic of article 16 of the decree approved by the Emperor concerning measures for the maintenance of state security and public order, and by agreement with the governor-general of St Petersburg, the midwife Maria Ivanovna Ivanova is forbidden to reside in St Petersburg or Moscow, due to her political unreliability, concerning which matter I have the honour of informing Your Excellency. Captain Shipov, for the head of section." ' What nonsense was this?

The general turned the piece of paper this way and that. 'An ordinary circular letter! What has this to do with the briefcase?'

'Surely it's s-simple enough,' the collegiate assessor in tramp's clothes said wearily, so upset that he had even begun to stammer. 'Someone cunningly exploited the fact that Masa does not understand Russian and has infinite respect for military uniforms, especially if they include a sword.'

'Ask him what the officer looked like,' the general instructed.

After listening to a few words of the Oriental's incoherent speech, the young functionary merely waved his hand despairingly: 'He says yellow hair, watery eyes … We all l-look alike to him.'

He turned to the adjutant: 'Did you get a good look at this m-man?'

'Afraid not,' the adjutant replied, spreading his hands in apology and blushing slightly. 'I didn't pay close attention. Blond. Above average height. Standard gendarme uniform. Captain's shoulder straps.'

'Are you telling me you were not taught observation and description?' the functionary enquired angrily. 'From this desk to that door is no more than ten paces!'

The adjutant said nothing and blushed an even deeper red.

'A catastrophe, Your Excellency,' the man in disguise stated. 'The million roubles has disappeared! But how did it happen? It's like some kind of black magic. What are we to do now?'

'Nonsense,' said Karachentsev dismissively. 'The million roubles is not the point, is it? They'll find it; it won't disappear. There are more important matters to be dealt with. We need to pay our dear friend Pyotr Parmyonovich Khurtinsky a little visit. Oh, what a character!' said Karachentsev with a grim smile. 'He'll soon clear up all our questions for us. Well, well, how interestingly everything has turned out. Yes, indeed, this will mean the end of our old beau Dolgorukoi as well. He warmed the viper at his breast, and very lovingly too!'

Collegiate Assessor Fandorin started. 'Yes, yes, let's go to see Khurtinsky. And let's hope that we are not too late.'

'We'll have to go to the prince first,' sighed the chief of police. 'We can do nothing without his sanction. Never mind, I shall enjoy watching the old fox squirm. Curtains, Your Excellency, you can't wriggle out of it this time. Sverchinsky!' The general glanced at the adjutant. 'My carriage, and look lively. And a droshky with an arrest detail – to follow me to the governor-general's house. In civilian clothes. Three will do, I think. We should manage without any shooting in this instance.' And he smiled another carnivorous smile.

The adjutant ran off quickly to carry out the order, and five minutes later a carriage harnessed with a foursome went dashing at full speed along the cobblestones of the road, followed by a droshky swaying gently on its springs, carrying three agents in civilian clothes.

Having watched the brief procession depart from the window, the adjutant picked up the earpiece of the telephone and wound the handle. He gave a number. Glancing at the door, he asked in a low voice: 'Mr Vedishchev, is that you? Sverchinsky.'

They had to wait in the reception room for an audience. The governor's secretary, after apologising extremely politely to the chief of police, nonetheless declared firmly that His Excellency was very busy, had said that no one was to be admitted and even ordered that no one was to be announced. Karachentsev glanced at Erast Petrovich with an ironical grin, as if to say: Let the old man put up one last show of strength. At last – at least a quarter of an hour must have gone by – there was the sound of a bell ringing behind the monumental gilded door.

'Now, Your Excellency, I shall announce you,' said the secretary, getting up from behind his desk.

When they entered the study, it became clear what significant matters had been occupying Prince Dolgorukoi's attention: he had been eating breakfast. Breakfast as such was already over, and the impatient visitors were admitted in time for the very last stage of the meal: Vladimir Andreevich had started on his coffee, sitting there, neatly bibbed with a soft linen napkin, and dunking a bun from Filippov's bakery in his cup. He appeared complacent in the extreme.

'Good morning, gentlemen,' the prince said with a warm smile, and swallowed a piece of bun. 'Please don't think badly of me for keeping you waiting. My Frol is so strict, and he says I must not be distracted when I am eating. Can I offer you some coffee? The buns are quite excellent; they simply melt in your mouth.'

At this point the governor looked a little more closely at the general's companion and began blinking in surprise. On the way to Tverskaya Street Erast Petrovich had pulled off his grey beard and wig, but there had been no chance to change out of his rags, so his appearance really was quite unusual.

Vladimir Andreevich shook his head disapprovingly and coughed. 'Erast Petrovich, of course I did tell you that you need not wear your uniform to visit me, but my dear fellow, this is really going too far. Have you lost all your money at cards, is that it?' There was an unaccustomed severity in the prince's voice. 'Of course, I am a man without prejudices, but even so, I would ask you in future not to come here in such a state. It simply won't do.'

He shook his head reproachfully and began munching on

his bun again, but the chief of police and the collegiate assessor had such very strange expressions on their faces that Dolgorukoi stopped chewing and asked in bewilderment: 'What on earth has happened, gentlemen? Is there a fire somewhere?'

'Worse, Your Excellency, much worse,' Karachentsev said with voluptuous emphasis and sat down in an armchair without waiting to be invited. Fandorin remained standing. 'Your head of the secret chancellery is a thief, a criminal and the protector of all the criminals in Moscow's underworld. Collegiate Assessor Fandorin has the proof of this. Most embarrassing, Your Excellency, most embarrassing. I really have no idea how we are going to deal with this.' He paused briefly to let the old man grasp what he had said and continued ingratiatingly, 'I have had the honour on numerous occasions of reporting to Your Excellency concerning the unseemly behaviour of Mr Khurtinsky, but you paid no attention to me. However, it naturally never even occurred to me that his activities might be criminal to such a degree.'

The governor-general listened to this short but impressive speech with his mouth half-open. Erast Petrovich expected an exclamation, a cry of indignation, questions about the proof; but the prince's composure was not shaken in the least. While the chief of police maintained an expectant silence, the prince thoughtfully finished chewing his piece of bun and took a sip of coffee. Then he sighed reproachfully.

'It is really most unfortunate, Evgeny Osipovich, that it never occurred to you. You are, after all, the head of Moscow's police, our pillar of law and order. I am no gendarme, and I am encumbered with rather more important matters than you; I have to carry the entire arduous business of municipal government on my shoulders, and I have long had my suspicions concerning Petrushka Khurtinsky.'

'Indeed?' the chief of police asked sarcastically. 'Since when would that be?'

'Oh, for quite a long time,' the prince drawled. 'I lost my liking for Petrusha a long time ago. Just three months ago I wrote to inform your minister, Count Tolstov, that according to information in my possession, Court Counsellor Khurtinsky was not merely a bribe-taker, but also a thief and general miscreant.' The prince rustled the papers on his desk. 'There was a copy here somewhere, of my letter, that is ... Ah, there it is.' He picked up a sheet of paper and waved it from a distance. 'And there was a reply from the count. Where could it be? Aha.' He picked up another sheet, with a monogram. 'Shall I read it to you? The minister reassured me absolutely that I had no need to feel concerned about Khurtinsky.'

The governor put on his pince-nez. 'Listen to this. "*As to any doubts that Your Excellency may happen to entertain concerning the activities of Court Counsellor Khurtinsky, I hasten to assure you that this functionary, while he may on occasion behave in a way that is hard to explain, does so by no means out of any criminal intent, but only in the execution of a secret state mission of immense importance, which is known both to me and to His Imperial Majesty. Allow me, therefore, to reassure you, my dearest Vladimir Andreevich, and in particular to mention that the mission that Khurtinsky is carrying out is in no way directed against ...*" Mm-m, well that is nothing to do with the matter. All in all, gentlemen, as you can see for yourselves: if anyone is at fault here, then it is certainly not Dolgorukoi, but rather your department, Evgeny Osipovich. What grounds could I possibly have for not trusting the Ministry of Internal Affairs?'

The shock was too much for the police chief's self-control and he stood up abruptly, reaching out for the letter, which was rather stupid, since in such a serious matter any subterfuge on the prince's part would have been entirely out of the question – it was too easy to verify. The prince complacently handed the sheet of paper to the ginger-haired general.

'Yes,' muttered Karachentsev. 'That is Dmitry Andreevich's signature. Not the slightest doubt about it ...'

The prince enquired solicitously: 'Did your superiors really not consider it necessary to inform you? Ai-ai-ai, that was very bad of them. So it would appear that you do not know what kind of secret mission Khurtinsky was carrying out?'

Karachentsev said nothing, absolutely stunned.

Meanwhile Fandorin was pondering an intriguing circumstance: how had it come about that the prince had three-months-old correspondence to hand, among his current paperwork? However, what the collegiate assessor said out loud was: 'I am also not aware of the nature of Mr Khurtinsky's secret activity; however, on this occasion he has clearly overstepped its limits. His connection with bandits in Khitrovka is indubitable and cannot be justified by any interests of state. And most importantly of all: Khurtinsky is clearly implicated in the death of General Sobolev.' Then Fandorin related in brief, point by point, the story of the stolen million roubles.

The governor listened very attentively. At the end he said decisively: 'A scoundrel, a palpable scoundrel. He must be arrested and questioned.'

'That is why we c-came to you, Vladimir Andreevich.'

Speaking in a completely different tone now – bright and respectful – the chief of police enquired: 'Will you permit me to do that, Your Excellency?'

'Of course, my dear fellow,' said Dolgorukoi with a nod. 'Let that villain answer for everything.'

They walked quickly down the long corridors, the officers in civilian clothes clattering along in step behind them. Erast Petrovich did not utter a word and tried not to look at Karachentsev – he understood how excruciatingly he was suffering following his débacle. And it was even more unpleasant and alarming that apparently there were certain secret matters that the top brass preferred not to entrust to

Moscow's chief of police, but to his eternal rival, the head of the secret section of the governor's chancellery.

They went up to the second floor, where the offices were located. Erast Petrovich asked the attendant on duty at the door if Mr Khurtinsky was in. It turned out that he had been in his office since early in the morning.

Karachentsev took heart and stepped out even faster, hurtling along the corridor like a cannonball, spurs jingling and aiguillettes clattering.

The reception room of the head of the secret section was overflowing with visitors.

'Is he in?' the general asked the secretary abruptly.

'Yes, he is, Your Excellency, but he asked not to be disturbed. Shall I announce you?'

The chief of police brushed him aside. He glanced at Fandorin, smiled into his thick moustache and opened the door.

At first sight Erast Petrovich thought that Pyotr Parmyonovich Khurtinsky was standing on the window sill and looking out of the window. But a moment later he saw quite clearly that he was not standing, but hanging.

Chapter Eleven

IN WHICH THE CASE TAKES AN UNEXPECTED TURN

Vladimir Andreevich Dolgorukoi knitted his brows as he read the lines written in that familiar hasty scrawl for the third time: '*I, Pyotr Khurtinsky, am guilty of having committed a crime against my duty out of avarice and of having betrayed him whom I should have served faithfully and assisted in every way possible in his onerous obligations. God is my judge.*' The lines were written crookedly, overlapping each other, and the last line even ended with a blot, as if the writer's strength had been totally drained by his excess of repentance.

'What was the secretary's account of events again?' the governor asked slowly. 'Tell it to me once more, please, Evgeny Osipovich, my dear fellow – in greater detail.'

Karachentsev related what they had managed to discover for the second time, more coherently and calmly than at his first attempt: 'Khurtinsky came to work, as usual, at nine o'clock. He appeared normal; the secretary noticed no signs of anxiety or agitation. After perusing the correspondence, Khurtinsky began receiving visitors. At about five to eleven the secretary was approached by a gendarme officer who introduced himself as Captain Pevtsov, a courier from St Petersburg who had come to see the court counsellor on urgent business. The captain was holding a brown briefcase described as precisely matching the stolen one. Pevtsov was immediately shown into the study and the reception of visitors was halted. Shortly after that Khurtinsky put his head out and instructed that no one else was to be allowed in until he gave specific instructions and in general he was not to be disturbed for any reason whatever. According to the secretary, his chief appeared extremely anxious. About ten minutes later the captain left and confirmed that the counsellor of state was busy and had given instructions that he was not to be disturbed, since he was studying secret documents. And a quarter of an hour after that, at twenty minutes past eleven, Erast Petrovich and I arrived.'

'What did the doctor say? Could it be murder?'

'He says it is a typical case of suicide by hanging. He tied the cord from the transom window round his neck and jumped. A standard fracture of the cervical vertebrae. And then, as you can see for yourself, there is no reason to doubt the note. Forgery is out of the question.'

The governor-general crossed himself and remarked philosophically: ' "And he cast down the pieces of silver in the temple, and departed, and went and hanged himself." Well, now the criminal's fate is in the hands of a judge more righteous than you or I, gentlemen.'

Erast Petrovich had the feeling that such an outcome suited Prince Dolgorukoi better than any other. In contrast, the chief of police was quite clearly downcast: just when he thought that he had laid hold of the precious thread that would lead him to the crock of gold, the thread had simply snapped.

Erast Petrovich's thoughts were concerned, not with state secrets and interdepartmental intrigues, but with the mysterious Captain Pevtsov. It was perfectly obvious that he was the same man who, forty minutes before appearing in Khurtinsky's reception room, had tricked poor Masa into giving him Sobolev's million roubles. From Malaya Nikitskaya Street the captain of gendarmes (or, as Fandorin was inclined to presume, some individual dressed in a blue uniform) had set out directly for Tverskaya Street. The secretary had got a clearer look at this individual than the police chief's adjutant and described him as follows: height approximately two *arshins* and seven *vershoks*, broad shoulders, straw-blond hair. One distinctive feature was that he had very light, almost transparent eyes. This detail made Fandorin shiver. In his youth he had had an encounter with a man who had eyes exactly like that, and he preferred not to recall that story from long ago, which had cost him too dear. However, the painful memory had nothing to do with this case, and he drove the gloomy shadow from his mind.

His questions arranged themselves in the following sequence. Was this man really a gendarme? If he was (and – more interestingly – even if he was not), then what was his role in the Sobolev case? But most importantly of all: how could he possibly be so fiendishly well informed and so incredibly ubiquitous?

Just at that moment the governor-general began stating the questions that interested him, which naturally had a somewhat different slant: 'Now what are we going to do, my esteemed detectives? What would you have me report to my superiors? Was Sobolev murdered, or did he die a natural death? What was Khurtinsky doing right under my – or rather, your – nose, Evgeny Osipovich? Where have the million roubles got to? Who is this fellow Pevtsov?' There was a note of menace underlying the feigned benevolence of the prince's voice. 'What do you say, Your Excellency, our dear defender and protector?'

The agitated chief of police wiped his sweaty forehead with a handkerchief. 'I have no Pevtsov in my department. Perhaps he really did come from St Petersburg and was dealing directly with Khurtinsky, bypassing the provincial administration. I surmise the following ...' Karachentsev tugged nervously on one ginger sideburn. '... Acting in secret from you and from me ...' The chief of police swallowed. '... Khurtinsky was carrying out certain confidential assignments from high up. These assignments evidently included provisions for Sobolev's visit. To what end this was necessary, I do not know. Obviously Khurtinsky found out from somewhere that Sobolev had a very large sum of money with him and that his retinue knew nothing about it. On Thursday night Khurtinsky was informed of Sobolev's sudden death in one of the apartments at the Hotel Anglia – probably by agents who were secretly observing the general – Well, and … As we already know, the court counsellor was greedy and not particularly choosy about his methods. He succumbed to the temptation to snatch this unbelievable booty and sent his minion, the housebreaker Little Misha, to extract the briefcase from the safe. However, Khurtinsky's dubious enterprise was discovered by Captain Pevtsov who, in all probability, had been assigned to observe the observer – that happens quite often in our department. Pevtsov confiscated the briefcase, came to Khurtinsky and accused him of double-dealing and theft. Immediately after the captain left, the state counsellor realised that his goose was cooked, so he wrote a repentant note and hanged himself … That is the only explanation that occurs to me.'

'Well, it is certainly plausible,' allowed Dolgorukoi. 'What action do you propose?'

'Immediately forward a query to St Petersburg concerning the identity of Captain Pevtsov and what authority he has been granted. Meanwhile, Erast Petrovich and I will examine the suicide's papers. I shall take the contents of his safe, and Mr Fandorin will study Khurtinsky's notebook.'

The collegiate assessor could not suppress a wry smile at the deft way in which the general had divided up the booty: in one half the contents of the safe, and in the other an ordinary notebook for business appointments, lying openly on the desk of the deceased.

Dolgorukoi drummed his fingers on the table and adjusted his wig, which had slipped slightly to one side, with a habitual gesture. 'It would seem, Evgeny Osipovich, that your conclusions amount to the following: Sobolev was not murdered, but died a natural death; Khurtinsky fell victim to inordinate avarice; Pevtsov is a man from St Petersburg. Are you in agreement with these conclusions, Erast Petrovich?'

Fandorin's reply was terse: 'No.'

'Interesting,' said the governor, brightening up. 'Well then, speak your piece: what conclusions have your calculations produced – "that is one", "that is two", "that is three"?'

'By all means, Your Excellency ...' The young man paused – evidently for greater effect – and began resolutely: 'General Sobolev was involved in some secret business, the essence of which is not yet clear. P-Proof? Concealing his actions from everybody, he gathered together an immense sum of money. That is one. The hotel safe contained secret papers, which were hidden from the authorities by the general's retinue. That is two. There is the very fact that Sobolev was under secret observation – I think Evgeny Osipovich is right when he says he was being observed – that is three.' At this point Erast Petrovich mentally added: The testimony of the young woman Golovina – that is four. However, he chose not to involve the teacher from Minsk in the investigation. 'I am not yet ready to draw any conclusions, but I am prepared to venture a few surmises. Sobolev was murdered – by some cunning means that imitates a natural death. Khurtinsky fell victim to his own greed, the illusion of impunity went to his head. Here I am once again in agreement with Evgeny Osipovich. But the true criminal – the man pulling the strings behind the scenes – is the person whom we know as "Captain Pevtsov". Khurtinsky, a sly, cunning villain whose like would be hard to find anywhere, was mortally afraid of this man. This man has the briefcase. "Pevtsov" knows everything and appears everywhere. I very much dislike such supernatural agility. A blond man with pale eyes who has twice appeared in a gendarme uniform – that is the person we must find at any cost.'

The chief of police rubbed his temples wearily. 'It could well be that Erast Petrovich is right and I am mistaken. When it comes to deduction the collegiate assessor can easily give me a hundred points' start.'

Prince Dolgorukoi got up from his desk with a grunt, walked across to the window and gazed out for about five minutes at the incessant stream of carriages flowing along Tverskaya Street.

Then he turned round and spoke in an untypically brisk and businesslike manner. 'I shall report to the top. Immediately, by coded telegram. As soon as they reply, I shall summon you. Remain at your posts and do not leave them. Evgeny Osipovich, you are where?'

'In my office on Tverskoi Boulevard. I shall go through Khurtinsky's papers.'

'I shall be at the Dusseaux,' Fandorin announced. 'To be quite honest, I can hardly stay on my feet. I have hardly slept at all for two days now.'

'Go on then, my dear fellow, get an hour or two of sleep, and make yourself look respectable while you're at it. I shall send for you.'

Erast Petrovich did not actually intend to sleep, as such, but he did intend to refresh himself – by taking an ice bath, and a massage afterwards would be good. Sleep – how could he take any sleep when there was business like this afoot? How could he possibly fall asleep?

Fandorin opened the door of his apartment and started back sharply as Masa threw himself at his feet, pressed his cocooned head to the floor and began jabbering: 'Masters it is unforgivable, it is unforgivable. I failed to protect your *onshi* or to guard your leather briefcase. But that was not the end of my offences. Unable to bear such shame, I wished to lay hands on myself and dared to make use of your sword for that purpose; but the sword broke, and so I have committed yet another terrible crime.'

The small ceremonial sword was lying on the table, broken in half.

Erast Petrovich sat down on the floor beside his miserable servant. He stroked his head cautiously – he could feel the immense bump even through the towel.

'Masa, you are not to blame for anything. I am responsible for Grushin-*sensei*'s death, and I shall never forgive myself for it. Your courage did not fail you; you showed no weakness. It is just that life here is different and there are different rules, to which you are not accustomed. And the sword is worthless trash, a knitting needle; it is quite impossible to cut yourself open with it. We shall buy another; they cost fifty roubles. It is not my family sword.'

Masa straightened up with tears running down his contorted face. 'But I still insist, master. It is not possible for me to live after I have failed you so terribly. I deserve to be punished.'

'All right,' sighed Fandorin. 'You will learn off by heart the next ten pages of the dictionary.'

'No, twenty!'

'All right. But not now, later, when your head has healed. Meanwhile, prepare an ice bath.'

Masa dashed downstairs with an empty bucket while Erast Petrovich sat down at the table and opened Khurtinsky's notebook. It was not actually an ordinary notebook, but an English schedule book – a diary in which every day of the year is allotted its own page. A convenient item: Fandorin had seen others like it before. He began leafing through it without really hoping to find anything significant. Of course, the state counsellor had kept everything that was in the least degree secret or important in the safe and only written various minor items that he needed to remember, such as the times of business meetings, audiences and reports, in the book. Many names were indicated by only one or two letters. Fandorin would have to make sense of all of it. The collegiate assessor's glance halted on Tuesday, 4 July (that is, Tuesday, 22 June in our Russian style), attracted by a strangely elongated blot. So far there had not been a single blot or even correction in the book – Khurtinsky was obviously an extremely neat individual. And the form of the blot was very odd – as if the ink had not fallen from a pen, but been deliberately smeared. Fandorin held the page up against the light. No, he could not make it out. He carefully ran the tip of his finger over the paper. There seemed to be something written there. The dead man had used a steel nib and pressed hard with it. But there was no way to read it.

Masa brought a bucket of ice and flung it into the bath with a crash and a clatter. There was the sound of running water. Erast Petrovich picked up the travelling bag that held his tools and took out the device that he required. He turned over the page with the blot, applied an extremely thin sheet of rice paper to its reverse side and ran a rubber roller over it several times. This was not ordinary paper: it had been impregnated with a special solution that reacted sensitively to the slightest irregularity in the surface. The collegiate assessor's fingers were trembling with impatience as he lifted the sheet of paper away. Against the matt background he could make out the pale but distinct words: *Metropole No. 19 Klonov.*

It had been written on 22 June. What had happened on that day? The commander of the Fourth Army Corps, Infantry General Sobolev, had concluded his manoeuvres and submitted his application for leave. Well, and a certain Mr Klonov had been in apartment 19 at the Hotel Metropole. What connection was there between these two facts? Most likely, none. But why would Khurtinsky have wanted to obscure the name and address? Very interesting.

Erast Petrovich undressed and climbed into the bath of ice,

which obliged him to abandon extraneous thoughts for a moment, as usual straining his mental and physical powers to the utmost. Fandorin ducked his head under the water and counted to a hundred and twenty, and when he surfaced and opened his eyes, he gasped and blushed bright red: standing in the doorway of the bathroom, rooted to the spot in amazement, was the Countess Mirabeau, the morganatic wife of His Highness Evgeny Maximilianovich, Duke of Lichtenburg. Her face was also crimson.

'I beg your pardon, Monsieur Fandorin,' the countess babbled in French. 'Your servant admitted me to the apartment and pointed to this door. I assumed that it was your study …'

Good breeding would not allow the panic-stricken Erast Petrovich to remain seated in the presence of a lady and he instinctively leapt to his feet, but a second later he plunged back down into the water in even greater panic. Blushing even more deeply, the countess backed out of the doorway.

'Masa!' Fandorin roared in a wild voice. 'Masa!'

The villainous rogue appeared, holding a dressing gown in his hands, and bowed. 'What can I do for you, master?'

'I'll give you "what can I do for you"!' screeched Erast Petrovich, his dignity totally undermined by his embarrassment. 'For that I *will* make you disembowel yourself, and not with a knitting needle, but with a chopstick! I already explained to you, you brainless badger, that in Europe the bathroom is a private place! You have put me in an impossible position and made a lady burn with shame!' Switching into Russian the collegiate assessor shouted: 'I do beg your pardon! Make yourself comfortable, Countess, I'll just be a moment!' And then again in Japanese: 'Bring me my trousers, frock coat and shirt, you repulsive bandy-legged insect!'

Fandorin emerged into the room fully dressed, with an impeccable parting in his hair, but still red-cheeked and unable to imagine how he could possibly look the countess in the face after the scandalous incident that had just taken place. Contrary to his expectations, however, the countess had completely recovered her composure and was scrutinising the Japanese prints hanging on the walls with a curious eye. She glanced at the functionary's disconcerted face and the ghost of a smile even glimmered in her blue Sobolev eyes; but it was immediately replaced by an extremely serious expression.

'Mr Fandorin, I have taken the liberty of calling on you because you are an old comrade of Michel's and are investigating the circumstances of his demise. My husband left Moscow yesterday with the grand duke – some urgent business or other. I shall take my brother's body to the estate for burial.'

Zinaida Dmitrievna hesitated, as though uncertain whether to continue, but she plunged on resolutely: 'My husband left with only light luggage and a servant found this in one of his frock coats that remained here.' The countess handed him a folded sheet of paper, and as he took it Fandorin noticed that she had kept hold of another sheet.

The message in French below the letter head of the Fourth Army Corps was written in Sobolev's sprawling hand: *'Eugène, be in Moscow on the morning of the 25 for the final explanation of the matter already known to you. The hour draws near. I shall stay at the Dusseaux. I embrace you. Your Michel.'*

Erast Petrovich glanced enquiringly at his visitor, anticipating clarification.

'This is very strange,' she said, whispering for some reason. 'My husband did not tell me that he was due to meet Michel in Moscow. Eugène said only that we had to make a few visits, and then we would go back to St Petersburg.'

'That really is strange,' Fandorin agreed, noting from the date stamp that the message had been sent from Minsk by courier on the sixteenth of the month. 'But why did you not ask His Highness about this?'

Biting her lip, the countess held out the second sheet of paper. 'Because Eugène concealed this from me.'

'What is it?'

'A note from Michel, addressed to me. Evidently it must have been attached to the other message. For some reason Eugène did not pass it on to me.'

Erast Petrovich took the sheet of paper. It had clearly been written in haste, at the very last moment: '*Dear Zizi, you must come to Moscow together with Eugène. It is very important. I do not want to explain anything to you now, but it could be that* (then half a line had been crossed out) *we shall not see each other again for a long time.*'

Fandorin went over to the window and pressed the note against the glass in order to read what had been crossed out.

'Don't waste your time, I have already made it out,' Zinaida Dmitrievna's trembling voice said behind him. 'It says: "*... that this meeting will be our last*".'

The collegiate assessor ruffled up his wet, freshly combed hair. So, it seemed that Sobolev had known that his life was in danger? And the duke also knew this? That was very interesting ...

He turned towards the countess: 'There is nothing that I can say to you now, madam, but I promise that I shall investigate all the circumstances as thoroughly as possible.' Glancing into Zinaida Dmitrievna's perplexed eyes, he added: 'Naturally, as t-tactfully as possible.'

The moment the countess left, Fandorin sat down at the table and as usual, when he wanted to concentrate, turned to a calligraphic exercise: he began drawing the hieroglyph for 'serenity'. However, at only the third sheet of paper, when perfection was still very far off, there was another knock at the door – sharp and peremptory.

With a fearful backward glance at his master's solemn ritual, Masa tip-toed across to the door and opened it.

There stood Ekaterina Alexandrovna Golovina, the

golden-haired lover of the deceased Achilles. She was fuming with rage, which only made her seem even more beautiful.

'You disappeared!' the young lady exclaimed instead of greeting him. 'I have been waiting, going out of my mind with all the uncertainty. What have you discovered, Fandorin? I gave you such important information, and you are sitting here, drawing. I demand an explanation!'

'Madam,' the collegiate assessor interrupted her sharply, 'it is I who demand an explanation from you. Please be seated.' He took his unexpected visitor by the hand, led her over to an armchair and sat her down. He pulled up a chair for himself.

'You told me less than you knew. What was Sobolev planning? Why was he in fear of his life? What was so d-dangerous about his journey? What did he need so much money for? Why all this mystery? And finally, what did you quarrel about? Because of your omissions, Ekaterina Alexandrovna, I assessed the situation incorrectly and a very good man was killed as a result – as well as several bad ones, who nonetheless still had souls.'

Golovina hung her head. Her delicate face reflected an entire gamut of powerful feelings that clearly sat together rather uncomfortably.

She began with a confession: 'Yes, I lied when I said that I did not know what Michel's passion was. He thought that Russia was dying, and he wanted to save her. All he ever spoke about recently was Constantinople, the German menace, the greatness of Russia ... And a month ago, during our final meeting, he suddenly began talking about Bonaparte and asked me to be his Josephine ... I was horrified. Our views had always differed. He believed in the historic mission of Slavdom and some special Russian destiny, but I believed and still believe that what Russia needs is not the Dardanelles, but enlightenment and a constitution ...' Unable to control her voice any longer, Ekaterina

Alexandrovna shook her fist in annoyance, as if that would help her over some difficult spot on her road. 'When he mentioned Josephine, I was frightened – frightened that Michel would be consumed like some intrepid moth in the bright, alluring flame of his own ambition ... and even more afraid that he might be successful. He could have been. He is so single-minded, so strong, so fortunate in everything ... He *was*, that is. What would he have become, given the chance to control the fates of millions? It is terrible even to think of it. He would no longer have been Michel, but an entirely different person.'

'And did you report him to the authorities?' Erast Petrovich demanded sharply.

Golovina shrank away in horror. 'How could you think such a thing? No, I simply told him: choose – either me, or this undertaking of yours. I knew what the answer would be ...' She wiped away an angry tear. 'But it never even occurred to me that everything would end in such a vile and vulgar farce. The future Bonaparte killed for a bundle of banknotes ... As it says in the Bible: ' "The Lord will destroy the house of the proud." '

She fluttered her hands as if to say: No more, I cannot say any more – and burst into bitter tears, no longer attempting to restrain herself.

Fandorin waited for the sobbing to pass and said in a low voice: 'It would appear that what happened had n-nothing to do with the banknotes.'

'With what, then?' wailed Ekaterina Alexandrovna. 'He was killed after all, wasn't he? Somehow I believe that you will uncover the truth. Swear that you will tell me the whole truth about his death.'

Erast Petrovich turned away in embarrassment, thinking that women were incomparably better than men – more loyal, more sincere, more truly all of a piece. Naturally, that is, if they truly loved. 'Yes, yes, definitely,' he mumbled, knowing perfectly well that never, no matter what, would he ever tell Ekaterina Alexandrovna the whole truth about the way the man she loved had died.

At this point the conversation had to be broken off, because a messenger from the governor-general had arrived for Fandorin.

'How did the contents of the safe look, Your Excellency?' Erast Petrovich asked Karachentsev. 'Did you discover anything of interest?'

'Plenty,' replied the chief of police with an air of satisfaction. 'A great deal of new light has been cast on the shady dealings of the deceased. It will take a bit more fiddling about to decode his financial records, though. Our bee was busy collecting nectar from many flowers, not just from Little Misha. And what have you got?'

'I do have something,' Fandorin replied modestly.

The conversation was taking place in the governor-general's study. Dolgorukoi himself, however, was not yet there – according to his secretary, His Excellency was finishing his lunch.

Eventually Dolgorukoi appeared, entering the room with an air of mysterious importance. He sat down and cleared his throat in a formal manner.

'Gentlemen, I have received a telegram from St Petersburg in reply to my detailed report. As you can see, the matter was considered so important that there was no procrastination at all. In this case I am merely conveying a message from one party to another. This is what Count Tolstov writes:

'Highly esteemed Vladimir Andreevich, in reply to your message, I beg to inform you that Captain Pevtsov is indeed attached to the chief of the Corps of Gendarmes and is at present in Moscow on a special assignment. To be specific, the captain was instructed to confiscate a briefcase which might contain documents of state importance. His Imperial Majesty has instructed that the case of the death of Adjutant-General Sobolev should be considered closed, concerning which appropriate formal notification will be forwarded to Evgeny Osipovich. His Majesty has further instructed that for exceeding his authority and involving a private individual in a secret investigation, which resulted in the death of the aforesaid individual, your Deputy for Special Assignments Fandorin is to be removed from his post and placed under house arrest until further instructions. Minister of Internal Affairs D.A. Tolstov.'

The prince spread his hands regretfully and addressed the astounded Fandorin. 'There, my dear fellow, see how things have turned out. Well, the people at the top know best.'

Erast Petrovich rose slowly to his feet, pale and feeling desperately disheartened, not because his sovereign's punishment was harsh, but because it was essentially just. The worst thing of all was that the account of the case that he had proposed with such cool self-assurance had collapsed ignominiously. He had taken a secret government agent for the main villain of the piece! What a shameful error!

'Please don't be offended if Evgeny Osipovich and I have a little talk now; go on back to your hotel and take some rest,' Dolgorukoi said sympathetically. 'And chin up! I have taken quite a liking to you, and I shall put in a word for you with Petersburg.'

The collegiate assessor set off dejectedly towards the door. Just as he reached it, Karachenstsev called to him. 'What was it that you discovered in the notebook?' asked the chief of police with a discreet wink, as if to say, Never mind, it will all blow over soon.

Erast Petrovich paused for a moment and replied: 'Nothing of any real interest, Your Excellency.'

Back at the hotel Fandorin declared from the threshold of his apartment: 'Masa, I am disgraced and have been placed under arrest. It is my fault that Grushin died. That is one. I have no more ideas. That is two. My life is over. That is three.'

Erast Petrovich walked to the bed and, without bothering to undress, collapsed on the pillow and instantly fell asleep.

Chapter Twelve

IN WHICH A TRAP IS SPRUNG

The first thing that Fandorin saw on opening his eyes was the rectangle of the window, filled with the pink glow of sunset.

Masa was sitting on the floor by the bed, wearing his black formal kimono, with his hands resting ceremonially on his knees and a fresh bandage on his head. His face was set in an austere expression.

'Why are you all dressed up like that?' Erast Petrovich asked curiously.

'You said, master, that you are disgraced and that you have no more ideas.'

'Well, what of it?'

'I have a good idea. I have thought everything over and can propose a worthy way out of the distressing situation in which we both find ourselves. To my numerous misdeeds I have added yet another: I have broken the European rule of etiquette that forbids allowing a woman into the bathroom. That I do not understand this strange custom is no justification. I have learned off twenty-six whole pages from the dictionary – from the short word *ab-ster-use*, which means "difficult to conceive of or apprehend", to the long word *aff-fran-chise-ment*, which means "release from servitude or an obligation"; but not even this severe trial has lifted the weight from my heart. And as for you, master, you yourself told me that your life was over. Then let us leave this life together, master. I have prepared everything – even the brush and the ink for the death poem.'

Fandorin stretched, savouring the languorous aching in his joints. 'Forget that, Masa,' he said; 'I have a better idea. What is it that smells so delicious?'

'I bought fresh bagels, the finest thing there is in Russia after a woman,' his servant replied sadly. 'The sour-cabbage soup that everyone here eats is absolutely terrible, but bagels are an excellent invention. I wish to comfort my *hara* one last time, before I slice it in half with my dagger.'

'I'll slice you in half,' the collegiate assessor threatened him. 'Give me one of those bagels; I'm dying of hunger. Let's have a bite and get down to work.'

'Mr Klonov from number 19?' echoed the *koelner* (that was what the senior floor staff in the Metropole were called, after the German fashion). 'Why, of course, we remember him very well. Such a gentlemen – a merchant he was. Would you happen to be a friend of his then, mister?'

That evening's idyllic sunset had beaten a rapid retreat, ousted by a cold wind and rapidly gathering gloom. The sky had turned bleak and loosed a fine scattering of raindrops that threatened to develop into a serious downpour by night-time. In view of the weather conditions, Fandorin had dressed to withstand the elements: a cap with an oil-cloth peak, a waterproof Swedish jacket of fine kidskin, rubber galoshes. His appearance was extravagantly foreign, which obviously must have been the reason for the *koelner*'s unexpected comment. *Might as well be hung for a sheep as a lamb*, the collegiate assessor decided – after all, he was a fugitive arrestee.

He leaned across the counter and whispered: 'I don't know him at all, dear chap. I am C-Captain Pevtsov of the gendarme corps, and this is an extremely important matter – top secret.'

'I understand,' the *koelner* replied, also in a whisper. 'One moment and I'll find everything for you.'

He began rustling through the register. 'Here it is, sir. Merchant of the first guild Nikolai Nikolaevich Klonov. Checked in on the morning of the twenty-second, arrived from Ryazan. The gentleman checked out on Thursday night.'

'What!' cried Fandorin. 'Actually during the night of the twenty-fourth to the twenty-fifth?'

'Yes, sir. I was not present myself, but here is the entry – please look for yourself. The full account was settled at half past four in the morning, during the night shift, sir.'

Erast Petrovich's heart thrilled to that overwhelming passion known only to the inveterate hunter. He enquired with feigned casualness: 'And what does he look like, this Klonov?'

'A well-set-up sort of gentleman, respectable. In a word: a merchant of the first guild.'

'You mean a beard, a big belly? Describe his appearance. Does he have any distinctive features?'

'No, no beard, sir, and he's not a fat man. Not your average old-style merchant, more one of your modern businessmen. Dresses European-style. And his appearance ...' The *koelner* pondered for a moment. 'An ordinary appearance. Blond hair. No distinctive features ... Except for his eyes. They were very pale – the kind that Finns sometimes have.'

Fandorin slapped his hand down on the counter like a predator pouncing. Bull's eye! Here was the central character of the plot. Checked in on Tuesday, two days before Sobolev's arrival, and checked out at the very hour when the officers were carrying the dead general into the plundered apartment 47. He was getting warm now, very warm!

'You say he was a respectable-looking man? I suppose people came to see him, business partners?'

'Not a one, sir. Only messengers with telegrams a couple of times. It was plain to see the man didn't come to Moscow on business – more likely to enjoy himself.'

'What made it so plain?'

The *koelner* smiled conspiratorially and spoke into Fandorin's ear: 'The moment the gentleman arrived, he started enquiring about the ladies. Wanted to know what little lovelies Moscow had with a bit of extra style. She had to be blonde, and slim, with a waist. He was a gentleman of great taste.'

Erast Petrovich frowned. This was a strange turn of events. 'Captain Pevtsov' ought not to be interested in blondes.

'Did he speak about this with you?'

'Not at all, sir; Timofei Spiridonich told me about it. He used to work as *koelner* in this very spot.' He sighed with affected sorrow. 'Timofei Spiridonovich passed on last Saturday, Lord bless his soul. The mass is tomorrow.'

'And how did he "pass on"?' asked Fandorin, leaning forward. 'In what way?'

'In a very ordinary way. He was on his way home in the evening and he slipped and banged the back of his head against a stone. Not far from here, walking through one of the courtyards. Gone, just like that. We're all of us in God's hands.' The *koelner* crossed himself. 'I used to be his assistant. But now I've been promoted. Eh, poor old Timofei Spiridonich ...'

'So Klonov spoke with him about the ladies?' asked the collegiate assessor, with the acute intuition that the veil was about to fall away from his eyes at any moment, revealing the full picture of what had happened in its clear and logical completeness. 'And did Timofei Spiridonovich not tell you any more details?'

'Why, of course, the deceased was a great man for talking. He said he'd described all the high-class blondes in Moscow for number nineteen (that's the way we refer to the guests between ourselves, sir – by their numbers) and number nineteen was interested most of all in Mamselle Wanda from the Alpine Rose.'

Erast Petrovich closed his eyes for an instant. The thread had led him along a tangled path, but now its end was in sight.

'You?'

Wanda stood in the doorway, wrapping herself in a lace shawl and gazing in fright at the collegiate assessor, whose wet kidskin jacket reflected the light of the lamp and seemed to be enveloped in a glowing halo. Behind the late caller's back the rain hissed down in a shifting wall of glass, and beyond that the darkness was impenetrable. Rivulets of water ran off the jacket on to the floor.

'Come in, Mr Fandorin; you are soaked through.'

'It is most amazing,' said Erast Petrovich, 'that you, mademoiselle, are still alive.'

'Thanks to you,' said the songstress, with a shrug of her slim shoulders. 'I can still see that knife creeping closer and closer to my throat … I can't sleep at night. And I can't sing.'

'I was not thinking of Herr Knabe at all, but of Klonov,' said Fandorin, staring keenly into those huge green eyes. 'Tell me about this interesting gentleman.'

Wanda was either genuinely surprised or play-acting. 'Klonov? Nikolai Klonov? What has he got to do with this?'

'That is what we are going to try to discover.'

They went into the drawing room and sat down. The only light came from a table lamp covered with a green shawl, which gave the whole room the appearance of some mysterious underwater world. *The kingdom of the Enchantress of the Sea*, thought Erast Petrovich, and then immediately banished all inappropriate thoughts from his mind.

'Tell me about merchant-of-the-first-guild Klonov.'

Wanda took his wet jacket and put it on the floor, without appearing at all worried about damaging the fluffy Persian carpet. 'He is very attractive,' she said in a dreamy tone of voice, and Erast Petrovich felt something akin to a prick of envy, to which, of course, he had absolutely no right whatever. 'Calm, confident. A good man, one of the best kind of men, the kind that you rarely meet. At least I almost never come across them. Like you in some ways.' She smiled gently and Fandorin felt strangely perturbed: she was bewitching. 'But I don't understand why you are so interested in him.'

'This man is not who he says he is. He is not a merchant at all.'

Wanda half-turned away and her gaze went blank. 'That does not surprise me. But I have grown used to the fact that everyone has his own secrets. I try not to interfere in other people's business.'

'You are a very perceptive woman, mademoiselle; otherwise you would hardly be so successful in your ... profession.' Erast Petrovich was embarrassed, realising that he had not chosen the happiest way to express himself. 'Are you quite sure that you never sensed any danger emanating from this m-man?'

The songstress swung round to face him: 'Yes, yes, I did. Sometimes. But how do you know?'

'I have substantial grounds for believing that Klonov is an extremely dangerous man,' said Fandorin, and then continued without the slightest transition, 'Tell me, was it him who brought you and Sobolev together?'

'No, not at all,' Wanda replied just as quickly – perhaps a little too quickly. She also seemed to sense this and feel it necessary to elaborate on her answer: 'At least, he is in no way involved in the general's death, I swear to you! Everything happened just as I told you.'

Now she was telling the truth – or believed that she was telling the truth. All the signs – the modulation of the voice, the gestures, the movements of the facial muscles – were precisely as they should be. But then, perhaps the world had lost an exceptional actress in Miss Tolle?

Erast Petrovich changed tactics. The masters of detective psychology teach us that if one suspects a person under interrogation of not being entirely frank, but merely pretending to be so, he or she should be peppered with a hail of rapid, unexpected questions that require an unambiguous answer.

'Did Klonov know about Knabe?'

'Yes, but what …'

'Did he mention the briefcase?'

'What briefcase?'

'Did he mention Khurtinsky?'

'Who's that?'

'Does he carry a weapon?'

'I think so. But surely that is not illeg—'

'Are you going to meet him again?'

'Yes. That is …' Wanda turned pale and bit her lip.

Erast Petrovich realised that from now on she would lie to him, and before she could start, he began speaking quite differently, in an extremely serious voice, sincerely and from the heart: 'You have to tell me where he is. If I am mistaken and he is not the man I take him for, it is best for him to clear himself of suspicion now. If I am not mistaken, he is a terrible man, not at all what you imagine him to be. And as far as I can follow his logic, he will not allow you to stay alive; it would be against his rules. I am astounded you are not already lying on a slab in the mortuary at Tverskaya Street Police Station. Well then, how can I find him, your Mr Klonov?'

She did not answer.

'Tell me,' said Fandorin, taking her by the hand. The hand was cold, but the pulse was pattering rapidly. 'I have saved you once already and I intend to do it again. I swear to you, if he is not a murderer, I shall not touch him.'

Wanda gazed at the young man through dilated pupils. There was a struggle taking place inside her, and Fandorin did not know how to tilt the scales in his favour. While he was feverishly trying to think of something, Wanda's gaze hardened: the scales had been tipped by some thought that remained unknown to Erast Petrovich.

'I do not know where he is,' the songstress stated definitively.

Fandorin slowly stood up and left without saying another word. What was the point? The important thing was that she was going to see Klonov–Pevtsov again. In order to locate his target, all that was needed was to arrange for her to be competently shadowed. The collegiate assessor stopped dead in the middle of Petrovka Street, oblivious to the rain, and in any case the downpour was no longer as vehement as before.

How could he arrange any damned thing at all! He was under arrest and supposed to be sitting quietly in his hotel. He would have no assistants and on his own it was impossible to carry out proper surveillance – that would require at least five or six experienced agents.

To force his thoughts out of their well-worn rut, Fandorin clapped his hands rapidly and loudly eight times. Passers-by hidden under their umbrellas shied away from this madman, but a smile of satisfaction appeared on the collegiate assessor's lips. An original idea had occurred to him.

On entering the spacious vestibule of the Dusseaux, Erast Petrovich immediately turned to the desk. 'My dear man,' he addressed the porter in a haughty voice, 'connect me to the apartments in the Anglia on Petrovka Street, and step aside, will you; this is a confidential conversation.'

The porter, who was by now well used to the mysterious behaviour of the important functionary from number 20, bowed, ran his finger down the list of telephone subscribers hanging on the wall, found the one required and lifted the earpiece of the telephone.

'The Anglia, Mr Fandorin,' he said, handing the earpiece to the collegiate assessor.

Someone hissed: 'Who is calling?'

Erast Petrovich looked expectantly at the porter, and he tactfully moved away into the furthest corner of the vestibule.

Only then did Fandorin set his lips close to the mouthpiece and say: 'Be so good as to ask Miss Wanda to come to the telephone. Tell her Mr Klonov wishes to speak with her urgently. Yes, yes – Klonov!'

The young man's heart was pounding rapidly. The idea that had occurred to him was new and daringly simple. For all its convenience, communication by telephone, which was rapidly gaining in popularity among the inhabitants of Moscow, was technically far from perfect. It was almost always possible to make out the sense of what was said, but the membrane did not convey the timbre and nuances of the voice. In the best case – which was not every time – one could hear if it was a man's voice or a woman's, but no more than that. The newspapers wrote that the great inventor Mr Bell was developing a new model which would transmit sound much more precisely. However, as the wise Chinese saying has it, even imperfections have their own charm. Erast Petrovich had not actually heard of anyone pretending to be someone else in a telephone conversation. But why should he not try it?

The voice in the earpiece was squeaky, interrupted by crackling, not at all like Wanda's contralto: 'Kolya, is that you? How delighted I am that you decided to telephone me!'

Kolya? Delighted? Hmm!

Wanda shouted through the telephone, running the syllables together. 'Kolya, you're in some kind of danger. A man has just been here looking for you.'

'Who?' asked Fandorin, and froze in expectation: now she would give him away.

But Wanda answered as if it were not that important: 'Some detective. He is very shrewd and clever. Kolya, he says terrible things about you!'

'Rubbish,' Erast Petrovich responded curtly, thinking that this *femme fatale* seemed to be head over heels in love with her gendarme captain of the first guild.

'Really? Oh, I just knew it! But even so I was terribly upset! Kolya, why are you telephoning? Has something changed?'

He said nothing, feverishly trying to think of what to say.

'Are we not going to meet tomorrow-morrow?' An echo had appeared on the line, and Fandorin plugged his other ear with his finger, because it had become difficult to follow Wanda's rapid speech. 'But you promised that you wouldn't go away without saying goodbye-oodbye! Kolya, why don't you say something? Is the meeting cancelled?'

'No.' Taking his courage in his hands, he uttered a rather longer phrase. 'I only wanted to check that you remembered everything correctly.'

'What? Check what?'

Evidently Wanda could not hear very well either, but that was actually rather helpful.

'Whether you remember everything!' Fandorin shouted.

'Yes, yes, of course! The Troitsa Inn at six, number seven, from the yard, knock twice, then three times, then twice again. Maybe instead of six we could make it a bit later? I haven't got up that early in a hundred years.'

'All right,' said the emboldened collegiate assessor, mentally repeating: six, number seven, from the yard, two-three-two. 'At seven. But no later. I've got business to deal with.'

'All right, at seven,' shouted Wanda. The echo and the crackling had suddenly disappeared and her voice came through so clearly that it was almost recognisable. It sounded so happy that Fandorin suddenly felt ashamed.

'I'm hanging up,' he said.

'Where are you telephoning from? Where are you?'

Erast Petrovich thrust the earpiece into its cradle and twirled the handle. Deception by telephone was quite exceptionally simple. He must remember that in future, in order not to be caught out himself. Perhaps he ought to invent a separate password for every person he spoke to? Well, not for everyone, of course, but for police agents, say, or simply for confidential occasions.

But he had no time to think about that now.

He could forget about his house arrest. Now he had something to offer his superiors. At six o'clock the next morning the elusive, almost incorporeal Klonov–Pevtsov would be at some place called the Troitsa Inn. God only knew where that place was, but in any case Fandorin would not be able to manage without Karachentsev. This was an arrest that required thorough planning, everything done by the book. The cunning opponent must not be allowed to get away.

The house of the chief of police on Tverskoi Boulevard was one of the sights of Russia's ancient capital. With a façade overlooking the respectable boulevard where in good weather the very finest of Moscow society performed its refined perambulations, the two-storey house (painted public-purse yellow) seemed to be watching over and even, in a certain sense, blessing the decent, honest folk in their elegant and tranquil recreation. Stroll on, my cultured ladies and gentlemen, along this narrow European promenade, breathe in the aroma of lime-tree blossom, and do not concern yourselves with the snuffling and snorting of this immense semi-Asiatic city, populated for the most part by people who possess neither education nor culture. Authority is close at hand; here it stands, on guard over civilisation and order; authority never sleeps.

Erast Petrovich was granted an opportunity to ascertain the correctness of this claim when he rang at the door of the famous mansion house shortly before midnight. The door was opened, not by a footman, but by a gendarme with a sword and a revolver, who listened austerely to what the nocturnal visitor had to say, but said not a single word in reply and left him standing there on the doorstep – after summoning the duty adjutant with an electric bell. Fortunately, the adjutant proved to be a familiar face: Captain Sverchinsky. He had no difficulty in recognising the anglicised gentleman as the ragged beggar who had caused such a commotion in the department that morning, and was instantly politeness itself. It emerged that Evgeny Osipovich was taking his usual stroll along the boulevard before retiring for the night; he was fond of his bed-time walk and never skipped it in any weather, not even if it was raining.

Erast Petrovich went out on to the boulevard and walked on a little in the direction of the bronze statute of Pushkin; and there, strolling towards him at a leisurely pace, he did indeed see a familiar figure in a long cavalry greatcoat with the hood pulled forward over his forehead. The instant the collegiate assessor began to dash towards the general, two silent shadows appeared out of nowhere at his sides, as if they had sprung up out of the earth, and two equally determined silhouettes appeared behind the police chief's back. Erast Petrovich shook his head: so much for the illusory solitude of a high state official in the age of political terrorism. Not a single step without guards. Good God, what was Russia coming to?

The shadows had already taken Collegiate Assessor Fandorin by the arms – gently, but firmly.

'Erast Petrovich, I was just thinking about you!' Karachentsev declared happily, and then shouted at the agents: 'Shoo, shoo! Would you believe it, out stretching my legs and thinking about you. Couldn't sit still under house arrest, eh?'

'I'm afraid n-not, Your Excellency. Let us go inside, Evgeny Osipovich; there is no time to waste.'

Asking no questions, the chief of police immediately turned in the direction of the house. He walked with broad strides, every now and then glancing sideways at his companion.

They went through into a spacious oval office, and sat down facing each other at a long table covered with green baize.

Karachentsev shouted: 'Sverchinsky, stand outside the door! I might be needing you!'

When the leather-bound door silently closed, Karachentsev asked impatiently: 'Well, what is it? Have you picked up the trail?'

'Better,' Fandorin informed him. 'I have found the criminal. In person. M-May I smoke?'

The collegiate assessor puffed on a cigar as he related the results of his investigations.

Karachentsev's frown grew deeper and deeper. Having heard the story out, he scratched his tall forehead anxiously and tossed back a stray lock of ginger hair. 'And what do you make of this brainteaser?'

Erast Petrovich shook a long tip of ash off his cigar. 'Sobolev was planning some bold political initiative. Possibly an eighteenth-century-style coup – what the Germans call a *putsch*. You know yourself how popular Mikhail Dmitrievich was with the army and the people. Our supreme authority is held in such low esteem these days ... But I don't need to tell you that; you have the entire Department of Gendarmes working for you, gathering rumours.' The chief of police nodded.

'I know nothing of any conspiracy as such. Either Sobolev saw himself in the role of Napoleon or – which is more likely – he intended to place one of the Emperor's relatives on the throne. I do not know, and I do not wish to guess. In any case, for our purposes, it is not important.' At that Karachentsev merely jerked his head and unbuttoned his gold-embroidered collar. Beads of sweat stood out above the bridge of the police chief's nose.

'In general, our Achilles was planning something really serious,' the collegiate assessor continued, as if he had noticed nothing, and blew an elegant stream of smoke, a delight to behold, up towards the ceiling. 'However, Sobolev had certain secret, powerful opponents who were informed about his plans. Klonov, alias Pevtsov, is their man. The anti-Sobolev party decided to use him to get rid of the self-appointed Bonaparte, but quietly, with no fuss, imitating a natural death. And it was done. The executioner was assisted by our f-friend Khurtinsky, who had links with the anti-Sobolev party; indeed all the signs indicate that he represented their interests in Moscow.'

'Not so fast, Erast Petrovich,' the chief of police implored him. 'My head is spinning. What party? Where? Right here, in the Ministry of Internal Affairs?'

Fandorin shrugged: 'Very possibly. In any case, your boss Count Tolstov has to be involved. Remember the letter in justification of Khurtinsky, and the telegram shielding Pevtsov? Khurtinsky made a real mess of the job. The court counsellor was too greedy – he was tempted by Sobolev's million roubles and decided that he could combine business with pleasure. But the central figure in this entire story is undoubtedly the blond man with the pale eyes.'

At this point Erast Petrovich started, struck by a new idea. 'Wait now … perhaps everything is even more complicated than that! Why, of course!'

Fandorin leapt to his feet and began walking rapidly from one corner of the study to the other. Karachentsev merely watched him striding to and fro, afraid to interrupt the flow of the sagacious functionary's thoughts.

'The Minister of the Interior could not have organised the murder of Adjutant-General Sobolev, no matter what he was planning. That's sheer nonsense!' Erast Petrovich was so excited that he had even stopped stammering. 'Our Klonov is very probably not the Captain Pevtsov about whom Count

Tolstov writes. Probably there is no genuine Pevtsov. This business smacks of a cunning intrigue, planned in such a way that if things were to go wrong, all the blame could be shifted on to your department!' the collegiate assessor fantasised wildly. 'Yes, that's it, that's it.'

He clapped his hands rapidly several times and the general, who was listening intently, almost leapt into the air.

'Let us assume that the minister knows about Sobolev's conspiracy and arranges to have the general followed in secret. That is one. Someone else also knows about the conspiracy and wants Sobolev killed. That is two. Unlike the minister, this other person, or more probably, these other people, whom we shall call the counter-conspirators, are not bound by the law and are pursuing their own goals.'

'What goals?' the chief of police asked in a weak voice, totally confused.

'Probably power,' Fandorin replied casually. 'What other goals can there be when intrigue unfolds at such a high level? The counter-conspirators had at their disposal an extraordinarily inventive and enterprising agent, who is known to us as Klonov. There is no doubt that he is quite certainly no merchant. He is an exceptional man with quite incredible abilities. Invisible, elusive, invulnerable. Omnipresent – he has always appeared everywhere ahead of the two of us and struck the first blow. Even though we ourselves acted rapidly, he has always left us looking like fools.'

'But what if he really is an officer of the gendarmes acting with the sanction of the minister?' asked Karachentsev. 'What if the elimination of Sobolev was sanctioned from the very top? I beg your pardon, Erast Petrovich, but you and I are professionals, and we know perfectly well that the protection of state secrets sometimes involves resorting to untraditional methods.'

'But then why was it necessary to steal the briefcase, especially from the Department of Gendarmes?' Fandorin asked with a shrug. 'The briefcase was already in the Department of Gendarmes, and you would have forwarded it to St Petersburg by the appropriate channels, to Count Tolstov himself. No, the ministry has nothing to do with this business. And then killing a national hero – that's not quite as simple as strangling some General Pichegru in his prison cell. How could they raise their hand against Mikhail Dmitrievich Sobolev? Without benefit of trial and due process? No, Evgeny Osipovich; even with all the imperfections of our state authorities, that would be going too far. I can't believe it.'

'Yes, you're right,' Karachentsev admitted.

'And then the facility with which Klonov commits his murders does not look much like state service.'

The chief of police raised his hand: 'Hang on now, don't get carried away. What murders exactly? We still don't know whether Sobolev was killed or died of natural causes. The conclusion of the autopsy was that he died.'

'No, he was killed,' retorted Erast Petrovich, 'though it is not clear how the traces of the crime were concealed. If we had known at the time what we know now, we might possibly have instructed Professor Belling to conduct a more exhaustive investigation. He was, after all, convinced beforehand that death had occurred from natural causes, and initial assumptions always determine a great deal. And then ...' The collegiate assessor halted, facing the general. '... it didn't stop with Sobolev's death. Klonov has closed off every possible trail. I am sure that Knabe's mysterious death is his work. Judge for yourself: why would the Germans kill an officer of their own general staff, even if they were seriously alarmed? That's not the way things are done in civilised countries. If the worst came to the worst, they would have forced him to shoot himself; but stab him in the side with a butcher's knife? Incredible! For Klonov, however, the death would have been most timely – you and I were quite convinced that the case had been solved. If the briefcase with the million roubles had not turned up, we should have closed the investigation. The sudden death of the *koelner* from the Hotel Metropole is also extremely suspicious. Clearly, the only mistake that the unfortunate Timofei Spiridonovich made was to help Klonov to locate the agent he needed – Wanda. Ah, Evgeny Osipovich, everything looks suspicious to me now!' exclaimed Fandorin. 'Even the way Little Misha died. Even Khurtinsky's suicide!'

'That's taking things too far,' said the police chief, pulling a wry face. 'What about the suicide note?'

'Can you put your hand on your heart and tell me that Pyotr Parmyonovich would have laid hands on himself if he had been threatened with exposure? Was he such a great man of honour then?'

'Yes, indeed, it is hardly likely.' Now it was Karachentsev who leapt to his feet and began striding along the wall. 'He would be more likely to try to escape. Judging from the documents that we discovered in his safe, the dead man had an account in a bank in Zurich. And if he didn't manage to escape, he would have begged for mercy and tried to bribe the judges. I know his kind: very concerned for their own skin. And Khurtinsky would most likely have got hard labour rather than the gallows. But even so, the note is written in his hand, there is no doubt about that ...'

'What frightens me most of all is that in every case either no suspicion of murder arises at all or, as in the case of Knabe or Little Misha, it is laid very firmly at someone else's door – in the first case German agents and in the second Fiska. That is a sign of supreme professionalism,' said Erast Petrovich, hooding his eyes. 'There is just one thing I can't make any sense of: how he could have left Wanda alive ... By the way, Evgeny Osipovich, we need to send a detail for her immediately and get her out of the Anglia. What if the real Klonov should telephone her? Or, even worse, decide to correct his incomprehensible oversight?'

'Sverchinsky!' the general shouted and left the reception room to issue instructions.

When he returned, the collegiate assessor was standing in front of a map of the city that was hanging on the wall and running his finger across it. 'This Troitsa Inn – where is it?' he asked.

'The Troitsa Inn is a block of apartments on Pokrovka Street, not far from Holy Trinity Church. Here it is,' said the general, pointing. 'Khokhlovsky Lane. At one time there was actually a monastery there, but now it's a labyrinth of annexes and extensions, semi-slums. The apartments are usually just called the Troitsa. Not a salubrious area, only a stone's throw from the Khitrovka slums. But the people who live in the Troitsa are not entirely lost souls – actresses, milliners, ruined businessmen. Tenants don't stay there for long: they either scramble their way back up into society or fall even lower, into the Khitrovka abyss.'

As he gave this lengthy answer to a simple question, Karachentsev was thinking about something else, and it was clear that he was having difficulty in reaching a decision. When the chief of police finished speaking, there was a pause.

Erast Petrovich realised that the conversation was entering its most crucial phase. 'Naturally, this is an extremely risky step to take, Evgeny Osipovich,' the collegiate assessor said quietly. 'If my suppositions are mistaken, you could ruin your career, and you are an ambitious man. But I have come to you, and not to Prince Dolgorukoi, because he would definitely not wish to take the risk. He is too cautious – that is the effect of his age. On the other hand, his position is also less delicate than yours. In any case, the ministry has plotted and intrigued behind your back and – pardon my bluntness – assigned you the role of a dummy hand in the game. Count Tolstov did not think it possible to initiate you, the head of the Moscow police, into the details of the Sobolev case, and yet he trusted Khurtinsky, a dishonourable individual and a criminal to boot. Someone more cunning than the minister has conducted a successful operation of his own here. You were not involved in all of these events, but in the final analysis responsibility will be laid at your door. I am afraid that it will be you who foots the bill for damaged goods. And the most annoying thing of all is that you will still not find out who damaged them and why. In order to understand the true meaning of this intrigue, you have to catch Klonov. Then you will be holding an ace.'

'And if he is a state agent, after all, then I shall find myself rapidly shunted into retirement. In the best case, that is,' Karachentsev objected gloomily.

'Evgeny Osipovich, it is hardly likely in any case that you will be able to hush the matter up, and it would be a sin – not even so much because of Sobolev as because of one terrible question: what mysterious p-power is toying with the fate of Russia? By what right? And what ideas will this power come up with tomorrow?'

'Are you hinting at the Masons?' the general asked in amazement. 'Count Tolstov is a member of a lodge, certainly, and so is Vyacheslav Konstantinovich Plevako, the director of the Department of Police. Well nigh half the influential people in St Petersburg are Masons. But they have no use for political murder; they can twist anyone they like into a ram's horn by using the law.'

'I don't mean the Masons,' said Fandorin, wrinkling up his smooth forehead in annoyance. 'Everybody knows about them. What we have here is an absolutely genuine conspiracy, not the operetta kind. And if we are successful, Your Excellency, you could discover the key to an Aladdin's cave that would take your breath away.'

Evgeny Osipovich shuffled his ginger eyebrows in agitation. It was an enticing prospect, very enticing. And he could show that Judas Vyacheslav Konstantinovich (his so-called comrade) and even Count Tolstov a thing or two. Don't trifle with Karachentsev, don't go trying to make a fool out of him. You've overplayed your hand, gentlemen, now look what a mess you're in! Secret surveillance of a conspirator is all well and good – in a case like that discretion is required. But to allow a national hero to be killed under the very noses of your agents – that is scandalous. You've botched the job, you St Petersburg know-alls! And now you are probably quaking in your armchairs, tearing your hair out. And here comes Evgeny Osipovich offering you the cunning rogue on a plate: here's your villain, take him! Hmm, or perhaps he should be offered up on a plate to someone a little higher? Oh, this was truly momentous business!

In his mind's eye the chief of police pictured prospects of such transcendental glory that they took his breath away. But at the same time he had a sinking feeling in the pit of his stomach. He was afraid.

'Very well,' Karachentsev said tentatively. 'Let us say we have arrested Klonov. But he just clamps his mouth shut and won't say a word. Relying on his patrons to protect him. Then what are we going to do?'

'A perfectly reasonable hypothesis,' said the collegiate assessor with a nod, betraying no sign of his delight that the conversation had moved on from the theoretical stage to the practical. 'I have been thinking about that too. To take Klonov will be very difficult, and to make him talk will be a hundred times harder. Therefore, I have a proposal.'

Evgeny Osipovich pricked up his ears at that, knowing from experience that this bright young man would not propose anything stupid and would take the most difficult part on himself.

'Your people will blockade the Troitsa from all sides, so that the cockroach cannot slip out,' said Fandorin, prodding passionately at the map. 'A cordon here, and one here, and here. Close off all the open courtyards throughout the entire district – fortunately it will be early in the morning and most people will still be sleeping. Around the Troitsa itself just a few of your best agents, three or four men, no more. They must act with extreme caution, and be well disguised in order not to frighten him off, God forbid. Their job is to wait for my signal. I shall go into Klonov's room alone and play a game of confessions with him. He will not kill me straight away, because he will want to discover how much I know, where I come from and what my interest is in all this. He and I will perform an elegant *pas de deux*: I shall part the curtain slightly for him, he will tell me a few frank truths; then I shall have another turn, and then so will he, quite certain that he can eliminate me at any moment. This way Klonov will be more talkative than if we arrest him. And I do not see any other way.'

'But think of the risk,' said Karachentsev. 'If you are right and he is such a virtuoso in the art of murder, then, God forbid …'

Erast Petrovich shrugged his shoulders flippantly: 'As Confucius said, the noble man must bear responsibility for his own errors.'

'Well then, God be with you. This is serious business. They'll either give you a medal or take your head off.' The police chief's voice trembled with feeling. He shook Fandorin's hand firmly. 'Go to your hotel, Erast Petrovich, and catch up on your sleep as well as you can. Do not be concerned about anything: I shall organise the operation in person and make sure everything is absolutely right. When you go to the Troitsa in the morning you will see for yourself how good my lads' disguises are.'

'You are just like Vasilisa the Wise in the fairy tale, Your Excellency,' the collegiate assessor laughed, displaying his white teeth: 'Sleep Ivanushka, morning is wiser than evening.' Well, I really am a little tired, and tomorrow is an important day. I shall be at the Troitsa at precisely six o'clock. The signal at which your men should come to my assistance is a whistle. Until there is a whistle they must not interfere, no matter what ... and if something happens – do not let him get away. That is a p-personal request, Evgeny Osipovich.'

'Don't be concerned,' the general said seriously, still holding the young man by the hand. 'The whole thing will go off like clockwork. I'll detail my most valued agents, and more than enough of them. But take care and don't do anything rash, you daredevil.'

Erast Petrovich had long ago trained himself to wake at the time that he had determined the day before. At precisely five o'clock he opened his eyes and smiled, because the very edge of the sun was just peeping over the window sill and it looked as if someone bald and round-headed was peering in at the window.

As he shaved, Fandorin whistled the aria from *The Love Potion* and even took a certain pleasure in admiring his own remarkably handsome face in the mirror. A samurai is not supposed to take breakfast before battle, and so instead of his morning coffee the collegiate assessor worked with his weights for a while and prepared his equipment thoroughly and unhurriedly. He armed himself to the very fullest extent of his arsenal, for he was facing a serious opponent.

Masa helped his master equip himself, demonstrating an increasingly noticeable concern.

Eventually he could hold back no longer. 'Master, your face is the one you have when death is very near.'

'But you know that a genuine samurai must wake every day fully prepared to die,' Erast Petrovich joked as he put on his jacket of light-coloured wild silk.

'In Japan you always took me with you,' his servant complained. 'I know that I have already failed you twice, but it will not happen again. I swear – if it does may I be born a jellyfish in the next life! Take me with you, master. I beg you.'

Fandorin gave him an affectionate flick on his little nose: 'This time there will be nothing you can do to help me. I must be alone. But in any case, I am not really alone, I have an entire army of policemen with me. It is my enemy who is all alone.'

'Is he dangerous?'

'Very. The same one who tricked you into giving him the briefcase.'

Masa snorted, knitted his sparse eyebrows and said no more.

Erast Petrovich decided to make his way on foot. Ah, how lovely Moscow was after the rain! The freshness of the air, the pink haze of daybreak, the quietness. If he had to die, then let it be on just such a heavenly morning, the collegiate assessor thought, and immediately rebuked himself for his predisposition to melodrama. Walking at a comfortable stroll and whistling as he went, he came out on to Lubyanka Square, where the cabbies were watering their horses at the fountain. He turned on to Solyanka Street and blissfully inhaled the aroma of fresh bread wafting from the open windows of a bakery in a semi-basement.

And now here was his turning. The houses here were a bit poorer, the pavement a bit narrower, and on the final approach to the Troitsa the landscape shed its final remaining picturesque elements: there were puddles in the roadway, rickety, lopsided fences, flaking walls. Erast Petrovich was very pleased that for all his keen powers of observation, he had been unable to spot the police cordon.

At the entrance to the yard he looked at his watch: five minutes to six. Exactly on time. Wooden gates with a crooked sign hanging on them: 'Troitsa Inn'. A jumble of single-storey buildings, every room with a separate entrance. There was number 1, number 2, 3, 4, 5, 6. Number 7 ought to be round the corner, on the left.

If only Klonov would not start shooting straight away, before he was drawn into conversation. Fandorin needed to prepare some phrase that would disconcert him. For instance: 'Greetings from Mademoiselle Wanda.' Or something a bit more complicated than that: 'Are you aware that Sobolev is actually still alive?' The essential thing was not to lose the initiative. And then to follow his intuition. He could feel his trusty Herstahl weighing down his pocket.

Erast Petrovich turned in resolutely at the gates. A yard-keeper in a dirty apron was lazily dragging a broom through a puddle. He glanced at the elegant gentleman out of the corner of his eye and Erast Petrovich winked at him discreetly. A most convincing yardkeeper, no doubt about it. There was another agent sitting over by the gates, pretending to be drunk: snoring, with his cap tipped down over his face. That was pretty good too. Fandorin glanced over his shoulder and saw a fat-bellied woman in a shapeless coat, trudging along the street with a brightly patterned shawl pulled right down over her eyes. That was going a bit too far, the collegiate assessor thought, with a shake of his head. It almost bordered on the farcical.

Apartment number 7 was indeed the first one round the corner, in the inner yard. Two steps leading up to a low porch and 'No. 7' written on the door in white oil paint.

Erast Petrovich halted and took a deep breath, filling his lungs up to the top with air, then breathed it out in short, even jerks.

He raised his hand and knocked gently.

Twice, three times, then twice again.

PART TWO
Achimas

SKYROVSK

1

His father was called Pelef, which in Ancient Hebrew means 'Flight'. In the year of his birth disaster befell the Brothers of Christ, who had lived in Moravia for two hundred years: the emperor revoked the dispensation under which the community was exempted from military service, because he had begun a great war with another emperor and he needed many soldiers.

The community picked up and left in a single night, abandoning their land and houses. They moved to Prussia. The Brothers of Christ did not care what differences the emperors might argue about – their strict faith forbade them to serve earthly masters, to swear an oath of loyalty to them, to take weapons in their hands or to wear a uniform with buttons bearing coats of arms, which are impressions from the seal of Satan. This was why the Brothers' long brown camisoles, the cut of which had scarcely changed in two and a half centuries, had no buttons and only cord fastenings were tolerated.

There were fellow believers living in Prussia. They had come there long, long before, also fleeing from the Antichrist. The king had granted them the possession of land in perpetuity and exempted them from military service on condition that they would drain the boundless Prussian marshes. For two generations the Brothers had struggled with the impassable quagmire until finally the third generation conquered it, and then they had lived a life free of care and hunger on fertile lands rich in humus. They had greeted their fellow believers from Moravia warmly, shared with them everything that they had, and they had all lived a fine, peaceful life together.

Having attained the age of twenty-one years, Pelef married. The Lord gave him a good wife, and at the appointed time she bore him a son. But then the Most High chose to subject his faithful servants to grievous trials. First there was a plague, and many people died, including Pelef's wife and son. He did not complain, even though the colour of life had changed from white to black. But the Most High wanted more than this, and He chose to reveal his love to his favoured ones in the full measure of its rigour and intransigence. A new, enlightened king decreed that in his realm all were equal, and annulled the law granted by that other king who had lived so long, long before. Now even the Jews and the Mennonites and the Brothers of Christ were all obliged to serve in the army and defend their homeland with weapons in their hands. But the Brothers' true homeland did not lie among the drained marshes of Prussia: it lay in the heavens above; therefore the Convention of Spiritual Elders consulted and decided that they must travel to the east, to the lands of the Russian Tsar. There was a community there also, and from that place there sometimes came letters, which travelled for a long time, with trustworthy people, because the state post service was the handiwork of the Evil One. In their letters the fellow believers wrote that the land in those parts was rich, while the authorities were tolerant and content with only small bribes.

They gathered together their goods and chattels, sold what they could and abandoned the rest. Riding in carts for seven times seven days, they arrived in a country with the difficult name of Melitopolstschina. The land there was indeed rich, but twelve young families and the widower Pelef decided that they wanted to travel further, because they had never seen mountains but only read about them in holy books. They could not even imagine how it was possible for the earth to rise up into the firmament of heaven for a distance of many thousand cubits, right up to God's clouds. The young believers wished to see this, and Pelef did not care where he went. He liked to ride on a cart harnessed to bulls through forests and open fields, because this distracted him from thoughts of Rachel and little Ahav, who had remained behind for ever in the damp Prussian soil.

The mountains proved to be exactly as they were described in the books. They were called the Caucasus, and they stretched out along the horizon in both directions as far as the eye could see. Pelef forgot about Rachel and Ahav, because here everything was different, and they even had to walk differently – not like before, but down from above or up from below. In the very first year he married.

This was how it came about: the Brothers of Christ were cutting timber on the only shallow slope, clearing a field for plough land. The local girls watched as the foreign men in the long, funny coats deftly chopped down the centuries-old pines and rooted out the stubborn stumps. The girls laughed and giggled and ate nuts. One of them, fifteen-year-old Thetima, was taken by the looks of the giant with white hair and a white beard. He was big and strong, but calm and kind – not like the men from her *aul*, who were quick-tempered and rapid in their movements.

Thetima had to be christened and wear different clothes: a black dress and white cap. She had to change her name – instead of Thetima she became Sarah. She had to work in the house and on the farm from dawn till dusk, learn a foreign language, and on Sunday she had to pray and sing all day long in the prayer house, which had been built before the dwelling houses. But Thetima was not dismayed by all this, because she was happy with white-haired Pelef and because Allah had not promised woman an easy life.

The following summer, as Sarah-Thetima lay in the torment of childbirth, wild Chechens came down from the mountains, burned the crop of wheat and drove away the cattle. Pelef watched as they led away the horse, the two bulls and three cows and prayed that the Lord would not abandon him and allow his rage to break out. Therefore the father gave his son, whose first cry rang out at the very moment when the greedy tongues of flame began licking at the smoothly planed walls of the prayer house, the name of Achimas, which means 'Brother of Rage'.

The next year the Abreks came back for more booty, but they left with nothing, because a blockhouse now stood on the outskirts of the rebuilt village, and in it there lived a sergeant-major and ten soldiers. For this the brothers had paid the military commander five hundred roubles.

The boy was big when he was born. Sarah-Thetima almost died when he was coming out of her. She could not give birth again, but she did not wish to, because she could not forgive her husband for standing and watching as the brigands led away the horse, the bull and the cows.

In his childhood Achimas had two gods and three languages. His father's God, strict and unforgiving, taught that if someone smote you on the right cheek, then you must offer them the left; that if a man rejoiced in this life, he would weep his fill in the next; that grief and suffering were not to be feared, for they were a boon and a blessing, a sign of the special love of the Most High. His mother's God, whose name was not to be spoken out loud, was kind: he allowed you to feel happy and play games and did not demand that you forgive those who offended you. He could only speak of the kind God in a whisper, when no one but his mother was near, and this meant that his father's God was more important. He spoke in a language that was called 'Die Sprache', which was a mixture of Dutch and German. His mother's God spoke Chechen. Achimas's other language was Russian, which he was taught by the soldiers from the blockhouse. The boy was fascinated by their swords and rifles, but that was forbidden, absolutely forbidden, because the more important God forbade his people even to touch weapons. But his mother whispered: 'Never mind, you can if you want.' She took her son into the forest to tell him stories about the bold warriors from his clan, taught him how to trip people up and punch them with his fist.

When Achimas was seven years old, nine-year-old Melhisedek, the blacksmith's son, deliberately splashed ink on his primer. Achimas tripped him up and punched him on the ear. Melhisedek ran off, crying, to complain.

The conversation with his father was long and painful. Pelef's eyes, as pale and bright as his son's, became angry and sad. Then Achimas had to spend the whole evening on his knees, reading psalms. But his thoughts were directed to his mother's God, not his father's. The boy prayed for his white eyes to be made black like his mother's and her half-brother Chiran. Achimas had never seen his uncle Chiran, but he knew that he was strong, brave and lucky and he never forgave his enemies. His uncle travelled the secret mountain paths, bringing shaggy carpets from Persia and bales of tobacco from Turkey, and ferrying weapons in the opposite direction, out across the border. Achimas often thought about Chiran. He imagined him sitting in the saddle, surveying the slope of a ravine with his sharp eyes to see if border guards were waiting in hiding to ambush him. Chiran was wearing a tall shaggy fur hat and a felt cloak, and behind his shoulder he had a rifle with an ornamental stock.

Achimas spent the day when he reached the age of ten locked into the woodshed from early in the morning. It was his own fault: his mother had secretly given him a small but genuine dagger with a polished blade and a horn handle and told him to hide it. But Achimas had been too impatient: he had gone running out into the yard to try the keenness of the blade and been discovered by his father. Pelef had asked where the weapon had come from, and when he realised that there would be no answer, he had decreed that his son must be punished.

Achimas spent half the day in the shed. He felt wretched because his dagger had been taken away and, as well as that, he was bored. But after midday, when he had also begun to feel very hungry, he suddenly heard shooting and screaming.

The Abrek Magoma and four of his friends had attacked the soldiers, who were laundering their shirts in the stream, because it was their day for washing themselves. The bandits fired a volley from the bushes, killing two soldiers and wounding two more. The other soldiers tried to run to the blockhouse, but the Abreks mounted their steeds and cut all of them down with their swords. The sergeant-major, who had not gone to the stream, locked himself in the strong log house with the small, narrow windows and fired out with his rifle. Taking aim in advance, Magoma waited for the Russian to reload and show himself at the loophole again and shot a heavy, round bullet straight into the sergeant-major's forehead.

Achimas did not see any of this; but with his eyes pressed to a crack between the boards of the shed, he did see a man with a beard and one eye walk into the yard, wearing a white, shaggy fur hat and carrying a long rifle in his hand (it was Magoma himself). The one-eyed man stopped in front of Achimas's parents, who had come running out into the yard, and said something to them – Achimas could not make out what it was. Then the man put one hand on his mother's shoulder and the other under her chin and lifted her face up. Pelef stood there with his lion's head lowered, moving his lips. Achimas realised that he was praying. Sarah-Thetima did not pray; she bared her teeth and scratched the one-eyed man's face.

A woman must not touch a man's face, and therefore Magoma wiped the blood from his cheek and killed the infidel woman with a blow of his fist to her temple. Then he killed her husband too, because after this he could not leave him alive. He had to kill all the other inhabitants of the village as well – it was evidently what Fate had intended for that day.

The Abreks drove away the cattle, heaped all the useful and valuable items into two carts, set fire to the four corners of the village and rode away.

While the Chechens were killing the villagers, Achimas sat quietly in the shed: he did not want them to kill him as well. But when the hammering of hooves and squeaking of wheels had disappeared in the direction of the Karamyk Pass, the boy broke out a board with his shoulder and climbed out into the yard. It was impossible to stay in the shed in any case: the back wall had begun to burn, and grey smoke was already creeping in through the cracks.

His mother was lying on her back. Achimas squatted down and touched the blue spot between her eye and her ear. His mother looked as if she were alive, but instead of looking at Achimas, she was looking at the sky – it had become more important for Sarah-Thetima than her son. But of course: that was where her God lived. Achimas leaned down over his father, but his father's eyes were closed and his white beard had turned completely red. The boy ran his fingers over it, and they were stained red too.

Achimas went into all the farmyards in the village. There were dead men, women and children lying everywhere.

Achimas knew them very well, but they no longer recognised him. The people he had known were not really there any more. He was alone now. Achimas asked first one God and then the other what he should do. But although he waited, he heard no answer.

Everything was burning. The prayer house, which was also the school, gave a rumble and shot a cloud of smoke up into the air: the roof had collapsed.

Achimas looked around him. Mountains, sky, burning earth and not a single living soul. And at that moment he realised that this was the way things would always be from now on. He was alone and he must decide for himself whether to stay or to go, live or die.

He listened carefully to his heart, breathed in the smell of burning and ran to the road that led first upwards, into the mountain plateau, and then downwards, into the large valley.

Achimas walked for the rest of the day and the whole night. At dawn he collapsed at the side of the road. He felt very hungry, but even more sleepy, and he fell asleep. He was woken by hunger. The sun was hanging in the very centre of the sky. He walked on and in the early evening came to a large Cossack village.

At the edge of the village there were long beds of cucumbers. Before this Achimas would never even have thought of taking someone else's property, because his father's God had said: 'Thou shalt not steal'; but now he had no father and no God either, and he sank down on to his hands and knees and began greedily devouring the plump, pimply green fruits. The earth crunched in his teeth and he did not hear the owner, a massive Cossack in soft boots, come stealing up behind him. He grabbed Achimas by the scruff of the neck and lashed him several times with his whip, repeating: 'Don't steal, don't steal.' The boy did not cry and he did not beg for mercy; he just looked up with his white wolf's eyes. This drove the owner into a fury and he set about thrashing the wolf cub as hard as he could – until the boy puked up a green mess of cucumbers. Then the Cossack took Achimas by the ear, dragged him out into the road and gave him a kick to start him on his way.

As he walked along, Achimas thought that, although his father was dead, his God was still alive, and his God's laws were still alive too. His back and shoulders were on fire, but the fire consuming everything inside him was worse.

By a narrow, fast-running stream Achimas came across a big boy about fourteen years old. The little Cossack was carrying a loaf of brown bread and a crock of milk.

'Give me that,' said Achimas and grabbed the bread out of his hand.

The big boy put his crock down on the ground and punched him in the nose. Stars appeared in front of Achimas's eyes and he fell down; then the big boy – he was stronger – sat on top of him and began punching him on the head. Achimas picked up a stone from the ground and hit the little Cossack above his eye. The older boy rolled away, covered his face with his hands and began whimpering. Achimas lifted up the stone to hit him again, but then he remembered that God's law said: 'Thou shalt not kill' – and he stopped himself. The crock had been knocked over during the fight and the milk had been spilled, but Achimas was left with the bread, and that was enough. He walked on along the road and ate and ate and ate, until he had eaten it all to the very last crumb.

He ought not to have listened to God; he ought to have killed the boy. Achimas realised this later, when it was twilight, and he was overtaken by two riders. One was wearing a peaked cap with a blue band and the little Cossack was sitting behind him, with his face bruised and swollen.

'There he is, Uncle Kondrat!' the little Cossack shouted. 'There he is, the murderer!'

That night Achimas sat in a cold cell and listened to the

Cossack sergeant, Kondrat, and the police constable, Kovalchuk, deciding his fate. Achimas had not said a word to them, although they had tried to find out who he was and where he came from by twisting his ear and slapping his cheeks. Eventually they had decided the boy must be a deaf mute and left him in peace.

'What can we do with him, Kondrat Panteleich?' asked the constable. He was sitting with his back to Achimas and eating something, washing it down with some liquid from a jug. 'We can't take him into town, surely? Perhaps we should just keep him here until morning and throw him out on his ear?'

'I'll throw you out on your ear,' replied the sergeant, who was sitting facing him and writing in a book with a goose-quill pen. 'He almost broke the ataman's son's head open. Kizlyar's the place for him, the animal – in prison.'

'But it's a shame to put him in prison, the way they treat little lads in there! You know yourself, Kondrat Panteleich.'

'There's nowhere else to put him,' the sergeant replied sternly. 'We don't have any orphanages round here.'

'I heard that the nuns in Skyrovsk take in orphans.'

'Only girl orphans. Put him in prison, Kovalchuk, put him in prison. You can take him away first thing in the morning. I'll just sort out the papers.'

But when morning came Achimas was already far away. After the sergeant left and the constable lay down to sleep and began snoring, Achimas pulled himself up to the window, squeezed between two thick bars and jumped down on to the soft earth.

He had heard about Skyrovsk before: it was forty versts away in the direction of the sunset.

It turned out that God did not exist after all.

216

Achimas arrived at the Skyrovsk Convent orphanage dressed as a little girl – he had stolen a cotton-print dress and a shawl from a washing line. He told the mother superior, who had to be addressed as 'Mother Pelagia', that he was Lia Welde, a refugee from the village of Neueswelt, which had been devastated by mountain bandits. Welde was his real surname, and Lia was the name of his second cousin, another Welde, a horrid little girl with freckles and a squeaky voice. The last time Achimas had seen her she had been lying flat on her back with her face split in two.

Mother Pelagia stroked the little German girl's cropped white hair and asked: 'Will you take the Orthodox Faith?'

So Achimas became Russian, because now he knew for certain that God did not exist and prayers were nonsense, which meant that the Russian faith was no worse than his father's.

He liked it at the orphanage. They were fed twice a day and they slept in real beds. Only they prayed a lot and his feet kept getting tangled in the hem of his skirt.

On the second day a girl with a thin face and big green eyes came up to Achimas. Her name was Evgenia and her parents had also been killed by bandits, only a long time ago – last autumn. 'What clear eyes you have, Lia. Like water,' she said. Achimas was surprised – people usually found his strangely pale eyes unpleasant. When the sergeant was beating him, he had kept repeating over and over again: 'White-eyed Finnish scum.'

The girl Evgenia followed Achimas everywhere. Wherever he went, she went. On the fourth day she caught Achimas with the hem of his dress pulled up, urinating behind the shed.

So now he would have to run away again, only he didn't know where to go. He decided to wait until they threw him out; but they didn't throw him out. Evgenia had not told anyone.

On the sixth day, a Saturday, they had to go to the bathhouse. In the morning Evgenia came up to him and whispered: 'Don't go; say you've got your colours.'

Achimas did not understand. 'What colours?' he asked.

'It's when you can't go to the bathhouse because you're bleeding and it's unclean. Some of our girls already have them. Katya and Sonya have,' she explained, naming the two oldest wards of the orphanage. 'Mother Pelagia won't check; she's too prudish.'

Achimas did as she said. The nuns were surprised that it had started so early, but they allowed him not to go to the bathhouse. That evening he told Evgenia: 'Next Saturday I'll go away.'

Tears began running down her cheeks. She said: 'You'll need some bread for the road.'

But Achimas did not have to run way, because the following Friday evening, on the day before the next bath day, his uncle Chiran came to the orphanage. He went to Mother Pelagia and asked if there was a little girl here from the German village that had been burned down by the Abrek Magoma. Chiran said that he wanted to talk to the girl and find out how his sister and his nephew had died. Mother Pelagia summoned Lia Welde to her cell and left them there in order not to hear talk of evil.

Chiran was nothing at all like Achimas had imagined him. He was fat-cheeked and red-nosed, with a thick black beard and cunning little eyes. Achimas looked at him with hatred, because he looked exactly like the Chechens who had burned down the village of Neueswelt.

The conversation went badly. The orphan either would not answer questions or answered them in monosyllables, and the look in the eyes under those white lashes was stubborn and hostile.

'They did not find my nephew Achimas,' Chiran said in Russian punctuated with a glottal stutter. 'Perhaps Magoma took him away with him?'

The little girl shrugged.

Then Chiran thought for a moment and took a silver coin necklace out of his bag. 'A present for you,' he said, holding it up. 'Beautiful – all the way from Shemakha. You play with it while I go and ask the mother superior for a night's lodging. I've travelled a long way; I'm tired. I can't sleep out in the open …'

He went out, leaving his weapon on the chair. The moment the door closed behind his uncle, Achimas threw the coin necklace aside and pounced on the heavy sword in the black scabbard with silver inlay work. He tugged on the hilt and out slid the bright strip of steel, glinting icily in the light of the lamp. *A genuine Gurda sword*, thought Achimas, running his finger along the Arabic script.

There was a quiet creak. Achimas started violently and saw Chiran's laughing black eyes watching him through the crack of the door.

'Our blood,' his uncle said in Chechen, baring his white teeth in a smile, 'it's stronger than the German blood. Let us leave this place, Achimas. We'll spend the night in the mountains. Sleep is sweeter under the open sky.'

Later, when Skyrovsk was left behind them, beyond the mountain pass, Chiran put his hand on Achimas's shoulder. 'I'll put you in school to learn, but first I'll make a man of you. You have to take vengeance on Magoma for your father and mother. This you must do, it is the law.'

Achimas realised that this was the true law.

4

They spent the night wherever they could: in abandoned houses, in roadside inns, with his uncle's friends, and sometimes out in the forest, wrapped up in their felt cloaks. 'A man must know how to find food and water and a path through the mountains,' said Chiran, teaching his nephew his own law. 'And he must be able to defend himself and the honour of his family.' Achimas did not know what the honour of his family was. But he wanted very much to be able to defend himself and was willing to study from morning till night.

'Hold your breath and imagine a fine ray of light stretching out of the barrel. Feel for your target with that ray,' Chiran taught him, breathing down the back of his neck and adjusting the position of the boy's fingers where they clutched the gunstock. 'You don't need strength. A rifle is like a woman or a horse: give it affection and understanding.'

Achimas tried to understand his rifle; he listened to its high-strung iron voice, and the metal began droning into his ear: 'A little more to the right, more – and now fire.'

'*Vai!*' said his uncle, clicking his tongue and rolling up his eyes. 'You have the eye of an eagle! To hit a bottle at a hundred paces! And that is how Magoma's head will be shattered!'

Achimas did not want to fire at the one-eyed man from a hundred paces. He wanted to kill him in the same way as he had killed Thetima – with a blow to the temple – or, even better, slit his throat, as Magoma had slit Pelef's.

Shooting with a pistol was even easier. 'Never take aim,' his uncle told him. 'The barrel of the pistol is a continuation of your hand. When you point at something with your finger, you don't take aim, do you? You just point where you need to. Think of the pistol as your sixth finger.'

Achimas pointed the long metal finger at a walnut lying on a tree-stump, and the nut shattered in a spray of fine crumbs.

Chiran did not give his nephew a sword, telling him that his arm and shoulder had to grow first; but he gave him a dagger on the very first day and told him never to part with it, saying: 'When you swim naked in the stream, hang it round your neck.' As time went by, the dagger became a part of Achimas's body, like a wasp's sting. He could cut dry twigs for the campfire with it, bleed a deer that he had shot, whittle a fine sliver of wood to pick his teeth with after eating the deer meat. When they halted for a rest and he had nothing to do, Achimas would throw his dagger at a tree from a standing, sitting or lying position. He never wearied of this pastime. At first he could only stick the knife into a pine tree, then into a young beech, then into any branch on the beech.

'A weapon is good,' said Chiran, 'but a man must be able to deal with his enemy even without a weapon: with his fists, feet, teeth – it doesn't matter what. The important thing is that your heart must be blazing with holy fury; it will protect you against pain, strike terror into your enemy and bring you victory. Let the blood rush to your head, so that the world is shrouded in red mist, and then nothing will matter to you. If you are wounded or killed – you will not even notice. That is what holy fury is.' Achimas did not argue with his uncle, but he did not agree with him. He did not want to be wounded or killed. In order to stay alive, you had to see everything, and fury and red mist were no use for that. The boy knew that he could manage without them.

One day, when it was already winter, his uncle returned from the tavern in a cheerful mood. A reliable man had informed him that Magoma had arrived with his loot from Georgia and was feasting at Chanakh. That was close – only two days' journey.

At Chanakh, a large bandit village, they stayed with a

friend of his uncle. Chiran went to find out how things stood and came back late, looking dejected. He said things were difficult. Magoma was strong and cunning. Three of the four men who had been with him in the German village had also come and were feasting with him. The fourth – bandy-legged Musa – had been killed by Svans. Now his place had been taken by Djafar from Nazran. That meant there were five of them.

That evening his uncle ate well, prayed and lay down to sleep. Before he fell asleep he said: 'At dawn, when Magoma and his men are tired and drunk, we shall go to take our revenge. You will see Magoma die and dip your fingers in the blood of the one who killed your mother.'

Chiran turned his face to the wall and fell asleep immediately, and the boy cautiously removed a small green silk bag from around his neck. It contained the ground root of the poisonous irganchai mushroom. His uncle had told him that if the border guards caught you and put you in a windowless stone box where you could not see the mountains and the sky, you should sprinkle the powder on your tongue, muster up as much spit as you could and swallow it. Before you could repeat the name of Allah five times, there would be nothing left in the cell except your worthless body.

Achimas took the baggy trousers, dress and shawl of their host's daughter. He also took a jug of wine from the cellar and sprinkled the contents of the little bag into it.

In the tavern there were men sitting and talking, drinking wine and playing backgammon, but Magoma and his comrades were not there. Achimas waited. Soon he saw the son of the tavern-keeper take some cheese and flat bread cakes into the next room and he realised that Magoma was there.

When the tavern-keeper's son went away, Achimas went in and set his jug on the table without raising his eyes or saying a word.

'Is the wine good, girl?' asked the one-eyed man with the

black beard whom he remembered so well.

Achimas nodded, walked away and squatted down in the corner. He did not know what to do about Djafar from Nazran. Djafar was still very young – only seventeen years old. Should he tell him that his horse was agitated and chewing on its tethering post, so that he would go out and check? But Achimas remembered the little Cossack and realised that he should not do that. Djafar owed him nothing, but he would die anyway, because that was his fate.

Djafar was the first to die. He drank from the jug with all the rest and almost instantly slumped forward, banging his head down on the table. A second Abrek started laughing, but his laughter turned into a hoarse croak. A third said: 'There's no air in here,' clutched at his chest and fell. 'What's wrong with me, Magoma?' asked the fourth Abrek, stumbling over his words; then he slid off the bench, curled up into a ball and stopped moving. Magoma himself sat there without speaking, and his face was as scarlet as the wine spilled across the table.

The one-eyed man looked at his dying comrades, then stared at the patiently waiting Achimas. 'Whose daughter are you, girl?' Magoma asked, forcing out the words with an effort. 'Why do you have such white eyes?'

'I am not a girl,' replied Achimas. 'I am Achimas, son of Thetima. And you are a dead man.'

Magoma bared his yellow teeth, as if he were greatly pleased by these words, and began slowly pulling his sword with the gilded handle out of its scabbard; but he could not pull it out: he began wheezing and tumbled over on to the earthen floor.

Achimas stood up, took his dagger out from under the girl's dress and, gazing into Magoma's single unblinking eye, he slit his throat – in a rapid, gliding movement, as his uncle had taught him. Then he dipped his fingers in the hot, pulsing blood.

EVGENIA

1

At the age of twenty Achimas Welde was a polite, taciturn young man who looked older than his years. For the visitors who came to the famous springs of Solenovodsk for the good of their health, and to local society in general, he was simply a well-brought-up young man from a rich merchant's family, a student from Kharkov University on a long vacation to restore his health. But among *people in the know*, who shared their knowledge with very few others, Achimas Welde was regarded as a serious and reliable individual who always finished what he began. *Those in the know* referred to him behind his back as 'Aksahir', which means the 'White Wizard'. Achimas accepted the sobriquet as his due – he really was a wizard, though his wizardry had nothing to do with magic: everything was determined by careful calculation, a cool head and skilful psychology.

His uncle had bought him a student's identity card for the Kharkov Imperial University for three hundred and fifty paper roubles – not an expensive price. The grammar-school certificate, with the heraldic seal and genuine signatures, had been more expensive. After Chanakh, Chiran had sent his nephew to school in the quiet town of Solenovodsk, paid for a year in advance and gone away into the mountains. Achimas had lived in the boarding school with the other boys, whose fathers were serving in distant garrisons or leading caravans west to east, from the Black Sea to the Caspian, or north to south, from Rostov to Erzerum. Achimas was not really close to any of his peers – he had nothing in common with them. He knew what they did not know and were unlikely ever to learn. This gave rise to a certain difficulty while Achimas was studying in the preparatory class at the grammar school. A stocky, broad-shouldered boy by the name of Sykin, who had subjugated the entire boarding school to his rule of fear, took a dislike to the pale-eyed 'Finn', and the other boys followed his lead and joined in the persecution. Achimas tried to put up with it, because he would not be able to deal with them all on his own, but it only kept getting worse. One evening in his bedroom he discovered that his pillowcase had been smeared all over with cow dung and he realised that something had to be done.

Achimas considered all the possible solutions to his problem. He could wait for his uncle to return and ask for his help. But he did not know when Chiran would be coming back. And it was extremely important to him that the spark of respectful interest that had appeared in his uncle's eyes after Chanakh should not be extinguished.

He could try to give Sykin a beating, but he was unlikely to succeed: Sykin was older, stronger, and he would not fight one against one.

He could complain to his tutor. But Sykin's father was a colonel, and Achimas was a nobody, the nephew of some wild mountain tribesman, who had paid for his board and lessons at the grammar school in Turkish gold coins out of a leather pouch.

The simplest and most correct solution would be for Sykin to die. Achimas racked his brains and thought up a neat and tidy way in which this could be done.

While Sykin delighted in kicking the 'Finn', tipping drawing pins down the back of his collar and blowing spit-balls of chewed paper at him out of a little tube, Achimas was waiting for May to come. Summer began in May, and the pupils began running to the River Kumka to bathe. From the beginning of April, when the water was still scaldingly cold, Achimas began learning to dive. By the beginning of May he could already swim under water with his eyes open, had studied the bottom of the river and could hold his breath for an entire minute without any difficulty. Everything was ready.

It all turned out to be very simple, just as he had imagined it. Everybody went to the river. Achimas dived, tugged Sykin down by the leg and dragged him under the water. Achimas was holding a piece of string, the other end of which was firmly attached to a sunken log. Chiran had once taught his nephew a Kabardinian knot – it is tied in a second, and there is no way that anyone who does not know the secret can possibly untie it.

In one swift movement Achimas tied the knot over his enemy's calf, surfaced and climbed out on to the bank. He counted to five hundred and then dived again. Sykin was lying on the bottom. His mouth was open, and so were his eyes. Achimas looked inside himself and discovered nothing apart from calm satisfaction with a job well done. He untied the knot and surfaced. The boys were shouting and splashing each other with water. It was some time before Sykin was missed.

After that particular difficulty was resolved, life in the boarding house improved greatly. Without Sykin as ringleader there was no one left to persecute the pale-eyed 'Finn'. Achimas moved on from one class to the next. He was neither a good pupil, nor a poor one. He sensed that in his life not very much of all this knowledge would be required. Chiran came only rarely, but each time he took his nephew away into the mountains for a week or two – to hunt and spend the night under the starry sky.

When Achimas was about to finish sixth class, a new difficulty arose. Outside the town, three versts along the Stavropol highway, there was a bawdy house to which the men who had come to take the waters repaired in the evenings. And for some time Achimas, who at the age of sixteen had shot up and broadened in the shoulders so that he could quite easily be taken for a twenty-year-old, had also been making the three-verst journey. This was real life, not learning chunks of Ancient Greek from the *Iliad*.

One day Achimas was unlucky. In the public hall downstairs, where the painted girls drank lemonade while they waited to be taken upstairs, he ran into an inspector from the grammar school, Collegiate Counsellor Tenetov – wearing a frock coat and a false beard. Tenetov realised from the boy's glance that he had been recognised and, although he said nothing to Achimas, from that day on he conceived a fierce hatred for the white-haired sixth-class pupil. It soon became clear what the inspector was aiming at: he was determined to fail Achimas at the summer examinations.

Staying back for a year would be shameful and boring. Achimas started thinking about what he ought to do.

If it had been one of the other teachers instead of Tenetov, Chiran would have paid a bribe. But Tenetov did not take bribes and he was very proud of it. He had no need to take them: two years earlier the collegiate counsellor had married a merchant's widow and taken as his dowry a hundred thousand roubles and the finest house in the entire town.

It was clearly not possible to improve relations with Tenetov: one glance at Achimas was enough to set the inspector trembling with fury.

Achimas ran through all the possible solutions and settled on the most certain.

That spring there were bandits operating in Solenovodsk; wicked men would approach a late stroller, stab him in the heart and take his watch, wallet and – if he had any – rings. The word was that it was the 'Butchers', a famous gang from Rostov, working away from home.

One evening, when the inspector was walking home from Petrosov's restaurant along the dark, deserted street, Achimas walked up to him and stabbed him in the heart with his dagger. He took a watch on a gold chain and a wallet from the fallen man, then threw the watch and the wallet in the river and kept the money – twenty-seven roubles – for himself.

He thought the difficulty had been resolved, but things turned out badly. The maidservant from the next house had seen Achimas walking quickly away from the scene of the murder and wiping a knife with a bunch of grass. She informed the police and Achimas was put in a cell.

It was fortunate for him that his uncle happened to be in town at the time. His uncle threatened the maidservant that he would cut off her nose and ears, and she went to the superintendent of police and said that she had identified the wrong man by mistake. Then Chiran himself went to the superintendent and paid him five thousand roubles in silver – everything that he had amassed from his smuggling – and the prisoner was released.

Achimas felt ashamed. When Chiran sat Achimas down to face him, he could not look his uncle in the eye. Then he told him the whole truth – about Syskin and about the inspector.

After a long silence, Chiran sighed. He said: 'Allah finds a purpose for every creature. No more studying, boy; we're going to do real work.'

And a different life began.

Previously Chiran had imported contraband goods from Turkey and Persia and sold them to middlemen. Now he began transporting them further afield himself – to Ekaterinodar, Stavropol, Rostov and the market at Nizhny Novgorod. His goods sold well, because Chiran did not ask a high price. He and his buyer would shake hands and drink to the deal. Then Achimas would catch up with the buyer, kill him and bring the goods back again – until the next time they were sold.

Their most profitable trip of all was to Nizhny Novgorod in 1859, when they sold one and the same lot of lambskin – ten bales – three times over: the first time for one thousand three hundred roubles (Achimas overtook the merchant and his bailiff on the forest road and killed both of them with his dagger); the second time for one thousand one hundred roubles (the young gentleman barely had time to grunt in surprise when the polite student travelling with him thrust the double-edged blade into his liver); the third time for one thousand five hundred roubles (and by a stroke of good luck they found almost three thousand roubles more in the Armenian's belt).

Achimas killed calmly and was only distressed if the death was not instantaneous. But that rarely happened – he had a sure hand.

Things continued in this way for three years. During this time Prince Baryatinsky captured the Imam Shamil and the great war in the Caucasus came to an end. Uncle Chiran married a girl from a good mountain-tribe family, then took a second wife from a poorer family – according to the official documents she was his ward. He bought a house in Solenovodsk with a big garden, in which peacocks strutted and screamed. Chiran became fat and developed a taste for drinking champagne on his veranda and talking philosophy. He was too lazy now to travel into the mountains for contraband, so *people in the know* brought the goods to him themselves. They would sit drinking tea and arguing at length over prices. If the negotiations proved difficult, Chiran sent for Achimas, who entered with a polite touch of his hand to his forehead and gazed silently at the obstinate trader with his pale, still eyes. It was very effective.

One day in autumn, the day after the serfs were liberated in Russia, Chiran's old friend Abylgazi came to tell him that a new man had appeared in Semigorsk, a baptised Jew whose name was now Lazar Medvedev. He had come the year before to take the cure for his stomach, taken a liking to the place and stayed. He had married a beautiful girl without a dowry, built a house with columns up on a hill and bought three springs. Now all the visitors drank only Medvedev's water and bathed only in his baths, and they also said that every week he sent ten thousand bottles of mineral water to Moscow and St Petersburg. This was interesting, but by far the most interesting thing was that Lazar had an iron room. The baptised Jew did not trust the banks – and he was wise not to do so, of course. He kept all his immense fortune in the basement under his house, where he had a chamber in which all the walls were made of iron, with a door so thick that not even a shot from a canon could break it in. It was hard to get into such a room, said Abylgazi, and therefore he was not asking to be paid in advance for telling Chiran all this; he was prepared to wait as long as necessary, and the fee he was asking was modest: only ten kopecks from each rouble that Chiran managed to take.

'An iron room – that is very difficult,' said Chiran, nodding solemnly. He had never heard of such rooms before. 'And, therefore, if Allah assists me, you will receive five kopecks from each rouble, respected friend.'

Then he called his nephew, recounted old Abylgazi's story

to him and told him: 'Go to Semigorsk and see what this iron room is like.'

To see what the iron room was like proved easier than Achimas had expected.

He went to Medvedev's house, dressed in a grey morning coat and matching grey top hat. While still in his hotel he had sent on his card, which was printed with words in gold lettering:

Chiran Radaev Trading House

AFANASY PETROVICH WELDE

PARTNER

Medvedev had replied with a note saying that he had heard of the trading house of the respected Chiran Radaev and requested an immediate visit. So Achimas had set out to the beautiful new house on the outskirts of the town, which stood at the top of a steep cliff and was surrounded on all sides by a tall stone wall. It was a fortress, not a house. A place where you could sit out a siege.

When Achimas entered the oak gates, this impression became even stronger: there were two sentries with carbines strolling about in the yard, and the sentries were wearing military uniform, only without shoulder straps.

His host was bald, with a bulging forehead, a firm pot belly and shrewd black eyes. He sat the young man down at the table and offered him coffee and a cigar. After ten minutes of polite, leisurely conversation about politics and the price of wool, he asked how he could be of assistance to the estimable Mr Radaev.

Achimas then expounded the business proposal that he had invented as an excuse for his visit. 'An exchange of mineral waters between Solenovodsk and Semigorsk ought to be arranged,' he said. 'Your springs heal the stomach and our springs heal the kidneys. Many visitors come here to take a cure for both. So that these people will not have to travel a hundred versts over bumpy mountain roads, why should the firm of Medvedev not set up a shop in Solenovodsk, and the firm of Radaev set up a shop in Semigorsk? It would be profitable for both of us.'

'A good idea,' the baptised Jew said approvingly. 'Very good. Only there are many bandits on the road. How shall I transport my earnings here from Solenovodsk?'

'Why bring them here at all?' Achimas asked in surprise. 'You can put them in the bank.'

Medvedev stroked the thin wreath of curly hair surrounding his bald patch and smiled: 'I don't trust the banks, Afanasy Petrovich. I prefer to keep my money at home.'

'But it is dangerous to keep it at home: you could be robbed,' said Achimas, shaking his head in disapproval.

'They won't rob me,' said Medvedev, with a cunning wink. 'In the first place, I have retired soldiers, lifelong professionals, living here in the house, they guard the yard day and night in shifts. But I have even more confidence in my armour-plated room. No one except me can get into it.'

Achimas was about to ask what this room was like, but before he had a chance his host himself made the suggestion: 'Perhaps you would like to take a look?'

While they were walking down into the basement (it had a separate entrance from the yard), Medvedev told the story of how an engineer from Stuttgart had build him a repository for his money with a steel door eight inches thick. The door had a numerical lock with an eight-digit combination which only he, Medvedev, knew, and he changed it every day.

When they entered the underground premises, in which a

kerosene lamp was burning, Achimas saw a steel wall and a forged metal door with round rivets.

'A door like that can't be forced or blown open,' his host boasted. 'The governor of the town himself keeps his savings with me, and the chief of police, and the local merchants. I charge them well for the security, but it is still worth people's while. This is safer than any bank.'

Achimas nodded respectfully, interested to hear that it was not only Medvedev's own money that was kept in the iron room.

At this point, however, the baptised Jew said something unexpected: 'So please tell your respected uncle, may God grant him health and prosperity in his business affairs, that he need not trouble himself any more. I am a new man in the Caucasus, but I know about those people who I need to know about. Convey my humble greetings to Chiran Muradovich and my gratitude for taking an interest in me. But that idea about the water is a good one. Was it yours?' He slapped the young man on the shoulder patronisingly and asked him to pay another visit – on Thursdays the cream of Semigorsk society gathered at the house.

The fact that the baptised Jew had proved to be clever and well informed was not in itself a difficulty. The difficulty arose on Thursday, when Achimas, having accepted the invitation, arrived at the house at the top of the cliff in order to study the disposition of the rooms.

So far the plan had been conceived as follows: overpower the guards at night, hold a knife to the householder's throat and see which he loved more: the iron room or his own life. It was a simple plan, but Achimas did not really like it. Firstly, it could not be managed without additional helpers. And secondly, there were people who loved their money more than their lives, and the young man's intuition told him that Lazar Medvedev was one of them.

At that Thursday's gathering there was a large number of

guests, and Achimas was hoping that later, when they took their seats at table and drank their fill, he would be able to slip away unnoticed and look round the house. But matters never reached that point, because the aforementioned difficulty manifested itself at the very beginning of the evening.

When the host introduced his guest to his wife, Achimas merely noted that old Abylgazi had not lied when he said she was young and attractive: ash-blonde hair with a golden tinge and beautifully shaped eyes. She was called Evgenia Alexeevna. But Madam Medvedev's charms had no connection with his business and, therefore, having pressed his lips to the slim white hand, Achimas walked through into the drawing room and took up a position in the farthest corner, by the door curtain, from where he had a good view of the entire company and the door that led into the inner rooms.

It was there that the hostess sought him out. She walked up to him and asked quietly: 'Is that you, Lia?' Then she answered herself. 'It is you. No one else has eyes like that.'

Achimas said nothing, overcome by a strange stupefaction that he had never experienced before, and Evgenia Alexeevna continued in a rapid, fitful half-whisper: 'What are you doing here? My husband says that you are a bandit and a murderer, that you wish to rob him. Is it true? Don't answer; it is all the same to me. How I waited for you. And now, when I stopped waiting and married, you suddenly turn up. Will you take me away from here? You don't mind that I didn't wait until you came, do you; you're not angry? You remember me, don't you? I'm Evgenia from the orphanage at Skyrovsk.'

Suddenly Achimas had a vivid recollection of a scene that he had not remembered even once in all those years: Chiran carrying him away from the orphanage, and a thin little girl running silently after the horse. He thought that at the end he had heard her shout: 'Lia, I'll wait for you!'

This difficulty could not be resolved by the usual means. Achimas did not know how to explain the strange behaviour of Medvedev's wife. Perhaps this really was the love that they wrote about in novels? But he did not believe in novels and had not touched a single one since grammar school. This was alarming and uncomfortable.

Achimas left the soirée without giving Evgenia Alexeevna any answer. He mounted his horse and rode back to Solenovodsk. He told his uncle about the iron room and the difficulty that had arisen. Chiran thought for a moment and said: 'For a wife to betray her husband is a bad thing. But it is not for us to untangle the artful designs of Fate; we should simply follow its wishes. And it is Fate's wish for us to enter the iron room with the help of Medvedev's wife – this much is clear.'

4

Chiran and Achimas walked up the hill to Medvedev's house in order to avoid alerting the sentries with the clattering of hooves. They left their horses in a copse at the bottom of the cliff. Down below in the valley, there were only scattered points of light – Semigorsk was already sleeping. Transparent clouds skudded across the greenish-black sky, and the night constantly changed from bright to dark and back again.

The plan had been drawn up by Achimas. Evgenia would open the small garden gate at the special knock that they had agreed. They would creep through the garden into the yard, stun both sentries and go down into the basement. Evgenia would open the armoured door, because her husband had shown her how to do it, and he wrote down the number of the combination on a piece of paper that he hid behind the icon in the bedroom. He was afraid of forgetting the combination, which would mean that he had to take up the stonework of the floor – there would be no other way of getting into the iron room. They would not take everything – only as much as they could carry away. Achimas would take Evgenia with him.

While they had been making their arrangements, she had suddenly looked into his eyes and asked: 'Lia, you won't deceive me, will you?'

He did not know what to do with her. His uncle gave him no advice. 'When the moment comes to decide, your heart will tell you what to do,' said Chiran. But they took only three horses: one for Chiran, one for Achimas and one for the spoils. The nephew watched silently as his uncle led the chestnut, the black and the bay out of the stable, but he said nothing.

As he walked along beside the white wall without making a sound, Achimas wondered what those words meant: his heart would tell him. As yet his heart was silent.

The garden gate opened immediately on oiled hinges that did not squeak. Evgenia was standing in the opening, wearing a tall fur hat and a felt cloak. She had prepared for a journey.

'Walk behind us, woman,' Chiran whispered, and she moved aside to let them through.

Medvedev had six retired soldiers. They stood guard in pairs, changing every four hours.

Achimas pressed himself up against an apple tree and began watching what was happening in the yard. One sentry was sitting on a bollard beside the gates, dozing with his arms round his rifle. The other was striding at an even pace from the gates to the house and back: thirty steps to the house, thirty steps back.

Of course, the sentries would have to be killed – when Achimas had agreed in his conversation with Evgenia that he would only stun them and tie them up, he had known that the promise could not be kept.

Achimas waited until the wakeful sentry halted to light

his pipe, ran up behind him without a sound in his soft leather shoes and struck him slightly above the ear with his brass knuckles. Brass knuckles were a quite indispensable item when someone had to be killed very quickly. Better than a knife, because a knife had to be withdrawn from the wound, and that cost an extra second.

The soldier did not cry out, and Achimas caught the limp body in his arms, but the second sentry was sleeping lightly and he stirred and turned his head at the sound of crunching bone.

Achimas pushed the dead body away and in three massive bounds he was already at the gates. The soldier opened his dark mouth, but he had no time to call out. The blow to his temple flung his head backwards and it smashed against the oak boards with a dull thud.

Achimas dragged one dead man into the shadows and positioned the other one as he had been sitting before. He waved his hand, and Chiran and Evgenia came out into the moonlit yard. The woman glanced at the seated corpse without speaking and wrapped her arms round her shoulders. Her teeth were chattering rapidly. Now, by the light of the moon, Achimas could see that under her cloak she was wearing a Circassian coat with cartridge belts and she had a dagger at her waist.

'Go, woman, open the iron room,' Chiran prompted her.

They walked down the steps into the basement; Evgenia opened the door with a key. Down below, one wall of the square chamber was made of steel. Evgenia lit a lamp. She took hold of the wheel on the armoured door and began turning it to the right and the left, glancing at a piece of paper. Chiran looked on curiously, shaking his head. Something clicked in the door and Evgenia tried to pull the massive slab outwards, but the steel was too heavy for her.

Chiran moved the woman aside, grunted with the effort and the door began swinging out, reluctantly at first, but then more and more freely.

Achimas took the lamp and went inside. The room was smaller than he had imagined: about six paces wide and fifteen paces long. It contained trunks, bags and files of papers.

Chiran opened one trunk and immediately slammed it shut again – it was full of silver ingots. You couldn't take many of those; they were too heavy. But the bags were filled with jangling gold coins, and the uncle smacked his lips in approval. He began stuffing bags inside his coat and then heaping them up on his cloak.

Achimas was more interested in the files, which turned out to contain share certificates and bonds. He began selecting the ones that came from mass issues and had the highest face value. Shares in Rothschild, Krupp and the Khludov factories were worth more than gold, but Chiran was a man of the old breed and he would never have believed that.

Grunting again, he loaded his heavy bundle on to his back and glanced round regretfully – there were still so many bags left – then sighed and started towards the door. Achimas had a thick wad of securities inside his coat. Evgenia had not taken anything.

When Chiran began climbing up the shallow steps to the yard, there was a sudden volley of shots. Chiran tumbled backwards and slid down the steps head first. His face was the face of a man overtaken by sudden death. His cloak came untied and the gold scattered downwards, glittering and jingling.

Achimas went down on all fours, scrambled up the steps and peeped out cautiously. He was holding a long-barrelled American Colt revolver, loaded with six bullets.

The yard was empty. His enemies had taken up a position on the veranda of the house and could not be seen from below. But it was also unlikely that they could see Achimas, because the steps of the staircase were concealed by intense darkness.

'One of you is dead!' Lazar Medvedev's voice called out. 'Who is it – Chiran or Achimas?'

Achimas took aim at the voice, but did not fire – he did not like to miss.

'Chiran – it was Chiran,' the baptised Jew shouted triumphantly. 'Your figure, Mr Welde, is slimmer. Come out, young man. You have nowhere to go. Do you know what electricity is? When the door of the repository opens, an alarm bell sounds in my bedroom. There are four of us here – me and three of my soldiers. I've sent the fourth one for the superintendent. Come out; let's stop wasting time! The hour is getting late!'

They fired another volley – evidently trying to frighten him. The hail of bullets rattled against the stone walls.

Evgenia whispered from behind him: 'I'll go out. It's dark, I'm wearing a cloak; they won't understand. They'll think it's you. They'll break cover and you can shoot them all.'

Achimas pondered her suggestion. He could take Evgenia with him, now that there was a free horse. It was just a pity that they would never reach the copse. 'No,' he said, 'they are too afraid of me; they will start shooting immediately.'

'They won't,' Evgenia replied. 'I'll raise my hands high in the air.'

She stepped lightly over Achimas's recumbent form and walked out into the yard, her hands thrown out to the sides as if she were afraid of losing her balance.

When she had taken five steps a ragged volley of shots rang out. Evgenia was thrown backwards. Four shadows cautiously climbed down from the dark veranda and approached the motionless body. *I was right*, thought Achimas, *they did fire*. And he killed all four of them.

In the years that followed he rarely remembered Evgenia. Only if some chance occurrence happened to remind him of her.

Or in his dreams.

MAÎTRE LICOLLE

1

At the age of thirty Achimas Welde was fond of playing roulette. It was not a matter of money; he earned money, plenty of it – far more than he was able to spend – by other means. He enjoyed defeating blind chance and exercising control over the elemental force of numbers. It seemed to him that the spinning roulette wheel, with its pleasant clicking sound and bright gleam of metal and polished mahogany, followed laws of its own that no one else knew. Yet precise calculation, restraint and control of the emotions were just as effective here as they were in every other situation with which Achimas was familiar; therefore the basic law must be the same one he had known since his childhood. The underlying unity of life through all its infinite variety of forms – this was what interested Achimas above all else. Each new confirmation of this basic truth made the regular rhythm of his heartbeat just a little faster.

His life included occasional prolonged periods of idleness, when he had to find something to occupy his time. The English had come up with an excellent invention when they devised the so-called *hobby*, and Achimas had two of them: roulette and women. He preferred the very finest of women, the most genuine kind: *professional women*. They were undemanding and predictable; they understood that there were rules that had to be observed. Women were also infinitely varied, while still remaining the one, eternally unchanging Woman. Achimas ordered the most expensive from an agency in Paris – usually for a month at a time. If he happened to find a very good one, he would extend the contract for a second term, but never for longer than that – that was his rule.

For the last two years he had been living in the German resort of Ruletenburg, because here, in the jolliest town in Europe, both of his hobbies could be pursued without any difficulty. Ruletenburg was like Solenovodsk: it also had mineral springs, and a leisured, idle throng of people in which no one knew anyone or took any interest in anyone else. All that was missing was the mountains, but the overall impression of impermanence, of *artificiality*, was precisely the same. Achimas thought of the resort as a neat and accurate model of life made to a scale of 1:500 or 1:1000. A man lived five hundred months on this earth, or, if he were lucky, a thousand; but people came to Ruletenburg for one month. That is, the average lifetime of a resort resident had a length of thirty days and that was the precise rate at which the generations succeeded each other here. Everything was accommodated within this period: the joy of arrival, the process of habituation, the first signs of boredom, the sadness at the thought of returning to that other, bigger world. In the resort there were brief romances and tempestuous but short-lived passions, ephemeral local celebrities and transient sensations. But Achimas was a constant spectator at this puppet theatre, for, unlike all the other residents, he himself had determined the length of his own lifetime here.

He lived in one of the finest apartments in the Hotel Kaiser, the preferred accommodation of Indian nabobs, Americans who owned gold mines and Russian grand dukes travelling incognito. His intermediaries knew where to find him. When Achimas accepted a commission, his apartment was kept for him and sometimes it would stand empty for weeks, or even months – depending on the complexity of the matter he had to deal with.

Life was pleasant. Periods of exertion alternated with periods of recreation, when his eyes were gladdened by the dense green of baize and his ears by the regular clicking of the roulette wheel. All around him passions raged, heightened and intensified by their reduced time scale: respectable gentlemen blanching and blushing by turns, ladies swooning, someone shaking the final gold coin out of his wallet with trembling hands. Achimas never wearied of observing this fascinating spectacle. He himself never lost, because he had a System.

The System was so simple and obvious that it was amazing that no one else used it. They quite simply lacked patience, restraint and the ability to control their emotions – all the things that Achimas possessed in abundance. All that was needed was to bet on one and the same sector, constantly doubling up the stake. If you had a lot of money, sooner or later you would get back all that you had lost and win something into the bargain. That was the entire secret. But you had to place your bet on a large sector, not a single number. Achimas usually preferred a third of the wheel.

He walked over to the table where they played without any limits on stakes, waited until the ball had failed to land in one or another of the thirds for six times in a row, and then began to play. For his first bet he staked a single gold coin. If his third did not come up, he staked two gold coins on it the next time, then four, and then eight and so on until the ball eventually landed where it should. Achimas could raise his stake to absolutely any level – he had more than enough money. On one occasion, shortly before the previous Christmas, the third on which he was staking his money had failed to come up for twenty-two spins in a row – the six preliminary spins and sixteen on which he had placed bets. But Achimas had never doubted his eventual success, for each failure improved his chances.

As he tossed chips with ever longer strings of zeros on to the table, he had recalled an incident from his American period.

It was 1866, and he had received a substantial commission from Louisiana. He had to eliminate the commissioner of the Federal Government, who was interfering with the sharing-out of various concessions by the carpetbaggers – enterprising adventurers from the North, who came to the conquered South with nothing but an empty travelling bag and left in their own personal Pullman cars.

Those were troubled times in Louisiana and human life was cheap. But the money offered for eliminating the commissioner was good, because it was very difficult to get close to him. The commissioner knew that he was being hunted down, and he behaved wisely, never leaving his residence at all. He slept, ate and signed all his documents within the same four walls. His residence was guarded day and night by soldiers in blue uniforms.

Achimas put up at a hotel located only three hundred paces from the commissioner's residence – he was unable to obtain anything closer. From his room he could see the window of the commissioner's study. Every morning at precisely half past seven his target opened the curtains. This action took three seconds – not enough time to get a decent aim at such a great distance. The window was divided into two parts by the broad upright of the frame. An additional difficulty was caused by the fact that when the commissioner drew back the curtains, he stood either slightly to the right or slightly to the left of the upright. There would be only one chance to get off a shot – if Achimas missed, then he could forget about the job: he wouldn't get a second opportunity. Absolute certainty was imperative.

There were only two possibilities: the target would be either on the right or on the left. Then let it be the right, Achimas decided. What difference did it make? The long-barrelled rifle with its stock gripped tight in a vice was trained

243

on a spot six inches to the right of the upright, at exactly the height of a man's chest. The most certain way would have been to set up two rifles, aiming to the right and the left, but that would have required an assistant, and in those years (and still even now, except in cases of extreme need) Achimas preferred to manage without help from anyone else.

The bullet was a special one that exploded on impact, unfolding its petals to release the essence of ptomaine within. It was enough for even the tiniest particle to enter the blood to render the very slightest of wounds fatal.

Everything was ready. On the first morning the commissioner approached the window from the left. Likewise on the second. Achimas did not try to hurry things. He knew that tomorrow or the next day the curtains would be pulled back from the right, and then he would press the trigger.

It was as if someone had cast a spell on the commissioner. From the very day that the sights were set, for six days running he parted the curtains from the left, not once from the right.

Achimas decided that his target must have established a routine, and he shifted his sights to a spot six inches left of centre. Then, on the seventh day, the commissioner made his approach from the right! And again on the eighth day, and the ninth.

That was when Achimas realised that in a game played against blind chance the most important thing was not to get flustered. He waited patiently. On the eleventh morning the commissioner made his approach from the required direction, and the job was done.

Likewise last Christmas, at the seventeenth spin of the wheel, when his stake had risen to sixty-five thousand, the ball had finally landed where it should, and the house had paid out almost two hundred thousand to Achimas. His winnings had covered all the stakes that he had lost and left him slightly ahead of the game.

That September morning in 1872 had begun as usual. Achimas and Azalea had breakfasted alone together. She was a slim, loose-limbed Chinese girl with a remarkable voice like a small crystal bell. Her real name was something different, but in Chinese it meant 'Azalea' – or so the agency had informed him. She had been sent to Achimas on approval, as a sample of the oriental goods that had only recently begun to appear on the European market. The price asked was only half the usual, and if Monsieur Welde wished to return the girl early, his money would be reimbursed. In exchange for such preferential conditions the agency had requested him, as a connoisseur and regular client, to give his authoritative opinion both on Azalea's abilities and the prospects for yellow goods in general.

Achimas was inclined to award her the highest possible rating. In the mornings, when Azalea sang quietly to herself as she sat in front of the Venetian mirror, Achimas felt a strange tightness in his chest, and he did not like the feeling. The Chinese girl was simply too good. What if he were to grow accustomed to her and not wish to let her go? He had already decided that he would send her back ahead of time. But he would not demand a refund and he would give the girl excellent references, in order not to spoil her career.

Following his invariable custom, that afternoon Achimas entered the gaming hall at two fifteen precisely. He was wearing a jacket the colour of cocoa with milk, check trousers and yellow gloves. Attendants came dashing up to take the regular client's cane and top hat. Herr Welde was a very familiar figure in the gambling houses of Ruletenburg. At first his manner of gambling had been accepted begrudgingly as an inevitable evil, but then they had noticed that the constant doubling-up of the stake practised by the taciturn blond with the cold, pale eyes inflamed the passions of his neighbours at the table. Achimas had then become a most welcome guest.

He drank his usual coffee with liqueur and looked through the newspapers. England and Russia could not reach an agreement over customs duties. France was delaying the payment of reparations and in response Bismarck had sent a threatening diplomatic note to Paris. In Belgium the trial of the Pied Piper of Brussels was just about to begin.

After he had smoked a cigar, Achimas went over to table number 12, where they were playing for high stakes.

There were three players and a grey-haired gentleman simply sitting there, nervously clicking the lid of his gold watch. Catching sight of Achimas, he fastened his eyes on him like limpets. Experience and intuition told Achimas that he was a client. His presence here was not accidental; he was waiting. But Achimas gave the gentleman no sign – let him make the first approach.

Eight and a half minutes later the required third of the wheel had been selected – the last one, from 24 to 36. Achimas staked a *Friedrichsdor*. He won three. The grey-haired man carried on watching. His face was pale. Achimas waited for another eleven minutes before the next sector was determined. He staked a gold coin on the first third, from 1 to 12. Number 13 came up. The second time he staked two gold coins. Zero came up. He staked four gold coins. Number 8 came up. He had won 12 *Friedrichsdors* and was now five gold coins to the good. Everything was proceeding as usual, with no surprises.

At this point the grey-haired man finally stood up. He came over and enquired in a low voice: 'Mr Welde?' Achimas nodded, continuing to follow the spinning of the wheel. 'I have come to you on the recommendation of the Baron de —' The grey-haired man named Achimas's intermediary in Brussels. He was becoming more and more agitated and lowered his voice to a whisper as he explained: 'I have a very important matter to discuss with you—'

'Would you perhaps care to take a stroll?' Achimas interrupted, slipping the gold coins into his purse.

The grey-haired gentleman proved to be Leon Fechtel, the owner of a banking house famous throughout Europe: Fechtel and Fechtel. The banker had a serious problem. 'Have you read about the Pied Piper of Brussels?' he asked when they were seated on a bench in the park.

All the newspapers were full of the story: the maniac who had been kidnapping little girls had been captured at last. The *Petit Parisien* said that the police had arrested 'Mr F', the owner of a suburban villa outside Brussels. The gardener reported that he had heard the muffled groans of children coming from the basement at night. When the police entered the house in secret, in the course of their search they had discovered a concealed door in the basement, and behind it things so horrible that the newspaper claimed 'paper could never bear the description of this monstrous scene'. The scene was, however, described in lurid detail in the very next paragraph. In several oak barrels the police had discovered pickled parts of the bodies of seven of the little girls who had disappeared in Brussels and its environs during the previous two years. One body was still quite fresh and it bore the traces of indescribable tortures. In recent years fourteen girls aged from six to thirteen had disappeared without trace. On several occasions people had seen a respectably dressed gentleman with thick black sideburns offering a seat in his carriage to little flower-girls or cigarette-girls. On one occasion a witness had actually heard the man with sideburns urging the eleven-year-old flower-girl Lucille Lanoux to bring her entire basket of flowers to his house and promising that if she did, he would show her a mechanical piano that played wonderful melodies all on its own. This was the occasion that had prompted the newspapers to stop calling the monster 'Blue Beard' and christen him 'the Pied Piper of Brussels', by analogy with the fairy-tale Pied Piper who had lured the children of Hamelin away with the music of his magical flute.

Concerning the prisoner, Mr F, it was reported that he was a member of the gilded youth from the very highest social circles, that he did indeed possess thick black sideburns, and that he had a mechanical piano at his villa. The motive for the crimes was clear, wrote the *Evening Standard*: it was perverted sensual gratification in the manner of the Marquis de Sade. The date and location of the court hearing had already been determined: the 24 September in the little town of Merlain, only half an hour's journey from the Belgian capital.

'I have read about the Pied Piper of Brussels,' said Achimas, with an impatient glance at the banker, who had said nothing for a long time. Wringing his plump hands spangled with rings, Fechtel exclaimed: 'Mr F is my only son, Pierre Fechtel! He is destined for the gallows! Save him!'

'You have been misinformed about the nature of my activities. I do not save life; I take it away,' said Achimas, smiling with his thin lips. The banker whispered fervently: 'They told me that you work miracles. If you will not take this job, then there is no hope. I implore you. I will pay. I am a very rich man, Mr Welde, very rich.'

After a pause Achimas asked: 'Are you certain that you even want such a son?'

Fechtel senior replied without hesitation – it was clear that he had already asked himself that question: 'I have no other son and never shall have. He was always rather wild as a boy, but he has a good heart. If I can only extricate him from this business, he will learn a lesson that will last the rest of his life. I have been to see him in prison. He is so frightened!'

Then Achimas asked the banker to tell him about the forthcoming trial.

The 'rather wild' heir was to be defended by two extremely expensive lawyers. The line of defence was based on proving that the accused was insane. However, according to the banker, the chances of a favourable verdict from the medical experts were slim – they were so obdurately set against the boy that they would not even agree to an 'unprecedentedly high fee'. This latter circumstance had apparently astounded Fechtel senior more than any other.

On the first day of the trial the lawyers had to announce whether their client admitted his guilt. If he did, sentence would be pronounced by a judge; if he did not, the verdict would be delivered by a jury. If the conclusion of the psychiatric examination was that Pierre Fechtel was responsible for his own actions, the defence lawyers had recommended choosing the first route.

The inconsolable father explained angrily that the hangmen in the Ministry of Justice had deliberately chosen Merlain for the trial – three of the girls who had disappeared had lived in the little town. 'There can be no fair trial in Merlain,' the banker complained. The population of the small town was in a state of high fever. At night they lit bonfires around the court building. The day before yesterday a crowd had tried to break into the prison and tear the suspect to pieces – they had had to treble the guard.

Mr Fechtel had conducted secret negotiations with the judge, and he had proved to be a reasonable man. If the decision were to depend on him, the boy would receive a life sentence. But that would not really mean much. The general prejudice against the Pied Piper of Brussels was so great that the public prosecutor would be sure to appeal against such a verdict and a second court hearing would be scheduled.

'You are my only hope, Mr Welde,' the banker concluded. 'I have always regarded myself as a man for whom nothing is impossible. But in this instance I am powerless, and it is a matter of my own son's life.'

Achimas looked curiously at the millionaire's crimson

face. It was clear that here was a man unused to displaying emotions. For instance now, at a moment of the most powerful agitation, his thick lips were extended in an absurd smile and there was a tear dribbling from one of his eyes. It was interesting: a face unused to moulding itself for the expression of feeling was unable to portray a mask of grief.

'How much?' asked Achimas. Fechtel swallowed convulsively.

'If the boy remains alive, half a million francs. French francs, not Belgian,' he added hastily when his companion gave no reply.

Achimas nodded and an insane glow lit up the banker's eyes. It was exactly the same glow that lit up the eyes of the madmen who staked all their money on zero at the roulette wheel. This glow had a name: it was called 'just maybe'. The only difference was that this was clearly not all the money that Mr Fechtel possessed. 'And if you succeed ...' The banker's voice trembled. 'If somehow you should succeed not only in saving Pierre's life but also in giving him back his freedom, you will receive a million.'

Achimas had never been offered such a huge fee. Following his usual habit, he translated the sum into pounds sterling (almost thirty thousand), American dollars (seventy-five thousand) and roubles (more than three hundred thousand). It was a very large amount indeed.

Narrowing his eyes slightly, Achimas said slowly and clearly: 'Your son must refuse the psychiatric examination, declare himself not guilty and demand trial by jury. And you must dismiss your expensive lawyers. I shall find a new lawyer.'

Etienne Licolle's only regret was that his mother had not lived to see this day. How she had dreamed of the time when her boy would qualify as an advocate and array himself in the black robe with the rectangular white tie! But paying for his studies at the university had consumed all her widow's pension, and skimping on doctors and medicine had shortened her life: she had died the previous spring. Etienne had gritted his teeth and refused to be defeated. Dashing from one lesson to another in the afternoon and poring over his textbooks at night, he had completed his studies after all – and the coveted diploma with the royal seal had been duly awarded. His mother could be proud of her son.

His fellow graduates and new-fledged advocates had invited him to go to a restaurant in the country – to 'christen the gown'; but Etienne had refused. He had no money for revels, but more importantly than that, on a day like this he wanted to be alone. He walked slowly down the broad marble staircase of the Palais de Justice, where the solemn ceremony had taken place. The entire city, with its spires, towers and statues on rooftops, lay spread out below him, at the foot of the hill. Etienne stopped and admired the view, which seemed to be offering him a hospitable welcome: as if Brussels had opened its arms wide to embrace the new Maître Licolle, enticing him with the prospect of every possible kind of surprise – for the most part, of course, pleasant ones.

Who, though, could dispute the fact that a diploma was only the beginning? Without useful connections and acquaintances he would not be able to find good clients. And in any case he lacked the means required to establish his own firm. He would have to work as an assistant to Maître Wiener or Maître Van Gelen. But that was not so bad – at least they would pay him some kind of salary.

Etienne Licolle pressed the folder containing the diploma with the red seal against his chest, turned his face towards the warm September sunshine and squeezed his eyes tight shut in an excess of emotion.

He was surprised in this absurd position by Achimas Welde.

Achimas had picked the young lad out while the hall was echoing to the boring, pompous speeches of the award ceremony. The youth's appearance was ideally suited to requirements: pleasant-looking, but no Adonis; slim, with narrow shoulders; wide, honest eyes. When he stepped up to pronounce the words of the oath, his voice had proved ideally suited too: clear, boyish, trembling with excitement. But best of all, it was immediately obvious that he was no rich gentleman's son, but genuine plebeian stock and a hard worker.

While the interminable ceremony continued, Achimas had been able to make enquiries. His final doubts had been laid to rest; this was indeed ideal material. The rest could not have been simpler. He walked up to the thin youth without making a sound and then cleared his throat.

Etienne started, opened his eyes and turned round to find himself facing a gentleman in a travelling coat with a walking cane who had appeared out of nowhere. The stranger's eyes were regarding him with keen seriousness. They were a rather unusual colour too: very pale.

'Maître Licolle?' the man enquired with a slight accent. It was the first time Etienne had been addressed as 'Maître' and he liked the feeling.

As was only to be expected, the boy was at first exultant to learn that he was being offered a case, but when the client's name was mentioned he was horrified. Achimas remained silent while he indignantly objected, gesticulating wildly and declaring that he would never defend that villain, that monster, for anything. He only spoke after Licolle had

252

exhausted his reserves of indignation and finally muttered: 'Anyway, I could not cope with a case like that. You see, monsieur, I am still very inexperienced, I have only just received my diploma.'

Now it was Achimas's turn. He said: 'Do you wish to work for a pittance for twenty or even thirty years, earning money and glory for other lawyers? Yes, some time about 1900 you may manage to scrape together enough centimes to set up in practice for yourself, but by that time you will be a bald, toothless failure with a sick liver and life will already have squeezed you dry. Your vital juices will have oozed out through your fingers drop by drop, Maître, in exchange for those hard-earned centimes. But I am offering you far more than that right here and now. Now, while you are still twenty-three, you can earn good money and make a big name for yourself – even if you should happen to lose the case. In your profession a name is even more important than money. Certainly, your reputation will be tinged with scandal, but that is better than wasting your entire life as someone else's errand-boy. You will receive enough money to open your own firm. Many people will hate you, but there will be others who will appreciate the courage of a young lawyer who was not afraid to stand up against the whole of society.'

Achimas waited for a minute, to give the lad time to grasp what he had said. Then he moved on to the second stage of his argument, which, as he understood matters, ought to prove more decisive for the boy's response. 'Or could it be that you are simply afraid? Have I not just heard you swear "to uphold justice and a man's right to legal representation regardless of all obstacles and pressures"? Do you know why I chose you out of all the graduates? Because you are the only one who pronounced those words with genuine feeling. Or, so at least, it seemed to me.'

Etienne said nothing, horrified as he felt himself being swept away by a raging torrent that was quite impossible to resist.

'And most important of all,' said the stranger, lowering his voice suggestively, 'Pierre Fechtel is innocent. He is no Pied Piper; he is the victim of a confluence of circumstances and the zealous determination of the police. If you do not intervene, an innocent man will go to the scaffold. Yes, it will be very difficult for you. You will be overwhelmed with insults; no one will want to testify in defence of a "monster". But you will not be alone. I shall be helping you. I shall remain in the shadows, your eyes and ears. I am already in possession of certain items of evidence which, while they do not entirely confirm Pierre Fechtel's innocence, do at least cast doubt on the prosecution's case. And I shall obtain more.'

'What items of evidence?' Etienne asked in a weak voice.

4

At least three hundred people were crammed into the little hall of the Merlain Municipal Court, designed to hold only a hundred, and there were even more people thronging the corridor, standing under the windows and waiting on the square outside.

The appearance of Public Prosecutor Renan was greeted with a thunderous ovation. But when they brought in the felon – a pale, thin-lipped man with close-set black eyes and sideburns that had once been well groomed but had now grown ragged and uneven – a deadly silence fell in the hall, followed by such thunderous uproar that the judge, Maître Viksen, broke his bell trying to call the assembly to order.

The judge called out the counsel for the defence and for the first time everyone noticed the puny young man whose advocate's robes were clearly too large for him. First turning pale, then bright red, Maître Licolle babbled a few barely audible words and then, in reply to the judge's impatient question as to whether the accused admitted his guilt, he suddenly squeaked quite clearly: 'No, Your Honour!'

The hall erupted indignantly once again. 'And such a decent-looking young man too,' shouted one of the women.

The trial continued for three days.

On the first day the witnesses for the prosecution testified. First came the policemen who had found the terrible room and then interrogated the accused. According to the commissioner of police, Pierre Fechtel had trembled and given contradictory answers to questions, been quite unable to explain anything and offered the police huge sums of money if they would leave him alone.

The gardener who had reported suspicious screams to the police did not appear in court, but his presence was not necessary. The public prosecutor summoned witnesses who provided vivid descriptions of Fechtel's debauchery and depravity and his constant demands for the youngest and slenderest girls in brothels. The madam of one of these bawdy houses told the court how the accused had tortured her 'little daughters' with red-hot curling tongs, but the poor little things had put up with it because the villain paid them a gold coin for every burn.

The hall burst into applause when a man who had seen the flower-girl Lucille Lanoux ride away in the carriage (her head had later been found in a barrel with the eyes gouged out and the nose cut off) identified Fechtel as the very same man who had described the miraculous abilities of his mechanical piano in such glowing terms.

The jurors were presented with items of evidence: implements of torture, a photographic camera and photographic plates discovered in the concealed room. There was also testimony from Monsieur Brühl, who had taught Pierre Fechtel the art of taking photographs three years previously.

In conclusion the jurors were shown an album of photographic cards found in the ghastly basement. These photographs were not shown to the public and the journalists, but one of the jurors fainted and another vomited.

The advocate Licolle sat there with his head bowed like a student at a lecture, assiduously taking down all the testimony in a notebook. When he was shown the photographs, he turned as white as chalk and swayed on his feet.

'That's right, take a good look, you puny weakling!' someone shouted from the hall.

That evening there was an unpleasant incident at the end of the session: as Licolle was leaving the hall, the mother of one of the murdered girls came up to him and spat in his face.

On the second day the witnesses were questioned by the counsel for the defence. He asked the police if they had shouted at the accused.

'No, we gave him a hug and a kiss,' the commissioner replied sarcastically, to approving laughter from the hall.

The advocate asked the witness to the abduction of Lucille Lanoux if he had seen the full face of the man with whom the flower-girl had driven away.

No, he had not, the witness replied, but he did remember the sideburns very clearly.

After that Maître Licolle wanted to know what kind of photographs Pierre Fechtel had taken in the course of his amateur studies. It turned out that he used to take photographs of still lives, landscapes and newborn kittens. (This announcement was greeted with whistling and jeering, after which the judge ordered half of the spectators to be removed from the courtroom.)

In conclusion the counsel for the defence demanded that the main witness, the gardener, must be brought into court, and the session was adjourned for an hour.

During the break in proceedings the local curé approached Licolle and asked if he believed in our Lord Jesus Christ.

Licolle replied that he did, and that Jesus had taught charity to sinners.

When the proceedings continued, an inspector declared that the gardener could not be found and no one had seen him for the last three days. The counsel thanked him politely and said that he had no more questions for the witnesses.

Then came the public prosecutor's opportunity to shine. He conducted his interrogation of the accused brilliantly and Pierre Fechtel was unable to give a satisfactory answer to a single question. When he was shown the photographic cards, he stared at them for a long time, swallowing hard. Then he said that he had never seen them before. When he was asked if the 'Weber and Sons' camera belonged to him, after whispered consultation with his counsel, he said: Yes, it did, but he had lost interest in photography a year ago, put the camera away in the attic and not laid eyes on it since then. When the question: Could the accused look the parents of the little girls in the eye? was asked, it evoked thunderous applause, but it was withdrawn on the insistence of the defence.

When Etienne got back to his hotel that evening, he saw that his things had been thrown out into the street and were lying in the mud. Blushing painfully, he crawled around on all fours, gathering up his long drawers with darned patches and soiled shirt-fronts with paper collars.

A large crowd gathered to enjoy this spectacle and shower the 'mercenary swine' with abuse. When Etienne had finally packed his things into his new travelling bag, purchased especially for this trip, the local tavern-keeper came up to him, slapped him resoundingly across both cheeks and declared in a voice of thunder: 'You can add that to your fee!'

Since none of the other hotels in Merlain would take Licolle in, the mayor's office provided him with lodgings in a little house used by the guard at the railway station – the old guard had retired a month before and had not yet been replaced.

In the morning there were several words scrawled in charcoal on the white-painted wall of the little house: 'You will die like a dog!'

On the third day Public Prosecutor Renan surpassed himself. He delivered a magnificent denunciatory speech that lasted from ten in the morning until three in the afternoon. People in the hall sobbed and cursed freely. The members of the jury, all of them respectable men who paid at least five hundred francs in taxes each year, sat with their faces set in sullen scowls.

The counsel for the defence was pale and they noticed in the hall that several times he seemed to glance enquiringly at his client, but the latter was sitting with his shoulders hunched up, his head lowered and his face in his hands. When the public prosecutor demanded a death sentence, the public sprang to its feet as one man and began chanting 'String-him-up, string-him-up!' Fechtel's shoulders began twitching spasmodically and he had to be given smelling salts.

The defence was given the floor after the break, at four o'clock in the afternoon.

For a long time Licolle was not even allowed to speak – people deliberately scraped their feet, creaked their chairs and blew their noses loudly. The advocate waited, bright crimson in his trepidation, clutching a crumpled sheet of paper covered with the neat handwriting of a star pupil. But once he began speaking, Etienne did not glance at the sheet of paper even once. This is his speech, word for word, as it was printed in the evening editions of the newspapers with the most disparaging of commentaries:

Your Honour, gentlemen of the jury, my client is a weak, spoiled and even depraved man. But that is not what you are judging him for ... One thing is clear: in the home of my client, or rather in a secret room in the basement, the existence of which *might or might not* have been known to Pierre Fechtel, a terrible crime was committed. A whole series of crimes. The question is: who committed them? [A loud voice: 'Yes, that's a real riddle.' Laughter in the hall.] The defence has its own explication of events. I surmise that the murders were committed by the gardener Jean Voiture, who reported the mysterious screams to the police. This man hated his master because he had reduced his salary for drunkenness. There are witnesses who can be called if necessary – they will confirm this fact. The gardener has an awkward, quarrelsome character. Five years ago his wife left him, taking the children with her. It is well known that people of the same type as Voiture often become morbidly sensitive and develop aggressive tendencies. He knew the lay-out of the house very well and could easily have installed a secret room without his master's knowledge. He could also have taken the camera with which Monsieur Fechtel had become bored down from the attic and learned how to use it. He could have taken his master's clothes during his frequent absences. He could have glued on false sideburns, providing easy identification. You must surely agree that if Pierre Fechtel had committed these heinous crimes, he would long ago have rid himself of such a distinctive feature. Please understand me correctly, gentlemen of the jury: I am not stating that the gardener did all of this – only that he *could* have done it all. But the main question is: why has the gardener, who set the entire investigation in motion, disappeared so suddenly? There can be only one explanation: he was scared that in court his true involvement in the affair would be revealed, and then he would suffer the punishment that he deserves ... [Up to this point Maître Licolle had spoken smoothly and rather impressively, but now he suddenly began stammering out his words.] And what I would like to say to you is this: there is a great deal that is unclear in this story. To be quite honest, I myself do not know if my client is guilty. But while there remains even the shadow of a doubt – and, as I have just demonstrated to you, there are indeed many doubts concerning this whole business – it is absolutely impermissible to send a man for execution. In the faculty of law I was taught that it is better to acquit a guilty man than to condemn an innocent one ... That is all that I wish to say, gentlemen.

The speech was over at ten minutes past four. The advocate resumed his seat, wiping the sweat from his brow.

There were jeers here and there in the hall, but all in all the speech received a mixed reception. The reporter from *Le Soir* heard (and afterwards reported in his newspaper) the famous advocate Jan Van Brevern say to his neighbour, also a lawyer: 'In essence the boy is right. From the higher perspective of essential jurisprudence. But in this particular case that changes nothing.'

The judge rang his bell, and shook his head reproachfully, with a glance at the lamentable counsel for the defence: 'I had assumed that Maître Licolle's address would continue until the end of today's session and then all of tomorrow morning. But now I find myself in some difficulty ... I therefore declare today's session at an end. I shall sum up for the jury tomorrow morning, following which you, gentlemen, will withdraw to consider your verdict.'

But the next morning there was no session of the court.

During the night there was a fire. The railway guard's hut was torched and Maître Licolle was burnt alive, because the door had been locked from the outside. The inscription 'You will die like a dog' was left on the smoked-blackened wall – no one had taken the trouble to remove it. No witnesses were found to this act of arson.

The trial was interrupted for several days. Certain intangible but quite definite shifts in public opinion took place. The newspapers reprinted Maître Licolle's final address to

the court, this time without any scoffing remarks, accompanied by sympathetic commentaries from respected lawyers.
Touching reports appeared concerning the short and difficult
life of a young man from a poor family, who had studied at
university for five years in order to be an advocate for just
over a week. His portrait gazed out at readers from the front
pages: a boyish face with large, honest eyes.

The Lawyers' Guild published a declaration in defence of
free and objective jurisprudence, which should not be held to
ransom by an emotionally imbalanced public baying for
vengeance.

The concluding session was held on the day after the
funeral.

To begin with, at the judge's suggestion, everyone present
honoured the memory of Etienne Licolle with a minute's
silence. They all stood – even the parents of the dead girls. In
his summing-up, Judge Viksen recommended the jurors not
to bow to external pressure and reminded them that in capital cases a majority of two thirds of the jurors was required
for a 'guilty' verdict to be carried.

The gentlemen of the jury consulted for four and a half
hours. Seven of the twelve said 'not guilty' and demanded
that the judge release Pierre Fechtel for lack of evidence.

A difficult task had been carried off very neatly. The gardener's body was lying in a pit of quicklime, and as for the boy
lawyer, he had died without any suffering or fear: Achimas
had killed him in his sleep before he set fire to the railway
guard's hut.

THE TROITSA INN

1

In the year of his fortieth birthday Achimas Welde began wondering whether it was time for him to retire.

No, he had not become blasé about his work – it still gave him the same satisfaction as ever and set his impassive heart beating slightly faster. Nor had he lost his touch – on the contrary, he was now at the very peak of his maturity and prowess. The reason lay elsewhere: there was no longer any point to his work.

In itself, the process of killing had never given Achimas any pleasure, apart from on those very rare occasions when personal scores were involved. The situation with the killings was simple. Achimas existed alone in the universe, surrounded on all sides by the most varied forms of *alien life* – plants, animals and people. This life was in constant motion: it came into existence, changed and was broken off. It was interesting to observe its metamorphoses, and even more interesting to influence them through his own actions. But trample down life in one sector of the universe, and it changes the overall picture very little: life fills in the breach that has been formed with quite wonderful tenacity. Sometimes life seemed to Achimas like a tangled, overgrown lawn through which he was trimming the line of his fate. Precision and careful deliberation were required, in order not to leave any blades of grass sticking up in the wrong place, while not touching any more blades than was necessary in order to maintain the smoothness and evenness of the line. Glancing back at the path he had travelled, what Achimas saw was not trimmed grass but the ideal trajectory of his own movement.

Until now there had been two stimuli for his work: finding solutions and earning money. However, Achimas no longer found the first of these as fascinating as he once had: for him there remained few truly difficult problems that were genuinely interesting to solve.

The second stimulus had also begun to make less and less sense. A numbered account in a Zurich bank contained very nearly seven million Swiss francs. A safe in Baring's Bank in London held securities and gold ingots worth seventy-five thousand pounds sterling.

How much money did a man need, if he did not collect works of art or diamonds, if he was not building a financial empire or consumed by political ambition?

Achimas's outlays had stabilised: two or three hundred thousand francs a year went on ordinary expenses, and the upkeep of his villa cost another hundred thousand. The price of the villa had been paid in full the year before last, all two and a half million francs of it. It was expensive, of course, but a man who was getting on for forty had to have a house of his own. A man of a certain psychological constitution might not have a family, but he had to have a house.

Achimas was satisfied with his residence, a house that suited the character of its owner perfectly. The small villa of white marble stood on the very edge of a narrow outcrop of rock overlooking Lake Geneva. On one side there was free, open space, and on the other – cypress trees. Beyond the cypress trees there was a high stone wall, and beyond that a sheer descent into a valley. Achimas could sit for hours on his veranda overhanging the smooth surface of the water, looking at the lake and the distant mountains. The lake and the mountains were also forms of life, but without the constant agitation intrinsic to fauna and flora. It was hard to affect this form of life in any way; Achimas had no control over it and therefore it commanded his respect.

In the garden, among the cypresses, stood a secluded retreat, a white house with small round towers at its corners, in which the Circassian woman Leila lived. Achimas had brought her here from Constantinople the previous autumn. He had long ago abandoned the Parisian agencies and the monthly rotation of professional women – the moment had arrived when they no longer seemed so very different to Achimas. He had developed his own taste.

This taste required that a woman should possess a beauty and natural grace that were not cloying, and not be too talkative. She should be passionate without being forward, not too inquisitive and – above all – she should possess a female instinct that made her unerringly sensitive to a man's mood and desires.

Leila was almost ideal. She could spend the whole day from morning till evening combing her long black hair, singing and playing herself at backgammon. She was never sulky, never demanded attention. In addition to her native tongue she knew only Turkish and Chechen, which meant that Achimas was the only one who could talk to her and she communicated with the servants by means of gestures. If he wanted to be entertained, she knew numerous amusing stories from the life of Constantinople – Leila had formerly lived in the harem of the grand vizier.

Recently Achimas had accepted work only rarely: two or three times a year, either for very big money or for some special reward. For instance, in March he had received a secret commission from the Italian government: to seek out and eliminate the anarchist Gino Zappa, known as 'the Jackal', who was planning to kill King Umberto. The terrorist was regarded as extremely dangerous and quite impossible to catch.

In itself the job had proved to be rather simple (the Jackal had been traced by Achimas's assistants, and he had only needed to take a trip to Lugano and press the trigger once); but the fee he had been promised was quite outstanding. Firstly, Achimas received an Italian diplomatic passport in the name of the Cavaliere Welde, and secondly, he was granted the option of buying the island of Santa Croce in the Tyrrhenian Sea. If Achimas should decide to realise this option and buy this small scrap of land, in addition to the title of the Count of Santa Croce he would also be granted the right of extra-territoriality, which was particularly attractive. He could be his own sovereign, his own police, his own court. Hmm.

Out of curiosity Achimas made the trip to take a look at the island and was captivated. There was nothing remarkable about it, nothing but rocks, a couple of olive groves and a bay. It was possible to walk round the entire shoreline of the island in one hour. For the last four hundred years no one had lived here and the only visitors had been occasional fishermen seeking to replenish their supplies of fresh water.

The title of count held little attraction for Achimas, although in travelling around Europe a fine-sounding title could sometimes have its uses. But an island of his own?

There he could be alone with the sea and the sky. There he could create his own world, belonging to nobody but him. It was tempting. To withdraw into peaceful retirement. To spend his time sailing and hunting mountain goats, to feel time stand still and fuse with eternity.

No more adventures; he was not a boy any more.

Perhaps he could even start a family?

But the idea of a family was not really serious – it was more of a mental exercise. Achimas knew that he would never have a family. He was afraid that, once deprived of his solitude, he would begin to fear death – as other people feared it. As he was, he had no fear of death at all. It was the foundation underpinning the sturdy edifice that went by the name of Achimas Welde. If a pistol should happen to misfire, or a victim prove too cunning and lucky, then Achimas would die. That was all there was to it. It simply meant that nothing would exist any longer. One of the ancient philosophers – he thought it was Epicurus – had said all there was to say on that score: while I exist, death does not exist; and when it comes, I shall not exist.

Achimas Welde had lived long enough and seen enough of the world. One thing he had never known was love, but that was because of his profession. Attachment made you weak and love made you completely defenceless. As he was, Achimas was invulnerable. What leverage is there against a man who fears nothing and holds nothing and nobody dear?

But an island of his own – that was worth thinking about.

There was only one difficulty with the idea: finance. The redemption of his option would cost a lot of money; it would consume all of his funds in the banks in Zurich and London. How would he pay for the equipping and appointment of his count's fiefdom? He could sell his villa, but that would probably not be enough. Somewhat more substantial capital would be required.

Perhaps he should simply put these idle fantasies out of his head?

Yet an island was more than your own cliff, and the sea was more than a lake. How was it possible to rest content with a little if you were offered more?

These were the reflections with which Achimas was occupied when he received a visit from a man in a mask.

First his butler Archibald brought him a calling card – a piece of white cardboard with a gold coronet and a name in ornamental Gothic script: *Baron Eugenius von Steinitz*. A brief note in German was attached to the card: '*Baron von Steinitz requests Mr Welde to receive him today at ten o'clock in the evening on a confidential matter.*'

Achimas noted that the top edge of the sheet of paper had been torn off. Apparently the prospective visitor did not wish Achimas to see his monogram, which meant that he might perhaps be a genuine 'von', but he was certainly not Steinitz.

The visitor arrived at precisely ten o'clock, not a single minute earlier or later. With such punctuality, it could safely be presumed that he was indeed German. The baron's face was concealed by a velvet half-mask, for which he apologised politely, citing the extremely delicate nature of his business. Achimas noted nothing special about von Steinitz's appearance – light hair, neat sideburns, blue eyes with a troubled expression. The baron was dressed in a cloak, top hat, starched shirt, white tie and black tails.

They sat on the veranda with the lake glittering below them in the moonlight. Von Steinitz did not even glance at the tranquil view; instead he scrutinised Achimas continually through the openings in his operetta mask, seeming in no hurry to begin the conversation. He crossed his legs and lit a cigar.

Achimas had seen all of this many times before and he waited calmly for his visitor to make his mind up to begin.

'I am applying to you on the wecommendation of Mr Du Vallet,' the baron eventually began. 'He asked me to give you his most humble gweetings and to wish you the utmost … no, it was the most complete pwospewity.'

Achimas acknowledged the name of his Paris intermediary and his password with a silent nod.

'I have come on a matter of immense importance and absolute confidentiality,' von Steinitz declared, lowering his voice.

'Precisely the kind of matter that is usually brought to me,' Achimas remarked impassively.

Until this point the conversation had been conducted in German, but now the visitor suddenly switched to Russian, which he spoke perfectly and correctly, with only that distinctive burring of the r's.

'The work has to be carried out in Wussia, in Moscow. The job has to be done by a foweigner who knows the Wussian language and is familiar with Wussian customs. You are ideally suited. We have made enquiwies about you.'

Made enquiries? And who might 'we' be? Achimas did not like the sound of that. He was on the point of breaking off the conversation immediately, but then his lisping visitor said: 'For performing this difficult and delicate task, you will weceive a million Fwench fwancs in advance, and on the completion of our … mm … contwact, a million woubles.'

That changed matters. A sum like that would be a worthy consummation of a brilliant professional career. Achimas recalled the whimsical outline of Santa Croce when the island first hove into view on the horizon – exactly like a bowler hat lying on green velvet.

'You, sir, are an intermediary,' he said coolly, speaking in German. 'And it is my principle only to deal directly with the client. My terms are as follows. You immediately transfer the advance payment to my account in Zurich. After that I meet with the client at a place of his choosing and he recounts all the ins and outs of this matter to me. If for some reason I do not find the terms acceptable, I shall return half of the advance.'

'Baron Eugenius von Steinitz' indignantly fluttered a pampered hand (an old sapphire glinted on the middle finger), but Achimas had already risen to his feet.

'I will only speak with the principal. If I cannot, you must find another man for the job.'

3

The meeting with the client took place in St Petersburg, on a quiet little street to which Achimas was delivered in a closed phaeton. The carriage wound through the streets this way and that for a long time, with its blinds completely obscuring the windows. This precaution made Achimas smile.

He made no attempt to remember the route, although he knew the geography of Russia's capital intimately – in times past he had fulfilled several serious contracts here. In any case, Achimas had no need to peep stealthily through the crack beside the blind and count the turns in the road. He had taken steps to ensure his own safety: firstly by arming himself in an appropriate fashion, and secondly by bringing four assistants with him.

They had travelled to Russia in the next carriage of his train and now they were following the phaeton in two droshkies. His assistants were professionals, and Achimas knew that they would not fall behind or give themselves away.

The phaeton halted. The taciturn driver, who had met Achimas at the station and – to judge from his military bearing – was no driver at all, opened the door and gestured for Achimas to follow him.

Not a soul on the street. A single-storey detached mansion. Modest, but neat and tidy. Only one unusual feature: although it was summer, all the windows were closed and covered by curtains. One of the curtains quivered slightly and once again Achimas's thin lips extended in a momentary smile. He was beginning to find these dilettante attempts at cunning amusing. It was all quite clear: aristocrats playing at conspiracy.

His guide led him towards their destination through an enfilade of dark rooms. When they reached the last one he stopped to let Achimas go on ahead. Once Achimas stepped inside, the double door closed behind his back and he heard the sound of a key turning in the lock.

Achimas glanced around curiously. An intriguing room – not a single window. The only furniture was a small round table with two tall-backed armchairs beside it. It was hard, however, to get a clear impression of the interior, since it was only lit by a single candle that did not cast its feeble light as far as the gloom in the corners.

Achimas waited for his eyes to grow accustomed to the darkness before he examined the walls with a practised glance. He failed to discern anything suspicious – no secret spy-holes from which a gun could be trained on him, no additional doors. But there proved to be another chair positioned in the far corner.

Achimas sat down in an armchair. Five minutes later the doors swung open and a tall man entered. He did not take the second armchair, but walked across the room and sat on the chair in the corner without greeting Achimas in any way.

So the client was not so stupid after all. An excellent arrangement: Achimas sitting in full view, illuminated by the candle, and his partner in conversation enveloped in dense shadow. And his full face was not visible – only the silhouette.

Unlike 'Baron von Steinitz', this individual wasted no time in getting straight to the point.

'You wished to meet the principal party in this matter,' the man in the corner said in Russian. 'I have consented. Be certain not to disappoint me, Mr Welde. I shall not introduce myself; to you I am Monsieur N.N.'

To judge from his pronunciation, he was a man from the very highest levels of society. He sounded about forty years old, but might be younger – his was a voice accustomed to command, and they always sounded older. His grand manner suggested that he was a man to be taken seriously.

The conclusion? If this was a high-society conspiracy, it was certainly no laughing matter.

'Please explain the gist of the proposal,' said Achimas.

'You speak Russian well,' said the shadow with a nod. 'I was informed that at one time you were a Russian subject. That is most convenient. There will be no need for superfluous explanations. And it will certainly not be necessary to impress upon you the importance of the individual who has to be killed.'

Achimas noted the remarkable directness of expression – no equivocations, nothing about 'eliminating', 'removing' or 'neutralising'.

Meanwhile Monsieur N.N. continued in the same even tone, without the slightest pause: 'It is Mikhail Sobolev.'

'The one they call the White General?' Achimas enquired. 'The hero of recent wars and the most popular general in the Russian army?'

'Yes, Adjutant-General Sobolev, commander of the Fourth Army Corps,' the silhouette confirmed dispassionately.

'I beg your pardon, but I must refuse your request,' Achimas declared politely and crossed his arms on his chest.

The science of gestures defined the meaning of this pose as calm composure and adamant determination. In addition, it happened to set the fingers of his right hand against the handle of the little revolver lying in a special pocket in his waistcoat. The revolver was called a 'velodog' and it had been invented for cyclists who were pestered by stray dogs. Four little round-headed twenty-two-calibre bullets. A mere trinket, of course, but in situations like today's it could prove very useful.

A refusal to accept a commission after the target had already been named was an extremely dangerous move. If complications should arise, Achimas intended to act as follows: put a bullet in the client's brain and jump back into the darkest corner. It would be no simple job to subdue Achimas there. There had been no search at the entrance, so his entire arsenal was still intact: the Colt manufactured to his personal order, the throwing knife and the Spanish knife with the sprung blade. Therefore Achimas was tense but calm.

'Surely you are not also one of Sobolev's devotees?' the client enquired with irritation.

'I have no interest in Sobolev; I am a devotee of common sense. And common sense requires me not to involve myself in matters that entail the subsequent elimination of the agent employed – that is, in the present case, myself. No witnesses are ever left alive after an act of such immense importance. My advice is to find yourself another agent, some novice. An ordinary political assassination is not such a very tricky job.' Achimas stood up and began backing cautiously towards the door, ready to fire at any second.

'Sit down.' The man in the corner pointed imperiously to the armchair. 'What I need is not some beginner, but the very finest master of your trade, because this is a very tricky job indeed – as you will see for yourself. But first allow me to inform you of certain circumstances which will allay your suspicions.'

Achimas could tell that Monsieur N.N. was not used to providing explanations and was restraining the urge to fly into a fury.

'This is neither a political assassination nor a conspiracy. On the contrary, the conspirator and offender against the state is Sobolev, who dreams of rivalling the glory of Napoleon. Our hero is planning a military coup, no more and no less. The conspiracy includes officers from his army corps and also the general's former comrades-in-arms, many of whom serve in the Guards. But the most dangerous thing of all is that Sobolev's popularity extends beyond the army to every class of society, while we at court and in the government are regarded by some with resentment and by others with open hatred. The prestige of the ruling house has fallen very low following the shameful hounding and murder of the previous emperor. They ran down the Lord's anointed as if they were running down a hare with dogs.'

The speaker's voice was suddenly suffused with a menacing power, and the door behind Achimas immediately gave a creak. The individual for whom the court and the government were included in the concept of 'we' impatiently waved a white-gloved hand and the door closed again.

The mysterious gentleman continued, speaking more calmly now, without anger: 'We are aware of the conspirators' plans. At the present moment Sobolev is conducting manoeuvres that are in actual fact a rehearsal for the coup. He will then set out for Moscow, accompanied by his retinue, in order to meet with certain Guards officers far away from St Petersburg, assure himself of their support and work out his final disposition of forces. The blow will be struck at the beginning of June, during a parade at Tsarskoe Selo. Sobolev intends to take the members of the royal family into "temporary custody" – for their own good and in the name of the salvation of the fatherland.' His intonation became intensely sarcastic. 'The fatherland itself will be declared in such grave danger that a military dictatorship will have to be established. There are serious grounds to suppose that this insane project will be supported by a significant part of the army, the gentry, the merchantry and even the peasantry. The White General is ideally suited to the role of saviour of the fatherland!'

Monsieur N.N. got to his feet and strode angrily along the wall, cracking his knuckles. Nonetheless, he remained in the shadows as before and did not show his face. Achimas could only make out an aristocratic nose and lush sideburns.

'So you should be aware, Mr Welde, that in this case you will not be committing any crime, because Sobolev has been condemned to death by a court which included the most senior dignitaries in the empire. Of the twenty judges appointed by His Imperial Majesty, seventeen voted for the death penalty. And the Emperor has already confirmed the verdict. It was a secret court, but no less legitimate for that. The gentleman whom you took for an intermediary was one of the judges and was acting in the interests of security and peace in Europe. As you are probably aware, Sobolev is the leader of the militant Slavist party, and his accession to power would inevitably lead to war with Germany and Austro-Hungary.'

The man of state stopped speaking and looked at his imperturbable listener.

'Therefore you have no reason to fear for your life. You are not dealing with criminals, but with the supreme authority of a great empire. You are being asked to play the role of an executioner, not a murderer. Do you find my explanation satisfactory?'

'Let us assume so,' said Achimas, placing his hands on the table. There was apparently no prospect of any shooting. 'But what exactly is it that makes the job so difficult? Why can the general not simply be poisoned, or even shot, if it comes to that?'

'Aha, you would appear to have accepted our proposal.' Monsieur N.N. nodded in satisfaction and lowered himself on to the chair. 'Now I shall explain why we needed such an authoritative specialist. Let us start with the fact that it is very difficult to get close to Sobolev. He is surrounded day and night by adjutants and orderlies who are fanatically devoted to him. And he cannot simply be killed – that would set the whole of Russia up in arms. He must die naturally, without any ambiguities or suspicions. But even that is not enough. We ourselves could eliminate the criminal by using poison, but the conspiracy has already gone too far. Even the

274

death of their leader cannot stop the conspirators. They will carry their cause through to the end, believing that they are acting out Sobolev's behest. It is most probable that without their leader they will achieve nothing, but Russia will be plunged into bloody chaos and the supreme authority will be totally compromised. By comparison with Sobolev's gentlemen the Decembrists will come to seem like naughty children. And now allow me to lay the task before you in all its baffling complexity.' He summed up briskly, slashing at the darkness with a white-gloved hand: 'Sobolev must be eliminated in such a way that his death will appear natural to the general public and not provoke its indignation. We shall organise a sumptuous funeral, set up a monument to him and even name some ship or other in his honour. Russia cannot be deprived of her only national hero. At the same time, however, Sobolev must die in such a way that his co-conspirators will be demoralised and unable to rally round his banner. While remaining a hero in the eyes of the common crowd, for the conspirators he must be stripped of his halo. And so you can see for yourself that such a task is far beyond any novice. Tell me, is it really possible at all?'

For the first time the speaker's voice betrayed a note of something akin to uncertainty.

Achimas asked: 'How and when shall I receive the remainder of the money?'

Monsieur N.N. sighed in relief. 'When Sobolev leaves for Moscow, he will be carrying all the funds for the conspiracy with him – about a million roubles. Preparations for a coup require substantial expenditure. After killing Sobolev, you will take the money for yourself. I trust that you can manage that task with no difficulty?'

'Today is the twenty-first of June by the Russian calendar. You say that the coup has been set for the beginning of July. When is Sobolev leaving for Moscow?'

'Tomorrow. Or the day after at the very latest. And he will

be there until the twenty-seventh. Then he will pay a visit to his estate in Ryazan and go directly from there to St Petersburg. We know that he has arranged meetings with his generals for the twenty-fifth, twenty-sixth and twenty-seventh, for which they will make a special journey from St Petersburg to Moscow ... but I will not name any unnecessary names. Without Sobolev these people are not dangerous. In time we shall retire them quietly, with no publicity. But it would be better if Sobolev had no chance to meet with them. We do not wish distinguished generals to besmirch their reputations with state treason.'

'In your circumstances you cannot afford to be so considerate,' said Achimas with sudden abruptness. The task was difficult enough without the time allowed being shortened unnecessarily. 'You wish me to complete the task before the twenty-fifth of June – that is, you are giving me only three days. It is rather short notice. I shall do my best, but I can promise nothing.'

That same day Achimas paid his assistants what was due to them and dismissed them: he had no more need of their services.

He himself boarded the night train to Moscow.

4

According to a system of classification that Achimas had developed earlier in his life, the current task belonged to the fourth and highest category of difficulty: the disguised murder of a celebrity with an extremely tight deadline and the complication of additional conditions. There were three difficulties.

Firstly, the target's strong and devoted bodyguards.

Secondly, the need to imitate a natural death.

Thirdly, the fact that in the eyes of the general public the death had to appear respectable, but a narrow circle of initiates must regard it as shameful.

Interesting.

In anticipation of fruitful mental endeavour, Achimas settled himself comfortably on the small velvet divan in the first-class carriage. Ten hours of travelling ought to suffice. He did not have to sleep – when necessary, he could go without sleep for three or even four days. He had his training with Uncle Chiran to thank for that.

Also, der Reihe nach. [So, everything in order.]

He took out the information that the client had provided at his request. This was a complete dossier on Sobolev that had clearly taken several years to compile: a detailed biography including his service record, interests and connections. Achimas failed to discover in it a single useful eccentricity that might have offered some leverage – Sobolev was not a gambler, or an opium addict, or a dipsomaniac. His character reference was dominated by the word 'excellent': an excellent horseman, an excellent marksman, an excellent billiards player. Very well.

Achimas moved on to the 'Interests' section. Drinks in moderation, prefers Château d'Yquem, smokes Brazilian cigars, likes Russian romances, especially 'The Rowan Tree' (composer Mr I. Surikov). Yes, yes.

'Intimate habits'. Alas, disappointment awaited Achimas here also. Not a homosexual, not a disciple of the Marquis de Sade, not a paedophile. Formerly, it seemed, he had been a well-known womaniser, but for the last two years he had remained faithful to his mistress Ekaterina Golovina, a teacher at the Minsk girls' grammar school. There was information to the effect that a month ago he had offered to legitimise their relationship, but for some unknown reason Golovina had refused him, and the relationship had been broken off. Right, there was something in this.

Achimas looked pensively out of the window. He picked up the next document: the names and character references of the officers in Sobolev's retinue. For the most part men of the world who had seen military action. When he travelled, the general was always accompanied by at least seven or eight men. Sobolev never went anywhere alone. That was bad. Even worse was the fact that the food the general ate was checked, not just by one taster but by two: his senior orderly, the Cossack captain Gukmasov, and his personal valet.

However, the only possible way to imitate a natural death without arousing suspicion was to use poison. An accident would not suit – they always left a lingering odour of suspicion.

How could he bypass the tasters and give his mark the poison? Who was closer to Sobolev than his orderly and valet?

Apparently no one was. There was his old flame in Minsk – no doubt he had eaten from her hands without any check. But the relationship had been broken off.

Stop! That thought clearly pointed in the right direction. A woman could get closer to a man than anyone else, even if he had only made her acquaintance recently. Always assuming, naturally, that they entered into intimate relations. In that case the adjutants and the valets would have to wait outside the door.

So, when had Sobolev broken things off with his mistress? A month ago. He must be famished by now – he would have had no time for love affairs on manoeuvres, and they would have been reported in the file. He was a hot-blooded man, in the very prime of life. And in addition he was plotting an enterprise so risky that he could not possibly know how it would turn out for him.

Achimas half-closed his eyes.

Sitting opposite him were a lady and her son, a junior cadet. She was talking to him in a low voice, trying to persuade him to behave himself and stop wriggling. 'You see, Serge, that gentleman is trying to work and you're being naughty,' the lady said in French.

The boy looked at the neat, blond-haired man in the fine-quality grey jacket. The German had spread out some boring papers on his knees and was moving his lips without speaking. He glanced at the cadet from under his eyebrows and suddenly winked with a pale eye.

Serge scowled.

The renowned Achilles did have a vulnerable heel, and one that was not particularly original, Achimas concluded. There was no point in trying to be too clever and reinvent the bicycle. The simpler the method, the surer.

The logic of the operation defined itself:

1. A woman was the most appropriate bait for a strong, healthy male of Sobolev's character who was weary of abstinence.

2. The easiest way of all to give the mark poison was by using a woman.

3. In Russia debauchery was regarded as shameful and certainly unworthy of a national hero. If a hero gave up the ghost not on the field of battle, or even in a hospital bed, but in a bed of vice with his mistress, or even better, with some slut, according to the Russian way of thinking, that would be a) indecent, b) comical, c) simply stupid. Heroes were not forgiven for such behaviour.

The retinue would take care of everything else. The adjutants would go to any lengths to conceal the unseemly circumstances of the White General's death from the public. However, the word would spread in a flash among those close to him, among the conspirators. It is hard to oppose an emperor without a leader, especially if the place of the knightly banner fluttering above one's head has been taken by a stained bed sheet. The White General would no longer appear so very white to his own devotees.

Well then, the general method had been determined. Now for the specifics.

Among the various useful things he carried in his trunk Achimas had a rather good selection of chemical substances. The one that was ideally suited to the present case was an extract of the juice of an Amazonian fern. Give two drops of this colourless and almost tasteless liquid to a healthy man and a slight increase in the rate of his heartbeat would induce respiratory paralysis and heart failure. The death, moreover, appeared perfectly natural and it would never enter anyone's head to suspect poisoning. In any case, after two or three hours it was quite impossible to detect any trace of the poison.

It was a reliable method, proved repeatedly in practice. Achimas had used it most recently the year before last, in carrying out a commission for a certain idle parasite in London who wished to get rid of his millionaire uncle. The operation had been completed simply and elegantly. The loving nephew had arranged a dinner in honour of his dear uncle. Achimas had been among the guests. First he had drunk poisoned champagne with the old man, and then whispered to the millionaire that his nephew wished to do away with him. The uncle had turned scarlet, clutched at his heart and collapsed as if his legs had been scythed from beneath him. The death had occurred in the presence of a dozen witnesses. Achimas had walked back to his hotel at a slow, measured pace – in order to allow the poison to disperse and become ineffective.

The target had been an elderly man in poor health. Experience had shown that the substance took effect in a strong, young man when his pulse reached a rate of eighty to eighty-five beats a minute.

The question, therefore, was whether the general's heart would accelerate to eighty-five beats a minute at the climax of his passion.

The answer was that it was certain to do so, for that was the very nature of passion. Especially if its object were sufficiently sultry.

Only one trifling matter remained: to find a suitable *demimondaine*.

5

Following his instructions, in Moscow Achimas put up at the fashionable new Hotel Metropole under the name of Nikolai Nikolaevich Klonov, a merchant from Ryazan. Using the number provided by Mr N.N., he telephoned his client's representative in Moscow, whom he had been told to address as 'Mr Nemo'. Achimas no longer found these absurd aliases laughable – it was clear that these people were deadly serious.

'Hello,' said a crackling voice in the earpiece.

'This is Klonov,' Achimas said into the mouthpiece. 'I would like to speak to Mr Nemo.'

'Speaking,' said the voice.

'Please tell them to send me a verbal portrait of Ekaterina Golovina urgently.' Achimas repeated the name of Sobolev's mistress one more time and disconnected the telephone.

Well now, the defenders of the throne were not very good conspirators. Achimas took the telephone directory from the *koelner* and looked to see which subscriber was registered under the number 211. Court Counsellor Pyotr Parmyonovich Khurtinsky, head of the governor-general's secret chancellery. Not bad.

Two hours later a courier delivered a sealed envelope to the hotel. The telegram was brief: '*Blonde, blue-grey eyes, slightly aquiline nose, thin, well-proportioned, height two arshins and four vershoks, small bust, slim waist, mole on right cheek, scar on left knee from a fall from a horse. N.N.*'

The information concerning the left knee and the mole was superfluous. The important thing was that the type was clearly defined: a short, slim blonde.

'Tell me, my dear fellow, what's your name?'

Number 19 was regarding the *koelner* uncertainly, as if he were embarrassed. The *koelner*, a man of some experience, was well acquainted with that tone of voice and that expression. He wiped the smile off his face, in order not to embarrass the guest with his excessive perspicacity, and replied: 'Timofei, your honour. Can I be of any service to you?'

Number 19 (according to the register, a merchant of the first guild from Ryazan) led Timofei away from the counter to the window and handed him a rouble. 'I'm feeling bored, brother. Lonely. I could do with a bit of … pleasant company.' The merchant fluttered his white eyelashes and blushed a pale pink. How pleasant it was to deal with such a sensitive individual.

The *koelner* shrugged and raised his hands: 'Why, nothing could be simpler, sir. We have plenty of jolly young ladies here in Moscow. Would you like me to give you an address?'

'No, no address. What I'd like is someone special, who can think a bit. I don't like the cheap ones,' said the merchant from Ryazan, taking heart.

'We have some like that too.' Timofei began bending down his fingers as he counted. 'Varya Serebryanaya sings at the Yar – a very presentable girl; she won't go with just anyone. Then there's Mamselle Carmencita, a very modern individual; she makes her arrangements on the telephone. Mamselle Wanda sings at the Alpine Rose – a young lady of very discriminating taste. There are two dancers at the French Operetta, Lisette and Anisette; they're very popular, sir. And as for the actresses …'

'That's it, I'd like an actress,' said number 19, brightening up even further. 'Only to suit my taste: I have no time for over-fleshy women, Timofei. What I like is a slim woman with a waist, not too tall; and she has to be blonde.'

The *koelner* thought for a moment and said: 'Then that means Wanda from the Rose. Blonde and skinny. But very popular. Most of the others are on the fleshy side. Can't be helped, sir; it's the fashion.'

'Tell me what this Wanda's like.'

'She's a German. With the manners of an aristocrat. Thinks very highly of herself. Lives in grand style in an apartment at the Anglia, with a separate entrance. She can afford it, sir: she takes five hundred for the satisfaction. And she's choosy; she'll only go with someone she likes.'

'Five hundred roubles? My goodness!' The merchant seemed to be interested. 'And where could I take a look at this Wanda, Timofei? What is this place the Alpine Rose like?'

The *koelner* pointed out of the window: 'It's just here, on Sofiiskaya Street. She sings there most evenings. The restaurant's nothing special – doesn't compare with ours or the Slavyansky Bazaar. It's mostly Germans, begging your pardon, who go there. Our Russian men only go to gawk at Wanda. And engage her services, if their intentions are serious.'

'And how are her services engaged?'

'You have to go about it the right way,' said Timofei, amused, and he set about describing it. 'First of all you have to invite her to your table. But if you just call her over, she won't sit with you. The very first thing you do is send her a bunch of violets, and it has to be wrapped in a hundred-rouble note. The mamselle will take a look at you from a distance. If she takes a dislike to you straight away, she'll send the hundred roubles back. But if she doesn't, it means she'll come and sit with you. But that's only the half of it, sir. She might sit down and chat about this and that and still refuse you afterwards. And she won't give the hundred roubles back, because she's spent time on you. They say she earns more from the hundred-rouble rejects than from the five-hundred-rouble fees. That's the way this Miss Wanda's set herself up.'

That evening Achimas sat in the Alpine Rose, sipping a decent Rhein wine and studying the songstress. The young German woman really was attractive. She looked like a bacchante. Her face was not German at all – it had a bold, reckless look to it, and there was a glint of molten silver in her green eyes. Achimas knew that special tint very well as the exclusive trait of the most precious members of the female species. It was not plump lips or a finely moulded little nose that caught men's fancy; it was that silver sheen that blinded them with its deceptive glimmer and drove them out of their minds. And what a voice! As an experienced connoisseur of female beauty, Achimas knew that half the enchantment lay in the voice. When it had that chesty resonance and that slight hint of hoarseness, as if it had been seared by frost or, on the contrary, scorched by fire, it was dangerous. The best thing you could do was follow Odysseus' lead and tie yourself to the mast, otherwise you would drown. The bold general would never be able to resist this siren – not for the world.

However, Achimas still had a certain amount of time in hand. Today was only Tuesday and Sobolev would arrive on Thursday, so he had an opportunity to take Mademoiselle Wanda's measure more precisely.

During the evening she was sent a bouquet of violets twice. One – from a fat merchant in a scarlet waistcoat – Wanda returned straight away, without even touching it. The merchant left immediately, stamping his heels and cursing.

The second bouquet was sent by a colonel of the Guards with a scar across his cheek. The songstress raised the bouquet to her face and tucked the banknote into her lacy sleeve, but it was some time before she took a seat beside the colonel and she did not stay with him for long. Achimas could not hear what they were talking about, but the conversation ended with Wanda throwing her head back with a laugh, smacking the colonel across the hand with her fan and walking away. The colonel shrugged his gold-trimmed shoulders philosophically and after a while sent another bouquet, but Wanda returned it immediately.

Yet when a certain red-cheeked, blond-haired gentleman, whose appearance was clearly far less impressive than the officer's, casually beckoned the proud woman to him with his finger, she took a seat at his table immediately, without making him wait. The blond man spoke to her indolently, drumming on the tablecloth with his short fingers covered in ginger hairs, and she listened without speaking or smiling, nodding twice. *Surely not her pimp*, Achimas thought in surprise. He didn't look the part.

However, when Wanda emerged from the side entrance at midnight (Achimas was keeping watch outside), it was the red-cheeked man who was waiting for her in a carriage and she drove away with him. Achimas followed them in a single-seater carriage, prudently hired in advance at the Hotel Metropole. They drove across the Kuznetsky Bridge and turned on to Petrovka Street. Outside a large building on the corner with a glowing electric sign that said 'Anglia', Wanda and her companion got out of their carriage and dismissed the driver. The hour was late and the unattractive escort was clearly going to stay the night. Who was he – a lover? But Wanda did not look particularly happy.

He would have to ask 'Mr Nemo' about this.

6

In order to avoid any risk of simply wasting his time, Achimas did not wrap his violets in a hundred-rouble note, but threaded them instead through an emerald ring bought that afternoon at Kuznetsky Most. A woman might refuse money, but she would never refuse an expensive trinket.

Naturally, the ploy was successful. Wanda inspected the present curiously and then looked around, seeking out the giver with equal interest. Achimas bowed slightly. Today he was wearing an English dinner jacket and a white tie with a diamond pin, which lent him an appearance somewhere between an English lord and a modern entrepreneur – the new cosmopolitan breed that was just beginning to set the tone in Europe and Russia.

Yesterday's peremptory blond, concerning whom Achimas had received exhaustive (and extremely interesting) information, was not in the restaurant.

When she finished her song, Wanda sat down facing Achimas, glanced into his face and suddenly said: 'What transparent eyes. Like a mountain stream.'

For some reason Achimas's heart fluttered momentarily at that phrase. It had triggered one of those vague, elusive memories that the French call *déjà vu*. He frowned slightly. What nonsense! Achimas Welde was not one to be hooked by cunning feminine wiles.

He introduced himself: 'Merchant of the first guild Nikolai Nikolaevich Klonov, chairman of the Ryazan Commercial Association.'

'A merchant?' the green-eyed woman asked in surprise. 'You don't look like one. More like a sailor. Or a bandit.' She laughed gruffly and for the second time Achimas was caught off guard. No one had ever told him that he looked like a bandit before. He had to appear normal and respectable – it was a necessary condition of his profession.

The songstress continued to surprise him. 'And you don't have a Ryazan accent,' she remarked with casual mockery. 'You wouldn't happen to be a foreigner, would you?'

Apparently Achimas's speech really was marked by an

extremely slight, almost indistinguishable accent – a certain non-Russian metallic quality retained from his childhood; but to detect it required an extraordinarily subtle ear. Which made it all the more surprising to hear such a comment from a German.

'I lived in Zurich for a long time,' he said. 'Our company has an office there. Russian linen and calico.'

'Well, and what do you want from me, Swiss-Ryazan businessman?' the woman continued, as if it were a perfectly ordinary question. 'To strike some lucrative deal, perhaps? Have I guessed right?'

Achimas was relieved – the songstress was merely flirting. 'Precisely,' he said seriously and confidently, in the manner he always used when speaking to women of this type. 'I have a confidential business proposition to put to you.'

She burst into laughter, exposing her small, even teeth. 'Confidential? How elegantly you express it, Monsieur Klonov. Generally speaking, the propositions put to me are extremely confidential.'

Then Achimas remembered that he had said the same thing in almost the same words to 'Baron von Steinitz' a week before. He smiled despite himself, but immediately continued in a serious voice: 'It is not what you think, madam. The Ryazan Commercial Association, of which I have the honour to be the chairman, has instructed me to give an expensive and unusual present to a worthy and famous individual who hails from our district. I may choose the present at my own discretion, but our compatriot must be pleased with it. This person is greatly loved and esteemed in Ryazan. We wish to present our gift tactfully and unobtrusively. Even anonymously. He will never even know that the money was collected by subscription from the merchants of his home town of Ryazan. I thought for a long time about what to give the fortunate man. Then when I saw you I realised that the very finest gift is a woman like yourself.'

It was amazing, but she blushed. 'How dare you!' Her eyes flashed in fury. 'I am not a thing, to be given as a gift!'

'Not you, mademoiselle – only your time and your professional skills,' Achimas declared sternly. 'Or have I been misled, and you do not trade in your time and your art?'

She looked at him with hatred in her eyes. 'Do you realise, merchant of the first guild, that one word from me would be enough to have you thrown out into the street?'

He smiled, but only with his lips. 'No one has ever thrown me out into the street, madam. I assure you that it is quite out of the question.' Leaning forward and looking straight into those eyes glittering with fury, he said: 'It is not possible to be only half a courtesan, mademoiselle. Honest business relations are best: work in exchange for money. Or do you ply your trade for the pleasure of it?'

The sparks in her eyes faded and the wide, sensuous mouth twisted into a bitter smile. 'What pleasure? Order me some champagne. It's the only thing I drink. Otherwise in my "trade" you'd never stop drinking. I'm not going to sing any more today.' Wanda made a sign to a waiter, who evidently knew her habits, for he brought a bottle of Cliquot. 'You are quite right, Mr Philosopher. It is only deceiving yourself to be half for sale.' She drained her glass to the last drop, but would not allow him to fill it again.

Everything was going well and the only one thing that was causing Achimas any concern was the way everyone around them was staring at him, Wanda's favoured client. But never mind, he would leave the restaurant alone; they would think him just another loser and immediately forget him.

'People don't often speak to me like that.' The champagne had not lent her gaze sparkle – on the contrary, it had rendered it sad. 'They mostly cringe and fawn. At first. And then they start talking to me in a familiar fashion, trying to persuade me to be their kept woman. Do you know what I want?'

'Yes. Money. The freedom that it brings,' Achimas

remarked casually as he thought out the details of his subsequent actions.

She gaped at him, astounded. 'How did you know?'

'I am exactly the same,' he replied curtly. 'So how much money do you need in order finally to feel that you are free?'

Wanda sighed. 'A hundred thousand. I worked that out a long time ago, when I was still a stupid fool scraping a living from giving music lessons. I'm not going to talk about that … It's not interesting. I lived in poverty for a long time; I was almost destitute. Until I was twenty years old. And then I decided, that's enough, no more. I'm going to be rich and free. And that was three years ago.'

'Well, and are you rich and free?'

'In another three years I shall be.'

'Then that means you already have fifty thousand?' Achimas laughed. He liked this songstress very much.

'Yes,' she laughed, this time without bitterness or defiance, but fervently, the way she sang her Parisian *chansonettes*.

He liked that too – the fact that she did not wallow in self-pity.

'I can shorten your term of hard labour by at least six months,' he said, spearing an oyster with a little silver fork. 'The Association collected ten thousand for our gift.'

Realising from the expression on Wanda's face that she was in no mood to think things over coolly and was about to tell him to go to hell and take his ten thousand with him, Achimas added hurriedly: 'Don't refuse, or you will regret it. And in any case, you don't yet know what I have in mind. Oh, Mademoiselle Wanda, he is a great man. Many women, even from the very best society, would gladly pay handsomely to spend the night with him.'

He stopped, knowing that now she would not walk away. The woman had not yet been born whose pride was stronger than her curiosity.

Wanda glared angrily at him. Then she gave way and snorted: 'Well, tell me then, don't torment me like this, you serpent of Ryazan.'

'It is none other than General Sobolev, the incomparable Achilles and Ryazan landowner,' Achimas declared with a solemn air. 'That is whom I am offering you, not some rough merchant with a belly down to his knees. Later, when you are free, you can write about it in your memoirs. Ten thousand roubles and Achilles into the bargain – that sounds like a good arrangement to me.'

He could see from the young woman's face that she was in two minds. 'And there's something else I can offer you,' Achimas added in a very quiet voice, almost a whisper. 'I can rid you for ever of the society of Herr Knabe. If you would like that, of course.'

Wanda shuddered and asked in a frightened voice: 'Who are you, Nikolai Klonov? You're no merchant, are you?'

'I am a merchant.' He clicked his fingers to get them to bring the bill. 'Linen, calico, duck. Don't be surprised at how well informed I am. The Association has entrusted me with a very important job, and I like to be thorough in my work.'

'That's why you were staring so hard yesterday, when I was sitting with Knabe,' she said suddenly.

Observant, thought Achimas, not yet sure if that was good or bad. And that intimate tone that had appeared in her voice required some kind of response too. What would be more convenient: closeness or distance?

'But how can you rid me of him?' Wanda asked avidly. 'You don't even know who he is ...' Then, suddenly seeming to remember something, she interrupted herself. 'Anyway, what gives you the idea that I want to get rid of him?'

'It is up to you, mademoiselle,' Achimas said with a shrug, deciding that in the present case distance would be more effective. 'Well then, do you accept the proposal?'

'I do.' She sighed. 'Something tells me that I won't be able to shake you off anyway.'

Achimas nodded. 'You are a very intelligent woman. Don't come here tomorrow. But be at home at about five in the evening. I shall call for you at the Anglia and we will finalise everything. And do try to be alone.'

'I shall be.' She looked at him rather strangely – he did not understand the meaning of that look.

'Kolya, you won't deceive me, will you?'

Not only the words themselves, but the very intonation with which they were spoken, suddenly sounded so familiar that Achimas's heart skipped a beat. He remembered. It really was *déjà vu*. This had happened before. Evgenia had said the same thing once, twenty years earlier, before they had robbed the iron room. And the words about his transparent eyes – they were hers too, spoken when she had still been a little girl in the Skyrovsk orphanage.

Achimas unfastened his starched collar – he had suddenly found it hard to breathe. He said in a steady voice: 'On my honour as a merchant. Well then, mademoiselle, until tomorrow.'

7

At the hotel there was a courier waiting for Achimas with a telegram from St Petersburg:

He has taken a month's leave and left for Moscow by train. He will arrive tomorrow at five in the afternoon and stay at the Hotel Dusseaux, Theatre Lane, apartment 47. He is accompanied by seven officers and a valet. Your fee is in a brown briefcase. His first meeting is set for 10 a.m. on Friday with the commander of the Petersburg district

Ganetsky. I remind you that this meeting is undesirable.
N.N.

From early in the morning on Thursday, 24 June Achimas, wearing a striped blazer and straw boater and with his hair neatly parted and brilliantined, was hard at work in the vestibule of the Dusseaux. He managed to establish sound business relations with the porter, the doorman and the janitor who serviced the wing destined for the honoured guest. Two important factors had greatly facilitated the establishment of these relations: the first was a correspondent's identity card from the *Moscow Provincial Gazette*, thoughtfully provided by Mr Nemo, and the second was his generous greasing of palms (the porter had received a twenty-five-rouble note, the doorman a tenner and the janitor three roubles). The three roubles proved to be the most profitable investment, for the janitor sneaked the reporter into apartment 47.

Achimas gasped and sighed at the luxurious appointments, noted which way the windows looked (out into the yard, in the direction of Rozhdestvenka Street – very good), and also took note of the safe built into the wall of the bedroom. That was helpful too: he would not need to turn everything upside down searching for the money. The briefcase would naturally be lying in the safe, and the lock was a perfectly ordinary Van Lippen – five minutes' fiddling at the most. In gratitude for services rendered, the correspondent of the *Moscow Gazette* handed the janitor another fifty kopecks, but so clumsily that the coin fell out of his hand and rolled under the divan. While the janitor was crawling around on all fours, Achimas adjusted the latch on the frame of one half of the window, positioning it so that it was just barely held in place and the window would open at the slightest push from the outside.

At half past five Achimas was standing in the crowd of

correspondents and idlers at the entrance of the hotel, waiting with a reporter's notebook in his hand to observe the great man's arrival. When Sobolev emerged from his carriage in his white uniform, some people in the crowd made an attempt to shout 'hurrah', but the hero gave the waiting Muscovites such an angry glance and his adjutants began gesturing so frantically that the cheering petered out before it had really begun.

Achimas's first thought was that the White General bore a remarkable resemblance to a catfish: protruding forehead, slightly bulging eyes, drooping moustache and flared sideburns so broad that they reminded him of gills. But no: a catfish was lazy and good-natured, whereas the general looked around him with such a steely gaze that Achimas immediately reclassified him among the large marine predators. A hammerhead shark at the very least.

Swimming along ahead of him was his pilot-fish, a bold Cossack captain, cleaving ferociously through the crowd with broad sweeps of his white gloves. Three officers walked on each side of the general. Bringing up the rear was a valet, who walked as far as the door and then turned back to the carriage and began supervising the unloading of the luggage.

Achimas noticed that Sobolev was carrying a large and apparently rather heavy calfskin briefcase – a comical touch: the mark had brought along the fee for his own elimination.

The correspondents dashed into the vestibule after the hero, hoping for at least some small pickings – the chance to ask a quick question or spot some telling detail. But Achimas behaved differently. He walked slowly across to the valet and cleared his throat respectfully to draw attention to his presence. Then he waited to be noticed before bothering the man with any questions.

The valet, a bloated old man with bushy, cross-looking grey eyebrows (Achimas knew his entire life story, with all his habits and weaknesses, including a fatal predisposition for taking an early-morning drink for his hangover), squinted in annoyance at the fop in the straw hat, but, appreciating his tact, graciously condescended to turn halfway round towards him.

'I'm a correspondent with the *Moscow Provincial Gazette,*' Achimas said quickly, eager to exploit his opportunity. 'I would not dare to bother His Excellency with tiresome questions, but on behalf of the people of Moscow I would like to enquire as to the White General's intentions concerning his visit to the old capital. And who should know that if not yourself, Anton Lukich?'

'We know right enough, but we don't tell just anyone,' the valet replied pedantically; but it was clear that he felt flattered.

Achimas opened his notebook and assumed the pose of someone ready to jot down every precious word. Lukich drew himself erect and began speaking in elevated style: 'The schedule for today is relaxation. His Excellency is tired following the manoeuvres and his railway journey. No visits, no formal banquets, and instructions are: God forbid that any of your colleagues should get anywhere near him. And no speeches or deputations either, oh no. Instructions are to book dinner in the hotel restaurant for half past eight. If you want to gawk at him, book a table before it's too late. But you have to keep your distance and not bother him with any questions.'

Achimas pressed his hand to his heart prayerfully and enquired in a sugary voice: 'And what plans does His Excellency have for the evening?'

The valet frowned. 'That's none of my business and even less of yours.'

Excellent, thought Achimas. *The target's business meetings start tomorrow, but it seems that this evening is indeed reserved for relaxation. On that point our interests coincide.*

Now he had to make sure that Wanda was ready.

Just as she had promised, the young woman was waiting for him in her apartment – and she was alone. She glanced at

Achimas rather strangely, as if she were expecting something from him, but when her guest began talking of business, Wanda's eyes glazed over with boredom.

'We agreed everything, didn't we?' she remarked carelessly. 'What's the point in wading through all the details? I know my trade, Kolya.'

Achimas glanced round the room that served simultaneously as salon and boudoir. Everything was just as it should be: flowers, candles, fruit. The songstress had laid in some champagne for herself, but she had not forgotten the bottle of Château d'Yquem that she had been told to get the day before.

In her claret-coloured dress with its plunging neckline, tight-fitting waist and provocative bustle, Wanda looked stunningly seductive. That was all very well, but would the fish bite?

In Achimas's estimation, he was bound to: 1) No normal, healthy man could resist Wanda's advances; 2) If his information was correct – and Mr N.N. had not disappointed him so far – Sobolev was not merely a normal man, but a man who had endured a forced fast for at least a month; 3) Mademoiselle Wanda was precisely the same physical type as the general's amour in Minsk, the old flame to whom he had proposed, only to be rejected and later abandoned.

Taking everything together, the powder keg was ready and waiting. But to make detonation certain, a spark would be required.

'Why are you wrinkling up your forehead like that, Kolya? Afraid your compatriot won't like the look of me?' Wanda asked defiantly, but Achimas caught a hint of suppressed anxiety in her intonation. Every great beauty and incorrigible heartbreaker needed to be constantly reassured that she was absolutely irresistible. Nestled in the heart of every *femme fatale* there was a little worm that whispered: 'But what if the magic doesn't work this time?'

Depending on her particular character, a woman needed

either to be given assurances that she was the fairest in the land, more radiantly lovely than all the rest or, on the contrary, to have her competitive spirit aroused. Achimas was certain that Wanda belonged to the second type.

'I saw him today,' he said with a sigh and a doubtful glance at the songstress. 'I am afraid I might have chosen the wrong present. In Ryazan Mikhail Dmitreevich has the reputation of a great breaker of hearts, but he looks so very serious. What if it doesn't work? What if the general is not interested in our little gift?'

'Well, that's for me to worry about, not you,' said Wanda, flashing her eyes at him. 'All you have to do is pay the money. Did you bring it?'

He put the wad of notes on the table without speaking.

Wanda took the money and made great play of pretending to count it. 'All ten thousand? All right, then.' She tapped Achimas lightly on the nose with her finger. 'Don't you be concerned, Kolya. You men are a simple-minded bunch. Your great hero won't escape my clutches. Tell me, does he like songs? As I recall, there's a baby grand in the Dusseaux.'

That's it, thought Achimas. *The spark to detonate the powder keg.* 'Yes, he does. His favourite romance is "The Rowan Tree". Do you know it?'

Wanda thought for a moment and shook her head. 'No, I don't sing many Russian songs – mostly European ones. But that's no problem: I can find it in a moment.'

She picked up a songbook off the piano and leafed through it until she found the song. 'This one, you mean?'

She ran her fingers over the keys, hummed the tune without any words, then began singing in a low voice:

> In vain the rustling rowan
> Reaches out to the oak tree.
> Forever a poor orphan,
> I tremble, sad and lonely.

'What pathetic nonsense! Heroes are such sentimental souls.' She glanced rapidly at Achimas. 'You go now. Your Ryazan general will snatch at his present; he'll grab it with both hands.'

Achimas did not go. 'A lady is not supposed to arrive at a restaurant unaccompanied. What can we do about that?'

Wanda rolled her eyes up in mock mortification. 'Kolya, I don't interfere in your dealings in calico, so don't you meddle in my professional arrangements.'

He stood there for a moment, listening to that low, passionate voice pouring out the torment of its longing to throw itself into the embrace of the oak tree. Then he quietly turned round and walked to the door.

The melody broke off. Behind his back Wanda asked: 'Don't you regret it, Kolya? Giving me away to someone else?'

Achimas turned round.

'All right, go,' she said with a wave of her hand. 'Business is business.'

8

In the restaurant at the Hotel Dusseaux all the tables were taken, but Achimas's domesticated porter had kept his word and saved the most convenient one for his newspaperman – in the corner, with a view of the entire hall. At twenty minutes to nine three officers entered with a jangling of spurs, followed by the general himself and then another four officers. The other diners, who had been strictly cautioned by the maître d'hôtel not to pester the general with any unwanted expressions of esteem, behaved with appropriate tact and pretended that they had simply come to the restaurant for dinner, not to gawk at the great man.

Sobolev took the wine list, failed to discover Château d'Yquem in it and ordered some to be brought from Levet's shop. His retinue elected to drink champagne and cognac.

The military gentlemen talked among themselves in low voices, with several outbursts of general merriment, in which the general's lilting baritone could be clearly distinguished. The overall impression was that the conspirators were in excellent spirits, which suited Achimas very well.

At five minutes past nine, when the Château d'Yquem had been delivered and duly uncorked, the doors of the restaurant swung inwards as though wafted open by some gust of magical wind and Wanda appeared on the threshold, poised picturesquely, her lithe figure leaning bodily forwards. Her face was flushed and her huge eyes glowed like midnight stars. The entire hall turned round at the sound and froze, entranced by the miraculous spectacle. The glorious general seemed to have turned to stone, the pickled mushroom on his fork suspended halfway to his mouth.

Wanda paused for just a moment – long enough for her audience to admire the effect, but too brief for them to stick their faces back in their plates.

'There he is, our hero!' the miraculous vision declared resoundingly. And with a loud clattering of heels, she rushed impetuously into the hall.

The claret silk rustled and the ostrich feather on her wide-brimmed hat swayed. The maître d'hôtel fluttered his hands in horror, recalling the prohibition on any public displays of feeling; but he need not have been alarmed: Sobolev was not in the least bit indignant. He wiped his glistening lips with a napkin and rose gallantly to his feet.

'Why do you remain seated, gentlemen, and not pay tribute to the glory of the Russian land!' the ecstatic patriot cried, appealing to the hall and not allowing the initiative to slip out of her grasp for a moment. 'Hoorah for Mikhail Dmitrievich Sobolev!'

It was as if this was what the diners had all been waiting for. They jumped up out of their chairs and began applauding, and the thunderous enthusiasm of their 'hoorah' set the crystal chandelier swaying beneath the ceiling.

Blushing most fetchingly, the general bowed to all sides. Despite being famous throughout the whole of Europe and loved throughout the whole of Russia, he still seemed unaccustomed to public displays of enthusiastic admiration.

The vision of beauty dashed up to the hero and flung her slim arms open wide: 'Permit me to embrace you on behalf of all the women of Moscow!' she cried and, clasping him firmly round the neck, she kissed him three times in the old Moscow manner – full on the lips.

Sobolev turned an even deeper shade of crimson. 'Gukmasov, move over,' he said, tapping the Cossack captain on the shoulder and pointing to an empty chair. Please do me the honour, madam.'

'No, no, what are you saying?' the delightful blonde exclaimed in fright. 'How could I possibly? But if you will permit me, I would be glad to sing my favourite song for you.' And with the same impetuous abandon, she launched herself towards the baby grand piano standing in the middle of the hall.

In Achimas's view, Wanda's approach was too direct, even a little coarse; but he could see that she was quite sure of herself and knew perfectly well what she was doing. It was a pleasure to work with a true professional. He was finally persuaded when the first notes of that deep, slightly hoarse voice set all the hearts in the hall quivering:

> Why do you stand so weary,
> My slender rowanberry,
> With murmurs sad and dreary
> Bowing down your head?

Achimas stood up and walked out quietly. Nobody took any

notice of him – they were all listening to the song.

Now he could sneak into Wanda's apartment and switch the bottles of Château d'Yquem.

9

The operation went so smoothly that it was almost boring. All that was required of him was a little patience.

At a quarter past twelve three droshkies pulled up outside the Anglia: Wanda and the mark were in the first and all seven officers were in the other two.

Achimas (wearing a false beard and spectacles, quite unmistakably a university lecturer) had earlier taken a two-room apartment at the hotel with windows looking out in both directions: on to the street and into the courtyard with the annexe. He extinguished the light so that his silhouette would not give him away.

The general was well guarded. When Sobolev and his female companion disappeared behind the door of Wanda's apartment, the officers prepared to stand watch over their leader's recreation: one remained in the street, at the entrance to the hotel, another began patrolling the inner courtyard, while a third quietly slipped inside the annexe and evidently took up a position in the hallway. The other four set off to the buffet. They were evidently going to stand watch by turns.

At twenty-three minutes to one the electric light in the windows of the apartment was extinguished and the curtains were illuminated with a dull red glow from within. Achimas nodded approvingly – the songstress was playing her part with true Parisian virtuosity.

The officer strolling about in the courtyard glanced around stealthily, walked over to a red window and stood on tip-toe, but then recoiled as if he were ashamed and resumed his striding back and forth again, whistling with emphatic cheerfulness.

Achimas gazed intently at the minute hand of his watch. What if the White General, so famous for his coolness in battle, never lost his head and his pulse never raced, not even from passion? That was unlikely, for it contradicted the laws of physiology. In the restaurant he had blushed violently at Wanda's kisses and more than mere kisses would be involved now.

A more likely possibility was that he would not touch the Château d'Yquem. But the laws of psychology said that he should. If lovers do not throw themselves into each other's arms in the first instant – and a good twenty minutes had passed before the lamp in the boudoir was extinguished – they had to amuse themselves with something. The best thing of all would be for him to drink a glass of his favourite wine, which happened quite fortuitously to be close at hand. And if he did not drink it today, then he would drink it tomorrow. Or the next day. Sobolev would be in Moscow until the twenty-seventh and there could be little doubt that from now on he would prefer to spend the night here instead of in apartment number 47 at the Dusseaux. The Ryazan Commercial Association would be only too glad to pay the cost of a season ticket for their compatriot – Monsieur N.N. had provided more than enough money for expenses.

At five minutes past one Achimas heard a woman's muffled scream, then another, louder and more prolonged; but he could not make out any words. The officer in the courtyard started and set off towards the annexe at a run. A moment later bright light flooded the windows and shadows began flitting about on the curtains.

That was all.

Achimas walked unhurriedly in the direction of Theatre

Lane, swinging his cane as he went. There was plenty of time. It took seven minutes to reach the Dusseaux at a leisurely pace – that afternoon he had walked the shortest route twice, timing himself with his watch. The fuss and panic, the attempts to bring the general round, the arguments about whether or not to call a doctor to the hotel or first take Sobolev to the Dusseaux for the sake of appearances – these would take at least an hour.

His problem lay elsewhere: what was he to do with Wanda now? The elementary rules of hygiene required him to clean up after the job was done, to leave no loose ends behind. Of course, there would not be any enquiry – the officers and gentlemen would make certain of that – and Monsieur N.N. would not allow it in any case. Wanda was extremely unlikely to have noticed that the bottle had been switched. However, if the subject of the bearer of gifts from Ryazan should come up, if it should be discovered that the real Nikolai Nikolaevich Klonov had never set foot outside his own fabric warehouse, there would be unnecessary complications. And in the words of the old saying: God helps those who help themselves.

Achimas frowned. Unfortunately, his line of work did have its unpleasant moments.

It was with these gloomy but unavoidable thoughts in mind that he turned off Sofiiskaya Street into the opening of an entryway that led most conveniently to the rear courtyard of the Dusseaux, directly beneath the windows of Sobolev's apartment. With a quick glance at the dark windows (all the hotel's guests had been sleeping for a long time already), Achimas set a crate that he had spotted earlier against the wall. The bedroom window opened at his gentle push with only a quiet jingling of its latch. Five seconds later Achimas was inside.

He clicked the spring of his pocket torch and it sprang to life, slicing through the darkness with a narrow, faint beam of light that was still quite strong enough for him to pick out the safe. Achimas pushed a picklock into the keyhole and began methodically twisting it to the left and the right in a regular rhythm. He regarded himself as an amateur in the art of safebreaking, but in the course of a long career you could learn many different things. After three minutes there was a click as the first of the lock's three tumblers yielded. The remaining two required less time – only about two minutes.

The iron door squeaked open. Achimas put his hand inside and felt some papers or other. He shone the torch in: lists of names and diagrams. Monsieur N.N. would probably have been very glad to get his hands on these papers, but the terms of Achimas's contract did not specify the theft of any documents. In any case, just at that moment Achimas was not interested in the papers.

He was pondering a surprise: the briefcase was not in the safe.

10

Achimas spent all Friday lying on his bed, thinking hard. He knew from experience that when you found yourself in a difficult spot, rather than give way to your first impulse, it was best to stop moving, to freeze the way a cobra does just before its deadly, lightning-fast strike – provided, of course, that circumstances permitted a pause in the action. In this particular case they did, since the basic precautions had already been taken. Last night Achimas had checked out of the Metropole and moved to the Troitsa Inn, a collection of cheap apartments. The crooked, dirty alleyways around Pokrovsky Boulevard were only a stone's throw away from Khitrovka, and that was where he would have to search for the briefcase.

When he left the Metropole, Achimas had not taken a cab. In the hours before dawn he had circled through the streets for a long time, checking to see if he was being tailed, and he had signed in to the Troitsa under a different name.

His room was dirty and dark, but it was conveniently located, with a separate entrance and a good view of the courtyard.

He had to think over what had happened very carefully.

The previous night he had searched Sobolev's apartment thoroughly and still failed to find the briefcase. But he had found a small pellet of mud on the sill of the end window, which was tightly closed. When he raised his head, he had noticed that the small upper window frame was open. Someone had climbed out through it not long before.

Achimas had stared intently at the small window as he thought for a moment and drew his conclusions.

He had brushed the dirt off the window sill and closed the window through which he had climbed in. He had then left the apartment via the door, which he had locked from the outside with a picklock.

It was quiet and dark in the hotel foyer, with only a single smoky candle burning on the night doorman's counter. The doorman himself was half-asleep and had failed to notice the dark figure that slipped out of the corridor. When the little bell on the door jangled, he had leapt to his feet, but the stealthy visitor was already outside. *I'll never get any sleep, God help me*, the doorman thought. He yawned and made the sign of the cross over his mouth, then went across to close the latch.

Achimas had walked briskly in the direction of the Metropole, trying to work out what to do next. The sky was beginning to turn grey – at the end of June the nights are short.

A droshky appeared from behind a corner. Achimas had

recognised the silhouette of Sobolev's Cossack captain, sitting with his arms wrapped round a figure in white. The figure was supported from the other side by another officer. Its head swayed loosely to the clattering rhythm of hoof-beats. There were two other carriages following behind.

Interesting, Achimas had thought absent-mindedly; *how will they carry him past the doorman? But they're military men; they're bound to think of something.*

The shortest route to the Metropole lay through an open courtyard, a route that Achimas had followed more than once during the last few days. As he was walking through the yard's long, dark archway with his footsteps echoing hollowly on the stone flags, Achimas had suddenly been aware of someone else's presence. It was not his vision or even his hearing that detected the presence, but some other, inexplicable, peripheral sense that had saved his life several times in the past. It was as if the skin on the back of his neck sensed a movement behind him, some extremely faint stirring of the air. It might have been a cat darting by or a rat making a dash for a heap of rotten garbage, but in such situations Achimas was not afraid of making himself look foolish: without pausing to think, he had thrown himself to one side.

He felt a sudden downward draft of air sweep past his cheek. Out of the corner of his eye, he caught the dull glint of steel slicing through the air close beside his ear. With a rapid, practised movement, he pulled out his 'velodog' and fired without taking aim.

There was a muffled shriek and a dark shadow went darting away from him.

Achimas overtook the runner in two swift bounds and swung his cane down hard from a height.

He shone his torch on the fallen man: a coarse, bestial face; dark blood oozing from under greasy, tangled hair. The stubby fingers clutching at the man's side were also wet with blood.

The attacker was dressed in the Russian style: collarless

shirt, wool-cloth waistcoat, velveteen trousers, blacked boots. Lying on the ground beside him was an axe with an unusually short handle.

Achimas leaned lower, pointing the finger of light straight into the man's face. It glinted on two round eyes with unnaturally dilated pupils.

There was the sound of a whistle from the direction of Neglinny Lane, then another from the Theatre Lane side. He didn't have much time. He squatted down, set his finger and thumb just below the fallen man's cheekbones and squeezed. He tossed the axe aside.

'Who sent you?'

'It's poverty that's to blame, your honour,' the wounded man croaked. 'We beg forgiveness.'

Achimas pressed his finger hard into the facial nerve, allowed the man on the ground to squirm in agony for a while and repeated his question: 'Who?'

'Let go … Let go, you gull,' wheezed the wounded man, hammering his feet against the flagstones. 'I'm dying …'

'Who?' Achimas asked for the third time, and pressed hard on an eyeball. Blood flooded out of the dying man's mouth, almost drowning his low groan. 'Misha,' the faint voice gurgled. 'Little Misha … Let go! It hurts!'

'Who is this Misha?' asked Achimas, pressing down more heavily.

But that was a mistake. The would-be murderer was already at his last gasp. His groan became a wheeze and a torrent of blood gushed out on to his beard. He was obviously not going to say any more.

Achimas straightened up. A police constable's whistle trilled somewhere very close.

By midday he had reviewed all the possible courses of action and formulated his decision.

He started from the facts: first someone had robbed Achimas and then someone had attempted to kill him. Were

306

these two events connected with each other? Undoubtedly. The man who had been lying in wait for Achimas in the dark archway had known what route he would take and when.

That meant: 1) He had been followed the previous day, when he was checking the route – and followed very cleverly: he had not spotted his tail; 2) Someone was well aware of what Achimas had been doing last night; 3) The briefcase had been taken by someone who was certain that Sobolev would not be coming back to his apartment – otherwise why would he have bothered to lock the safe after himself so carefully and climb out through the small window frame? The general would have discovered the loss in any case.

Question: Who knew about the operation and about the briefcase?

Answer: Only Monsieur N.N. and his people.

If they had simply tried to eliminate Achimas, that would have been annoying but understandable: annoying, because in that case he, a top-flight professional, would have misread the situation, miscalculated the risk and allowed himself to be deceived; understandable, because in a major undertaking like this, fraught with a multitude of possible complications, the agent should, of course, be eliminated. That was precisely what Achimas would have done in the client's place. The secret imperial court was a fiction, of course. But it was a clever invention, and even the worldly-wise Mr Welde had been taken in by it.

Taking everything together, it could all have been explained, if not for the disappearance of the briefcase.

Monsieur N.N. and crude housebreaking? Absurd. Take the million roubles, but leave the documents for the conspirators? Improbable. And the idea that the killer with the bestial face from the archway had any connection at all with N.N. or 'Baron von Steinitz' was absolutely unbelievable.

The wielder of the axe had addressed Achimas as a 'gull'. In Russian criminal argot this was a term of abuse that expressed the most extreme level of contempt – not a thief, not a bandit, but an ordinary, law-abiding citizen.

So the attacker was a professional criminal? Perhaps a character from the notorious Khitrovka district? His behaviour and manner of talking had certainly suggested it. What had he to do with N.N., whose lowly coach driver had the bearing of a military officer? Something here didn't add up.

Since he had insufficient information for genuine logical analysis, Achimas tried approaching the problem from a different angle. If the initial data were inadequate, it was more convenient to start by defining your objectives.

What needed to be done?

Clean up after his own operation.

Find the briefcase.

Settle accounts with the person or persons who had tried to cheat Achimas Welde.

And in that precise order. First protect himself, then get back what belonged to him, and then exact vengeance, as dessert. For there must be a dessert. It was a matter of principle and professional ethics.

At the practical level, the three stages of the plan were as follows:

Eliminate Wanda. A pity, of course, but it was necessary.

Deal with the mysterious Little Misha.

He would get Misha to provide his dessert. Someone among Monsieur N.N.'s people obviously kept strange company.

Once he had worked out his programme of action, Achimas turned over on to his side and instantly fell asleep.

Point number one was scheduled for implementation that evening.

He managed to sneak into Wanda's apartment without being noticed. As he had anticipated, the songstress had not yet returned from the Alpine Rose. Between the boudoir and the hallway there was a cloakroom, crammed with dresses on hangers and stacks of shoe- and hat-boxes. The room was ideally positioned, with one door leading into the boudoir and another into the hallway.

If Wanda came back alone, it would all be over quickly, without any complications. She would open the door in order to get a change of clothes and die that very second, before she had any time to feel afraid. Achimas very much did not want her to suffer any fear or pain before she died.

He pondered the question of what would be more appropriate – an accident or suicide – and settled on suicide. There were surely many reasons why a woman of the *demi-monde* might decide to take her own life.

The task was simplified by the fact that Wanda did not employ a maid. If you had been used to looking after yourself all your life, then it was more convenient to manage without servants – he knew that from his own experience. On the island of Santa Croce the servants would live separately; he would build a house for them at a good distance from the count's residence. They could always be summoned if they were needed.

But what if Wanda did not come back alone?

Well, in that case it would be a double suicide. That was quite fashionable nowadays.

He heard the sound of a door opening and light footsteps.

She was alone.

Achimas grimaced as he recalled her voice asking him: 'You won't deceive me, will you, Kolya?' At that very instant the door from the boudoir into the dressing room half-opened and a slim, naked arm reached in and pulled a Chinese dressing gown decorated with dragons off its hanger.

The moment had been missed. Achimas looked through the chink of the door. Wanda was standing in front of the mirror, still in her dress, holding the dressing gown in her hand.

Three quick, silent steps and the job would be done. She would hardly even have time to catch a glimpse of the figure behind her in the mirror.

Achimas opened the door slightly and then pulled back at the sound of a brief trill from the electric doorbell.

Wanda went out into the hallway, exchanged a few brief words with someone and came back into the drawing room, examining a small piece of cardboard. A calling card?

She was standing with her profile towards Achimas now and he saw her face quiver.

Almost immediately there was another ring at the door.

Again he was unable to hear what was said in the hallway – the door on that side of the little room was firmly shut; but Wanda and her late visitor came straight through into the drawing room, and then he could hear and even see everything.

Fate had an unexpected surprise in store for him. When the visitor – a well-proportioned young man in a fashionable frock coat – entered the circle of light cast by the lampshade, Achimas recognised his face immediately. In the years that had passed it had changed greatly, matured and shed the soft contours of youth; but it was definitely the same man. Achimas never forgot what his targets looked like; he remembered every last little detail of every one, and especially of this one.

It was an old story from a long time ago, from the interesting period when Achimas had been contracted to work for an organisation that called itself 'Azazel'. They were very serious people who paid the top rate, but they were romantics.

That was clear enough from the absolute requirement to utter the word 'Azazel' before every strike. Sentimental nonsense. But Achimas had observed this ludicrous condition: a contract is a contract.

He found it disagreeable to look at the handsome young man with black hair – above all because he was still walking about and breathing. In his entire professional career Achimas had only failed in his task three times and now he saw before him the living proof of one of those occasions. He ought surely to have been content with such a low failure rate after twenty years of work, but his mood, which had been bad enough already, was now completely spoiled.

What was the name of this young novice? Something beginning with 'F'.

'Mr Fandorin, on your card it said "I know everything". What is "everything"? And who are you, as a matter of fact?' Wanda asked in a hostile tone of voice.

Yes, yes, Fandorin. That was his name: Erast Petrovich Fandorin. So now he was the governor-general's deputy for special assignments, was he?

Achimas listened carefully to the conversation taking place in the next room, trying to understand the significance of this unexpected encounter. He knew that extraordinary coincidences like this were never accidental; they represented some kind of sign from the fates. Was this a good sign or a bad one?

The habit of tidiness prompted him to kill the black-haired young man, although the term of the contract had expired long ago, and the clients themselves had disappeared without trace. It was sloppy to leave a job unfinished. On the other hand, it would be unprofessional to give way to his emotions. Mr Fandorin could continue on his way. After all, even six years ago Achimas had not had anything personal against him.

But when the young functionary brought up a highly dangerous subject – the Château d'Yquem – Achimas was ready to reverse his decision: Mr Fandorin could not be allowed to leave this place alive. Then Wanda surprised him by saying not a single word about the merchant from Ryazan and how incredibly well informed he had been concerning the habits of the deceased hero. She led the conversation off in a completely different direction. What could that mean?

Shortly after that the young man took his leave.

Wanda sat at the table with her face in her hands. Nothing could be easier than to kill her now, but Achimas still hesitated.

Why kill her? She had withstood questioning without giving anything away. If the authorities had shown themselves perceptive enough to see through the officers' primitive conspiracy and find Mademoiselle Wanda, it would be better not to touch her for the time being. The sudden suicide of a witness would appear suspicious.

Achimas shook his head angrily. He must not deceive himself: it was a violation of his code. These reasons were merely excuses for letting her live. At this precise moment the suicide of a chance witness to a national tragedy would seem perfectly understandable: remorse, a nervous breakdown, fear of possible consequences. He had wasted enough time. It was time to get the job done!

There was another ring at the door. Wanda was in great demand this evening.

Once again the visitor proved to be a familiar face – not an old acquaintance like Fandorin, but a recent one: the German agent Hans-Georg Knabe.

The spy's very first words put Achimas on his guard. 'You serve me badly, Fräulein Tolle.'

A fine turn of events this was! As he listened, Achimas could hardly believe his ears. What 'substance' was this? Wanda had been instructed to poison Sobolev? God preserved Germany? It was raving lunacy! Or perhaps some incredible series of coincidences that he could exploit to his own advantage?

As soon as the door closed behind the German, Achimas emerged from his hiding place.

When Wanda came back into the room, she did not notice at first that there was someone standing in the corner, and when she did she clutched at her heart and uttered a thin shriek.

'Are you a German agent?' Achimas asked curiously, ready to put his hand over her mouth if she tried to make any noise. 'Have you been making a fool of me?'

'Kolya ...' she blurted out, raising her hand to her mouth. 'Were you listening? Who are you? Who?'

He shook his head impatiently, as though shaking off a bothersome fly. 'Where is the substance?'

'How did you get in here? What for?' Wanda muttered, as if she had not heard his questions.

Achimas took her by the shoulders and sat her down. She gazed at him through wide, black pupils. He could see two miniature reflections of the lampshade in them.

'This is a strange conversation we are having, mademoiselle,' he said, sitting down facing her: 'all questions and no answers. Someone has to begin and it might as well be me. You have asked me three questions: who am I? how did I get in here? and what for? Here are my answers: I am Nikolai Nikolaevich Klonov. I got in here through the door. And as for why – I think you already know that. I engaged your services to provide a pleasurable surprise for our famous compatriot, Mikhail Dmitrievich Sobolev, and not only did he receive very little pleasure, he lost his life. Surely I am obliged to make enquiries? It would be irresponsible not to, a violation of the merchant's code. What shall I report to the Association? After all, money has been spent.'

'I'll give you back your money,' said Wanda, ready to rush away and get it.

'It is not a question of the money,' said Achimas, stopping her. 'After standing in there for a while, listening to your conversations with your visitors, I realised I had no idea of what had been going on. Apparently, you and Herr Knabe were playing your own little game. I should like to know, mademoiselle, what you did to our national hero.'

'Nothing! I swear!' She dashed across to a little cupboard and took something out of it. 'Here is the bottle that Knabe gave me. See, it's still full. I don't play other people's games.'

The tears were streaming down her face, but there was no entreaty in the gaze that she turned on him, and certainly nothing hysterical. She hadn't thrown in her hand, even though the situation she was in was truly desperate: caught between the Russian police, German intelligence and Achimas Welde, who would be worse than any police force and intelligence service combined. But then, she knew nothing about that. He glanced at the tense expression on her face. Or did she?

Achimas shook the bottle, examined its colour, sniffed the cork. Apparently crude cyanide.

'Mademoiselle, do not try to hide anything from me. How long have you been connected with German intelligence? What instructions did Knabe give you?'

A rather peculiar change came over Wanda. She stopped trembling, her tears dried up and a strange expression appeared in her eyes, an expression that Achimas had seen once before – the previous evening, when she had asked him if he regretted giving her away to someone else. She moved closer and sat on the arm of his chair, put her hand on his shoulder.

She spoke in a voice that was quiet and tired. 'Of course, Kolya. I'll tell you everything. I won't try to hide anything. Knabe is a German spy. He has been coming to me for three years now. I was a fool when it all started; I wanted to get my money as quickly as possible, and he paid very well. Not for love – for information. All sorts of men come to see me, most of them big shots of one kind or another. Some of them are from the very top. Like your Sobolev. And men like to wag their tongues in bed.' She ran a finger across his cheek. 'Someone like you probably wouldn't. But there aren't many like you. Do you really think I earned that fifty thousand in my bed? No, my dear, I'm too choosy; I have to like a man. Sometimes, of course, Knabe would deliberately offer me to someone. The way you did with Sobolev. I tried to resist, but he had me locked too tightly in his vice. At first he sang me a sweet song: "What are you doing living here in Russia, Fräulein? You're German; you have a homeland of your own. Germany will not forget the services you have rendered; honour and safety await you there. Here you will always be a courtesan, but in Germany no one will ever find out about your past. The moment you wish it, we will help you to settle down comfortably, with honour." But later he changed his tune and kept telling me how long his reach was, that German citizenship had to be earned. I don't want their damned citizenship, but there was nothing I could do. He tightened his noose round my throat. He could even kill me. Without the slightest problem. As an example to the others. He has plenty more like me.'

Wanda shivered, but then she shook her luxuriant hair almost lightheartedly. 'The day before yesterday, when Knabe heard about Sobolev – like a fool I told him myself, I wanted to get into his good books – he almost nagged me to death. He started saying that Sobolev was Germany's sworn enemy and muttering about a conspiracy in the army. He said that if Sobolev was not eliminated, there would be a great war, and Germany was not yet prepared. "I've been racking my brains," he said, "wondering how to stop this Scythian, and now I have this stroke of luck! It's providential!" He brought me the bottle of poison. He promised me mountains of gold, but I wasn't interested. Then he started threatening me. He was like a madman. I decided not to argue with him and promised to do it. But I didn't give Sobolev the poison, honestly. He just died; it was his heart. Believe me, Kolya. I may be a despicable, cynical, fallen woman, but I'm not a murderer.'

There was a hint of entreaty in her green eyes now, but still not a trace of hysterics. A proud woman. But even so, she could not be allowed to live. A pity.

Achimas sighed and placed his right hand on her exposed neck. His thumb was on her artery, his middle finger on her fourth vertebra, just below the base of the skull. He only needed to squeeze and the light in those eyes looking down at him so trustingly would fade and die.

Then something unexpected happened: Wanda put her arm round Achimas's neck, pulled him closer and pressed her hot cheek against his forehead. 'Is it you?' she whispered. 'Is it you I've been waiting for all this time?'

Achimas looked at her white, delicate skin. Something strange was happening to him.

12

When he left at dawn, Wanda was sleeping soundly with her mouth half-open like a child. Achimas stood looking down at her for a moment, feeling a bizarre stirring sensation in the left side of his chest. Then he went out quietly.

She wouldn't tell anyone, he thought, as he came out on to Petrovka Street. If she hadn't told Fandorin yesterday, why would she tell today? There was no reason to kill her.

But in his heart he felt uneasy. It was inexcusable to confuse business with personal matters. He would never have allowed himself to do it before. 'What about Evgenia?' asked a voice that came from the same spot where he could feel that alarming stirring. The time had obviously come for him to retire. What had happened the night before would never be repeated. No more contact with Wanda.

Who could link the merchant Klonov, resident until the previous day at the Metropole, with the singer from the Alpine Rose? No one. Except perhaps the *koelner* Timofei. It was unlikely, but he had better not take the risk. It would tidy things up and not take up too much of his time. The voice whispered: 'The *koelner* will die so that Wanda can live.'

Never mind, that was all right. Things had not gone so well with Knabe, however. Fandorin was almost certain to have run into the German agent as he was on his way out from Wanda's apartment yesterday evening, and being a meticulous and quick-witted detective, he was bound to have made enquiries about her late visitor. It was also only reasonable to assume that the true nature of Herr Knabe's activities was well known to the Russian authorities. A senior intelligence agent was a rather conspicuous individual.

He discerned the possibility of an excellent manoeuvre that would divert the investigation into a safe channel. 'And Wanda will be free of her noose,' the perspicacious voice added pitilessly.

Achimas set up his observation post in the attic opposite Knabe's house. It was a convenient position offering a good view of the windows on the third floor, where the German agent lived.

Fortunately it turned out to be a hot day. Of course, the roof above the attic was scorching hot by eight o'clock and it was stifling up there, but Achimas was never bothered by minor inconveniences and the heat meant that Knabe's windows were thrown wide open.

He could see quite clearly what was happening in every single room of the German agent's flat: he saw him shave in front of the mirror, drink his coffee and leaf through the newspapers, marking them in some places with a pencil. If the cheerful way he moved and the expression on his face were anything to go by (Achimas was conducting his observation through binoculars with a magnification factor of twelve), Mr Knabe was in an excellent mood.

Some time after ten he emerged from the entrance to the building and strode off in the direction of Petrovsky Square. Achimas fell in behind him. From his appearance he could have been taken for an office clerk or a shop assistant: a cap with a cracked lacquer peak, a good-quality long-skirted frock coat and a little grey goatee beard. Knabe walked on, swinging his arms energetically, and in a quarter of an hour he had reached the central post office.

Inside the building Achimas reduced the distance between them and when the German agent walked over to the telegraph window, he stood behind him.

Knabe said a cheery hello to the counter clerk, who had obviously taken telegrams from him before, and handed him a sheet of paper.

'As always, to Kerbel und Schmidt in Berlin. Stock quotations. But please,' he added with a smile, 'if you would be so kind, Panataleimon Kuzmich, don't give it to Serdiuk like the last time. He confused two figures and it caused me great unpleasantness with my superiors afterwards. Please, as a friend, give it to Semenov; let him send it.'

'All right, Ivan Egorich,' the counter clerk replied in an equally merry voice. 'So be it.'

'There should be a reply for me soon; I'll call back,' said Knabe, and with a fleeting glance at Achimas's face, he set off towards the door.

The German agent was moving at an unhurried pace now, strolling along. He whistled a frivolous little tune as he walked along the pavement. Just once he checked to see if he was being tailed – no doubt purely out of habit. He didn't look as if he suspected he was under observation.

Nonetheless, he was being observed, and rather skilfully. Achimas himself did not spot the tail immediately. But the workman on the opposite side of the street was studying the window displays of the expensive shops, where there was clearly nothing that he could afford, really much too intently; and the reason was clear: he was following Knabe through his reflection in the glass. And five to ten paces further back, there was a cabby barely even trundling along. Someone hailed him and he turned them down, and then the same thing happened again. An interesting kind of cabby.

Mr Fandorin had apparently not wasted any time the evening before.

Achimas took precautionary measures to avoid becoming too obvious. He turned into an entryway, tugged off his beard in one swift movement, put on a pair of spectacles with plain lenses, dumped his cap and turned his frock coat inside out. The frock coat had an unusual lining – a state functionary's uniform coat with the collar tabs removed. A shop assistant went into the entryway and ten seconds later a retired bureaucrat came out.

Knabe had not moved on very far yet. He stood in front of the mirror-doors of a French pastry shop for a moment and then went in.

Achimas went in after him.

The German agent was eating crème-brûlée ice cream with great gusto, washing it down with seltzer water. A young man with extremely lively, prying eyes, dressed in a summer suit, appeared out of nowhere at the next table. He hid his face behind a fashionable magazine, but every few moments he glanced quickly over the top of its cover. The cabby previously noticed halted at the pavement outside. The workman, though, had disappeared. They were really giving Herr Knabe the full treatment. But that was all right; in fact, it was helpful. Just as long as they didn't arrest him.

But all the signs indicated that they wouldn't – what point would there be in tailing him then? They wanted to identify his contacts. But Herr Knabe didn't have any contacts, or he wouldn't be maintaining contact with Berlin by telegram.

The German spy sat in the pastry shop for a long time. After his ice cream, he ate a marzipan cake, drank a hot chocolate and then ordered a tutti-frutti. His appetite was prodigious. The young sleuth was replaced by another, rather older. The first cabby's place at the pavement was taken by a different one, who was equally stubborn in refusing to accept any fares.

Achimas decided that he had exposed himself to the eyes of the police for long enough and he left the pastry shop first. He took up a position in the post office and began to wait. Along the way he had changed his social status: he had got rid of the frock coat, pulled his shirt out of his trousers and put his belt on top of it, removed his spectacles and pulled a cloth cap on to his head.

When Knabe turned up, Achimas was standing right beside the telegraph window and moving his lips intently as he traced out words in a telegram blank with a pencil. 'Tell me, old fellow,' he said to the attendant, 'will it definitely get there tomorrow?'

'I already told you: it'll get there today,' the attendant replied patronizingly. 'And you keep it short: it's not a letter; you'll bankrupt yourself. Ivan Egorich, there's a telegram for you!'

Achimas pretended to be glaring angrily at the pink-cheeked German as he stole a glance at the piece of paper thrust out from behind the window. A brief text and columns of figures – it looked like stock quotations. Their working methods in Berlin were obviously rather crude. They under-estimated the Russian gendarmes.

Knabe gave the telegram a cursory glance and thrust it into his pocket. Naturally, it was in code; now he would be bound to go home and decipher it.

Achimas broke off his surveillance and returned to the observation point in the attic.

The German agent was already at home – he must have come back in a cab (could it have been the same one?). He was sitting at the table, leafing through the pages of a book and copying something out on to a sheet of paper.

Then things began to get interesting. Knabe's movements became more rapid. He wiped his forehead nervously several times. He flung the book to the floor and clutched his head in his hands. He leapt to his feet and began running round the room. He read through what he had written again.

Apparently the news he had received was not very pleasant.

Then things became even more interesting. Knabe dashed away somewhere into the back of his apartment and came back holding a revolver. He sat down in front of a mirror. Raised the revolver to his temple three times. Stuck the barrel into his mouth.

Achimas nodded his head. How very timely. A fairy-tale ending. *Go on then, shoot yourself.*

What could have been in that message from Berlin? The answer seemed fairly obvious. The initiative taken by their Moscow agent had not met with approval. To put it mildly. The career of the would-be killer of General Sobolev lay in hopeless ruins.

No, he didn't shoot himself. He lowered the hand holding the revolver and began running round the room again. He put the revolver in his pocket. A pity.

Achimas did not see what happened in the apartment after that, because Knabe closed the windows, and for about three hours all he could do was admire the bright spots of sunlight glittering on the window panes. Glancing down every now and then at the sleuth loitering in the street, he imagined to himself how his castle would look when it sprang up on the tallest cliff of the island of Santa Croce some time in the near future. The castle would be reminiscent of the kind of towers that guarded the peace of mountain villages in the Caucasus, but at the flat-roof level there had to be a garden. The palm trees would have to be planted in tubs, of course, but turf could be laid for the shrubs.

Achimas was trying to solve the problem of providing water for his hanging garden when Knabe emerged from the entrance to the building. First the sleuth in the street started fidgeting, then he skipped away from the door and hid round a corner, and a second later the German agent appeared in person. He halted outside the entrance, waiting for something. It soon became clear what it was.

A single-seater carriage harnessed to a dun horse rolled out of an entryway. The groom jumped down from the coach box and handed the reins to Knabe, who leapt nimbly into the carriage, and the dun set off at a brisk trot.

This was all quite unexpected. Knabe was escaping surveillance and there was absolutely no possibility of following him. Achimas peered hard through his binoculars just in time to see the spy put on a ginger beard. What idea had he come up with now?

The sleuth, however, reacted quite calmly. He watched the carriage drive off, jotted something down in his notebook and walked away. He apparently knew where Knabe had gone and what for. Well, since the German agent had taken nothing with him, he was certain to come back again. It was time for Achimas to prepare his operation.

Five minutes later Achimas was already in the apartment. He took a leisurely look around and found two secret caches. The first contained a small chemical laboratory: invisible ink, poisons, an entire bottle of nitroglycerine (was he planning to blow up the Kremlin, then?). In the other there were several revolvers, some money – about thirty thousand roubles at a glance – and a book of logarithmic tables, which had to be the key to the code.

Achimas did not touch the contents of the caches. The gendarmes could have them. Unfortunately, Knabe had burnt the decoded telegram – there were traces of ash in the kitchen sink.

It was bad that the apartment had no rear entrance. A window in the corridor overlooked the roof of an extension. Achimas climbed out, walked around for a while on the rumbling iron sheeting and confirmed that the roof was a dead end. The drainpipe was rusted through; you couldn't climb down it. All right.

He sat down by the window and prepared himself for a long wait.

Some time after nine, when the light of the long summer day had begun to fade, the familiar single-seater carriage came hurtling out from behind a corner. The dun was pushing as hard as it could, scattering thick flakes of lather behind it. Knabe was standing in the carriage and brandishing his whip frantically.

A chase?

Apparently not, Achimas could not hear anything.

Knabe dropped the reins and vanished into the entrance of the building.

It was time. Achimas took up the position he had spied out in advance, behind the coat stand in the hallway. He was holding a sharp knife he had taken from the kitchen.

The apartment was already prepared – everything turned upside down, the contents of the cupboards scattered about; even the eiderdown had been slit open. A crude imitation of a burglary. Mr Fandorin ought to conclude that Herr Knabe had been eliminated by his own people, who had made a clumsy attempt to fake an ordinary, everyday crime.

The act itself took only a moment.

The key scraped in the lock, and Knabe had only run a few steps along the dark corridor before he died without realising what had happened.

Achimas looked around carefully to make sure everything was in place and went out on to the staircase.

A door slammed downstairs and he heard voices talking loudly. Someone was running up the stairs. That was bad.

He backed away into the apartment and slammed the door perhaps a bit louder than was necessary. He had fifteen seconds at the most.

He opened the window at the end of the corridor and hid behind the coat stand again.

Literally the very next instant a man burst into the apartment. He looked like a merchant. The 'merchant' was holding a revolver, a Herstahl-Agent. A fine little gun. At one time Achimas had used one himself. The 'merchant' froze over the motionless body for a moment, then did what he was supposed to and went dashing round the rooms and finally out through the window on to the roof.

There wasn't a sound on the staircase. Achimas slipped silently out of the apartment. Now he only had to take care of the *koelner* at the Metropole and he could consider the first point of his plan completed.

13

Before he could proceed to the second point of his plan, a little brain work was required. That night Achimas lay in his room in the Troitsa, staring up at the ceiling and thinking.

The tidying-up had been completed. The *koelner* had been dealt with. There was no need to worry about the police. The German line of enquiry would keep them busy for a long time yet.

Now for the matter of his stolen fee.

Question: How could he find the bandit called Little Misha?

What did he know about him?

He was the leader of a gang – otherwise he would not have been able to track Achimas down and then send someone to kill him. So far that seemed to be all.

Now for the safebreaker who had stolen the briefcase. What could be said about him? No normal-sized man could have squeezed though the small window opening. So it was a juvenile? No, it was unlikely that a juvenile could have opened the safe so skilfully; that required experience. On the whole it had been a rather neat job: no broken glass, no signs of breaking and entering. The thief had even locked the safe when he was finished. So it was a small man, not a juvenile. And the gang leader was called Little Misha. Which made it reasonable to assume that he and the safebreaker were one and the same person. So this Misha must have the briefcase.

To sum up: he had a slim, agile little man known as Little Misha who knew how to crack safes and was the leader of a serious gang. That was really quite a lot. He could be quite sure that a conspicuous specialist like that would be well known in Khitrovka.

But that was precisely why he would be far from easy to find. Pretending to be a criminal would be pointless – you had to know their customs, their patois, their rules of etiquette. It would make more sense to play the part of a 'gull' who required the services of a good safebreaker – say, a shop assistant who dreamed in secret of getting his hands into his master's safe.

Early on Sunday, before he set out for Khitrovka, Achimas was unable to resist the temptation to turn on to Myasnitskaya Street and watch the funeral procession.

It was an impressive spectacle. None of the many operations he had carried out in the course of a long career had produced such an impressive result. Standing in the crowd of people weeping and crossing themselves, Achimas felt as if he were the central character in this grandiose theatrical production, its invisible centre. It was an unfamiliar, intoxicating feeling.

Riding behind the hearse on a black horse was a pompous-looking general. Arrogant and pretentious. Certain that in this spectacle he was the only star of the first magnitude. But like all the others, he was no more than a puppet. The puppet master was standing modestly on the pavement, lost to view among the sea of faces. Nobody knew him, nobody looked at him, but the awareness of his unique importance set his head spinning faster than any wine.

'That's Kirill Alexandrovich, the Tsar's brother,' someone said, referring to the mounted general. 'A fine figure of a man.'

Suddenly a woman in a black shawl pushed aside one of the gendarmes in the cordon and dashed out of the crowd to the hearse. 'Whose care have you left us to, our dear father?' she keened in a shrill whine, pressing her face down against the crimson velvet.

The grand duke's Arabian steed flared its nostrils in fright at this heart-rending wail and reared up on its hind legs. One of the adjutants made to seize the panicking horse's bridle, but Kirill Alexandrovich checked him with his powerful resonant voice: 'Back, Neplyuev. Don't interfere! I'll handle it!' Retaining his seat without any difficulty, he brought his mount to its senses in an instant. Snorting nervously, it began ambling sideways in small steps, then straightened up again.

The hysterical female mourner was taken by the arms and led back into the crowd, and the minor incident was over.

But Achimas's mood had changed. He no longer felt like the master pulling the strings in the puppet theatre. The voice that had ordered the adjutant not to interfere had been only too familiar. Once heard, a voice like that could never be confused with any other.

What a surprise to meet you like this, my dear Monsieur N.N.

Achimas cast an eye over the portly figure in the Cavalry Guards' uniform. This was the true puppet master, the one who pulled all the strings, and the Cavaliere Welde, otherwise the future Count of Santa Croce, was a mere stage prop. So be it.

He spent the whole day in Khitrovka. The funeral chimes of Moscow's forty times forty churches reached even here, but the denizens of Khitrovka had no interest in the respectable city's mourning over some general or other. This was a microcosm teeming with its own secret life, like a drop of dirty water under a microscope.

Achimas, dressed as a shop assistant, had suffered two attempts to rob him and three to pick his pocket, one of which had been successful: someone had slit his long-waisted cloth coat open with something sharp and pulled out his purse. There was hardly any money in it, but the skill was very impressive.

For a long time his attempts to find the safebreaker produced no results. Most of the local inhabitants would not enter into conversation at all, and those who would suggested people he didn't want – someone called Kiriukha, or Shtukar, or Kolsha the Gymnast. It was after four in the afternoon when he first heard Little Misha's name mentioned.

It happened while Achimas was sitting in the 'Siberia' tavern, where second-hand dealers and the more prosperous professional beggars gathered. He was chatting with a promising ragamuffin whose eyes shifted their focus with that particular alacrity found only among thieves and dealers in stolen goods.

Achimas treated his neighbour to some cheap vodka and made himself out to be a cunning but none too bright assistant from a haberdashery shop on Tverskaya Street. When he mentioned that his master kept an enormous fortune in cash in the safe, and if only some knowledgeable person would teach him how to open the lock, it would be no problem to take two or three hundred out of it once or twice a week – nobody would miss it – the ragamuffin's eyes glittered: his foolish prey had delivered itself straight into his hands.

'Misha's the one you need,' the local expert said confidently. 'He'll do a nice neat job.'

Achimas put on a doubtful expression and asked: 'Is he a man with brains? Not some cheap beggar?'

'Who, Little Misha?' said the ragamuffin, giving Achimas a disdainful look. 'You look into the Hard Labour this evening; Misha's lads are in there on the spree every evening. I'll call round and give them the whisper about you. They'll give you a grand reception.'

The ragamuffin's eyes glittered – he evidently had high hopes that Little Misha would pay him a commission for such a nice fat lead.

Achimas was ensconced in the Hard Labour from early in the evening. But he had not arrived dressed as a shop assistant; now he was a blind beggar, dressed in rags and bast sandals, and he had slipped small transparent sheets of calf's bladder under his eyelids. He could see through them as if he were looking through fog, but they gave a convincing impression of his eyes being obscured by cataracts. Achimas knew from experience that blind men roused no suspicion and nobody paid any attention to them. If a blind man sat quietly, the people around him stopped noticing him altogether.

He sat quietly. Not so much watching as listening. A company of tipsy men who were clearly bandits had gathered at a table a short distance away. They could be from Misha's gang, but the agile little burglar was not among them.

Events started moving when darkness had already fallen

outside the dim glass of the basement windows.

Achimas took no notice of the new arrivals when they first came in. There were two of them: a junk dealer and a bandy-legged Kirghiz in a greasy kaftan. A minute later another one arrived: a hunchback doubled right over to the ground. It would never have occurred to him that they might be detectives. You had to give the Moscow police their due; they certainly knew their job. Yet somehow the disguised undercover agents were spotted.

It was all over in a moment. Everything was peaceful and quiet and then two of them – the junk dealer and the Kirghiz – were stretched out, probably dead, the hunchback was lying stunned on the floor and one of the bandits was rolling about and screaming that it 'hurt something awful' in a repulsive voice that sounded fake.

The one Achimas had been waiting for appeared on the scene soon after that. A nervous, agile little dandy wearing European clothes, but with his trousers tucked into a pair of box-calf boots polished to a high gleam. Achimas was familiar with this particular criminal type, which he classified according to his own system as 'weasels' – minor, but dangerous, predators. It was strange that Little Misha had risen to a position of such prominence in Moscow's criminal underworld. 'Weasels' usually became stool pigeons or double agents.

Never mind, it would be clear soon enough what kind of character he really was.

They dragged the dead police agents behind a partition and carried the stunned one away somewhere else.

Misha and his cut-throats sat down at their table and began eating and drinking. The one who had been lying on the floor, groaning, soon fell silent, but the event passed unnoticed. It was half an hour later before the bandits suddenly remembered and drank 'to the repose of the soul of Senya Lomot', and Little Misha, with his thin voice, delivered a heartfelt speech, half of which consisted of odd words that Achimas didn't understand. The speaker respectfully described the dead man as a 'smooth operator', and all the others nodded in agreement. The wake did not last for long. They dragged Lomot away by the legs to the same place where they'd taken the two dead police agents, and the feasting continued as if nothing special had happened.

Achimas tried not to miss a single word of the bandits' conversation. The longer it continued, the more convinced he became that they knew nothing about the million roubles. Perhaps Misha had pulled the job on his own, without any help from his comrades in crime. In any case, he couldn't get away now. Achimas only had to wait for the right moment to have a confidential little talk with him.

When it was almost morning and the inn had emptied, Misha stood up and said loudly: 'That's enough chinwagging. I don't know about you, but I'm going to cuddle up close with Fiska. But first let's have our little chat with the nark.'

Laughing and guffawing, the entire gang went behind the bar and disappeared into the depths of the basement.

Achimas looked around. The innkeeper had been snoring away behind the planking partition for a long time already, and the only two customers left were a man and a woman who had drunk themselves unconscious. This was the right time.

Behind the counter there was a dark corridor. Achimas could see a dimly lit rectangle ahead of him and hear muted voices coming from it. A cellar?

Achimas removed the membrane from one eye and cautiously glanced down. All five of the bandits were there. He would have to wait for them to finish off the fake hunchback and take them down quietly one by one when they started climbing back up.

But things didn't turn out that way.

The police agent turned out to be nobody's stooge. Achimas had never seen skill like it before. The 'hunchback' dealt with the entire gang in a matter of seconds. Without even getting up, he jerked one hand and then the other and two of the bandits grabbed frantically at their throats. Were those knives he had thrown at them? The police agent broke the skulls of another two bandits with a most curious device – a stick of wood on a chain. Would you believe it? – so simple and yet so effective.

But Achimas was even more impressed by the deftness with which the 'hunchback' carried out his interrogation of Misha. Now he knew everything that he needed to know. He hid in the shadows and followed the detective and his prisoner through the dark labyrinth without making a sound.

They went in through a door and a moment later he heard the sound of shots. Who had come out on top? Achimas was sure that it wouldn't be Misha. And if he were right, it made no sense to go barging in and getting himself shot by such an adroit police agent. Better ambush him in the corridor. No, it was too dark. He might miss and not kill him with the first shot.

Achimas went back to the inn and lay down on a bench.

The dexterous detective appeared almost immediately and – what a pleasant surprise – he had the briefcase. Should Achimas shoot or wait? The 'hunchback' was holding his revolver at the ready; his reactions were lightning-fast, and he would start shooting at the slightest movement. Achimas squinted with the eye that had no membrane in it. Was that the familiar Herstahl? Could this be the same 'merchant' who had been at Knabe's apartment?

Events unfolded with dizzying speed as the detective arrested the innkeeper and found his men, one of whom, the Kirghiz, was still alive.

An interesting detail: when the 'hunchback' was bandaging his friend's head with a towel, they spoke to each other in Japanese. Miracles would never cease – a Japanese in Khitrovka! Achimas was familiar with the fluent rolling sounds of that exotic tongue from a job of three years before, when he had carried out a commission in Hong Kong. The police agent called the Japanese 'Masa'.

Now that the disguised detective was no longer imitating an old man's trembling voice, Achimas thought that he sounded familiar. He listened more closely – was that really Mr Fandorin? A truly resourceful young man – there was no denying it. You didn't meet many of his kind.

Achimas decided that it was definitely not worth taking any risks. You had to be doubly careful with an individual like that, especially since the detective was not letting his guard down – he kept darting glances in all directions and his Herstahl was always close at hand.

The three of them – Fandorin, the Japanese and the innkeeper with his hands tied – went outside. Achimas watched them through the dusty window. The detective, still clutching the briefcase, went off to look for a cab, the Japanese stayed behind to guard the prisoner. The innkeeper tried to kick out, but the short oriental hissed angrily and knocked the strapping Tartar off his feet with single swift movement.

I'll have to keep chasing the briefcase, thought Achimas. *Sooner or later Mr Fandorin will calm down and relax. Meanwhile I should check to see if my debtor Little Misha is dead or alive.*

Achimas walked quickly through the dark corridors and pulled at the half-open door. The little room behind it was dimly lit. There didn't seem to be anyone there.

He went across and felt the crumpled bed: it was still warm.

Then Achimas heard a low groan from the corner. Swinging round sharply, he saw a huddled figure. It was Little Misha, sitting on the floor, clutching his stomach with both hands.

He raised his moist, gleaming eyes and his mouth twisted pathetically as he uttered a thin, plaintive whine. 'Brother, it's me, Misha ... I'm wounded ... Help me ... Who are you, brother?'

Achimas clicked open the blade of his clasp knife, leaned down and slit the sitting man's throat. There would be less bother that way. And it was a debt repaid.

He ran back to the inn and lay down on the bench.

Outside hooves clattered and wheels squeaked. Fandorin came running in, this time without the briefcase, and disappeared into the corridor. He had gone to get Little Misha. But where was the briefcase? Had he left it with the Japanese?

Achimas swung his legs down off the bench.

No, there was no time.

He lay down again, beginning to feel angry. But he must not allow his exasperation to affect him – that was the source of all mistakes.

Fandorin emerged from the bowels of the underground labyrinth with his face a contorted mask, swinging the Herstahl in all directions. He glanced briefly at the blind man and dashed out of the inn.

Outside a voice shouted: 'Off you go! Drive hard to Malaya Nikitskaya Street, to the Department of Gendarmes!'

Achimas pulled out his cataracts. He had to hurry.

14

He drove up to the Department of Gendarmes in a fast, smart cab, jumped out as it was still moving and asked the sentry impatiently: 'Two of our men just brought in a prisoner; where are they?'

The gendarme was not at all surprised by the peremptory tone of the determined man who was dressed in rags, but had a gleam of authority in his eyes. 'They went straight through to see His Excellency. Less than two minutes ago. And the prisoner's being registered; he's in the duty office.'

'Damn the rotten prisoner!' the disguised officer exclaimed with an irritable gesture. 'I need Fandorin. You say he went to see His Excellency?'

'Yes, sir. Up the stairs and along the corridor on the left.'

'I know the way well enough!'

Achimas ran up the shallow stairs from the vestibule to the first floor. He looked to the right. From behind the white door at the far end of the corridor he could hear the clash of metal on metal. It must be the gymnastics hall. Nothing dangerous there. He turned to the left. The broad corridor was empty, with only occasional bustling messengers in uniforms or civilian clothes emerging from one office door only to disappear immediately into another.

Achimas froze where he stood: after a long sequence of absurd misfortunes and reverses, Fortune had finally exchanged her wrath for favour. The Japanese was sitting outside a door bearing a plaque that read 'Reception', holding the briefcase in his hands. Fandorin must be reporting to the chief of police about the events of the night. Why had he gone in without the briefcase? He wanted to flaunt his success; he was playing for effect. The night had been full of events – the detective would have a long story to tell – so Achimas had a few minutes to spare.

Walk up without hurrying. Stab him under the collarbone. Take the briefcase. Leave the same way he had come. All over in a moment.

Achimas considered the Japanese more closely. Gazing straight ahead, holding the briefcase with both hands, he looked like a taut spring. In Hong Kong Achimas had been able to observe the Japanese mastery of unarmed combat. The masters of English boxing or French wrestling could not possibly compare with it. This short fellow had thrown the massive Tartar innkeeper to the ground in a single movement. All over in a moment.

He couldn't take the risk. If there was a hitch, the slightest commotion would bring people running from every direction.

He had to think, time was slipping away!

Achimas swung round and walked quickly towards the sound of clashing rapiers. When he opened the door marked 'Officers' Gymnastics Hall', he saw a dozen or so figures in masks and white fencing costumes. All playing at musketeers.

Aha, there was the door to the changing room. He took off his rags and bast sandals, put on the first uniform jacket that came to hand and chose a pair of boots that were his size – that was important. Hurry, hurry.

As he trotted back briskly in the opposite direction, his eye was caught by a plaque with the words 'Post Room'. The petty functionary behind the counter was sorting envelopes.

'Is there any correspondence for Captain Pevtsov?' asked Achimas, giving the first name that came to mind.

'No, sir.'

'Well, just take a look, will you?'

The functionary shrugged, stuck his nose into the ledger and began rustling through the pages.

Achimas snatched an official envelope with seals off the counter and slipped it into his cuff. 'All right, don't bother. I'll come back later.'

He strode smartly up to the Japanese and saluted. 'Mr Masa.'

The Oriental jumped to his feet and greeted the officer with a low bow.

'I have come to you on the instructions of Mr Fandorin, do you understand?'

The Japanese bowed even lower.

Excellent: he didn't have a word of Russian.

'Here are my written instructions to collect the briefcase

335

from you.' Achimas held out the envelope, pointing at the briefcase with it.

The Japanese hesitated.

Achimas waited, counting off the passing seconds. The hand hidden behind his back was clutching a knife. Another five seconds and he would have to strike. He couldn't wait any longer. Five, four, three, two ...

The Japanese bowed once again, gave him the briefcase, took the envelope with both hands and pressed it to his forehead. Apparently his time to die had not yet come.

Achimas saluted, turned round and walked through into the reception area. He could not possibly leave by the corridor – the Japanese would have found that strange.

A spacious room. Straight ahead – the police chief's office. Fandorin must be in there. On the left – a window. On the right – a plaque with the words 'Secret Section'.

The adjutant was hovering outside his boss's door, which was most opportune. Achimas gestured reassuringly to him and disappeared through the door on the right. His luck held again – Fortune was growing kinder with every moment. It was not an office, where he would have had to improvise, but a short corridor with windows overlooking a courtyard.

Farewell, gentlemen and gendarmes.

Achimas Welde moved on to the third and final point in his plan of action.

The dashing captain of gendarmes walked up to the office floor of the governor-general's house and asked the attendant in a strict voice where Court Counsellor Khurtinsky's office was, then strode off in the direction indicated, swinging his heavy briefcase.

Khurtinsky greeted the 'urgent courier from St Petersburg' with a smile of phoney amiability.

Achimas also smiled, but sincerely, without a trace of pretence – he had been looking forward to this meeting for a

336

long time. 'Hello, you scoundrel,' he said, gazing into the dull grey eyes of Mr Nemo, Monsieur N.N.'s crafty helot. 'I am Klonov. This is Sobolev's briefcase. And this is your death.' He clicked open his clasp knife.

The court counsellor's face turned an intense white and his eyes an intense black, because the expanding pupils completely consumed the surrounding irises. 'I can explain everything,' the head of the secret chancellery mouthed almost soundlessly. 'Only don't kill me!'

'If I wanted to kill you, you would already be lying on the ground with your throat slit open. What I want from you is something else,' said Achimas, raising his voice in imitation of icy fury.

'Anything at all! Only for God's sake keep your voice down!' Khurtinsky stuck his head out into the reception area and told his secretary not to let anyone through.

'Listen, I can explain everything ...' he whispered when he came back.

'You can explain to the grand duke, you Judas,' Achimas interrupted. 'Sit down and write! Write!' He waved his knife in the air and Khurtinsky staggered backwards in horror.

'All right, all right. But what shall I write?'

'The truth.' Achimas stood behind the trembling functionary.

The court counsellor glanced round in fright, but his eyes were already grey again, not black. No doubt the cunning Mr Nemo was already pondering how he was going to wriggle out of this situation.

'Write: "*I, Pyotr Khurtinsky, am guilty of having committed a crime against my duty out of avarice and of having betrayed him whom I should have served faithfully and assisted in every way possible in his onerous obligations. God is my judge. I beg to inform Your Imperial Highness that ...*" '

As soon as Khurtinsky had written the word 'judge',

Achimas smashed his cervical vertebrae with a blow of his hand.

He hung the corpse up on the cord from the transom and regarded the look of surprise on the dead man's face with satisfaction. It was not profitable to play the fool with Achimas Welde.

That was all. His business in Moscow was concluded.

Still wearing his gendarme uniform, Achimas sent a telegram from the post office to Monsieur N.N. at his reserve address. He knew from the newspapers that Grand Duke Kirill Alexandrovich had left for St Petersburg the previous day. The text of the telegram was as follows: *'Payment has been received. Mr Nemo proved to be an untrustworthy partner. Difficulties have arisen with Mr Fandorin of the Moscow branch of the company. Your good offices are required. Klonov.'*

After a moment's hesitation, he gave his address at the Troitsa. It involved a certain degree of risk, of course, but only within the bounds of what he considered acceptable. Now that he knew who N.N. was, the likelihood of a double-cross seemed insignificant. N.N. was too important a figure to bother with such trivia. And he really did need the grand duke's help. The operation had been concluded, but the last thing he wanted was a police investigation following his trail into Europe. That would not suit the future Count of Santa Croce at all. Mr Fandorin was too perspicacious and quick-witted. Let them restrain him a little.

After that he dropped into the Bryansk Station and bought a ticket for the Paris train. Tomorrow, at eight o'clock in the morning, Achimas Welde would leave the city in which he had carried out his final commission. A brilliant professional career had been concluded with appropriate aplomb.

He suddenly felt like giving himself a present. A free man,

especially one who had retired from business, could afford to indulge himself.

He wrote a letter: '*Tomorrow at six a.m. be at the Troitsa Inn on Khokhlovksy Lane. My room is number 7, with an entrance from the courtyard. Knock twice, then three times, then twice again. I am leaving and I want to say goodbye. Nikolai.*' He sent the letter from the station by the municipal post, with the envelope addressed as follows: '*For delivery to Miss Tolle in person, the Anglia apartments, corner of Petrovka Street and Stoleshnikov Lane.*'

It was all right; he could do it. Everything had been neatly tidied away. Of course, he couldn't go sticking his own nose into the Anglia – Wanda might be under secret surveillance. But the surveillance would soon be lifted and the case closed: Monsieur N.N. would see to that.

He could give Wanda a goodbye present – the pitiful fifty thousand roubles she needed in order to feel free and live her life as she wished. And perhaps even arrange a further meeting? In a different, free life.

The voice that had settled in the left half of Achimas's chest a little while before, but had so far been drowned out by the louder considerations of business, suddenly began running riot. 'Why separate at all?' it whispered. 'The Count of Santa Croce is quite a different matter from Achimas Welde. His Excellency does not have to live alone.'

The voice was instructed to be silent, but even so Achimas went back to the ticket office, returned his ticket and bought one for a double sleeping compartment instead. The additional hundred and twenty roubles was a mere trifle, and it would be more pleasant to travel without any neighbours. 'Ha-ha,' commented the voice.

I'll decide tomorrow, when I meet her, Achimas argued to himself. *She will either get her fifty thousand or leave with me.*

Suddenly he remembered that this had happened before:

twenty-five years ago, with Evgenia. But then he had avoided making a decision and not taken a horse for her. This time the horse was ready and waiting.

For the rest of the day Achimas thought about nothing else. In the evening he lay in his room, unable to get to sleep – something that had never happened to him before. Eventually his thoughts became confused and unclear and gave way to a series of incoherent, fleeting images. Wanda appeared, then her face quivered slightly and changed imperceptibly until it was transformed into Evgenia's face. Strange: he thought her features had been erased from his memory long ago. Wanda–Evgenia looked at him tenderly and said: 'What transparent eyes you have, Lia. Like water.'

When the gentle knock came at the door Achimas, still not really awake, shot upright on the bed and grabbed his revolver from under the pillow. The grey light of dawn filled the window.

There was another knock, a simple sequence, with no intervals.

He went downstairs, stepping without making a sound.

'Mr Klonov!' a voice called out. 'An urgent telegram for you! From Monsieur N.N.!'

Achimas opened the door, holding the hand with the revolver behind his back.

He saw a tall man in a cloak. The face under the long peak of the cap was invisible, apart from the curled ends of the moustache. The messenger handed him an envelope and left without another word, disappearing into the hazy early-morning twilight.

Mr Welde, the investigation has been halted. However, a slight complication has arisen. Collegiate Assessor Fandorin, acting on his own initiative, has learned of your whereabouts and intends to arrest you. We were informed of this by the chief of police in Moscow, who requested our sanction. We ordered him to take no action, but not to inform the collegiate assessor. Fandorin will arrive at your apartment at six in the morning. He will come alone, unaware that there will be no police to assist him. This man is acting in a way that threatens the outcome of the entire operation. Deal with him as you see fit.

My thanks for a job well done. N.N.

Achimas experienced two feelings at once, one pleasant and the other very unpleasant.

The pleasant feeling was simple enough: killing Fandorin would make an impressive final entry in his service record and it would settle an old score; it would make everything neat and tidy.

But the second feeling was more complicated: how had Fandorin discovered the address? Obviously not from N.N. And then six o'clock was the time set for Wanda's visit. Could she really have betrayed him? That changed everything.

He looked at his watch. Half past four. More than enough time to prepare. There was absolutely no risk, of course: the advantages were all on Achimas's side; but Mr Fandorin was a serious individual and carelessness would be unpardonable. And there was an additional difficulty involved. It was easy to kill someone who was not expecting to be attacked, but first he needed Fandorin to tell him how he knew the address.

Only let it not be from Wanda. Nothing was more important than that to Achimas now.

From half past five he was at his post by the window, behind the curtain.

At three minutes past six a man in a stylish cream-coloured jacket and fashionable narrow trousers entered the courtyard bathed in the soft light of morning. Now Achimas had an opportunity to study the face of his old acquaintance in detail. He liked the face – it was energetic and intelligent. A worthy opponent. He had only been unlucky with his allies.

Fandorin halted at the door and filled his lungs with air. Then for some reason he puffed out his cheeks and released the air in short bursts. Was this some kind of callisthenics?

He raised his hand and knocked gently. Twice, then three times, then twice again.

PART THREE
White and Black

THE SVEIAN GATES

OR

THE PENULTIMATE CHAPTER IN WHICH
FANDORIN IS REDUCED TO ZERO

Erast Petrovich listened: there was no sound. He knocked again. Nothing. He pushed the door carefully and it yielded unexpectedly, with a hostile creak. Could the trap possibly be empty?

Holding his revolver out in front of him with one hand, he ran quickly up the stairs three steps at a time and found himself in a square room with a low ceiling. After the bright sunlight, the room seemed completely dark. On the right was the dark-grey rectangle of the window and further away, by the wall, stood an iron bed, a cupboard and a chair.

What was that on the bed? A vague form covered with a blanket. Someone was lying there.

The collegiate assessor's eyes had already adjusted to the dim light and he could make out an arm or, rather, a sleeve, dangling lifelessly from under the blanket. The gloved hand was turned palm upwards. On the floor lay a Colt revolver with a small, dark puddle beside it.

This was quite unexpected. His heart aching with disappointment, Fandorin put the now superfluous Herstahl in his pocket, walked across the room and pulled back the blanket.

*

Achimas stood absolutely still by the window, behind the thick curtain. He had been in a vile mood since the detective gave the coded knock at the door. So it had been Wanda after all ...

Everything in the room had been set up so that Fandorin would not bother to gaze around him but instantly focus his attention in the wrong direction, turn his back on Achimas and put his gun away.

All three goals had been achieved.

'Now then,' Achimas said in a low voice, 'put your hands behind your head. And don't even think of turning round, Mr Fandorin. I'll kill you.'

Annoyance was the first emotion that Fandorin felt when he saw the crude stuffed-clothing dummy under the blanket and heard that calm, self-assured voice. He had been duped like an idiot!

But annoyance was rapidly displaced by bewilderment. Why had Klonov–Pevtsov been ready for him? Had he been keeping watch at the window and seen that someone else had come instead of Wanda? But he had addressed him by name. That meant he had known and was waiting. How had he known? Could Wanda have managed to inform him after all? But then, why had he waited? Why had he not made his escape?

The conclusion was that his opponent had known about 'Mr Fandorin's' forthcoming visit, but not about the police operation. Very strange.

But then, this was not the time to be devising hypotheses. What should he do? Throw himself to the side? It was a lot more difficult than the ersatz captain of gendarmes might imagine to hit a man who had studied with the 'stealthy ones'.

But in that case, the sound of shots would bring the police running; they would open fire, and then it would not be possible to take the miscreant alive.

Fandorin put his hands behind his head. Calmly, in the same tone of voice as his opponent, he asked: 'And then what?'

'Take off your jacket,' Achimas told him. 'Throw it into the centre of the room.'

The jacket landed with a resounding clang. Evidently its pockets were stocked with more than just the Herstahl. The detective had a holster with a little pistol on the back of his belt.

'Take out the Derringer. Throw it under the bed. Right under. Now bend over. Slowly. Pull up your left trouser leg. Higher. Now the right one.'

There it was: a stiletto attached to his left ankle with its handle downwards. It was a pleasure doing business with such a prudent man.

'Now you can turn round.'

The detective turned round in the right way: with no hurry, in order not to strain his opponent's nerves unnecessarily.

Why did he have those four metal stars on his braces? Some other cunning oriental trick, no doubt.

'Take off your braces. Throw them under the bed.'

The detective's attractive features contorted in fury. The long eyelashes trembled – Fandorin was squinting in an attempt to make out the face of the man opposite him, who was standing with his back to the light.

Well, now he could show himself and see how good the young man's visual memory was.

It proved to be good. Achimas took two steps forward and was gratified to see the handsome fellow's cheeks blossom into patches of scarlet, then suddenly turn pale.

Now, young man, see what a capricious lady Fate is.

This was no man, but some kind of devil. He had even recognised the *sharinken* as weapons. Erast Petrovich was seething with anger at being entirely stripped of his arsenal.

Or almost entirely.

Out of all his numerous means of defence (and he had thought his selection was too generous!), the only one left was the arrow in the sleeve of his shirt – a slim shaft of steel attached to a strong spring. He only had to flex his elbow sharply and the spring would be released. But it was hard to kill anyone with an arrow – unless, that is, you could hit them precisely in the eye. And how could you make any sharp movements when you were looking down the barrel of a Baillard six-shooter?

At this point the dark silhouette moved closer and Fandorin finally had a clear view of his opponent's face.

Those eyes! Those white eyes! The same face that Erast Petrovich had seen in his dreams all these years. It was impossible! This was another nightmare. If only he could wake up.

He had to exploit his psychological advantage, before his opponent could gather his wits.

'Who told you the address, the time and how to knock?'

The detective did not answer.

Achimas lowered the barrel of his gun, aiming at a kneecap, but Fandorin did not seem to be frightened. On the contrary, he even seemed to turn a bit less pale.

'Wanda?' asked Achimas, unable to restrain himself, and there was a tell-tale note of hoarseness in his voice.

No, this one won't tell me, he thought. *He'll die before he says anything. That's his type.*

Then suddenly the detective opened his mouth and spoke. 'I'll tell you. In exchange for a question from me. How was Sobolev killed?'

Achimas shook his head. The boundless extent of human eccentricity never ceased to amuse him. But professional curiosity from a man about to die deserved some respect.

'All right,' he said with a nod. 'But the answer must be honest. Your word on it?'

'My word.'

'A substance extracted from an Amazonian fern. Paralysis of the heart muscle when the heartbeat accelerates. No traces. The Château d'Yquem.'

No further clarification was required. 'Ah, so that was it,' muttered Fandorin.

'It was Wanda, then,' Achimas asked through clenched teeth.

'No, she didn't give you away.'

The immense relief almost took Achimas's breath away – for an instant he even closed his eyes.

When he saw the features of this man tense in anticipation of his answer, Fandorin realised why he was still alive. But the answer to this question that was so important to the man with white eyes would be followed instantly by a bullet. He must not miss that brief instant when the finger shifted slightly on the trigger as it began to move. An armed man dealing with an unarmed inevitably suppressed his instinctive responses because he felt secure, and placed too much reliance in soulless metal. The reactions of such a man were retarded – this was basic to the art of the 'stealthy ones'.

The important thing was to divine the precise moment. First dart forwards to the left, and the bullet would pass you on the right. Then throw yourself at his feet, and the second bullet would pass over your head. And then an uppercut.

It was risky. Eight paces was quite a distance. And if his opponent decided to step back a bit, he could write the idea off.

But there was no choice.

Then the white-eyed man committed his first blunder: he closed his eyes for an instant.

That was enough. Erast Petrovich didn't waste any time diving under bullets; he launched himself upwards like a spring and shot through the window.

He broke out the frame with his elbows, flew on in a swirl of broken glass, somersaulted in the air and landed safely in a squatting position. He didn't even cut himself.

His ears were ringing – the man with white eyes must have fired a shot after all. But he had missed, naturally.

Fandorin began running along beside the wall. He snatched a whistle out of his trouser pocket and sounded the signal for the operation to begin.

Achimas had never seen a man move with such speed. One moment he was standing still, and the next his boots and white gaiters had disappeared through the window. He fired, but just a split second too late.

Without pausing for thought, he leapt over the glass-strewn window sill and landed outside on all fours.

The detective was blowing frantically on a whistle as he ran. Achimas even felt slightly sorry for him: the poor fellow had been counting on support from the police.

Moving as lightly as a boy, Fandorin was already turning the corner. Achimas fired from the hip and chips of plaster sprayed off the wall. Not good enough.

But the outer courtyard was bigger than the inner one. His opponent would never reach the gates.

There they were, the gates – with their wooden canopy and carved pillars. A primordially Russian structure from the days before Peter the Great, but for some reason they were called 'Sveian gates', from an old Russian word for 'Swedish'. Evidently, in ancient times the Muscovites must have been taught this marvel of carpentry by some Swedish merchant.

The yardkeeper holding the broom froze in the middle of the courtyard with his gap-toothed mouth hanging open. The man who had been pretending to be a drunk was still sitting there on his bench, gawking at the collegiate assessor as he ran. The strange woman in the patterned shawl and shapeless coat had pressed herself fearfully against the wall. Erast Petrovich suddenly realised that they weren't police agents! They were simply a yardkeeper, a lousy drunk and a street beggar.

He heard running steps behind him.

Fandorin began zigzagging, and just in time. Something hot seared his shoulder. Nothing serious, just a graze.

Outside the gates the street was drenched in golden sunshine. It looked so close, but he would never make it. Erast Petrovich stopped and turned round. What was the point of taking a bullet in the back?

The man with white eyes stopped too. There had been three shots, so there were three bullets left in the Baillard – more than enough to put an end to the earthly journey of Mr Erast Fandorin, twenty-six years of age, with no living relatives.

The distance was twenty-five paces: too far for him to try to do anything. Where was Karachentsev? Where were his men? But he had no time to think about that now.

The arrow under the cuff of his shirt would hardly be effective at that kind of distance. Nonetheless, Erast Petrovich raised his arm and prepared to flex his elbow.

The man with white eyes also took aim unhurriedly at his chest.

The collegiate assessor suddenly had a fleeting vision: the duel scene from *Eugene Onegin*. The man with white eyes was about to burst into song: 'If I should fall, pierced by an arrow ...'

Two bullets in the chest. Then walk up and put the third in his head.

Nobody would come running at the sound of shooting. In

these parts you couldn't find a constable for love or money. There was no need to hurry.

Then Achimas caught some rapid movement out of the corner of his eye: a low, squat shadow darting away from the wall.

Swinging round sharply, he saw a face with narrow slits for eyes contorted into a mask of fury beneath an absurd patterned shawl; he saw a mouth opened in a piercing shriek. The Japanese!

His finger squeezed the trigger.

The pitiful woman who had been huddling timidly against the wall suddenly uttered the war cry of the Yokohama *yakuza* and launched herself at the man with white eyes in exemplary jujitsu fashion.

The man turned adroitly and fired, but the woman ducked under the bullet and, with a perfectly executed *mawasagiri* from the fourth position, she knocked the gunman off his feet. The absurd patterned shawl slid down on to her shoulders, exposing a head of black hair bandaged with a white towel.

Masa! How could he be here? He'd followed him, the rogue! Fandorin had thought he was much too willing to let his master go alone! And that wasn't a shawl at all; it was a doormat from the Dusseaux. And the shapeless coat was the cover of an armchair!

But this was no moment for the retrospective exercise of powers of observation. Erast Petrovich dashed forwards, holding out the arm with the arrow; but he hesitated to shoot in case he might hit Masa.

The Japanese struck the man with white eyes across the wrist with the edge of his hand – the Baillard went flying into the air, landed on a stone and fired straight up into the bright blue sky.

The next moment a fist of iron struck the Japanese on the

temple with all its power and Masa went limp and fell to the ground nose down.

The man with white eyes glanced rapidly at Fandorin's advancing figure and the revolver lying out of reach. With an agile bound he was on his feet and dashing back towards the inner courtyard.

He couldn't reach the Baillard. His opponent was agile and skilled in unarmed combat. While he was busy with him, the Japanese would come round, and he could never deal with two skilful fighters like that alone.

Back to the room. The loaded Colt was lying up there, beside the bed.

Fandorin reduced his speed slightly and snatched up the revolver from the ground. It took less than half a second, but the man with white eyes had already disappeared round the corner. Another inappropriate thought flashed through his mind: they were just like children playing games – all running in one direction, then all turning round and running back again.

There had been five shots, so there was only one shell left in the cylinder. He couldn't afford to miss.

When he turned the corner, Erast Petrovich saw the man with white eyes with his hand already on the handle of the door to room number 7. The collegiate assessor loosed his arrow without taking aim.

Pointless: his opponent disappeared through the doorway.

Inside the door, Achimas suddenly stumbled as his leg folded under his weight and refused to obey him.

He glanced down, baffled – there was a metal shaft protruding from the side of his calf. What kind of witchcraft was this?

Defying the acute pain, he managed somehow to get up the steps and crawl across the floor on all fours to where the black Colt was lying. Just as his fingers closed on the grooved handle, there was a clap of thunder behind him.

Got him!

The dark figure was stretched out at full length. The black revolver had slipped out of the nerveless fingers.

Erast Petrovich bounded across the room and grabbed up the weapon. He cocked the hammer and stepped back, taking no chances.

The man with white eyes was lying face down. There was a damp stain spreading across the middle of his back.

The collegiate assessor did not turn round at the pattering sound behind him – he recognised Masa's short, rapid steps.

He said in Japanese: 'Turn him over. But be careful, he's very dangerous.'

In all his forty years, Achimas had never once been wounded. He was very proud of this, but secretly afraid that sooner or later his good luck would run out. He was not afraid of death, but being wounded – the pain and the helplessness – yes, he was afraid of that. What if the torment should prove unbearable? What if he were to lose control over his body and his spirit as he had so often seen others do?

It wasn't painful. Not at all. But his body wouldn't obey him any more. *My spine's broken*, he thought. *The Count of Santa Croce will never reach his island*. It was an ordinary thought, without any regret.

Then something happened. His eyes had been looking at the dusty floorboards. Now suddenly they saw the grey ceiling, festooned with cobwebs in the corners.

Achimas moved his eyes. Fandorin was standing over him with a revolver in his hand.

How absurd a man appeared when you looked up at him from below. That was the way dogs and worms and insects saw us.

'Can you hear me?' the detective asked.

'Yes,' Achimas replied, and was surprised to hear how steady and strong his voice was. The blood was flowing out of him incessantly – he could feel it. If it wasn't stopped, everything would be all over soon. That was good. He had to make sure that the blood wasn't stopped. To do that he had to talk.

The man on the floor looked up intently, as if he were trying to discern something very important in Erast Petrovich's face. Then he started talking. In sparse, clear sentences.

'I propose a deal. I save your life: you carry out my request.'

'What request?' Fandorin asked in surprise, certain that the man with white eyes was raving. 'And how can you save my life?'

'The request later. You are doomed. Only I can save you. You will be killed by your superiors. They have crossed out your name. From the list of the living. I failed to kill you. Others will not fail.'

'Nonsense!' exclaimed Erast Petrovich, but he had a terrible sinking feeling in the pit of his stomach. Where had the police got to? Where was Karachentsev?

'Let's agree,' said the wounded man, licking his grey lips. 'I tell you what to do. If you believe me, you carry out my request. If not, you don't. Your word?'

Fandorin nodded, gazing spellbound at this man who had appeared out of his past.

'My request. There's a briefcase under the bed. You know the one. No one will look for it. It's a problem for everyone. The briefcase is yours. There's also an envelope. It contains fifty thousand roubles. Send the envelope to Wanda. Will you do it?'

'No!' the collegiate assessor exclaimed indignantly. 'All the money will be handed over to the authorities. I am no thief! I am a state official and a man of honour.'

*

Achimas turned his attention inwards, to what was happening to his body. It seemed there was less time left than he had thought. It was getting harder to talk. He had to finish this.

'You are nobody and nothing. You are a dead man.' The outline of the detective's face began to blur and Achimas started speaking more quickly.

'Sobolev was condemned to death by a secret court. An imperial court. Now you know the whole truth. They will kill you for that. *Raison d'état*. There are several passports in the briefcase. And a ticket for the Paris train. It leaves at eight. You have time. Otherwise you die.'

It was getting dark. Achimas made an effort and forced the shroud of darkness back. *Think quickly*, he thought, urging Fandorin on. *You're a clever man and I have no time left.*

The man with white eyes was speaking the truth.

When the full realisation hit Erast Petrovich, he swayed on his feet. In that case he was done for. He had lost everything – his career, his honour, the very meaning of his life. That scoundrel Karachentsev had betrayed him and sent him to a certain death. No, it was not Karachentsev – it was the state, his country, his fatherland.

He was only alive now thanks to a miracle. Or rather, thanks to Masa. Fandorin glanced round at his servant, who stared back goggle-eyed, pressing his hand to his bruised temple.

The poor fellow. No head, not even the very thickest, could put up with that kind of treatment. Ah, Masa, Masa, what are we going to do with you? You have bound your life to the wrong man.

'The request. Promise,' the dying man whispered faintly.

'I'll do as you ask,' Erast Petrovich muttered reluctantly.

The man with white eyes smiled and closed his eyes.

Achimas smiled and closed his eyes. Everything was all right: a good life, a good ending.

Die, he told himself.

He died.

THE FINAL CHAPTER IN WHICH EVERYTHING
COULD NOT POSSIBLY WORK OUT BETTER

The station bell sounded for the second time and the Ericsson locomotive began panting out smoke impatiently, eager to dart off and away along the gleaming rails in pursuit of the sun. The Moscow–Warsaw–Berlin–Paris transcontinental express was preparing to depart.

The sullen young man sitting in one of the first-class sleeping compartments (bronze, velvet, mahogany) was wearing a badly stained cream-coloured jacket torn at the elbows. He gazed blankly out of the window, chewing on a cigar and occasionally puffing out smoke, but without any trace of the enthusiasm displayed by the locomotive.

Twenty-six years old, and my life is over, the departing passenger thought. *When I returned to Moscow only four days ago I was so full of hope and energy. And now I am obliged to forsake my native city, never to return. Dishonoured, victimised, forced to abandon my career, to betray my duty and my fatherland. But no, no – I have betrayed nothing; it is my fatherland that has betrayed its faithful servant! These wonderful reasons of state that first transform an honest worker into an inconsequential cogwheel and then decide to eliminate him altogether! You should read Confucius, you fine gentlemen who watch over the throne – where it says that the noble man can never be anyone else's tool.*

What now? They will slander me, declare me a thief, a

wanted man throughout the whole of Europe.

But no, of course, they won't declare me a thief: they will prefer to keep silent about the briefcase.

And they won't pursue me openly: publicity is not in their interest. But they will hunt for me, and sooner or later they will find me and kill me. It will not be too difficult to find a traveller accompanied by a Japanese servant. But what can I do with Masa? He won't survive in Europe alone.

And where is he, by the way?

Erast Fandorin took out his Bréguet watch. There were two minutes left until the train was due to leave.

They had arrived at the station in good time and the collegiate assessor (or rather, former collegiate assessor) had been able to dispatch a package of some kind to the Anglia, addressed to a Fräulein Tolle; but at a quarter to eight, when they were already sitting in the compartment, Masa had rebelled, declaring that he was hungry and had absolutely no intention of eating the chicken eggs, loathsome cow's butter and raw pig meat smelling of smoke that they served in the restaurant car, and he had set out in search of hot bagels.

The bell sounded for a third time and the locomotive gave a cheerful, exuberant hoot of its whistle.

That knock-kneed baby had better not have strayed too far. Fandorin stuck his head out of the window, concerned.

There he was, tearing along the platform, clutching a prodigious paper bag. He had two white bandages in different places on his head: the bump at the back was still there and now he had a bad bruise on his temple as well.

But who was that with him? Erast Petrovich shaded his eyes against the sun with his hand. Tall, thin with luxuriant sideburns, wearing livery.

Frol Grigorievich Vedishchev, Prince Dolgorukoi's personal valet! What was he doing here? Ah, how very inopportune.

Vedishchev spotted him and waved: 'Mr Fandorin, Your Honour! I've come to fetch you!'

Erast Petrovich started back from the window, but immediately felt ashamed. It was stupid. And senseless. And he ought to find out what was behind this incredible coincidence.

He went out on to the platform, holding the briefcase under his arm.

'Oof, I was only just in time ...' Vedishchev puffed and panted, mopping at his bald patch with a gaudy handkerchief. 'Let's go, sir; His Excellency is waiting.'

'But how did you find me?'

The young man glanced round as the carriage slowly started to move.

Let it go. What point was there in trying to escape by railway if the authorities already knew his route? They would send a telegram and have him arrested at the first station. He would have to find some other way to get out of Moscow.

'I can't go to His Excellency, Frol Grigorievich; my circumstances now are such that I am obliged to resign the state service. I ... I have to leave as soon as possible. But I will send the prince a letter explaining everything.'

Yes, yes! He could write to Dolgorukoi and tell him everything. Then at least someone would know the full background to this appalling and sordid story.

'Why waste the paper?' Vedishchev asked with a good-natured shrug. 'His Excellency is perfectly well aware of your circumstances. Let's go; you can tell him all the details yourself. All about that murderer – may he rot in hell; and how that Judas of a police chief deceived you.'

Erast Petrovich choked. 'But ... but, how on earth? How do you know everything?'

'We have our ways and means,' the valet replied vaguely. 'We learned about today's business in good time. I even sent one of my men along to see what would happen. Didn't you spot him there – wearing a cap and pretending to be drunk? In fact he's an extremely sober individual – never touches a drop, not even after Lent. That's why I use him. He was the one who told me you ordered the cab to go to the Bryansk Station. Oh, the effort it cost me to get to you in time! And I'd never have found you without the Providence of God: I just happened to spot your squinty-eyed servant here in the buffet. Could you see me running along all these carriages? I'm not a fit twenty-year-old like you, sir.'

'But is His Excellency aware that this is a matter of ... exceptional delicacy?'

'There's no delicacy involved here; it's a simple matter – one for the police,' Vedishchev snapped. 'You arranged with the chief of police to arrest a suspicious character, a swindler who was passing himself off as a merchant from Ryazan. A highly respectable gentleman, they say – the genuine Klonov; seven *poods*, he weighs. That addle-head Karachentsev got the time confused and you had to risk your own life. It's a pity you didn't manage to take that scoundrel alive. Now we'll never know what his intentions were. But at least you're fit and well, old chap. His Excellency described the entire business in a letter to St Petersburg, to the sovereign himself. It's clear enough what's going to happen: they'll throw the chief of police out on his ear, appoint a new one, and there'll be a decoration for Your Honour. It's all very simple.'

'Very s-simple?' Erast Petrovich asked, staring curiously into the old man's colourless eyes.

'Couldn't be simpler. Or was there something else?'

'... No, there wasn't anything else,' Fandorin replied after a moment's thought.

'There, you see. Oh, just look at that briefcase you have there. A really fine piece of work. Foreign, I suppose.'

'It's not my briefcase,' declared the collegiate assessor (no longer former, but quite current once again). 'I'm going to send it to the municipal Duma. It's a large contribution from an anonymous benefactor, for the completion of the cathedral.'

'Really large, is it?' the valet asked, with a keen glance at the young man.

'Almost a million roubles.'

Vedishchev nodded approvingly.

'That's certainly good news for Vladimir Andreich. We'll finally get that cathedral off our hands, damn the thing; it's swallowed more than enough money out of the city's coffers.' He began crossing himself fervently. 'Oh, there are still generous people left in Russia, God grant them good health; and when they die may they rest in peace.'

But halfway through crossing himself, Frol Grigorievich suddenly remembered something and threw his arms up in the air: 'Let's go, Erast Petrovich, let's go, dear fellow. His Excellency said he won't sit down to his breakfast if you're not there. And he has a regime to follow: he must take his porridge at half past eight. The governor's carriage is waiting out on the square, we'll be there as quick as a flash. Don't you worry about your Oriental here; I'll take him with me. I haven't had any breakfast yet either. I've got a potful of yesterday's cabbage soup with chitterlings – really tasty. And we'll throw these bagels away; it's bad to stuff yourself full of dough – just swells up the stomach.'

Fandorin looked pityingly at Masa, who was flaring his nostrils and sniffing blissfully at the aroma coming from his paper bag. The poor fellow was in for a terrible ordeal.